"*Readers and cyclists beware! Mother Nature Ain't Nobody's Mom by Lloyd Mardis may be a bit bawdy and naughty in places, like a few thorny stickers in a field of wild flowers, but it is well worth the romp. Mardis' witty and insightful observations about life and human nature–gathered during bicycle trips all over Texas (and a mention of trips to the Great Plains including Oklahoma) make this a book you will treasure.*"

Susie Kelly Flatau, Texas author and editor
*Red Boots & Attitude,*
*From My Mother's Hands,*
*Counter Culture Texas,*
and *Antonelli's River Inn.*

Jerry Billmeier
901.767.5311

# Mother Nature Ain't Nobody's Mom

by

Lloyd Mardis

# Mother Nature

# Ain't Nobody's Mom

Copyright 2003
by
Lloyd Mardis

Illustrations by Lloyd Mardis
Front cover photo by Larry Edgeman
Back cover photo by Donna Edgeman
Cover Design by Stephen J. Neubauer

ISBN 1-932196-16-1

*A Park Imprint*
P.O. Box 1785
Georgetown, TX 78627
WordWright.biz

Printed in the United States of America

*An inspirational, provocative and humorous journal*
*by a bicycling senior who discovers*
*Mother Nature and learns that*
*strangers become family.*

# Table of Contents

**Word Snapshots** ......................................................... i
*Memorize these and folks will think you read the book*

**Foreword**.................................................................... v
*By Fred Meredith--a great guy.*

**Introduction** .............................................................. xi
*I share how I made this simple story complex.*

**Map of Tours**............................................................xv
*Shows how mixed up a bicyclist can get.*

**Chapters One through Eight**.......................................1
*My adventures in that "whole other country" Texas.*

**Great Pictures of the Tour** .......................................119
*A little bit of what I saw and did in Texas.*

**Chapters Nine through Fifteen** .................................129
*More of my adventures in Texas.*

**The Bawdy and Romantic Scenes** ............................249
*From a thoroughly fictional stalled Texas novel*

**Poetic Attempts** .......................................................259
*Guaranteed to start you scribbling--moments of the road*

**Hip Sufferers, Take Heart**.........................................280
*Or, hooray for the hammer and saw--a new lease on life.*

**Nuggets—As in Small Lumps of Great Value**..........................286
*An erudite survey and splendid advice on bicycling.*

**Self-Portrait** ...............................................................................308
*What you do when the camera doesn't do you justice.*

**About the Author**.........................................................................309

# *Word Snapshots*

Mother Nature's a hell of a bitch. She don't like you and she don't hate you and there's some comfort in that. No sir. Mother Nature ain't nobody's mom.

ଔ       ଔ       ଔ

Strangers become  family

ଔ       ଔ       ଔ

Naked, I lay flat on my back in a 70 mph wind, clutching at poles, fabric and belongings,  my tent ballooning and collapsing on me,  fearing at any moment the storm would cartwheel the whole mess,  including me, into the creek.  Then I saw the red and blue flashing lights rapidly approaching.

ଔ       ଔ       ଔ

On a West Texas desert highway, a young steer grazing contentedly on the wrong side of the ranch fence and, up to that point, totally ignoring the eighteen-wheelers thundering past, caught sight of my bicycle making its stealthy approach and interpreted this as an attack by some pre-historic predator. The stampede was on. Pecos was 20 miles away.

೮ಕ       ೮ಕ       ೮ಕ

No wonder the rates at the motel were so reasonable–over the past year, three trucks had plowed into the room I had rented. Would tonight be the fourth?

೮ಕ       ೮ಕ       ೮ಕ

One of several signs hand-painted at a café: "Notice to parents: Unattended children will be sold into slavery."

೮ಕ       ೮ಕ       ೮ಕ

Some ants are slackers.

೮ಕ       ೮ಕ       ೮ಕ

No matter how tired at night, when I began riding early the next morning, it was like Columbus discovering the New World.

ⱗ        ⱗ        ⱗ

In East Texas: "You better carry a gun. If the logging trucks don't get you–there's plenty of people who'll shoot you just for the hell of it."

ⱗ        ⱗ        ⱗ

When I gave a talk at an elementary school, they had been studying explorers–now they gaped at one in the flesh.

ⱗ        ⱗ        ⱗ

Children's questions: "Why don't you drive a pickup?" "How much money do you have?" "Where do you do number two?" "Where do you sleep?" "Do you have a gun?" "Are you married?" "Does your mother know you're doing this?" "Aren't you afraid?" "How old are you? Older than my dad? Older than my grandpa? Wow! Cool!"

ⱗ        ⱗ        ⱗ

I'm standing there in front of my tent, barefoot, still dripping from my river swim when I feel this tingling and look down to see both legs covered with a black wriggling mass of tiny bodies.

ⱗ        ⱗ        ⱗ

I usually ate two or three hundred fried pies per trip, lots of buttermilk and sardines and several plates of salad whenever I could.

☙          ☙          ☙

In the desert I kept hearing a raspy quacking sound. What was a duck doing in the desert?

☙          ☙          ☙

I went days without a bath or shower and stayed perfectly clean.

# *Foreword*

*Fred Meredith, Editor, Southwest Cycling News*

*Fred Meredith*

When I first met Lloyd Mardis I was already an addicted bicyclist. I don't know if you are, but it should be easy enough to find out.

Do you frequently think about bicycles when there are no bicycles in view, no bicycle rides just ridden and no bicycle rides about to be mounted? Do you ever find yourself looking at bicycles for the sheer joy of it and maybe imagining you are riding them? From your favorite easy chair can you see a bicycle, any bicycle parts or accessories? How about images—photos, paintings, sculptures—of bicycles? Do you have any bicycle jewelry—either in the image of a bicycle or made from bicycle stuff? Answer yes to one of the above and you are under suspicion, two or more and you are busted. You have the affliction.

Well, at that first encounter with Lloyd I don't think he was addicted, not yet, but he was engaged in the first serious step in that direction. I was doing the Austin Cycling Association's club newsletter at the time. It was still probably 4-6 pages and not a lot more than a ride schedule and whatever I could scrounge up in the way of a serious article. We didn't pay anybody but me, and I was only paid to do the layout. Writing, editing, proofing, dragging it to the printer and distributing the finished product to a number of bike shops was "volunteer" work. We've grown a bit since those days. It's a 20-page tabloid now and the name has evolved from *Austin Cycling Notes* to *Southwest Cycling News*, but that's another story.

So there I was in my big chainring, no, I'm just kidding. That's an inside cyclo-journalist joke and yet another story.

There I was in the little Texas town of Satler. Me and 30 or 40 other bicyclists were gathered near the shores of Canyon Lake, on the edge of the Texas Hill Country. It was December 12, 1992 and we were about to embark on a ride of some 40-odd miles that would circumnavigate the lake and end right where we started.

Slam, bam, thank you ma'am and the skinny-butt fast guys were away, headed down the road, never to be seen again until the next ride. They were pursued by the skinny-butt fast guy wannabes who were not quite so fast or near as skinny-butted. Bringing up the rear was the conscientious ride starter, the designated photographer/editor and Lloyd Mardis. With our official excuses for riding at the back firmly established, we set off like any "Laughing Group" and endeavored not to let anyone fall by the wayside. We were the "sweep."

As we rode, we talked, and we occasionally stopped. We offered moral support at another rider's "flat tire clinic" and, when the ride was over, we joined some other slow riders for lunch at the café.

In the manner of a smart woman capturing the attention of a gullible man, Lloyd did not proceed to tell us about himself or attempt to explain his shortcomings as a long-distance cyclist. Instead, he asked question after question about cycling and listened intently to each answer. He seemed to examine the answers and turn them into more questions. He drew the rest of us into telling all--everything we knew about riding bikes and could compress into a single ride and lunch.

Lloyd did admit to being retired and looking for something to do with his free time. He allowed as how he might like to do more cycling and he may have even mentioned doing some writing in the future. As we all went our separate ways, I encouraged Lloyd to ride with us again.

Weeks and months passed and I did not see much of Lloyd. He quietly attended an ACA meeting or two and joined, but I don't recall discussing bicycling in depth again as we had at the café at Canyon Lake. I assumed that the heavy hybrid bike he'd been riding had taken its toll or that Lloyd had found other things more to his liking for "retirement" time, but in July, I received a postcard.

"Hi, Fred. Left Seminole Canyon [on the Mexico border] at 7:15 am and on my way to Sanderson, then Pecos. Will cover 80 miles today. Total trip will be 1,800 miles as I make a big loop around Central and West Texas. Back in Austin September 16. Lloyd Mardis."

He'd done it. He'd become addicted. Trading in the hybrid for a real touring bike, Lloyd Mardis had set out on his series of adventures, over 8,000 miles in Texas and 6,500 miles on the Great Plains, mostly alone but never staying that way, making new friends everywhere.

Over the years, Lloyd has written many postcards and pages of entertaining copy for *Cycling News*. He has taken on West Texas in summer, the panhandle in winter and the whole perimeter of Texas in the face of hip replacement surgery then a jaunt to Canada and back covering ten states and four provinces. His readers have tried to imagine the taste of cold chili from the can and All Bran with water (It will do, when you're really, really tired, says Lloyd) and we've tried to visualize him standing in the motel shower with his bike, scrubbing the white caliche dust from both after taking a wrong turn. Well, maybe we haven't really tried to visualize that. But Lloyd has shared with us the fun and folly of his adventures on a bicycle.

I hope you enjoy reading Lloyd's book as much as I have enjoyed being a close spectator to his truly awesome accomplishments. I'd just like to leave you (and Lloyd) with something I wrote back then and still find an accurate assessment of my experiences.


## *Gettin' Happy! You?*

(originally published as "On the Ride" in *Austin Cycling Notes*, Vol. III, No. 10, July, 1993)

Somewhere in the middle of this year's Texas Chainring Challenge—I think it was between Wills Point and Sulphur Springs [Texas] on the day I decided to ride alone and "hammer it" just a bit—the inevitable question formed within my mind as I am sure it has for all cyclists at one time or another. Why do I ride?

It's a simple question on the surface, a question that makes little sense on, say, a 30-minute spin around Town Lake [Austin] at lunchtime, or even a 15-mile ride home from the office. That the question came to me 300 miles and five days into a week-long relationship with my bicycle seat is significant. Down low, tucked behind the aero bar, I had just muscled my way over a small rise at 20 mph. Still feeling leg-strong, I was in my top gear (yeah, that's the big chainring), accelerating on a slight downhill and cranking it up past 35.

Yes, I knew my quads would be sore in the morning. Yes, I knew there would be some fresh tender places where the saddle and I had not "moved as one." But, I felt great and that's when a little voice whispered in my ear, "Why do you do it? Why do you ride like this?

All of the physically prescriptive reasons came to mind. Well, because I am an over-weight, over 50, Type II diabetic who doesn't want to end up with any of those much-feared complications so vividly described in all the literature. That's what I told myself. But no, that wasn't it—not all of it.

That may have been my motivation to start cycling again, but I ride a bicycle because it makes me happy. It makes me happy to set a goal, to climb a hill. It makes me happy to look back down the hill as I suck in that suddenly rarefied air at the top. It makes me happy to feel the wind in my face racing down the hill, just a little scared by the speed. It makes me happy to feel tired after I ride. It makes me happy to look at the map and see where I have been—and where I'm going.

The riding itself—the activity—makes me happy. It makes me happy to ride with other people, enjoying their company. It also makes me happy to ride alone, enjoying my own company.

But, it's not all about some endorphin-induced high. There is a stranger side.

I am also very happy handling my bicycles—cleaning, polishing, lubing, repairing and even assembling bicycles of my own. It is all very soothing and satisfying. Sometimes I am content just sitting and looking at a bicycle—such a fine thing, such a beautiful and functional piece of work. Is that weird?

Maybe it is and maybe it isn't. The answer may have more to do with a capacity for happiness than the focus of the happiness. I recently cut from a magazine a piece by an accomplished writer without, unfortunately, saving the part that had his name on it. But I think there is some truth to what he said and if he is right, I feel very lucky.

Of happiness or actually the lack of it, he said, "There is a breed of men and women who cannot be made happy. Happiness eludes them as music eludes the tone deaf. They are solitary, they are sad, and they are beyond consolation. They act as if, long ago, they arrived too late to the ultimate, the divine rendezvous, and nothing can possibly console them for what they missed."

Perhaps that explains some people's dogged pursuit of other "things" such as money and material wealth, not bad things in their own right but not fair substitutes for the capacity to be truly happy. What would I like to tell them? I'd like to tell them what Lloyd and I already know.

When in doubt, ride your bike, or at least write about it.

# *Introduction*

The name of this book comes from a conversation with an old man like myself. On my fully loaded bicycle, I climbed a steep hill outside a small town and paused to rest. I heard no cars. Too early in the morning, I guessed. Mist and fog surrounded me and I savored the silence. I made ready to pedal on.

"Gawdamighty–how'd you do that?" a voice boomed. Startled, I looked around and there, his head just visible at first above the brow of the hill, came a guy my age or older aboard a racing bicycle. He wore black Lycra® riding shorts and a brightly colored racing shirt. His left leg was bound with elastic cloth. He strained up the final few feet and repeated his question–oath and all.

Apparently, it was incomprehensible how I had ridden up that same hill ahead of him with all that weight–my bike and equipment weighed about 160 pounds–not including me. We talked. We traded experiences on that quiet road. After I told him about storms that destroyed my tent, monstrous winds, knife-like cold, the heat of the sun, insects–and other stuff cyclists talk about–he shared his thoughts about Mother Nature.

"Mother Nature's a hell of a bitch. She don't like you and she don't hate you and there's some comfort in that. No sir, Mother Nature ain't nobody's mom."

I agreed–in spite of the double negative–his words rang true. I told my fellow cyclist how I had cussed her out once for sending me days and days of south wind roaring past my ears without a break. We laughed together. He knew. He cared. A stranger can suddenly be family. I discovered in my travels that a lot of people cared about me–and each other. Riding my bicycle in Texas, the Great Plains and Canada, I found that strangers do indeed, become family.

My plan is to use my third and longest trip in Texas–the perimeter tour–as the backbone of this book. Stymied on how to present all of my tours in an interesting manner, I presented the problem to my friend and a dedicated artist, Larry Smitherman, who magically solved it with this format. We shall begin with the perimeter tour and we shall end with it. Along the way I want to include the more interesting episodes from my other tours taken in Texas, both before and after the perimeter tour.

The Texas tours include my first tour in the summer of 1993 to Del Rio, Pecos, Fort Worth and back to Austin; my second tour in the winter of 1993 to Fort Worth, Amarillo in the Texas panhandle and back to Austin; my third tour in the spring of 1994 around the perimeter which will serve as the clothesline on which to hang the laundry of the other tours; my fourth tour in the autumn of 1995 to the east central section of Texas; and my fifth tour in the winter of 1996 to the south central section of Texas. An adventure or two from my Great Plains tour, which took place in the spring, summer and fall of 1997 exploring ten states and four Canadian provinces, will be used to further show the hospitality of strangers. As I write this, I have just ridden to Enid, Oklahoma (November 2002) and back to Austin, Texas, (approximately 1,000 miles) trying out my new recumbent bicycle and filling up on Thanksgiving turkey. I'll include some of that experience as well– so, you are embarking on a travel adventure that has spanned almost nine years–although it seems like it took place a few weeks ago.

Naturally, you will get confused, even though I have tried my best to orient you each time I leave the Texas perimeter tour and come back to it. Actually, the chronology isn't that important. I merely use it so it appears we're getting someplace in the story–

that there's a beginning and an end. As much as possible just ignore everything pertaining to where and when and you'll probably like it more. Without my journals I couldn't keep it straight in my head either. However, going day by day on each of the tours in chronological order would be quite boring, and I hope my technique will avert that. If not–thanks for buying the book anyway and don't tell your friends how you feel about it.

It is my hope I can inspire you, no matter your age, to hop on a bike some day and recapture the feeling you had as a youth when you pedaled for the first time out of sight.

Certainly, there are other ways of experiencing the countryside and although I grant there are valid arguments for each of them, I always come back to bicycling as the best for me. If you try it, I believe you will come under its spell as I have.

In addition to the bicycle tales which take up most of the book, I have added a couple of scenes from a stalled novel to highlight a bit of Texas history; a section of on-the-road poetry; an account of my hip replacement and some bicycle history and a riding tutorial.

My thanks go to my project helpers: Fred Meredith who started it all, Regan Marie Brown for nudging, Ann Friou for insights, Gwen Rutherford for marketing ideas, Larry Edgeman for technical support, Lyn Lacava for being Julie and Ginger, Susie Flatau for cheer-leading, and Donna Edgeman for inspiration.

A special thank you to Joan Neubauer of WordWright.biz., the publisher of this book. Joan was always positive and professionally helpful guiding me through the printing process. She was great to work with and kept things humming right along. Another thank you to Bobbie Mardis, my waswife and friend, for proofing the text, creating the index and offering excellent suggestions, some of which, I followed.

Traveling 30 to 100 miles per day allows one to stop and smell the flowers, listen to the birds, watch the cattle grazing, and come close to the deer, wild turkey, coyotes and armadillos that may cross your path. The warmth of the people you meet along the way is unbelievable. Even the so-called "trying" experiences are great–especially to look back upon, although at the time the only positive thing may be an improvement in your "cussin'" vocabulary.

The beginning of every day promised a new adventure. No matter how tired at night, when I began riding early the next morning, it was like Columbus discovering the new world. Helen Hayes, toward the end of her life, is reported to have said, "My one regret...I never rode a bicycle...I wish I had."
Please enjoy.

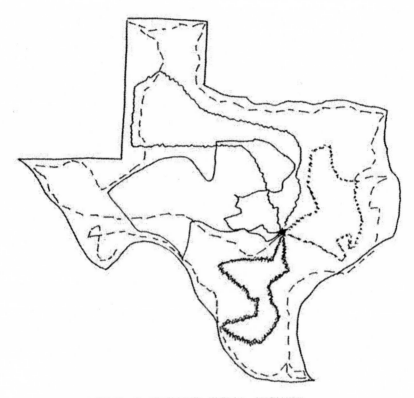

——— July 6 - September 15, 1993 - 72 days - 1,816 miles
∿∿∿ November 19 - December 30, 1993 - 42 days - 1,290 miles
- - - March 29 - August 3, 1994 - 128 days - 3,937 miles
·······• October 28 - November 12, 1995 - 16 days - 697 miles
∼∼∼∼ January 28 - February 10, 1996 - 14 days - 706 miles

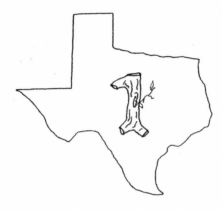

## *Planning for a New Way of Life*
### (Before the Tours Began)

I noticed during my 64th year a creeping depression as my mail box overflowed with circulars and glossy brochures marked URGENT. There appeared to be a preponderance of funeral insurance offers and invitations to visit trendy retirement homes "before it's too late."

One day during a fit of nostalgia, I sauntered through the front door of a bicycle store and gazed at row upon row of modern high-tech bicycles. On that day my life changed forever.

Who among us has forgotten the first taste of imminent freedom as we sat on the saddle of a handsome white-sidewall-tired Cruiser resplendent with chromed lights, fox tails waving from the tips of longhorn handlebars and a few of our mother's playing cards stuck in the spokes to mimic the sound of a powerful motorcycle?

Those memories stored away for half a century pedaled across the years and braked to a stop right in the middle of my heart. Naturally, I bought a bike–on the spot–as if I'd studied the matter carefully for months.

When I got it home I took it for a spin–all the way around the block. It had twenty-one gears and a shiny black paint job. Suddenly, I was transported to the carefree days of youth–free again with the wind whistling–this time–through my safety-inspected helmet. As I approached my driveway after the one-block circuit, the perfect distance for my first adventure, I realized I had not forgotten how to ride. It was October 6, 1992.

Daily practice resulted in longer and longer rides. I joined a bicycle club, The Austin Cycling Association, and went to meetings. Eventually, I accompanied the members on a club ride–forty-three miles of hills around Canyon Lake south of Austin. At the end of the ride my body pleaded to be laid to rest, but a hearty repast at a local country restaurant along with good-natured banter and support from my fellow club members saved me from collapse. Chief among those supporters, Fred Meredith, Editor of the Southwest Cycling News. He remains a valued friend and mentor to this day. After looking at the colorful lean and mean machines the other members straddled, I surmised my exhaustion was the fault of my bicycle and not my physical conditioning. How could I have felt warmly toward that, now so obviously, inferior mishmash of rubber and metal? And, that black paint job–yuck.

By January, 1993, my black slowpoke and I no longer spoke. Out I went to get another new bike. Do you sense something happening?

That time I purchased a skinny-tired bicycle named *Randonnee,* which I learned later connoted touring. Talk about prophetic. I had a *bona fide* touring bike with a purple paint job. I purchased a skin-tight purple riding shirt and another helmet–this time a purple beauty by Gyro. My *Randonnee* was light and strong. Low gears promised to flatten the steepest of hills. Drop handlebars wound in white leather-like material looked better than the fox tails of my youth. This was a serious bike. Immediately, I felt stronger. I brought it into my

2

apartment and gave it a place of honor by my bed. It said "go" to me. I looked at it a lot–waking up at night, I would look at it and listen to its call to adventure.

I bought panniers, filled them with books and magazines for ballast, and hung them on the sides of both wheels. Daily rides on a nearby highway developed stamina. On some days I persevered for 30 miles. Now, I was really ready. But for what? I outlined a trial run–a loop around west Texas of about 1800 miles. If anything went amiss I would be close enough for a friend to pop out and bring me home. Doing several tours never entered my mind when I began that first westward trek–just a medium-sized trip to prepare me to cross the country like every other self-respecting touring cyclist dreamed of doing.

Somehow, I put out of my mind a few things. The last time I went camping, at a church camp as a youth, I didn't like it. I hated mosquitoes, ants, sweat, and grimy clothes. I showered, shampooed and shaved every day. Clean clothes were *de rigueur*.

Scribbled-down reasons why that trip in the heat of summer was a perfectly sane undertaking cluttered my desk. Things like: staying active results in a healthy and energized life; being out-of-doors lifts the spirit; and, the elderly need a cheerleader. My predisposition toward the romantic played a part, too. I remembered devouring the adventure books of Richard Halliburton in my early teen years. He traveled the world in the 1930s long before the common man tried to swim in every ocean and sample a McDonald's hamburger in China.

Traveling was always a favorite daydream of mine. Amelia Earhart bedazzled me as she attempted to fly around the world. At the time I fantasized about having adventures like Halliburton and Earhart. But, like most of us, I got busy doing the expected and settled down to the usual and the ordinary. Now, thanks to the simple purchase of a bike, those dreams, buried and nearly forgotten, surged back to life. Like a dormant frog bursting from the baked mud of a dry creek bed after a good rain–I was reborn.

Nine months after my first ride around the block on that black

3

clunker, I eased across the Town Lake bridge pedaling west out of Austin, Texas, my beautiful purple *Randonnee* ladened with touring essentials. Jim Southard, a good friend, came to see me off offering moral support and a snack. West Texas called. I answered on July 6, 1993.

What started out as a trial run ended up as an obsession to see as much as possible of my adopted Lone Star state and, later, the beckoning lands beyond. I'm glad it turned out the way it did. I must confess to having fallen hopelessly in love with touring by bicycle. I would never be considered average again.

OUT WEST

## *Scenarios of Harm*
### (All Tours)

A woman acquaintance, after listening to some of my bicycle exploits, asked a question shared by many of my friends:

"Aren't you ever scared?"

"Of course." I hastened to add that most of my fears appeared before the trip began. Once on the road most worries disappear. Mostly, I'm afraid of the weather more than of man or animal, but not always.

I'm the kind of person who likes to figure things out as much as possible beforehand. I analyze, anticipate and play what-if games.

Let me share a few scenarios which repeat themselves, usually just before going to sleep and before I take off on a trip.

I see myself pedaling down a blacktop highway; it can be in a desert, a forest or anyplace devoid of houses, stores or the highway patrol. A pickup truck with three guys, unsavory types, passes me, pulls off the road and waits. Should I stop before I get to them? They might back up. They could do a U turn. If I keep on pedaling I may pass them and nothing will happen. But what if they pass me again and pull off and wait? Or, as I get close, they crawl out and wave me to a stop. Are they smiling? So, what difference does that make? Do I smile back? Do I stop?

At 10 miles an hour, I'm almost a sitting duck–at least a slow waddling one. Is this the time to pull out a shotgun, a slingshot loaded with poison pellets, a crossbow with steel flesh-cutting arrows? Perhaps I have strapped to my back a dozen throwing knives–and I have practiced and practiced before the trip to the point where I'm as accurate and as swift as a Ninja warrior. Maybe if I dress like one it would be enough–but would convenience store clerks let me come inside for an ice cream cone if I'm dressed all in black and have on a mask?

As one gun store owner offered: "Don't carry a shotgun–the laws are different in places–you'd be better off buying a machete. You can always say it's for cutting wood for your campfire. But don't ever cut wood with it–take it to a grinder and get a razor's edge put on it. You can separate a head from shoulders practically without effort. Very effective." I wondered what the other two guys would be doing while I lopped off the head of their friend.

Back to the shotgun. If I threaten them with it and they drive away, will they be waiting down the road in ambush? Will they drive home and get high-powered rifles with scopes, climb a hill and pick me off as I go by? Do they turn me in to their cousin who just happens to be the county sheriff? Would I go to jail for an extended stay for threatening law-abiding citizens? Would anyone believe me? Would my friends visit?

Can you see why I might toss and turn at night trying to work through these problems? Surely I could figure out something even though no answer would be fool-proof. My solution: I take along a hand-held inoperative cell phone. I'd never have enough time to actually dial someone. So, when someone stops down the road, I whip out the fake cell phone and pretend to be talking up a storm. If the characters wave me to a stop, I ask if they're having trouble and inform them that I've already reported the truck and that help is on the way. I've never had to do this, but I have passed trucks that looked as if they were waiting for me. I zip past talking on my dummy cell phone with its big antenna waving in the wind. So far, I've had no trouble. It's better than shooting them with a shotgun or separating their heads from their shoulders. If I were in their place, I know I would vote for the cell phone defense.

The other recurring, maddening scenario involves a night attack while I'm camping in my tent. Again, one could have a shotgun. Let's suppose I'm asleep, or almost asleep, and I hear a dry twig break–like in the movies. Instantly, the adrenalin flows and I'm alert and coiled for action like a steel spring. I reach for my short-barreled riot shotgun and pump in a shell. "Boy, anybody who hears the sound of a shotgun getting ready for action is sure to go in the opposite direction–and fast." But, what if they don't hear? What if they keep coming? Do they have a flashlight? Do I have my tent window or door unzipped so I can watch the intruder approach? Is this someone who wants to do me harm? Maybe it's the sheriff and he forgot to turn on his red and blue strobes. Am I going to kill the sheriff? A blast from the shotgun will put a mighty big hole in my tent, too. Are the mosquitoes out tonight? So, what if he/she/it doesn't have a flashlight and I've not unzipped my tent? Will I shoot a cow? And, again, what about that huge hole in my tent? What if there are several intruders? Maybe they are teenagers trying to scare a camper. Should I shoot them? Even one of them? Is she the daughter of the high school principal? What if I'm in bear country and a bear is lumbering toward me and I still have a half-eaten cupcake with crumbs in my lap? Do I know how to shoot a bear? Do I remember that shooting at a grizzly just makes him/her mad? Isn't there a fine for shooting a bear?

This scenario and all its variations have troubled me the most. I free-camped in over 100 roadside rest stops and I never had the slightest indication of trouble. But, I must admit that the specter of being attacked at night continues to haunt me and I cannot find a solution short of not camping alongside the road. In small city parks, deserted at night, I jump at every shadow. If I want a good night's sleep I stop at an RV park or a state park, or if I'm fortunate, I make arrangements to pitch my tent on someone's property–in the back yard or even in the driveway. If I must camp at a roadside park I select one with lots of lights and pitch my tent in as inconspicuous place as possible and hope for the best.

I continue to refuse to carry any kind of weapon, relying instead on my wit and physical strength to ward off trouble.

Some of my defenses sans weapons, I'll cheerfully admit are a bit bizarre.

Here are a few of them:

I could act crazy. I could pretend I have escaped from some institution and I'm sorry that I twisted someone's head off. I won't do it again, unless I get upset. I would laugh and snuffle a lot in sort of a maniacal way.

Perhaps I am deaf. I would use a lot of sign language and hope the intruder wasn't deaf too. I could listen to the intruder's plans and be ready to take advantage.

I have practiced barking like a large dog, usually a Rottweiler. I've got this down pretty good so that when I bark, all the Rottweilers hasten toward me. They sweep on by since they know that I, one of those dumb human beings, couldn't possibly have barked that insult about their mothers. Actually, I think this will work better than the sound of a shell being slammed into a shotgun chamber.

I have also taken up howling like a wolf. I use this when I'm traveling at night and I know there may be mountain lions lying in wait on the limestone highway cuts. This has really worked. No mountain lion has mistaken me for a tasty deer. Someone did mention a troubling thought however: "What makes you think they don't eat wolves?"

I've also thought about masquerading as a shaman with the ability to cast spells. "I have just planted a worm on your liver. You will not feel it at first. I will remove this curse only if I am alive and happy on..." here I would state a date sufficiently in the future to allow me adequate time to vacate the vicinity. I'll have to work on this–you know–invent some secret-sounding words and gestures that are devilishly authentic.

Usually, after going through these scenarios and solutions, I'm ready to close my eyes and snooze for the rest of the evening.

ROAD KILL

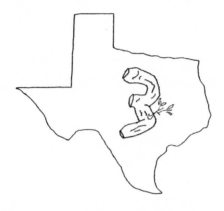

## *The Beginning*
(Perimeter Tour 1994)

In the summer of 1993 I rode my bicycle from Austin to Pecos in west Texas and back to Austin. The trip lasted seventy-two days and covered 1,816 miles. In November of that year I climbed aboard again, pedaled out of Austin and struck out for the Panhandle of Texas and back to Austin. The trip lasted forty-two days and covered 1,290 miles. Bicycle touring became old hat to me. I had no plans for another tour. Pain in my hip had shut me down.

In the spring of 1994, a friend invited me to go on a camping trip with her to the Black Gap Wildlife Management Area which consisted of 106,915 acres. As far as we knew, we had it all to ourselves. We spent ten days just roaming around trying not to get lost. She did the roaming. I hobbled about with a makeshift cane. Even so, one star-spangled night we took our bed rolls high up a mountain side hoping to see some of the newly introduced desert bighorn sheep, but not one of the two dozen or so mountain lions. After watching the stars and listening to the night sounds, she went right off to sleep while I kept wondering if the soft footfalls of a mountain lion approaching would give me adequate warning. None appeared and exhaustion finally closed my eyes.

Desert spring flowers enthralled me. As did the shrubs, cacti, sotol and yucca–the latter twelve feet high and higher and covered with masses of white blooms. Orange and red lantana shrubs carpeted the desert floor. The beginning buds of the ocotillo would soon burst forth with intense, red flowers, also the Indian blanket and Indian paintbrush began  to appear. Prickly pear's brilliant red bloom was here and there and soon to be joined by others. Agave plants–known as century plants sent their majestic spikes heavenward. And on the breeze the pungent, suffocating sweetness of Texas mountain laurel made me think there was a woman out there in the desert with too much perfume on. The area butted up against the Big Bend National Park in southwest Texas on the border with Mexico. We were home for a few days when my friend called wanting to go back. I had a problem with that. My hip made it almost impossible to walk and I didn't want to stay in camp while she had all the fun, so I said no, although I knew the desert would be in full bloom that time.

Earlier, my hip had been X-rayed and found to be in bad shape. Pain pills and no more long bicycle trips had been prescribed. Trying to hike around in the Black Gap WMA confirmed the need for a more sedentary life. Depression became my companion.

About the only time my hip felt somewhat pain free was while bicycling. After a few hours, I called my friend back to hitch a ride to Black Gap with my bike and baggage. Using some of the border with

Mexico, I would pedal back to Austin. A tour of a couple of thousand miles would be interesting and not too hard on me, I thought. I switched doctors. Dr. Joseph Abell, Jr. had set my leg after I broke it trying parachute jumping years before. I told him my plans and that I wanted an operation upon returning. No more pain pills and no more sedentary life style. Building hard muscles and getting a new hip became my new focus. Suddenly, without much thought, I was back in business. My spirits rose. I had a very noticeable limp and a wide smile.

Permit me to say here that I'll mention the hip pain sparingly–in the back is a section on the operation, if you're interested. Suffice it to say not a day went by during this period that I didn't limp and at times feel excruciating pain. After my perimeter trip of nearly 4,000 miles, I got my new hip. My remaining two trips were pain free and I am still pain free and active as all get out eight years later.

PRICKLY PEAR

## Arrival at the Stillwell Ranch
(Perimeter Tour 1994)

My wilderness loving friend and I arrived March 29, 1994 at the Hallie Stillwell ranch just outside the Big Bend National Park. There, we parted company. She went back packing and camping. I pitched my tent on the ranch and biked into and through the park the next day. The park's headquarters at Panther Junction would be my first long stop. It was only thirty-five miles away–unfortunately and unbeknownst to me–uphill all the way. My tactic was to rest for awhile at the park's headquarters and bike across the park to the town of Study Butte on the western side, an additional twenty-five miles for a total of sixty miles for my first day's ride. Not bad–except those miles twisted through mountains.

Morning arrived with an atonal chorus from a family of coyotes and the rasping quack of a raven in a nearby mesquite tree. On an earlier trip to west Texas I heard what I thought was a duck in the desert. I asked about it, but no one could offer an explanation. One day I saw a raven flying and making a quacking sound like a duck with a sore throat. Mystery solved. Well, it certainly sounded like a duck to me.

The wind blew at twenty-five to thirty miles per hour. Temperature stayed in the forties. The early morning clouds looped around the surrounding peaks like dirty gray ropes. Too much wind? I did a trial ride up a hill without my baggage. The cool wind pushed at my side–much better than head on. I could do it. I packed, had another cup of coffee; said goodbye to the friendly ladies at the ranch store and began what would become my longest bike ride yet. No more long bike rides–hah!

The demanding insistent notes of a cactus wren sounded across the range–one of my favorite desert sounds. The wren nests in a cactus and is nearly as large as a robin. The call is one of defiance–exactly the attitude one needs to ride in the desert of West Texas. The surrounding scrub land spread a panoply of blooms as far as I could see. Again I detected the strong sweet odor of the Texas mountain laurel playing against the oily smell of greasewood and a hundred other smells I breathed in but could not identify. The desert perfumes infused me with energy–for awhile. The miles came and went. I drank a lot of water and being the first day, I was woefully out of shape, struggling up the inclines to an ever higher altitude. A can of beans and a fistful of crackers helped for maybe thirty minutes.

Finally, with my energy level so low I couldn't measure it, three miles remained before reaching the headquarters building. I had to stop after each mile to rest. When I had only a half-mile left my body refused one more pedal. I peeled and consumed an orange which gave me permission to continue. What a wimp. I was tuckered.

PECCARY

## Park Headquarters
## (Perimeter Tour 1994)

A snack and a time-out at the check-in performed wonders on my body. Off I went across the park, still a little tired, but alert enough to scan the hollows and boulders for black bear, javelina (peccary), deer, bighorn sheep and mountain lion. I saw a peccary, more wild flowers, clouds, a few cars, sweeping vistas and listened to more staccato calls from cactus wrens. As before when I visited, I didn't really care if I missed seeing a mountain lion, although I would have classified it as "a life experience" if one had crouched in the middle of the park road. An acquaintance related how he had been stalked one night by a mountain lion in that very area. It had circled his tent at night. He saw the tracks the next morning. I read up on how to make noise, hold my ground, wave my arms, no bending over or crouching and generally how not to act like prey, which tries to run away as fast as possible. Never, never run. But, I was on a bike–hunched over–looking for all the world like prey trying to escape. Low cliffs I had to ride through made me particularly nervous. What could be up there waiting, watching me with those yellow eyes? No bears appeared either. I wouldn't have a close encounter with a black bear and a mamma grizzly for another three years when I biked the Great Plains and the Canadian Rockies

## Study Butte
### (Perimeter Tour 1994)

I arrived at Study Butte in the middle of the afternoon. Thus, my first day ended and I could relax in a delightful little RV park. Maps and brochures on my tent floor helped me plan the next day. Freshly laundered clothes soon filled a line from my tent to a tree. Dinner came and went and I looked at the blinking stars that night, admired the jagged hills about me, wrote in my journal and drifted off to sleep, content.

Detailing each day's adventures, no matter how exciting, can become boring. Realizing that, I promise only a few days where I spend time sharing my hour by hour experiences. You have heard one. Now you get to hear about two more–then we'll take a break.

Morning came. No breeze, but cool again. The sun was warm–just right. I had checked out possible camping sites between Study Butte and Alpine since I didn't think I could do the whole seventy-eight miles in one day–considering how pooped I was the day before. One ranch eighteen miles north, promised great accommodations, but to reach it another sixteen miles off the highway on a gravel road would have to be ridden. That gravel road would be spread with vulture food–me–if I attempted to ride my heavy bike through gravel–and back out again the next morning. Not wise. Not fun. The Longhorn Motel was twelve miles away–the first six hilly–right on the highway, which would leave sixty-six miles for the following day. That seemed quite reasonable to me; twelve miles I could do backwards. Besides, I had no choice. A possible problem: when I called, the owners told me there were no rooms available. When I suggested that I could stay in my tent, they said come on. Problem solved. Thankfully, the temperature topped out at sixty-eight degrees. Steep grades. Had to walk and push the bike up one. I was really happy I had only twelve miles to go–I would have traded them in for fifty flat ones, however.

## The Wild Horse Station
### (Perimeter Tour 1994)

I covered the first five miles in one and one-half hours–that's slow–hikers walk that fast.

A welcome surprise, The Wild Horse Station, not on my map, came into view. A picturesque trading post framed by six-foot-tall bougainvillea bushes ablaze with red blooms.

In a white wrought iron chair next to a matching table on a shaded veranda, I ate a microwaved pizza and a Snickers while the bougainvillea blossoms danced slowly in the breeze. Out back, a beautiful garden thrived–rose bushes, even.

"Anything will grow here–all you have to do is water it," said the attractive woman owner who had just returned from an Alpine shopping trip.

The station had furnished mountain cabins on the hillsides. Of course, I had not gone far enough to spend the night–but it was tempting.

Sharing my travel plans with her, she warned me that I still had some hills, but the mountains that started six miles this side of Alpine would really be hard to get over. Back on the highway, I ceased all forward motion trying to get up a hill. Time to walk again. I tried to console myself by saying that once my muscles got back into shape, in a couple of weeks, I would climb a hill like that with ease. I did notice cars and trucks had to gear down to get over it–so, it was truly steep.

## The Longhorn Ranch Motel
### (Perimeter Tour 1994)

I arrived at the Longhorn Ranch Motel in the late afternoon. John Brooks and Robyn Whyte, husband and wife owners, directed me to the desert–a beautiful, wild, scenic spot in a valley surrounded by lavender and pink mountains about a mile behind the motel on their ranch land. There would be no charge for my overnight stay.

BLACK BEAR

Spring in the desert. The ocotillo with densely packed small green leaves on long slender thorny stalks were adorned with orange-red flowers–small, delicate, intense. Desert daisies with white petals and yellow centers nodded. Staunch and immovable cacti filled with red blooms enticed me while the thorns said stay away. The yucca soared with their white flowers. The ocotillo vied for dominance throughout the spacious valley with bunches of purple flowers, probably verbena, and gray-green bushes of cenizo–also with purple blooms. It was only seventy degrees under a warm sun in a nearly cloudless dark-blue sky. Now and then, a gentle breeze carried desert scents to me.

Breaking my camping rule, I decided not to put up my tent. Instead, I would spread out my ground cover, anchor it by placing my panniers on the four corners, unroll my sleeping bag and gaze at the heavens that night for as long as I could keep my eyes open. It was a wonderful thought and plan. But alas.

I settled down while the sun still shone. In a few minutes, stretched out on my sleeping bag, I felt a stinging on my legs. Jumping up, I saw my ant sisters had come for a visit and a snack. They were not fire ants of the imported variety, but native fire ants whose stings and aggressive behavior are much more genteel.

Nevertheless, vigorous brushings and hoppings about were called for and I complied.

At last antless, I put up my ant-proof tent. Slabs of flat sandstone rock and pockets of loose dark-brown sand composed the land. Neither were conducive to holding tent stakes. I tied my guy ropes to bushes in all directions and hoped for the best. A ranch hand drove up in a pickup. He had a Blue Heeler with him that stared hard at me. They do that. "Don't worry, he won't bite–wind can get pretty strong out here–could blow you away." With more ifs, ands, buts, doubts and assurances, he and his staring Blue Heeler bounced back down the ranch road. The wind came up, a huge bank of storm clouds blossomed and dissipated. The half moon glowed. The stars dangled about twenty feet above me. My tent danced the fandango all night, but I didn't blow away.

Resolved to make an early start, I arose at four-thirty the next morning, packed up and pushed my bike through the sand to the highway and rode up to the motel–only to discover it didn't open until seven. As soon as the door unlocked, I jumped in ready to buy some supplies, eat breakfast and salvage as much of the day as possible. The waitress informed me about a bus load of tourists coming at seven-thirty for breakfast–so, I'd have to wait. I negotiated. Two large plates of biscuits and gravy graced my table. I ate. I drank coffee. I tried to buy something for the trip. Nothing available–except candy. I sped off. All things considered, it had been a good experience–terrific scenery and free camping. People were harassed, but friendly and the coffee, biscuits and gravy gave me a nice full feeling.

## To Alpine
### (Perimeter Tour 1994)

I had filled up my water containers resulting in a total of one gallon of water for the next sixty-six miles. I still did not appreciate the amount of water I needed on long trips in desert regions where stores are few or non-existent. Much, much later, it got through to me and I began carrying more water. Most days I ended up mildly or severely dehydrated. A cyclist uses around one gallon of water for each 30 or 40 miles in the heat of summer. A 90-mile day would require three gallons–maybe more–and that meant no emergencies like a break down that could cost another hour or two or all night. The possibility of spending the night out in the open because of a mechanical or physical failure of some sort should have rung a bell in my brain and caused me to reassess water needs. I learned. I learned. A night and a day with no water–not fun–not fun at all.

The highway climbed a few hills for the first three miles then rolled over gentle risings and fallings before becoming quite flat. Perched on one of the few fences I saw beside the highway, two vultures watched me with interest. I waved. At about ten miles I stopped at The Last Frontier Store–so, there was another place to camp after all. News I would have welcomed yesterday. My ride today would have been ten miles shorter–a big help–but I would have missed the desert camping and the staring Blue Heeler. I purchased Vienna sausages and a can of beef stew and filled up all my water bottles again. Bring on the Alpine hills. The manager warned me they were really mountains–not hills.

At eleven-fifteen I stopped for lunch. I still had most of a loaf of bread I had bought at a store in Big Bend. Because of the dry air, it tended to crumble. I wrapped one slice around each of the Vienna sausages–making seven sandwiches. I drank a quart or so of water. I ate the stew cold (by now kind of warm), opening the can with my Swiss Army knife. I have kept the same knife all these years. Once in Canada I left it at a store in the gravel driveway and had to back track fifteen miles to recover it. No one had found it. The opener has neatly detopped at least 5,000 cans over the years. I still use it.

Twenty-five miles out of Alpine, the highway began rising again in long sweeping curves of nearly half a mile each. After each curve a brief flat appeared followed by another long gradual rise. I ate seven more slices of bread. Just bread. I stopped at a beautiful roadside park that had large shade trees. I sat there for awhile toying with the idea of staying all night–but, you guessed it, I was running out of water. I hurt all over–especially my neck. The wrist that I had broken a few weeks earlier ached. I examined my Big Bend area guide and noticed a small advertisement of an RV park located six miles this side of Alpine. Right before the mountain grades. Perfect. I pressed on. I reached the park by six p.m. Totally empty–a field. No water. No restrooms. No trees for shade. No tables. Nothing. Just marked off parking places and a sign: "Register and we'll be back shortly–Fee $11.00–Enjoy." Enjoy what? I would have enjoyed twisting a couple of necks. What a joke. I wanted to tie the owners to an ant hill.

Soon it would be dark. I had to decide. Six miles of tortuous climbing. Maybe two hours of weariness before reaching Alpine. I gave myself two minutes to decide. Off I went–again.

There in front of me, another long and steep grade–no doubt about it–the mountains had arrived. I strained to reach the top and wonder of wonders, I faced a downhill! I coasted. I gained speed. The road swept around curves, the descent increased. I leaned to counteract the centrifugal force threatening to send me sailing into canyons on one side or the other. The curves were too tight for my increasing speed. I applied brakes carefully, alternating the front and rear pads so the rims wouldn't heat up and destroy the tires. Even so, I zoomed along at forty miles per hour hoping not to meet a truck coming from the other way. Everyone had been right. Entering Alpine one faced six miles of mountain roads–all down hill! I guessed in a car a person forgot–did I go up a hill or down a hill?–yawn. Sure made a difference when my legs supplied the power–only about one-quarter horsepower at that.

The views came and went. I snatched only a quick look before the next curve. One view, however, remained etched in my euphoric brain. Before me a wall of mountains. Above, a dark cloud almost hiding the sinking red-orange sun. A brilliant fan of rays shot out from the cloud. It was the kind of scene a painter would never paint–too gaudy–the kind of painting for a cheap calendar–over the top.

Mother Nature goes over the top sometimes–no taste for subtlety. I swooped into Alpine–having coasted for six fantastic miles. It was still daylight. I braked at a motel–I deserved a treat.

DALLAS, TX.

**Where the Cool Winds Blow**
(Perimeter Tour 1994)

If one used a little imagination–okay, a lot–and looked at a map of Texas, one would notice in the west, at a higher altitude than other Texas towns and cities, a triangle, described with somewhat wavy lines so as to sidestep a mountain or two, yet connected–an equilateral triangle where the cool winds hold forth, the year round. Of course, if one asked any of the citizens at any of the three points of the triangle about being equal with either of the other two points one would face an uncomprehending stare, followed by a conniption fit, and the unveiling of a lengthy factual brochure which would prove that the other two places could not possibly be thought of as equal to– and then one could plug in a choice–Alpine, Fort Davis or Marfa. Despite the protestations of local boosters, these three places belong together like Midland belongs with its kissin' cousin Odessa, or like Dallas belongs with its symbiotic twin Fort Worth. Alpine, Fort Davis and Marfa should go together and buy the inside of their triangle and do something spectacularly creative with it that would not only enrich west Texas, but the entire nation. Jurisdictional control might present a problem, since there are three huge counties involved, but it could be done.

Fort Davis is nearly a mile high, lacking just 230 feet and Marfa has a golf course nudging that altitude. Alpine is growing and has less than 800 feet to make it to mile high status. The marvelous thing about these places is the cool, cool breeze that wafts, or downright blows, away the summer temperatures.

Now back to my arrival in Alpine. Early in the morning, I journeyed to the friendly Pecan Grove RV park three miles west of town and put up my tent. Taking advantage of a few rest days, I visited the campus of Sul Ross State University, often called "the most beautiful college campus in Texas," maybe by Sul Rossians, and spent one morning in the handsome below-ground Big Bend Museum, located on the university grounds. I had a great dinner at the renowned Reata restaurant. I recommend it highly.

## Fort Davis
### (Perimeter Tour 1994)

Nothing impeded the cool wind coming from the west at my campsite. The nights were bracing and jacket-loving–the days sunny and bright, but not hot. I pedaled to Fort Davis, mostly uphill and against the cool winds, but only 26 miles away. The two most visited places at Fort Davis were the McDonald Observatory and the old fort. I arrived just in the nick of time to get a milkshake at the "Drugstore" which has no pharmacy and toured the Limpia Hotel–a venerable landmark, which has a gift shop and a great restaurant, where I had dinner ending with strong black coffee and the hotel's famous buttermilk pie.

Months before, I subscribed to **Star Date,** a bimonthly magazine, produced by the McDonald Observatory. Astronomy fascinates me. By musing about the hugeness of the universe or just our own galaxy and the vast distances out there, I maintain a better perspective on my moment of life. I wanted to see the observatory, but the nineteen miles northwest and the climb up to 6,800 feet–even though I knew I was already nearly a mile high at Fort Davis–dampened my spirits sufficiently and I passed on that tour. I needed more conditioning before I tested my leg muscles on that steep incline. McDonald Observatory is one of the ten most important observatories in the world—and some day I will return and climb that mountain.

The next day, I devoted several hours examining the army barracks, hospital, officers' quarters and headquarters buildings on the carefully reconstructed Fort Davis grounds. In the 1800s, it was the desire of every soldier to be assigned to Fort Davis because of the climate.

The fort was built up against jagged cliffs which figured in one of the two well-loved folk stories that make up a part of its history. The first legend featured an intensely romantic Mexican couple. The story, while embellished through the years, did have some basis in fact. Delores Gavino Doporto, reportedly demented, climbed the jagged cliffs above Fort Davis for years to build fires in an attempt to signal her young and handsome José who had been ambushed and killed by Indians in the mountains on the day they were to be married. If early records can be trusted, she lived into her fifties and died sometime in 1893. The name of the mountain near where she built the fires bears her name to this day. I wanted to climb up there and search for the fire site when I got my new hip. A long and very sentimentalized poem about Delores was written in 1885 by a Major Clapp for a reading at a party on the post by Mrs. Belle Marshall Locke, a one-time actress who lived on a local ranch.

The second legend grew up around Indian Emily. She was captured as a young girl after being injured in a fracas with Apaches. She responded well to treatment and grew up at the fort as a companion and servant to one of the officer's wives. She fell in love with a handsome officer who befriended her—more like a sister—subsequently marrying someone else, whereupon Indian Emily ran away disconsolate only to return late one night to warn the fort of a dawn attack. When she rushed into the fort with the news, she was shot by a sentry and died in the arms of her beloved officer.

One can visit the gravesite of Indian Emily, located about a quarter of a mile from the main part of the fort. Like most legends, the Indian Emily story does not stand the test of scrutiny. There never was an officer by the name of Easton, the supposed beloved, who served at the fort. There was a civilian clerk, however, named Easton and an early report by a post surgeon, of an alleged rape and murder of a captive Indian squaw which might have confirmed her existence. So, a mystery. I liked the folklore version, better. I paused several minutes at her grave site, which was hidden away from everyone except persevering tourists, who have Indian Emily's final resting spot at the top of their lists to see when they visit Fort Davis.

A more recent saga, infamous in nature, concerned a small unwelcome group headquartered close to Fort Davis which decided that Texas never legally became a part of the United States and was still not only a "whole other country" but a legal nation which owed neither taxes nor allegiance to the United States. I bicycled by the place where the gun-toting members eventually planted their Texas national flag in a trailer park. Things got out of hand and some were arrested, one of the charges being the filing of bogus liens. The short-lived movement appealed to several who felt disenfranchised by the government and who also wanted to turn the clock back to the 1800s. The dream of resurrecting the Texas nation was put on a back burner, where someday it may just slide off the stove completely.

## Marfa
### (Perimeter Tour 1994)

The third point of the triangle, Marfa, became my destination the following day. I ran into some road construction for four miles and climbed a few hills, but the twenty-one miles to Marfa's city limits turned into a pleasant ride through the high desert, largely due to the cooling breeze on my right shoulder.

My contact in Marfa, Gary Oliver, a cartoonist, invited me to camp out near his renovated adobe home. When I arrived, Gary was putting the finishing touches to a cartoon and soon joined me with a couple of bottles of Soporo Japanese beer. A house guest had just left, so I ensconced myself in the vacated artistic and book-lined apartment located at the rear of the lot, next to an outdoor shower and hot tub. The floors were brick laid in sand–rustic–and quite appealing.

I did notice one scorpion, but when it noticed me it quickly crawled into a crack between two bricks, and as far as I knew, stayed there all night–although scorpions do like to hunt at night. I put my shoes in bed with me.

In the morning, a gracious woman friend of Gary's served me hot coffee. The temperature gauge read 34 degrees–a cool start for the day, but invigorating with a brassy sun promising warmth within the hour.

I would call Marfa an artists' colony–laid back, peaceful with some mystery and a Hollywood past. The Chinati Foundation has been growing with a world-wide interest. It may become the one great claim to fame for Marfa. Begun by Donald Judd and chiefly for his huge works of art, it now includes several artists' works–especially those which are created on a grand scale. The exhibit area covers 340 acres of the old Fort D. A. Russell. Unfortunately, I missed it since the town was still caught up with the Mystery Lights and a movie which was filmed there years ago. These two items draw a lot of tourists. There is little or no publicity about the art museum, but the future of Marfa will be in the art world if enough people get behind it.

One of the biggest things that ever hit Marfa, a movie production, rejuvenated the town at a time when a long-running drought threatened its very existence. The year was 1955. James Dean, Elizabeth Taylor, Rock Hudson and others, plus an army of production people, invaded that vast land of sage brush and cactus near the town of Marfa during a hot summer and made movie history with one of the greatest of the super movies–*Giant*. The resulting movie captured the hugeness of the Texas story of intrigue, oil wealth, racism and ranch family jostling.

The great ranch house, a facade constructed on bleak ranch land, deteriorated quickly in the desert air. Only a few bare and weathered timbers existed when I rode by. Tourists still arrive, quietly poke around and meditate. It reminded me of the actions of African elephants, who handle and sniff tenderly the old bleached bones of their fallen comrades.

East of Marfa on Highway 90 I pulled up to read a marker. "The Marfa Lights, mysterious and unexplained lights that have been reported in the area for over one hundred years, have been the subject of many theories. The first recorded sighting of the lights was by rancher Robert Ellison in 1883. Variously explained as campfires, phosphorescent minerals, swamp gas, static electricity, St. Elmo's Fire, and "ghost lights," the lights reportedly change colors, move about, and change in intensity. Scholars have reported over seventy-five folk tales dealing with the unexplained phenomenon."

Unfortunately, it was not the time of day for me to witness the mysterious lights. Already, however, cars and RVs had parked, prepared to spend the approaching evening in anticipation of a magical viewing. The lights can not be counted on to appear each night. Some people have never been there at the right time to see them. Others testified seeing the blue and green lights, sometimes dark red, moving diagonally or up and down, or disappearing only to reappear at another place against the backdrop of the Chinati Mountains to the southwest across Mitchell Flat.

I read through at least 13 theories as to why the lights blink, run and slip about. None have been proven and some seem highly improbable. The folk tales were a delight to read, guaranteed to heighten one's interest, especially if camped out along the highway sipping on a six-pack and waiting for the show to begin. They ranged from Indian stories to government conspiracies; signals for German armies during World War I and also World War II; and earlier, lights to guide Pancho Villa to invade the United States. Of course, there were the stories of aliens using the lights for their own purposes. In the main, the lights were reported as helpful and friendly, showing ranchers, hopelessly lost in a blizzard, how to find their way back to their ranches or into Marfa.

One Indian story that I liked had two young people, an Indian herder and an Indian maiden who loved each other and each of whom had a flock of sheep which they brought down out of the Chinati Mountains in order to meet. One day when the maiden brought her flock to the meeting place, she saw a flash of light and going to investigate noted that the ground had been torn up. Nearby, one of the sheep had her lover's belt tied about its neck. The distraught maiden could not find the herder anywhere. Each week on the day he had disappeared the strange light would flash, and the maiden would move close to it to see if it held the answer to the disappearance of her true love. In the meantime, she had accumulated several suitors, but she spurned them all. One day as the light flashed she got too close and was blinded. The tribe moved away and she was left with but one suitor who remained faithful—and hopeful. She continued to wait and to search.

On one of her searches, she fell from a cliff and died. When her suitor found her, he decided to live the rest of his life at that spot. He believed the light he saw moving about was the grieving maiden still searching for her handsome herder.

The most bizarre story circulated at the end of World War II. Reportedly, the German prisoners held at the training base were turned loose. They headed for Mexico and were never seen again. The lights belonged to the ghost of Adolph Hitler, searching for his troops. For starters, there were never any prisoners held at the base. One of the funniest explanations I heard was from an old guy in a convenience store. "The annually elected 'Keeper of the Lights' just goes down the list of names in the Marfa phonebook and assigns each family a night to run out there in the desert and wave a couple of flashlights around."

Every few years, a group of students at Sul Ross State University get pumped up enough to conduct an expedition to get to the bottom of the mystery, but usually the expedition stalls soon after the beer runs out.

I pedaled on past the marker and the parked cars and RVs back into Alpine and the completion of my equilateral journey. In another day or two I would go east to Marathon and slant southeast to Del Rio along the border with Mexico.

My time spent in Alpine, Fort Davis, and Marfa reminded me of the Old West and the resourceful people who still lived there. I hope some day they will buy the inside of that triangle.

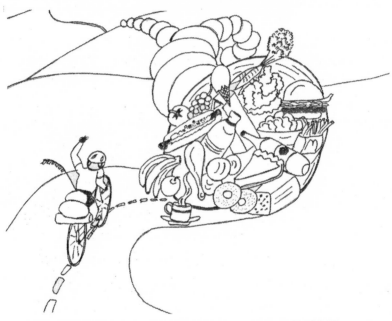

*Nope! Not a mirage. Definitely not a mirage. Nope!*

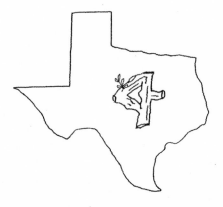

## *The Comanche War Trail*
(Perimeter Tour 1994)

The ride east on Highway 90 to Marathon and lunch at the Gage
Hotel in its Iron Mountain Grill proved delightful. A tail wind helped
me pedal at good speed along the desert highway. The weather stayed
cool and I had a warm sun. Having started late from Alpine, I arrived
in time for a late lunch. The hotel had been completely refurbished
and added to. It was truly a desert oasis. Built as headquarters in the
20s for a 500,000 acre ranch, it was abandoned and neglected decades
later. In 1978 J.P. and Mary Jon Bryan of Houston purchased it and
turned it into a show place again. The lunch of soup and a sandwich
was delicious. Once in awhile, I was tempted to just stay at a place
like Marathon for the rest of my days. Writing novels and spooning
up more of that soup–what could be better than that?

I rode on east a ways, as they say, and decided to camp out in the
open. To the north stretched the vast plains buttressed by red and blue

mountain ranges where some 150 years ago the Comanche bands would have thundered toward me on their superb horses. I wished it were September and a full moon–known by settlers as the Comanche moon–rose to cast its eerie glow–for that was the favorite time for raids. The bands would sweep south through the Marathon area on their way into Mexico. The trail was easily spotted in those days. The hooves of the horses kept the vegetation beaten back in a mile-wide swath. I wanted to recapture the sight, smell and noise of that ride, but only in my imagination. By camping out along the old trail, my mental recreation of the event could have free rein–and I would be perfectly safe as I pretended to be a raiding warrior or a hapless pioneer in the wrong place at the wrong time. Getting bludgeoned or speared by something sharp never impressed me as preferred ways to leave this life. A frontier assault usually meant a slow as well as a painful death. No, I'll take an eighteen-wheeler truck smacking me any day–not that I'm in any hurry for that either.

During my trips before and after this one, I visited several of the U.S. Military forts scattered throughout Texas. They were also called Indian forts, and I suppose to be politically sensitive they could be named Native American forts, but that wouldn't have been accepted by either side in the 1800s. The usual name that the Indians or Native Americans had for themselves invariably translated to mean "the people." There were several "plains tribes" in Texas at one time or another, but most people just think about the Comanche when the topic of a plains Indian comes up.

Along about the middle of the 17th century, the plains Indians grew increasingly dependent on the horses which either escaped or were stolen from the Spanish missions. The Spanish horse usually looked unkempt, maybe 14 hands high and weighed around 700 pounds. Looks deceived, since the Indian pony had no trouble bearing a 170 pound warrior quickly across the plains, seemingly never tiring. W. W. Newcomb, Jr. in his excellent book, *The Indians of Texas*, reported the telling of an encounter between officers at Fort Chadbourne, north of San Angelo and a group of Comanche warriors.

I have indulged in a bit of poetic license in the retelling–after all, that was how wild west stories grew. The basics, however, are faithfully reported.

The officers wanted to race their Kentucky mare, but the Comanche didn't seem much interested. When the Indians brought out their heavy-legged, long-haired "miserable sheep of a pony," the officers agreed to using a less imposing horse, reckoning any horse on the post could win the race. The Comanche warrior, using a war club smartly on his pony, won but not by much and the Indians collected the wager of flour, sugar and coffee they had bet against their buffalo robes. The officers demanded a rematch and brought on a much better horse. Again, the ill-formed decrepit-looking little horse won, but not by a wide margin. Then, the officers brought out the Kentucky mare and the stakes were raised. Betting became furious and a large amount of goods and money was on the line.

No undernourished Indian pony stood a chance against the fastest horse on the post–besides the pony had already run two races and would probably fall over before reaching the finish line. They lined up and as the signal was given, the Indian threw his war club away and let loose with a blood-curdling yell. The little pony shot across the ground as if from a gun. About 50 yards from the finish the warrior turned around on his horse's back and in a very unsportsmanlike way, made an obscene gesture at the laboring mare's rider. (Should have been a 15 yard penalty.) It was learned that the Comanche had used the same tactic earlier with the same pony and had won a considerable number of horses from the Kickapoo Indians. I thought only pool sharks knew how to play that game.

The forts were built to protect the colonists from Indian raids. They were usually in a line reaching north to south across Texas. No sooner was a line of forts built before the colonists were moving on west and crying out for another line of forts. The forts kept marching westward finally stopping when the colonists ran out of land at El Paso. Naturally, the Indians were hostile towards this westward push, as I would have been if someone were trying to take land away from

31

me.

However, it was interesting to note that the dominant groups of Indians at the time, the Comanche and their northern ally, the Kiowa, suffered no qualms of conscience in wiping out or subjugating most of the Indians already living in the Texas area before the "new settlers" arrived.

The "Lords of the Plains," as the Comanche were called, galloped out of the northern Rocky Mountains, transforming themselves from a servile and skulking society by leaping upon the backs of horses. The credit goes to the Comanche for learning to ride. Learning to ride horses ranked up there with learning how to walk and happened about the same time. They grew into exceptional horse handlers and conquered the vast space of the once-feared Great Plains, built a new culture around the American bison, known at that time as buffalo, and became the masters over other Indians who thought horses were to eat.

Judeo-Christian western civilization showed the Indians that when it came to "might makes right." sanitized later as the Manifest Destiny doctrine, the settlers and the army were no pikers. So, in this philosophy at least, the "savage Indian" and the "civilized settler" were remarkably alike. No quarter asked–none given.

Both sides regarded each other–using an analogy most modern Texans will recognize–as fire ants. Some would say the only good fire ant is a dead fire ant. I must admit that the fire ant analogy is particularly meaningful to me after I experienced a bunch of stings on my feet while standing on a flattened, and therefore, unnoticed fire ant mound after exiting from a river swim at Llano. My legs were covered with the black wriggling stinging mass. At the time, I made allowances, because, after all, I had invaded their home and I felt they had the right to defend it. At another time, however, I was attacked for no apparent reason with great enthusiasm by an advance patrol far from a mound. This time I felt no remorse about snuffing out as many miserable ant lives as possible as they marched resolutely across my blanket with malicious intent. With this rationalization I permitted myself to eliminate the intruders, and the home mounds as well. The Indian warriors, with their "unprovoked" attacks on "innocent" pioneers could have provided the army with a similar rationalization to punish not only the offenders but, in addition, to eliminate the Indian presence as much as possible. The fire ants sought to dominate their environment. The Indians wanted only to do the same. Apparently, the settlers liked that idea a lot, too.

*About how many bison burgers do we have here?*

The Indians were stubborn, however, and insisted on raising a ruckus at times, causing a scarcity of livestock, children, hard-working wives and several men caught out in the open tending herds or plowing up the prairie. It was a challenging time for settler and Indian alike.

On down the highway still heading east, I stopped at a campground and store and had a buffalo burger as a way of extending my mental trip into the past. Buffalo meat is very lean and therefore, comparatively healthy to eat. A few years later, when I went north into the Great Plains, I watched fifty bison being slaughtered for market at a processing plant in North Dakota.

The couple who owned the campground also managed 30,000

acres of wild life range close by. The range had a large herd of bison, elk, aoudad mountain sheep, foxes–but no coyotes. There was at least one mountain lion in residence. The husband said how he had spotted the lion one night along the highway with a freshly killed fawn. The lion gripped the fawn in its jaws and leaped over a fence with hardly any effort. I made a note not to travel at night in mountain lion territory. A note I apparently lost, since, toward the end of this trip, I did some night-time biking right through lion country. I made it without a scratch.

### Sanderson Cramps
(Summer Tour 1993)

The wind at my back meant I could get good mileage, so I decided to ride through Sanderson and see how close to Langtry I could get. I'll never forget Sanderson, a center for cattle and sheep ranching and fly breeding, built in a canyon with a large loss of life a few years ago when it flooded. My memory involved something less traumatic for the community, numbered at around 1,200 souls, but was plenty scary for me. It was on my first tour, the year before, when I arrived at Sanderson from the opposite direction.

The day's ride exhausted me–a stretch from Langtry without enough water. I arrived in Sanderson, opted for a thrifty motel, walked across the street to a drive-in and filled up on a hamburger and fries, a taco salad, two out-sized glasses of iced tea and a chocolate milkshake. I got another milkshake to suck on while walking back to my room.

Once inside, I turned on the air-conditioning unit full force–turned off the Spanish speaking TV station and lay down for what I thought would be a couple of minutes before showering. A half-hour later I attempted to get up and immediately cramps seized my right leg–the top of my thigh–the bottom of my thigh–the calf muscle and the top of my shin area–all at once. It happened too fast for me to straighten the leg. So, I grabbed it, bent it and held on.

The other leg followed suit. It felt as though every muscle would tear away. I could see myself being transported back to Austin on a stretcher and folks sadly shaking their heads because all my muscles had been ripped out of my legs and I would never walk again. I moaned and held the legs as close to me as I could. I thought about calling 911. Did they have that in Sanderson? No matter, I couldn't get off the bed. The two milkshakes decided my stomach was no place for them and began making overtures to my throat. We called a hasty conference and I put my foot down (Lordy, if only I could have) about them wanting to exit. After quelling about five rebellious uprisings, I won and the milkshakes, still grumbling, stayed below.

At last, I got hold of both legs with one arm which freed the other to massage my tormented muscles. In a few minutes I could straighten one leg and after more massaging, the other one straightened. So, there I was with two straight legs–rigid–trying to figure out how to get off the bed. Easy, I would just slide off an inch at a time–anyone watching would have had spasms of their own–laughing. When my toes touched the floor I was at an angle much like a big board leaning against a table. The table, in this case, was my bed. And I was anything but bored. Hoping not to fall, I hurled myself upright with a mighty arm push on the mattress. If only the room had been videoed for a "reality show"–I would have had everyone glued to the TV. Did I mention I was naked, too? The rest of the night I massaged muscles, walked around, took warm showers and possibly dozed. During the day I had become seriously dehydrated and my potassium had been depleted. Remember, I didn't know about that stuff on the first tour. That would not be my last leg cramping experience, but it definitely was the worst. I was scared stiff. There was no phone in the room.

As I went through Sanderson on the perimeter trip, I stopped a few minutes–just long enough for some ice cream and kept on pedaling. Unpleasant memories followed me to the city limits.

## Rattlesnakes
### (Perimeter Tour 1994)

A few miles before Langtry, I stopped to camp by the side of the highway. A rancher pulled up in his truck and invited me to camp on his ranch–just over the fence. "I'll lead you to a nice spot near the goat and sheep trails. Shearing's done and you won't do no harm." About an eighth of a mile inside the ranch I settled my tent on a rock-strewn knoll. Before he left he offered some advice.

"Be sure to stay in your tent tonight. We killed seven rattlers out here last week." I slept fitfully, careful not to let my toes touch the tent fabric. To a rattler in search of a meal, my big toe could be mistaken for a fat tasty rodent. For dinner I mixed soup powder with cold water and stirred in some crackers. More crackers helped me empty two sardine tins. I would never eat that kind of stuff at home, but out here on a sheep and snake infested ranch, it tasted just fine. Out my tent door I watched the finger-nail moon attempting to disperse the shadows that covered the nearby hills–not successful. The wind came up. My tent danced. I wondered if the shorn sheep would pay me a visit so I could count them.

A few years later, Sarah Jane English, a food and wine authority, invited me to go along on a whirlwind two-day trip to Alpine, Study Butte, Terlingua, Marathon and Del Rio. She was writing up some restuarants in the area and we did a little sightseeing. We left and returned to Austin in two days. It had taken me weeks. I remembered as we sped through Dryden, half-way between Sanderson and Langtry at 70 miles per hour, how I had spent a whole day just on that

lonely stretch of road and how I had run out of water and thought I
might die–quite a difference.

**The Law West of the Pecos**
(Perimeter Tour 1994)

I looked forward to visiting Langtry again. I had spent most of a
morning there the first time, writing postcards, eating sandwiches at
the little gift shop, visiting the museum, climbing into the small
building out back where Judge Roy Bean handed down sentences to
miscreants. He was the law west of the Pecos and he loved Miss
Langtry. I expected exclamations as I rode up to the gift
shop/postoffice and the museum.

"What? You again? Well, howdy! Gracious me! Welcome,
welcome!" I got off my steed and limped in–ready–it had been a year.
The ladies behind the gift shop counter were new. Friendly, but new.
The postmistress was new. The attendant at the museum was new. No
one remembered me. I felt old.

I walked out to visit the Judge. I knew he'd still be there–there's
sort of a security in dead people–they generally stay put. I stood
before the tiny building plastered on the outside with signs: Beer, The
Jersey Lilly, Justice of the Peace, Judge Roy Bean Notary Public,
Law West of the Pecos, Billiard Hall. Nothing had changed.

I climbed the weathered steps onto the weathered porch where the Judge often sat after being appointed Justice of the Peace in 1882. He moved from the tent city of Vinegaroon to Langtry in 1883 and the stories began. His one legal guide: The 1879 Revised Statutes of Texas. Mostly he used his own sense of justice backed up by the six-shooter he laid on the table beside the law book. He was not adverse to hanging evil doers, especially if they had borrowed a horse without permission.

The room off the porch measured 10 by 15 feet with a stand-up bar not more than eight feet long. A sturdy-looking table, four chairs, a bench and a pot-bellied stove completed the furnishings. In the old days, as folks told it, the saloon across the street paid a fine for disturbing the peace when it packed in a good crowd of drinking customers while Judge Bean's saloon remained nearly empty. Once, when an eastern lawyer made a motion to appeal a Judge Bean ruling that hadn't favored his client, the Judge, reportedly, put his finger on the trigger of his six-shooter with the muzzle pointed at the lawyer's mid-section. The motion was withdrawn.

Other tales involved Bruno, a pet bear, which Judge Bean chained up outside. If anyone had the misfortune of being "judged" drunk or disorderly, he joined Bruno on a nearby chain. The ensuing challenge to escape the lunges of the bear sobered a fellow up pretty quick.

The Judge named his saloon after Lillie Langtry, the great English actress, known as the Jersey Lily. A roaming sign painter, confused by her first name and the flower, painted "The Jersey Lilly" on the building's facade. A few years later she stopped by on the train to view her town, but the Judge had already retired to the cemetery. Miss Langtry's picture still hangs over the bar.

I didn't bother trying to get acquainted with the new people–I planned to stick with the Judge–he'd be there forever.

## Following Their Bliss
(Perimeter Tour 1994)

Farther on at a rest stop where I stopped to take a drink of water and stretch, I witnessed a pickup and trailer pulling in. Presumably a past-middle-aged husband and wife were spending time with each other on a trip out west. After a life of labor, at last they could do things together. The husband got out, opened the small door of the trailer, got in, stayed awhile then upon exiting, stumbled and fell on the ground nearly hitting a sharp guard rail. His wife watched from the pickup.

"What's the matter stupid, can't you see anything?"

"Shut your goddamned mouth!"

He got back in the pickup and they drove off. Togetherness–twenty-four hours a day.

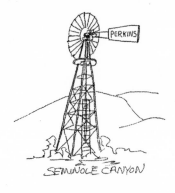

SEMINOLE CANYON

## The Devil's River
(Summer Tour 1993)

My next stop would be Seminole Canyon, just west of Del Rio. I had camped at the canyon the previous year riding south from Ozona alongside the Devil's River–it's earlier name, the San Pedro River, had only a brief tenure. Captain John Hays of the Texas Rangers came upon it while the country was still untamed Indian country. He sat on a bluff above it on a hot afternoon after a long grueling ride and proclaimed, "St. Peter's hell! It looks like the Devil's river to me." The new name stuck. Now, it snaked its jade-green way to the huge Amistad Reservoir near Del Rio. My ride that year of nearly 100 miles from Ozona to the Seminole Canyon had a break, thankfully, at Mayfield's Country Store. I followed an old stage coach trail at about the same speed as those coaches of old. Need I say it? I ran out of water before reaching the store. When I had drunk my last drop I became insanely thirsty–all at once. I considered slicing open a cactus–I had heard you could drink the stored water–but, fortunately, the store had appeared in the nick. I spent a weekend there in one of the most picturesque environments one could imagine. I scratched the ears of yellow-eyed goats. A retinue of turkeys, ducks and chickens followed me around gossiping and trying to figure me out. While there, I tasted, for the first time, the fruit of the strawberry cactus. Not only did it have a strawberry flavor, but it had tiny black seeds inside which, when bit into, popped like tiny, tiny firecrackers. I immediately thought of cornering the world's supply of strawberry cactus fruit, dipping them in chocolate and selling them in ultra chic shops throughout the world.

Emboldened by my strawberry cactus experience, I tried the fruit of the prickly pear. Instead of tiny, tiny firecrackers, I covered my lips and tongue with tiny, tiny hair-like stickers. I was told they would fester and pop right out in a couple of days. I spent an hour with a mirror and an eye brow plucker in lieu of the earlier recommendation.

I experienced my first storm at Mayfield's Country store, too. I t was quite mild–flattening my tent only a few times–but I thought it quite exciting and recorded it on tape along with my best imitation of a war correspondent caught behind enemy lines. I've got to go back there someday. My continuing ride to Seminole Canyon on that first tour bordered the beautiful river. The clouds cooled the temperature. The countryside was incredibly quiet. Wildlife crossed leisurely in front of my silent bike. Wild turkey, quail, rabbits, a snake or two, an armadillo, deer– hawks and vultures circling above me–everything, hills, trees, animals–all wrapped in a gentle breeze. The Devil's River wasn't the least bit devilish that day.

*Reading a Western Novel makes you forget your butt hurts*

## Seminole Canyon
(Perimeter Tour 1994 and Summer Tour 1993)

When I arrived at Seminole Canyon, known for its ancient shamanistic pictographs, I camped next to two motorcyclists from San Antonio. After our tents were up, they invited me over for a cup of herbal tea. I contributed some Mexican pastry I had purchased. Steve, a high school history teacher, and John, a high school counselor, planned to visit the Big Bend National Park before swinging about and going home. The camping area at Seminole Canyon was not in a canyon at all, but on a high plateau a mile from the park headquarters building. The 360 degree view, uninterrupted to the horizon was perfect for contemplation, and in the following few days, I did plenty of that.

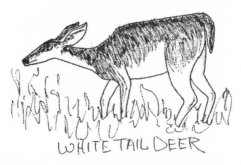

WHITE TAIL DEER

The obligatory thing at Seminole Canyon was to go down in it. For that, one joined a regular tour. Paintings of panthers, deer, birds and spiritual beings adorned the back walls beneath the overhangs. There, prehistoric groups of people, numbering around 15 or so, at any given time, lived and hunted. The paintings, in red, black, yellow and white dated back several thousands of years. A powerful hallucinogenic drug, ingested by chewing peyote cactus buttons, could have been the trigger for the visionary inspiration of those ancient painters. The artists used brushes made from sotol, a yucca-like plant with sharp stiff leaves. I counted our tour party–around fifteen–and international. I tried to imagine us thousands of years ago huddled around a fire and planning our next hunt.

"This place will be famous some day–just mark my words." There would be grunts from the group signaling the speaker to stick to the subject. I examined my fellow tourists with care–how helpful each one would or would not be in my prehistoric community. No doubt about it, we wouldn't have survived the winter. Maybe our paintings would have. I would have been the shaman. I wondered what a few peyote cactus buttons would have done for me. Party time–pass the paint!

In addition to a home and an art gallery, the cliffs above the canyon came in handy when the community got hungry. A bonfire belched smoke from below which obscured the edge of the towering cliff. Unable to see, the spooked bison fell to their deaths where they ended up, presumably, close enough to the fires for a Saturday night barbeque.

I learned the names of some local flora: black brush acacia, mountain laurel, buckeye, cenizo, also known as purple sage, ocotillo, resurrection plant, Gregg's ash and black persimmon. One can grind up the red flowers of the ocotillo for cough medicine. To kill something, just feed it some mountain laurel beans and buckeyes. Three beans

WILD TURKEY

would kill a cow, the guide said. We all gathered a few, presumably, to take care of an obstinate cow blocking our path some day. I studied all about the early railroads that came through this area and how a sheep ranch works. All good stuff should I decide to write a western novel.

At my campsite, a giant black bee-like bug visited me each morning around nine. Was it my brightly colored bandana that attracted it? Who knew? I could hear its approach through the black brush acacia, coming in low like a droning World War II bomber. The deep buzzing sound would get louder. Soon I could spot it in the distance and, as always, making a beeline toward me. I would wait, poised with my antiaircraft gun of insect repellent. When it finally lumbered into range, I bracketed its flight path with a couple of warning shots from my can. Invariably, its engine would stutter, cough and stop for an instant, causing a loss of altitude. But once below the shelling, bug-power would be regained and the black bomber would circle back into the desert drunkenly skirting Gregg's ash, a cenizo bush and possibly a greasewood shrub, not to be heard from nor seen until nine the following morning.

### The Helicopter Family
(Summer Tour 1993)

After the motorcyclists left, the adjacent campsite was occupied by a husband, wife and some boys–quite young boys–with incredible energy. The father was full of rules, always prefaced with, "Never,

NEVER..." and ending with "OK?" as in: "Never, NEVER argue with your mother, OK?" "Never, NEVER eat inside the tent because bugs will come in, OK?" "Never, NEVER put your eating utensils on the floor–ants will gather, OK?" I especially liked this one: "If you don't listen to exactly what I say, and do what I say–when I say it–we'll never, NEVER get anything done, OK?"

The mother limited her contributions to: "Don't do that!" and "Don't ever do that again!" Also heard from the father: "Never, NEVER touch wasps. Leave those wasps alone. We're not going to worry about those wasps, OK?"

I discovered, in addition to three small boys, a small girl. All of those arms and legs, big and small jammed themselves into a four-person tent. The father flew a helicopter in New Jersey for the Coast Guard and the family was on a fun trip across the country. In the first light of dawn the boys ran from the bath house chasing grasshoppers and anything that moved–not too wise in the desert, where practically everything had an array of protective devices. The father stopped them before they grabbed a 6 inch dark-green centipede with skin-puncturing orange legs. "Never, NEVER...OK?"

The mother explained they would be on their way to Carlsbad Caverns just after sunrise. "We're looking forward to it." She said this without smiling. Her face looked as if it hadn't smiled in a long time. I felt certain that the children and maybe even the parents would look back years later and pronounce that trip, white-washed of course, and with a good coat of nostalgia, as their most meaningful family-bonding experience.

### Ever Watch Ants?
(Summer Tour 1993)

I had a good time watching ants. No, that is not a misprint. And no, I wasn't bored out of my head to the point I would soon take up counting rocks. Actually, the little critters enchanted me–especially the Harvester ants. They made trails like super highways and brought in food after expeditions into the countryside surrounding their prominent hole in the ground.

They were fairly large and usually a brown and reddish-brown color. In the real world who would have the time and patience to watch ants–unless that was your profession, of course. I'm not going to give you an ant course–you can read the books. What I did was simple. I observed and learned just enough to appreciate their intricate society and come up with some questionable theories. I read some about them. They were really wasps. They didn't bite. They stung while using their pincers to hold on. They could do that stinging business a lot. The biggest news I learned about ants centered on the female ants. They did all the work in the mound and outside it. The male ants did absolutely nothing except wait for the day when they could fly off (they had wings) and attempt to mate with a new queen. Whether or not they were successful didn't matter, they died shortly after that flight and never made it back home. While they were waiting for this one flight, the female ants even fed them. What a life–or rather, what a short life.

Once the queen was caught in mid-air and received the love token from the male ant, she stored it away and parceled it out a little at a time as she needed it–in his ardor he had given her a life-time supply.

As I sat quietly and viewed an active Harvester mound I concluded that some of those female ants were slackers. This went against my Biblical knowledge, but I couldn't escape my conclusion. Some of those female ants simply did not pull their weight. Out they went, messed around for awhile, gazed at the sky and meandered back into the hole without picking up the slightest crumb of food. I even planted some crumbs for them and they passed right over or around them without showing the slightest interest. I did learn that Harvesters only picked up what their antennae touched. I reasoned that some of those females were wearing their antennae way too high off the ground.

One time I saw an ant carrying something that I didn't recognize.

So, with a small straw I made the ant drop her load. It was another ant–not a dead or injured ant either. The captive ant, once freed, took off in the opposite direction from the mound with zest. The other ant circled and circled looking for her captive. She spent at least 10 minutes searching. She gave up and went directly to the mound. She would need a good excuse.

"A huge alien attacked me, it was awful–right out of the blue, this huge THING and I mean HUGE–hit me with a log and...and..."
"Yeah, right–go to your tunnel and no TV tonight."

Another time I put a small mound of sand right on one of those trails. The ants struggled up one side and slid down the other side. It occurred to me that an ant cannot be deterred from a straight line to the mound. Therefore, I placed a twig on the incline and one on the decline so that the ants would not have to plow through the sand. Most ignored this new highway and continued to struggle laboriously up and down the hill. Occasionally, one would accidently find the twig and would speed over the hill leaving her comrades far behind, but the others refused to take the improved roadway. Given time, they probably would have adopted it, chemically.

One day I made the mistake of putting some food particles too close to the mound–almost on top of it–so those hard-working women would not have to go so far. Later, I found out they're kind of programmed to go out a certain distance before getting down to the business of gathering food. What happened to my particles? They were industriously picked up by the women in charge of keeping the hole clean and carted off nearly two feet and dumped as so much garbage.

Harvesters would appear beneath my picnic table scavenging. I scooped one up with my fly swatter and placed her on the table where I had some delectable tidbits. Immediately, she grabbed hold of one and ran to the edge of the table plunging without damage to the concrete far below. The force of the fall dislodged her prize however, and it took her a few seconds to locate it again, then she was off to the mound. The second ant refused to latch onto any food and ran around having a fit, eventually falling off the table. I put her back on top next to the delicious repast, but again, she refused it and nearly came unglued trying to get away. One of those slackers, no doubt, or perhaps just a highly-strung nervous ant that never got over not being selected as a queen.

I had a lot of experiences with ants, not only at Seminole Canyon, but at several of my stops. They never ceased to amaze me. I considered them fellow travelers and friends. The Harvesters never stung me.

COYOTE

**The Wolf Woman**
(Perimeter Tour 1994)

One night a family invited me to join them around their campfire. Bright stars, a moon, an erratic breeze which caused the flames to jump–perfect ingredients for story telling. We ringed the fire, watching the nervous orange-yellow flames tinged with hints of blue and green. There was an occasional pop as a droplet of sap exploded in the heat. We roasted a cut-up chicken. The talk turned to coyotes.

"Coyotes?" Manuel's eyes caught mine across the burning mesquite for a moment before refocusing on a chicken thigh impaled on his hand-held stick, twirling it slowly and expertly above some glowing embers near the edge. "No, we don't have as many coyotes anymore down here like in the old days. Ranchers keep thinnin' 'em out because of the stock and rabies, you know. But we used to have lots. Used to have wolves too, big ones–not afraid of anythin'." A drip of fat hit an ember and a small tongue of yellow flame leaped up. His two young sons sat together eyeing the marshmallow bag. Manuel's wife, Selena, had already turned in along with Monica, their six-year-old daughter. I had met the family the night before after they had pulled into the Seminole Canyon camping area in their bright aluminum Air Stream.

The boys opened the bag and fiddled with their marshmallows, arguing and laughing in turn as the blobs of sugar on the end of their sticks shaded from amber to brown to black and finally sprouted a blue flame. At that point the sticks were waved wildly to put out the small fires. Great blasts from puffed cheeks cooled the disfigured treats. They disappeared within sticky mouths amid expressions of delight only small boys can muster. Following the lead of Manuel, I roasted my own chicken thigh, but not as adeptly.

At the word wolves, the two boys turned their attention to their father. "Tell us about wolves. Tell us a wolf story," they pleaded. I added my interest. So, the teller of stories, slowly taking a bite of chicken leg, chewing thoughtfully for effect, like a good story teller should–making sure the audience could hardly stand the wait–began: "You ever hear about the Wolf Woman?" Manuel asked. Nope, we hadn't.

"Well, many years ago when Texas was young and there was a lot more land than folks, there was a trapper and his wife that camped out not far from here, where the Devil's River joined up with the Rio Grande. That's way before Amistad reservoir was built." He waited for his boys to nod agreement. "The trapper and his wife didn't have much to do with neighbors, not that there were many neighbors anyway because this area was near empty of everythin' except wolves and Indians."

"Well, his wife was agoin' to have a baby and the trapper wasn't sure she could make it on her own." Questions formed in the eyes of

48

the two youngsters, but they didn't dare ask anything that might have interrupted the story.

"The trapper lit out on his horse to find a neighbor. When he found some folks and explained the situation, they agreed to go back with him, but a terrible storm came up and a lightnin' bolt hit the trapper in the head and he was deader than that old mesquite wood you're holdin' onto," pointing to the boys' marshmallow sticks. Both boys gazed intently at the small blackened limbs.

"The folks decided to follow his trail back to see if they could find his wife. The storm had wiped out his tracks in places and they missed the trail two or three times, causin' the loss of several days. They finally found her lyin' under an old mesquite tree. They could tell she had died givin' birth, but there was no child–just wolf tracks– lots of wolf tracks. So, the folks buried the trapper's wife and went home and forgot all about it. But that's not the end of the story–not by a long shot." Here Manuel helped himself to another bite of leg and an interminable chew.

"Well, about ten years went by, and some cowboys were out huntin' some Longhorns in the brush and they came up on the strangest sight. There, eatin' a raw and bloody calf was a naked girl and two giant wolves." The boys scrunched up their knees and let their mouths drop open. I didn't know what my mouth was doing. I did know I was caught up in a Texas campfire tale. Manuel went on.

"The cowboys took out after the girl and the wolves. For awhile she ran on all fours, but all at once reared up and ran on two feet. The wolves got away, but they cornered her in a box canyon. She fought like the animal she was, but they got her roped and on a horse and brought her back to their ranch. Her yellow hair was so long it nearly hid her whole body but what they could see was burned brown by the sun and looked like leather. They put her in a room with just one small window that was boarded up.

"Some of the cowboys remembered the story of the trapper and his wife and decided that the wolves had taken the baby girl when she'd been born and raised her as one of their own. When the moon came up that night she started howlin'.

"But it wasn't like anythin' the cowboys had heard before. Part wolf and part human and so sad–it made a person want to cry. Hour after hour, she just howled and howled until the cowboys thought they couldn't take it any longer. Then they heard wolves far off in the hills answerin'. The howls got closer and closer–and closer. Every wolf in ten miles was acreepin' up on that cabin." The boys scooted together and their eyes darted out where the shadows swallowed up the bushes and the other campsites. Manuel took another bite of chicken, chewed a couple of times. He looked–scary-like, into the darkness.

"The wolves!" Manuel jerked his arm up. The boys squeaked two unboylike squeaks. "Wolves," he yelled again. "The wolves attacked the corrals. They went after the goats and the horses and the cattle, tryin' to slash and kill everythin' in sight. It was terrible. The growlin', the shrieks of the horses, the bleatin' of the goats, the bawlin' of the cows–it was like the Devil himself had showed up."

"The cowboys ran out with their guns ablazin'. They chased off the wolves, but not before the wolf woman knocked open the window and ran off in the desert. Her and the wolves went far away and for a long time no one saw any wolves near Devil's River or the Rio Grande."

The boys sighed and giggled nervously–trying to laugh but not doing a very good job at it.

A good story. I wondered if I could tell one like that.

"But that's not the end of it," said Manuel. "Six years later, two goat herders travelin' up the Rio Grande west of here, saw her–a full-grown woman covered with her long yellow hair and a bit darker–across the Rio Grande on the Mexican side. She was sucklin' two wolf cubs. When she saw the goat herders, she gathered up those cubs in her arms and lit out in the brush so fast no horse could ever catch her and she never showed herself again. But a lot of folks up the river seen wolves with faces that looked human.

"Of course, all the wolves are gone now, so we'll never know for sure." With those words, Manuel reared back his head and let out a long, mournful wolf howl. The sound echoed in the canyon below us. The boys grabbed onto each other and a light went on in the Air Stream.

Yep, it was a darn good tale. Later, I heard and read variations, but however the details differed, nothing could detract from its power around a dying mesquite campfire high on the mesa overlooking Seminole Canyon and told by a master story teller.

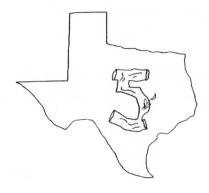

## *Del Rio*
### (Perimeter Tour 1994)

Out on the road again with Del Rio my target for the day, I noticed a slight change in the weather. More humidity, a touch of mugginess enveloping me. In the city a constable told me about a park fifteen miles farther on where I could camp free. I liked free.
Del Rio began in 1635 as a mission. I learned things didn't really take off, however, until 1883 when two railroad lines joined nearby. Irrigated farming proved successful because of the San Felipe Springs which pumped 90 million gallons of fresh water daily.

Across the border, the sister city, Acuña, bustled with a population of 150,000, four times larger than Del Rio. Several maquiladoras–twin plants– where products were assembled on the Mexican side in plants owned by U.S. firms and then exported back to the U.S. without tariffs were mainly responsible for its growth as had been also the case at Laredo, El Paso and Brownsville.

The big advantage for the U.S. firms lay with the greatly reduced wage scale of Mexican workers. The disadvantage for Mexico were the conditions under which the workers lived caused in the main by the lack of an adequate infrastructure to take care of the burgeoning population.

In the 50s and 60s, Wolfman Jack broadcasted with his gravelly voice across the U.S. thanks to the million watts of radio station power there. I remembered listening to him late at night. Earlier I crossed the great bridge across the Amistad Reservoir–an important body of water and a magnet for water tourists. I knew that Del Rio was also home to Texas' oldest winery, the Val Verde Winery. Since I had another fifteen miles to pedal, I resisted tasting the fruit of the grape.

I arrived at the park, and heard happy voices and the sounds of Mexican music. As I prepared my campsite, I could see the colorful group having a picnic, children playing, some men with accordians and guitars, people singing–having a great time–families gathered for an evening of food and fun. I put up my tent close enough to hear the music and chatter of happy voices only to have everyone leave at dusk. I didn't like the thought of camping by myself as I watched the trees beginning to disappear in the shadows. However, I would not be alone long–a dilapidated car swung in and parked beneath the high bridge that spanned the park. I got the feeling by the way the driver unhesitatingly swerved off the park road and headed for a secluded stand of small trees directly under the bridge that he had been here before–perhaps often. I barely got inside my tent for the evening before two ferocious dogs, freed from the car and in no mood for making new friends, rushed toward me, barking and growling. They patrolled the grounds until daybreak. Talk about feeling safe.

BROWNSVILLE, TX.

## Carrizo Springs
(Perimeter Tour 1994)

The next morning I ate a breakfast of oatmeal and coffee while still in my tent. Finally, I unzipped the front panel and stepped out into the heavy humid air alert for mosquitoes and anything else. The car and dogs were gone and singing birds–lots of birds–took their place. On the road at last, I noticed my very first palm tree. Although they grow as far north as Austin and beyond, I somehow took this sighting as a sign of welcome to the subtropical valley area of Texas. Suddenly, everything appeared greener.

The gray folds of fat clouds wrapped around me like a monk's cowl and I began to fantasize I had biked into Florida–a recurring phenomenon as the days passed and I drew close to Brownsville at the southern most tip end of Texas. The winds were light and I made it to Eagle Pass on Highway 277 where I debiked for a breather before continuing on to Carrizo Springs, still on Highway 277, a good day's bike ride–eighty-seven miles. Stopping for the evening at an RV park carpeted in lush green grass, I adopted a couple of homeless and hungry chiggers. After my shower, I set about the task of mending my tent. The zipper had given me fits since I left Alpine and it slowly but surely gave out. I had purchased strips of velcro, an upholstery needle and thread, then sewed the strips next to the damaged zipper.

The repair worked until I got back to Austin. In the meantime, the mosquitoes welcomed me as a new member to their blood bank. I must have donated at least ten times that night. I bought more cans of insect repellent resulting in nearly one-fourth of my daily budget going to fight mosquitoes and chiggers–an unexpected touring expense.

## Defender of Justice in Catarina
(Perimeter Tour 1994)

The next morning I got an early start for Laredo, a little over 80 miles away. Again, I had oatmeal and coffee to get my engine started. Out on Highway 83, I noted I had one small town to pass through, Catarina, which turned out to be an interesting experience. But first, as I stopped for a mid-morning snack of refried beans and fried apple pies, I noticed what I thought were two deer approaching the highway from the overgrown field across from me. I realized they were coyotes. Possibly, a male and his mate. She, smaller and more skittish, saw me first, although they both were on high alert. I didn't move a muscle, but they dashed at full speed into a field on my side of the road. I wondered if life were shortened by such a constant state of readiness to fight or flee.

To say that Catarina loomed into view down the road would certainly be an overstatement, even though there was an abandoned three-story hotel there which used to pack people in thanks to the supposedly medicinal springs close by. I didn't see any form of life until I was nearly out of town.

Seemingly out of nowhere, I heard this resonant voice announcing crime reports for the area. Someone had a very loud radio. As I got closer, I saw a trailer with loud speakers about one hundred feet off the highway. Apparently, the loud speakers spotted me and invited me to drop in. Rain had been threatening all day and I was ready for a break anyway, so off the highway I went to check it out. Signs with big letters were everywhere.

"Guardian of the Law." "Violators of the Law Will Be Prosecuted," "Crimes will be Immediately Reported," "No Drugs in This Area." There were several others, but those were all I copied down. As I stepped inside, a rather large man said howdy and proclaimed he was 71. A worse-for-wear black T-shirt covered his generous stomach. He had a nice-sized gap between his front teeth, wider than my favorite model's and a one-inch white beard. He explained he was the Watchman for Justice.

His assistant, a young Hispanic woman, got me a soda to drink for a quarter. Half of the trailer was set up as a radio station–except there was no station. A turntable, a recording device and a public address system that reached to the highway were located in front of a picture window. The Watchman had a good view of the highway. He told of a drug bust close by that had yielded several hundred pounds. "Helicopters, police cars, everybody was here." "When?" I asked. "Everyone knows when and where and that they let the driver go." He exuded good cheer until he looked across the highway where a few candy and pop machines were parked–like what are used in carnivals or on vacant lots in towns.

"That carney throws nails on the highway that causes flats. I've watched him do it." He stopped long enough to issue a small report about police negligence on his public address system. No one was listening as far as I could tell.

"Don't drink the water around here–it's got sulphur in it and bacteria. I just drink sodas–want another–on the house." I had another soda. It began to sprinkle and I left. I felt certain Catarina had the lowest crime rate in the entire country.

### Casa Blanca Park in Laredo
(Perimeter Tour 1994)

On the highway, I saw a wall of rain in front of me about half a mile away. Behind me I saw another wall of rain, also about half a mile away. I stayed dry in the middle by carefully adjusting my speed–keeping both walls at bay and doing quite well at the job when hunger intervened. At a crossroads I stopped and entered a small café where I heard only Spanish being spoken. I had biked into Mexico? Another fantasy. I downed a wonderful bowl of hot and spicy chili–chomped through two burritos and drank two cups of coffee. The other patrons seemed genuinely pleased to see me and we shook hands all around. Mexico is a friendly country. When I left the rain walls had disappeared and a hazy sun tried its best to shed some warm light on me and the countryside.

The cacti were in bloom and stands of mesquite still hugged the highway, but I noticed little by little a changing landscape. Palm trees, semi-tropical wild flowers, orchards of pecan trees and grazing cattle in green fields announced a new land. Fog appeared in the mornings, but burned off by ten.

I entered Laredo on the border where ninety percent of the 155,000 inhabitants are Hispanic. Across the river Mexican Nuevo Laredo with a population of over 400,000 and wonderful places to shop awaited me, but I didn't cross over. On non-bicycling trips to Nuevo Laredo, I had a great time in the shops. A large amount of the trade between Mexico and the U.S. takes place there.

In Laredo I got a map showing how to get to Casa Blanca park, where I would rest for a couple of days before reaching Brownsville. Actually, Boca Chica was the very tip end–and I planned to bike there and right into the Gulf. Before riding to the park, I stopped at a McDonalds and ordered a chocolate shake. The waitress didn't understand English–no one in there did. I did a lot of pointing. Amazing. Challenging. I didn't dislike it. I pointed at a picture of a hamburger and held up three fingers. I took them with me for dinner. The young people were full of laughter and had a good time with their "gringo."

At a grocery store I had purchased large black garbage bags. I was tired of everything getting wet. At the park I hung out everything to dry. While all my stuff was drying, I lined the inside of my panniers with the black plastic bags. I would use them also to cover my sleeping bag, mat, and tent which I piled on the back of my bike above the panniers. I would be ready for the next downpour.

In the morning my tent was crawling with tiny ants. The "picnic" ant presence is not uncommon where there are a lot of picnics. Casa Blanca park is quite popular with people and therefore, with ants as well. I thumped the fabric, from the inside, sending the little busy-bodies into orbit. None got in–the velcro worked. For breakfast I prepared my usual bowl of oatmeal and coffee which turned out to be not enough to eat. I made brown gravy from a mix and water which I boiled on my stove. Into the gravy I broke up seven slices of bread and the hunger pangs subsided.

White herons graced the lake in large numbers. After breakfast, I washed and oiled my bike and tightened everything in sight. I washed all my clothes, showered and shaved. In the afternoon I took time for a brief sun bath. Lazy, lazy. I couldn't go for a walk because of my hip, but I enjoyed my stay a lot. Just relaxing–one of my most favorite things to do.

A couple of years later I would be at the park again during a cold front that pushed the temperatures into the 20s and I would meet a beautiful young girl.

### Blue Eyes
(Winter Tour 1996)

So, jumping ahead to my next visit to the Casa Blanca park ( my fifth tour in Texas, and with my new hip, O joy!) we begin when I decided to explore the brushy country to the south of Austin. The two months I had not traveled in the Lone Star state by that time were January and February. So on the 28$^{th}$ of January 1996 away I went. Little did I know that Texas was in for a cold snap.

I made good time, because shortly after I left, the wind shifted to the north and I had what every bicyclist wants–a good tail wind. Apparently, I hadn't been watching my T.V. and the weather surprised me out on the road–or else, by then, a hardened traveler and tourer, I didn't care.

The only problem with this tail wind soon became apparent as my feet lost their feeling and numbing took charge of my hands. In addition, a misty, slightly sleety rain fell for most of the day and I got soaked through. At last I pulled up to a motel in Luling about 60 miles south of Austin and called it a day. Trying to extricate myself from the bicycle, my foot failed to clear the top tube, the bicycle moved, and my body, apparently shutting down in preparation for hibernation, didn't respond, as one might say, with alacrity. I fell over–just toppled, and on my recently replaced hip, too. As my helmet-clad head introduced itself to the pavement, the woman manager ran out to see if I had hurt myself. I thanked her. Nothing appeared damaged but my pride.

In the days that followed I attempted to out-pedal that cold spell. By the time I reached Hebronville, about 230 miles south of Austin, it swept southward in front of me. My plan had been to turn around at Hebronville and go back north toward Freer, famous for its rattlesnake roundups each year. The freezing wind still howled from the north when I lay down that night and it still howled the next morning–so instead of facing the "norther" to Freer, I opted to go to the Casa Blanca park at Laredo–due west 62 miles away. The cold wind stayed on my right shoulder, so I made it into Laredo and to the park with a minimum of discomfort. I could stay there over the weekend or as long as it took for the wind to play itself out. On the highway to Laredo, I was struck by the number of song birds which lay frozen on the road. Obviously, they were not made aware of the arctic blast sweeping south Texas the previous night.

However, to be fair, the passage in Matthew's Gospel about the birds of the air being fed did not say anything about warning them of cold fronts.

At four-thirty, I arrived in Laredo and wound my way through the city and back out on Highway 59 to the park. In a secluded valley I pitched the tent just as darkness settled in. I put on all my clothes and snuggled down into my sleeping bag. I thought my toes would never warm up. The wind found my valley and spent the night tugging and shoving my tent around. In the morning, I didn't want to unzip that sleeping bag. Maybe I would stay in it all weekend. At last, I steeled myself, unzipped and faced the frigid air–in the 20s.

There would be a wind chill suitable for an Oklahoma expedition. I packed everything up as fast as I could–loaded the bike– and pushed it up the hill to the south side of a large white-painted building containing the park's showers and restrooms. There I set up my tent again right against the wall and out of the wind. What a difference a wall made. The sun's rays warmed the wall and my tent. The numbing wind lurked around the corner. As I congratulated myself on the ingenious strategic plan and superb tactical maneuver that would ensure a pleasant weekend, I glanced in the direction of the entrance to the building and there, draped in a heavy blanket, stood an adorable young woman with bright blue eyes, looking at me. "Where did you come from?" she asked. I found out she stayed inside the women's restroom and had been there for several days. Apparently, the park officials looked the other way and allowed her free reign of the building. Since very few tourists were using the park anyway what could it hurt? The women from the RVs which did drive in insisted on buying her groceries and supplies–so even without heat and money, she managed.

We decided to go for a walk along the lake during which I found out she was in her early 20s and from Connecticut where it was too cold which was why she was here basking in Texas' warm weather. First, she had hitch-hiked to Kentucky, but it was almost as cold as Connecticut, so she got a ride with a truck driver to Texas. She had no money, but she was certain she would be able to make some soon and that it would also warm up.

"Maybe I'll move to Harlingen and get a job, there." Harlingen was close to the border about another 150 or so miles south.

"It would be warmer there, no doubt," I replied, noting that I wouldn't mind being there myself. I had biked through Harlingen on my third tour. It had been in late spring and very muggy and cloudy.

"You know," she said, "birds wake up in the morning and fly maybe twenty miles before breakfast. Maybe we should do that." Her bright blue eyes challenged me. "If you run really fast and wave a sheet over your head, it's almost like flying." She ran for a short distance waving her arms above her head. She danced with excitement and the cold wind reddened her cheeks.

"I'm going to get into weight-training. A person's body is the most wonderful thing. I want mine to be strong. I'll probably enter body-building contests and I'll win, too." She laughed.

She had broken up with her boyfriend because he used drugs. "Definitely not good for your body," I said.

She told me she left the city's shelter program because of a personality problem with the director.

"I'm going to be a millionaire in a couple of years. I can do it. Just start a lot of little businesses. I'm going to build a spaceship, too. Anyone can do it–out of old spare parts."

So, some delusional thinking. I knew it would be hard for me to build a space ship even out of new parts.

We got back to the tent and I told her I needed to write in my journal and take care of some chores. I didn't see her the rest of the day or evening, but I could hear her talking occasionally in an upbeat clear voice, as if she were conducting a class with herself as both teacher and student. She went over lists of things to do to stay on track. "Always be positive in everything you do if you want to succeed." "Winners win and losers lose." "Plan your work and work your plan." I thought I was listening to motivational speeches in a real estate office.

The next morning as I got up, she was standing outside with a tray of food. "I've got plenty so I wanted to bring you some breakfast." I thanked her for the cookies, fruit, cheese and a small bottle of orange juice. The early morning sun backlighted her tousled blonde hair.

"Let's have a picnic tonight," she said. "Build a fire and roast something. You can play your harmonica some more." She had heard me practicing yesterday afternoon, I supposed.

"It could be a little windy, but we can do it," she said with rock-solid assurance. Her optimism and can-do spirit seeped into my old bones. She told about the placards she taped on the walls inside including a calendar so she could plan her days efficiently.

"I have to keep focused. You have to stay focused or you never get to where you want to go. I have a definite schedule to keep." Sounded good to me.

Late in the afternoon I walked to the entrance of the restroom and called out to see if she wanted to help build the fire. No one answered. I called again and told her who I was. After a few seconds I could hear her moving around.

"Oh, I forgot. I have an appointment tonight, so I can't join you for the fire. I'm sorry, but it's impossible." Her voice sounded preoccupied and disinterested.

Blue Eyes

She didn't leave the restroom. She had no transportation. No one came to pick her up. In a way I was relieved. I hadn't really looked forward to hunkering about a small fire in freezing weather–trying to cook something edible. On the other hand, I was sorely disappointed that it hadn't worked out. We could have talked about flying some more and where she planned to go in her spaceship after she made her millions. All was quiet–no motivational speeches were heard that night. A psychiatrist might have labeled her as maybe manic-depressive, a little delusional and suspicious of relationships. Aren't we all a little like that at times? Maybe she could make it. I hoped so. At least she coped well enough to survive so far.

May your life be as promising as a sunrise.
And as peaceful as a quiet summer's sunset.
May each day be filled with beautiful dreams and wonderful
Moments of achievement.

I fastened the note near her door and wondered if somewhere, sometime, it would join the other placards taped up on a wall someplace.

In the predawn I packed up and by daybreak pedaled out of the park on my way to Freer. The wind had died down and because I was going to Freer from Laredo instead of from Hebronville, I could ride on a northeasterly slant with what wind there was on my left shoulder.

There would be no towns along the way for 65 miles. I could do it. I was focused.

If it had not been for the cold front, I would not have detoured to Laredo and I would not have met the blanket-draped blue-eyed girl who wanted to fly like a songbird.

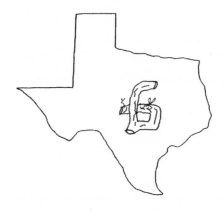

## *Into The Valley*
### (*Perimeter Tour 1994*)

One of the most important periods in the history of Texas took place along the Rio Grande. From the area around Del Rio to Brownsville in the early spring of 1836, Mexican forces entered Texas to teach the rebels a lesson. Texas gained independence because of those forays. Two of the most famous battles in Texas history were the Texan defeat at the Alamo in San Antonio and the Texan victory at San Jacinto, near present-day Houston. It appeared ironic to me that after the fracas, so much of south Texas appeared to be Hispanic. People who had been born and reared in south Texas and who were of Mexican, Indian and Spanish descent were fiercely Texan and firm citizens of the United States while at the same time jealous of their Hispanic heritage. A more balanced view of Mexico and Texas history over the past several years made room for both

Mexico and the United States to draw closer together in trade and appreciation.

A recent book by Stephen Harrigan, *The Gates of the Alamo*, went a long way in dispelling earlier myths and giving both sides in the conflict their due. I also read an earlier book by Stephen L. Hardin, *Texian Iliad*, which covered the battles in great detail and took an in-depth look at both sides. My bicycle ride through The Valley was certainly a highlight of my journey around the perimeter of Texas. What a rich cultural milieu welcomed me on my travels along the southern border. After Laredo, I selected Zapata as my next camping spot–an exotic sounding name. I remembered the movie, *Viva Zapata* and wondered if it had been filmed in Zapata. It turned out that another town named Roma received that honor–forty miles farther along the border. I would ride through there too.

As the fog burned away, the temperature climbed. The end of April signaled the beginning of summer in South Texas. Small cumulus clouds puffed up in the sky, looking as though someone had pulled a handful of cotton balls apart and then tossed them up to hang against the blue. One minute the countryside looked like a desert and the next minute there appeared the lush green fields of central Florida. The highway rolled up and down–up and down–not steep, just worrisome. Grackles and blackbirds flew about in large numbers. At a store I drank a quart of milk and ate a pint of strawberry ice cream. I planned to ride through Zapata to a camping site at the Falcon Lake State Park. I didn't make it–not even to Zapata.

## Flat Tires
### (Perimeter Tour 1994)

In the early afternoon the wind increased to 15 miles per hour with gusts up to 25. I shifted into lower gears and ground out the hills. I got a flat tire–the first on the perimeter tour. When I took the tire off to examine the tube, I saw that a plastic boot I had contrived last year had disintegrated allowing the tube to squeeze out through the damaged tire. To be safe I exchanged the tube for another. The tube I selected had come with the bike a year ago. Why I still had it, I didn't know. In addition, I put on a fold-up Michelin tire, since without a proper boot, I couldn't use the tire I had taken off.

The name "fold-up" means exactly that, the wire bead around the rim of the tire was not as rigid as a regular tire, thus allowing it to be folded up without taking up as much room in the pannier. (By the way, a boot can be made out of a credit card–preferably one you don't use anymore–even a folded up dollar bill will work and if you don't have one of those, you could use a twenty–more bucks for your bang.)

All fixed up at last, down the road I pedaled. I stopped to check on something and bam! the valve stem on my replacement tube blew out. So, flat number two and only eight miles between them. The tube and tire gods were definitely in a snit. I remembered that the valve stem had blown out on the other original tube as well–last year before my first trip. What a bummer. I took off the tire and inserted another tube–a new one purchased just last winter to have as an extra. I had a tough time getting the Michelin tire to clinch onto the rim because of the weaker bead. Finally, I got it on and started pumping in the air. At around 50 psi the bead on the tire separated from the rim at one point and the tube began mushrooming through the crack. Frantically, I tried to relieve the air pressure by poking at the valve stem with the back end of my pressure gauge. Too late! The tube expanded rapidly and blew up. My new tube with a ragged hole–unpatchable. Flat tire number three. I looked heavenward in despair. In that old TV drama *Mission Impossible*, the heroes were always able to save the situation at the very last second. I thought about that and how reality meant the tube blew up in your face.

Now, all my tubes had holes. One with a valve stem missing– couldn't repair that. One with a jagged hole–couldn't patch that. One that had gone flat because of the damaged tire. The hole was large. But I got a patch to cover it. That time I made certain the fold-up tire was well seated and I put in only 40 pounds of air, half the amount I normally carried in the tires. That time it held. The whole process had taken two hours out there on the open road. I was too hot and tired to go into Zapata. I camped off the road near Falcon Lake in some tall grass that shielded me from the highway. I covered myself with insect repellent before setting up the tent and once inside I washed thoroughly from head to toe with undiluted alcohol. Not a single chigger got to me. Even the mosquitoes were respectful. I wrote down in my journal about buying good spare tires and tubes. Across the lake, the clouds were purple and lavender. Beautiful.

## Falcon State Park
(Perimeter Tour 1994)

In the morning I doused myself with fresh insect repellent, took down the tent and emerged from the field of grass like some alien. No one paid any attention. I think I saw a Peregrine falcon. In Zapata, I ate a big breakfast. Jalapenos and eggs will lift anyone's spirits and mine needed an uplift. I left the café with new determination and a spring in my walk.

I crossed the handsome bridge across the reservoir. Falcon State park would be less than 30 miles–an easy ride. I needed to lay over, wash clothes, and rest. I noticed fields of onions. One field had been picked and the onions stuffed in small burlap bags. Some onions were shipped loose in trucks. Alongside the highway a few large onions had bounced out. I put a couple in a pannier and later had an onion sandwich. That will put a spring in your walk, too.

The wind remained in my face and gusty. I reached the state park, set up camp, washed clothes and relaxed, kind of. The wind increased with gusts to forty miles per hour. My tent dived to the ground–completely flat–in a strong gust, and popped up again as the wind died a way for a moment. Later in the day, Mother Nature calmed down.

Rabbit

## Road Kill
(Perimeter Tour 1994)

Coming from Zapata, I saw a small snake, a red-tailed hawk, a doe and a large dog–all road killed. There were a lot of animals killed each day on the highways as I made my tours. Since I ride by slowly, their presence makes more of an impact on me than if I were in a fast-moving car or truck. I decided not to list road kill each day–too depressing. The animals were there–smashed, their lives ended and there didn't seem to be a solution. At least the vultures didn't go hungry.

In a trash barrel I found a Sunday newspaper and caught up on world news. The comics were there too. And the Parade magazine! Things were still happening–life, death and the funnies.
The temperature reached 98. I wrote postcards to my friends and family. A bunny rabbit, nose twitching, came within ten feet and we looked at each other for a few moments. On the beach, car stereos blared sending great Mexican music my way– from about an eighth of a mile–just about right. Included in the sounds reaching me, the independent rhythmic clanks of several close by oil well derricks hoping to reward investors.

## Chachalaca
### (Perimeter Tour 1994)

In the morning, I awoke to overcast skies, the usual way days started in The Valley. The clouds and fog disappeared by ten. I saw lots of birds. For breakfast I had Turkey Tetrazini–another bird. I followed the turkey with oriental-flavored noodle soup. Two tins of sardines and coffee. I wanted some buttermilk, but I couldn't expect the perfect meal every time.

Around 7:30 I hit the highway on my way to Bentson Rio Grande State Park, south of McAllen and Mission. I met a very loud bird. If I wanted a perfect example of onomatopoeia I would just say cha-cha-la-ca at the top of my voice–chopping the syllables and if possible in a contralto range–or failing that–I could yell the syllables in falsetto. Now, I would put that sound on a tree limb ten feet above my tent (where it actually was!) and wait until dawn–then, let 'er rip.

If I kept the raucous cry going at irregular intervals so that I was constantly caught off guard, spilling coffee, bumping into something, dropping something, you would understand why I would want to shoot the damn thing and have it as an entree. People down there ate the Chachalaca and I didn't blame them one bit. On the other hand it was a splendid alarm clock.

*Lordy! my second breakfast today!*

# The Trail
## (Perimeter Tour 1994)

The Bentsen-Rio Grande Valley State Park provided the setting for a semi-tropical experience. Bird watching ranks as a popular pastime in The Valley along with trail walking to see some exotic plants. Markers told me what I looked at. Sometimes, what I looked at didn't look back. The guide book alerted me to that. Note: I saw a sign that said snake-eyes. The unusual shrub, when in flower gives the appearance of looking back at a person. The guide book reported it had died. I hated that. I wanted the experience of a plant looking at me. So, on to the next marker. Several markers reported accurately what appeared before my eyes until I got to the Huisaches marker: Dead. The sugar hackberries had also been hacked out.

Farther on some nincompoop had lettered a sign stating that in front of me grew a catclaw acacia. Rather than repaint the sign, the guide book announced the error. Not a catclaw acacia, but a Wright's catclaw. I felt trod upon mentally. I had to stand in front of the sign a long time repeating–sometimes out loud–Wright is right. Wright is right. Toward the end the Dryland willows had given up the ghost too. Actually, most of the items were alive and reaching for me as I walked by, but it bothered me to see some things dying off–was it the result of global warming? No, of course not. It's supposed to be hot and muggy in The Valley. Maybe not hot enough? Had I stumbled onto something? More heat! We needed more heat at Bentsen!

I read about all the birds: green jays, groove-billed anis, kites, hawks, chachalacas, herons, falcons, over a dozen species of ducks several species of warblers and six species of owls. I saw several birds but I didn't recognize some of them–none had markers.

Of interest to me was the mention that I might see a bobcat close to my tent that night. Also, there were snakes, but only the coral was poisonous. I didn't know if the snakes visited the tents at night like the bobcats so I zipped up tight and stared out through the mesh at dusk. Unfortunately, all the snakes and bobcats had died apparently, because nothing moved out there. I checked the guide book to see if I had missed a notation. I got sleepy, sleepier, sleepiest and fell over backwards onto my sleeping bag. Perhaps a bobcat came by after all and listened to my snoring.

*Pack up all my cares and clothes. . .*

### Mosquitoes
### (Perimeter Tour 1994)

Birds weren't the only things along the trail with wings. The mosquitoes were abundant and, according to them, underfed. I wore my insect repellent and had no trouble keeping the starving masses at bay. Four followed me into my tent after chasing me from the shower. They found out I did not see the humor in that.

### New Stuff
### (Perimeter Tour 1994)

I rode into Mission and purchased two tubes and a new water bottle. I cut a section out of the old one for a boot. Why didn't I buy a new tire? Over budget. Anyway, flat number four happened shortly thereafter. My patched tube gave out. But with my new boot and a new tube and a spare I could, once again, face the vicissitudes of south Texas bicycling.

## Brownsville
(Perimeter Tour 1994)

I could hardly believe I was closing in on Brownsville, only 50 or so miles away–the pointy end of Texas–the oldest town in The Valley. A Spanish explorer came through in 1519, but the resident Indians decided they didn't want the neighborhood infiltrated. Things went downhill for years until the Karankawa Indians moved away. They had a superb recipe for a fish dish. First, catch a fish. Second, put it on a rock in the sun for a few days and let the flies land all over it. Third, check to see if maggots are busy. Voila! Dinner! The fish flesh, soft and aromatic and the squirming little maggots, a taste treat and a lively chew. No wonder the Karankawa were unfriendly.

A Spanish settlement was established in 1748. Being on the south side of the Rio Grande, it became present Matamoros. The land across the river, present day Brownsville remained nearly vacant until the border dispute with Mexico was settled. The U.S. said the border with Mexico lay along the Rio Grande and Mexico liked the Nueces River–quite a ways farther north as the boundary. A fort was constructed and subsequently the commander, Major Jacob Brown was killed. Later, his name became the name of the fort and also of the new town that sprang up after 1845. The two cities buried the hatchet and increased trade, a bilingual culture and free movement back and forth made the area a bustling commercial center.

The Gladys Porter zoo in Brownsville, was ranked among the ten best in the United States. Again, I didn't go because by that time, walking for any extended period of time was definitely out of the question. The University of Texas established a campus in Brownsville and the Texas Southmost College also called the city home. Both institutions worked hard to provide a quality education, not only for the residents, but also for the increased numbers of winter visitors. Brownsville had a deep-water port and one of the largest shrimp boat fleets in the world.

I kept thinking I was in Florida. This feeling persisted even after I left Brownsville and had stopped at the King Ranch up the coast. "Nice ranch for Florida," I thought. I ate a lot of oranges along the way. I holed up at the Crooked Tree RV Park in Brownsville, a great place to camp. Green, green, green.

Beautiful trees including palm, evergreen, mesquite, mock olive and flowering hibiscus crowded the grounds in profusion. Brownsville could be Costa Rica. The camping grounds had a swimming pool, laundry, showers, restrooms, gift shop, black-topped drives, cement patios, and picnic tables. I relaxed for a day, just letting all the travel tiredness run out the ends of my toes.

## Boca Chica
### (Perimeter Tour 1994)

On May 1, I took off for Boca Chica–the absolute farthest southeast point of Texas. I left all my baggage in the RV park. Just me, a repair kit, three water bottles and my bike made the exhilarating trip. Instead of a tank, I was aboard a frisky filly. We dashed through the clouds, the spitting rain, the coastal breeze, the waist-high marsh grass and the "ancient" concrete highway with the regular "kabump–kabump" separations. My next highway like that was in Canada three years away.

Rain squalls lashed my face. I didn't care. The bar ditches brimmed with water. I saw terns, herons, sand pipers, gulls, swallows, but no pelicans. Near the coast I saw a subdivision of small houses packed together. One good-sized hurricane and goodbye subdivision. The day I rode it was cool, but I could imagine the high temperature and the mugginess of summer. Indicative of harsher times was a sign reading: "Don't drive while the dust is blowing."

The highway ended with a big red stop sign! Beyond it a narrow beach and the mighty Gulf. I rode–pushed my bike to the surf. The seas were running six to eight feet. A few people were surf casting into the waves. I was 25 miles east of Brownsville! I had done it! I had ridden across the southern border of Texas. I wished I had started at El Paso instead of Big Bend.

A spatter of rain followed me back to Brownsville. I was a happy camper. I couldn't have been happier even if I had dipped my bike in the Pacific and into the Atlantic. Besides, I thought I was in Florida.

I could have stayed longer. I really liked Brownsville. Right across the border Matamoros waved provocatively. I'd have to save that for another time.

If you consulted a map and located Brownsville, and looked north up the coast you would see no roads. You would need to come inland about 20 miles to find Highway 77. Fifty miles or less from Brownsville you would arrive at Raymondville (pop. 9,000) after passing through numerous towns and cities. As a matter of fact, the area around Brownsville (pop.100,000), Harlingen (pop. 50,000) , Mission (pop.30,000), Edinburg (pop. 30,000), Pharr (pop.33,000) and McAllen (pop. 90,000) was densely populated. After Raymondville–poof! Everyone disappeared. I know, I was there.

It was amazing, the density before Raymondville. I biked to Harlingen on my way north, and I took a trip over to Pharr, McAllen and Edinburg, too. In between these good-sized cities are numerous towns and villages, again predominately Hispanic. I counted at least thirty towns in the area. From 1,000 to 12,000 or more residents in each. I would wager anyone that if I counted everyone who came and went in this region you could double all those figures. So, in the extreme South Texas Valley there could be nearly a million residents. That was a great eye opener for me and I bet for most Texans.

When I got to Raymondville, before me stretched a straight uninhabited highway for miles. If you don't count Sarita–58 miles to the north and only one small store–and a couple more stops after Sarita, just like it, you are looking at about 75 miles of vacant highway. It was great. Most of that area constituted the mighty King Ranch.

The wind came from the east. Not exactly a tail wind but not in my face either. The road was straight and smooth and not hilly. Gray clouds hung low. On both sides of the highway, thousands of wild flowers bloomed. I recognized the Indian paint brush, the Texas or Russian thistle with its pink blooms and many species of daisy-like flowers. Some white and some yellow. I had mangos, oranges, bananas and apples to tide me over until I reached a store. I made it to Kingsville after dark. I had stopped at Sarita and asked permission to put my tent up beside the store, but the manager said it wouldn't be safe with all the "illegals" passing through. To the west the mighty King Ranch sprawled. I stayed over in Kingsville and rode out to the ranch the next day.

## The King Ranch
### (Perimeter Tour 1994)

I was heartily welcomed at the ranch's main house and had a fine visit and dinner–just kidding. I did ride to the visitor's center which provided ample material to impress me. It was almost impossible to imagine a working ranch that large. There was a giant ranch of three million acres in the panhandle, but it was parceled off and just a memory within 27 years of its creation.

By 1925, the King Ranch included well over a million acres. I read that it comprised 1.2 million acres in four counties–still one of the largest ranches in the world and larger than the state of Rhode Island. Income was derived from oil and gas exploration on the property as well as from successful Quarter Horse and English Thoroughbred breeding and racing enterprises. The ranch was best known, however, for the deep red Santa Gertrudis breed of cattle developed right there over a 30 year period in the ranch's early history. According to the flyer, the ranch was now home to approximately 60,000 head of Santa Gertrudis cattle and over 300 registered Quarter Horses. King Ranch was also a multinational livestock corporation controlling more than four million acres world wide on which it produced grain sorghum, sugar cane, rice, cotton turf grass, sweet corn and cattle. The fact that the ranch had lasted and doing well was a marvelous thing. Whoever heard of a ranch that made money?

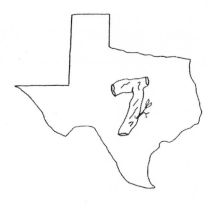

## *The Coast and East Texas*
### (Perimeter Tour 1994)

Big Bend National Park had disappeared in my rear view mirror over one thousand miles ago. Soon, I would cut this trip short and cut across the state for Austin. But not yet. I had no idea when, if ever, I would be in this part of the state again, so I decided to go on up the coast–maybe into the National Forests of East Texas before calling it quits.

I continued to parallel the coast about 25 miles inland. I made my way through Robstown near Corpus Christi, a crescent city overlooking Corpus Christi Bay that others have said reminded them of Buenos Aires. I stopped at an RV park with luscious green grass in the town of Sinton.

## Goliad
(Perimeter Tour 1994)

The next day I arrived in Goliad, a city steeped in early Texas history. It began as Santa Dorotea in the early 1700s and became La Bahia in 1749. In 1829 the name was changed again to Goliad. The two places I wanted to visit were the old fort and the mission. Presidio la Bahia was established in 1721 on the Matagordo Bay, hence its name "The Bay." It and the mission were moved to the lower banks of the San Antonio River in 1749. I was told the fort was the only restored Spanish colonial fort in the Americas.

In the space of one hundred years, the fort was involved in six separate independence wars and has had nine flags fly over it. For Texans the most infamous incident was the capture and execution of over three hundred soldiers under the command of Col. James Fannin during the war leading to the founding of the Republic of Texas in 1836.

I camped at the 178-acre Goliad State Historical Park. A few mosquitoes and "no seeums" camped with me. I pitched my tent right on the bank of the San Antonio River. I had just learned that when the Texans were executed there were some 25 or so who, feigning death, successfully escaped by easing into the river at nightfall and swimming away. I wondered if my tent sat on the exact spot where some soldier in 1836 had slipped into the river. The news he carried would have been a heavy burden, indeed.

Goliad was also the birthplace of General Ignacio Zaragoza, the hero of 1862 who forced the French from Mexico. That event is celebrated in Mexico and the southwestern U.S. as Cinco de Mayo.

ARMADILLO

## Armadillos and Alligators
(Perimeter Tour 1994)

My next stop was at Edna and the Texana State Park, some 60 miles away on Highway 59. I passed through the lovely southern city of Victoria. Beautiful old homes. I saw a lot of armadillos dead on the highway. It's reported that the natural habitat of the armadillo is dead at the side of the road. Unlike other animals who try to run for their lives across the road, the armadillo comes to a stop as the car or truck approaches and jumps straight up. There has to be a gene that can fix that someday.

At the park entrance, the attendant cautioned about alligators. Therefore, I set my tent facing the lake about twenty feet up the embankment. If an alligator came through the front door, I planned to go out the back window. The frogs entertained in the evening sounding much like a symphony orchestra tuning up. I heard clarinets, bass fiddles, violins, flutes, castanets and a very unsymphonic sound like a very rusty hinge. Other wild-things played around my tent during the night, but I tried my best to ignore them. In the morning, my clothes still dripped from last night's washing. I put them on–no matter–it rained most of the morning anyway. In the restroom a boy told me how he caught a small alligator on his fishing line. Also, how a raccoon had made off with a loaf of bread. Must have been raccoons around my tent last evening. In Austin I attended a party once where a raccoon came in the kitchen through the small "pets" entrance, slipped slyly to the refrigerator, opened it, selected some leftover chicken and sauntered away. He left without closing the refrigerator door, however. Bad raccoon.

Every morning in East Texas, where it's clammy, muggy and rainy in the spring, summer and fall, I sprayed, rubbed and splashed on DEET (thankfully shortened from N, N-diethyl-m-toluamide), the best insect repellent ingredient ever formulated. I also powdered my behind so liberally with baby powder that if I bumped into anyone I emitted a white fog around both of us. The DEET kept the mosquitoes at bay and the powder kept me smiling all day. So what if I looked like Linus. I was happy.

### A Snit and Self-Serve
(Perimeter Tour 1994)

I left early and 90 some miles later I camped at Surfside. To reach it I had to disobey the law. In front of me soared a huge awesome bridge that looked like Jacob's ladder ascending into heaven. About a fourth of the way up an unheavenly sign announced "Bicycles and pedestrians prohibited." I said a few unprintable words and went over anyway. What was I supposed to do–turn around on that narrow road–swim–walk or pedal on water? Of course, I knew the road was too narrow–saved a lot on the construction costs that way. They could have saved more and just made it a bicycle lane and foot path. "Cars prohibited." I was pissed.

Tired, sweaty and my DEET losing its potency, I stood, negotiating for a camping spot by the beach. The owner decided

$3.00 would be adequate. I lost a pint of blood as we bargained, probably worth $15.00 at any collecting clinic. I put up my tent, took an alcohol bath, put on fresh DEET and went for a ride up and down the beach on the packed sand. Like a busman on holiday–but hey, that was fun. The moon and crashing waves made it worthwhile. I got over my bridge snit.

In the morning, more DEET. Mosquitoes whined, but didn't land. I went next door for breakfast. My campsite negotiator sat at a table. He pointed to the coffee pot and to the menus in a box nearby. I got my coffee and sat down with a menu to plan the biggest breakfast known to western man. After I made my selections, he pointed to the kitchen. I walked into the kitchen where the cook, dishwasher and lone waitress greeted me and complained about the mosquitoes. The waitress was blonde, attractive and tired-looking. I was glad I had spared her the trip to my table. We went over my breakfast plans, doing a substitution here and there after conferring with the refrigerator, the cook, the waitress and the dishwasher. I didn't know what the dishwasher had to do with it, but I let it pass. Maybe he wanted to be included. Some of his teeth were gone, but he had a nice smile.

I won't tell what or how much I had to eat, because I don't want anyone reading this to faint. Suffice it to say, I got filled up. A nice feeling. Oh yes, after breakfast, I carried my dirty dishes back to the dishwasher. He thanked me. I left a tip for everyone on the kitchen table. We all hugged. It was a good moment.

### Galveston Island
(Perimeter Tour 1994)

With boundless energy pouring from every pore, I raced up the highway on Follet's Island to the toll bridge. Wonder of wonders–the toll man waved me through with a smile and a salute. At the other end of the bridge lay Galveston Island. Up that island I continued racing to the Galveston State Park where I would hang out at water's edge for a few days. The reason I used the words "raced" and "racing" should be evident by now. I had a terrific tailwind of 20 miles per hour all the way up. Being pushed by a tailwind counted as a religious experience for me. I passed several houses along the way. Every house ascended from the sand on poles. The landscaping favored blooming oleanders and bougainvilleas. Very colorful–white, red, pink. Bushes were ten feet high. Several properties had "For Sale" signs. Expecting a hurricane?

As I wrote that in Austin on September 9, 2002. "Fay," a tropical storm, threatened to lash Galveston with 10 to 15 inches of rain. I typed, with one eye on the T.V. By October 4 as I reread this section searching for errors, two hurricanes, Isadore and Lili, had visited the Louisiana coast just a week or so apart with winds close to 100 miles per hour, a big storm surge and plenty of rain. I decided I would pass on touring in Louisiana along about that time of year.

Galveston had a defining moment in 1900. Rapidly becoming a major port, it was nearly destroyed by a hurricane that year. Since then it has struggled to regain some of its former glory. As far as the threat from hurricanes, portions of the city of Galveston on the northern end of the island have been raised nearly two stories. A gigantic seawall erected after the 1900 disaster and along which I rode a few times on my trips into town from the park, also protected the city. The street atop the massive wall of boulders drew crowds of pedestrians. Some rode on and in two and four-wheeled cycles, the latter looking like the "surrey with a fringe on top" from *Oklahoma.* No one really knew if those hurricane barricades would work until a comparable hurricane hit again. It has been over 100 years.

Galveston fascinated me. Laid back, friendly, discovered by tourists, it's future appeared bright. I wouldn't mind living there at all. First, I would measure that seawall again. Second, I would rent and have a permanent U-Haul trailer parked close by. Third, I would have an excellent communications system with a meteorologist. Fourth, I would relax and enjoy the people, the beaches, the sun and the magic.

*Okay! Okay! You're the Boss*
**The Beach**
(Perimeter Tour 1994)

On the beach at the state park south of the city, I camped for $12.00 per night a few yards from the Gulf. I put my tent on grass next to a concrete structure that went with the camping site. There was a picture-window-sized round open hole in the sides permitting a nice view all around. The site also included a wooden and metal picnic table, a barbeque pit, a fire pit, water and electricity and a sewer hook-up–too small–I chose to use the restrooms. During the day I walked some along the beach watching the slow-moving ocean-going ships and fishing boats out in the Gulf looking like ghosts in the haze. Nearer at hand on the sand, I inspected a barnacle-covered coconut with a tale to tell, driftwood–probably from Africa, a Portugese Man-of-War–from Portugal?, iridescent pink and lavender jelly fish, people in various states of undress and sea gulls.

The so-called "laughing gull" had a black-capped head, eyes surrounded with a ring of white, white breast, gray wings with some black, an orange beak, knobby knees and webbed feet. After four or five laughing-like cries the head would jerk back sharply a couple of times accompanied by beeps. Sounded like my computer before crashing. After a brief interval the whole thing would start over. A generous poop was exported after some verses. For dinner I had two packages of noodles into which I broke up seven slices of bread. I don't know why I put that next to the poop sentence.

That night teenagers had the camping site next to me. Music and enthusiastic socializing abounded. Okay, I was young once. I remembered when loudness and giggling were equated with wit and charm.

All was quiet in the dawn hours. I didn't want to leave. Alas, off I pedaled northward to the ferry that would carry me to the "mainland." While the ferry throbbed its way across, I replenished my engine with pressed ham, tomatoes, two fried apple pies, a can of Vienna sausages, a beer and two quarts of buttermilk. The gas tank read full. When we docked I had 63 miles in front of me and a storm to beat to Winnie. I had a girlfriend once named Winnie. I received permission to camp in the city park and elected to put the tent under the pavilion. Lightning flashed, the sky rumbled, the clouds fell to the ground. Mother Nature upended her big bucket and tried to drown me. The park was inundated. The concrete floor of the pavilion got wet. I got wet. All my stuff got wet. Welcome to East Texas.

The next morning I swished out of there to Beaumont where I would begin my tour up through the Big Thicket and the National Forests. That was not my last time in East Texas. The following year after my successful hip operation I traveled into East Texas again and also into South Texas. I have related some of my experiences in South Texas already during that winter's ride (Blue Eyes.)

## The Mystique of East Texas
(Perimeter Tour 1994 and some of Fall Tour 1995)

Beaumont, Port Arthur and Orange formed what a lot of folks called the Cajun Triangle. The Cajun influence there on the Texas and Louisiana border shaped the culture of that fascinating area. The area also boasted the name Golden Triangle because of the influence of oil and the petrochemical industry. Just south of Beaumont on

January 10, 1901, a gusher blew in named Spindletop and became the richest oil field in the United States. Six hundred oil companies elbowed each other in the area over the following two years. It was an exciting and messy era as derricks nearly touched each other as they rose into the sky, hoping to cash in on the black gold.

The area also produced notable musicians. Janis Joplin, Gene Joseph Bourgeois, Harry Choates, George Jones, Joe Hunter, Tiny Moore, Barbara Lyn, Jules Richardson, Johnny Preston, Tex Ritter, Jerry LaCroix and the Winter brothers. And, who could pass up a big bowl of gumbo brimming with shrimp, chicken, crawfish and duck mixed with peppers, onions, celery and spices and who knows what else?

On this trip (perimeter trip of 1994) I pedaled through the Big Thicket, the Angelina and the Sabine National Forests. On my tour in the late fall of 1995 I slipped around in the Sam Houston and the Davy Crockett National Forests (Davy preferred to be called David, by the way–and he hardly ever dressed up in a coonskin cap and fringed buckskin leather).

The towering magnolias, the short and longleaf pines, cypress, hickory, oak, gum and several other species of trees, shrubs, clinging vines and Spanish moss grabbed at the narrow black-topped highways in an almost smothering hug.

There was a feeling of waiting and watching as I peered into the darkness of the trees and underbrush on either side of me. Birds could be heard but not easily seen. Other crackings and poppings testified to something going on in there just out of my sight, but real and alive. Man or beast who knew? It felt prudent to move silently, quickly and to watch carefully.

Occasionally, and more often than I wished, I heard the distant sound of a straining logging truck, gears grinding as it growled its way up and down the forest hills and ever closer to me. Would it move over? If not, off the road I would go into the weeds and grass, harvesting a new crop of chiggers to scratch that night. One truck came too close near Apple Springs in the Davy Crockett National

Forest. A November fog augmented by a light mist magnified the truck's engine as it approached. I knew those trucks were limited to 84,000 pounds, but a fellow down the way told me they usually weighed a lot more. Not that it mattered if it hit me. The horn signaled its passing. Enough room, I thought, until the rear of the truck whipped by. One crooked log sticking out whispered across the top of my helmet.

### Good Ol' Boys at Lunch
(Fall Tour 1995)

I visited Nacogdoches, which maintained it was the oldest city in Texas and staked that claim on a visit made by De Soto's men who stopped there awhile on their way to Mexico in 1541. But perhaps a more realistic starting point for the community was in the early 1700s by the Spanish. Nacogdoches was both modern and historical and a lovely city.

I stopped for lunch one day 12 miles or so west of Nacogdoches near the north end of Davy Crockett and Angelina forests at a village named Douglass, population 75–maybe. Several logging trucks had stopped too. The drivers knew each other and stories punctuated with laughter made the rounds. With a secret microphone and recording device, I could have gathered enough material for a whole book right there. If I had been included in the group, the stories would have been different, containing stuff for my benefit. So, since I had no secret spy machine on me, I just listened to the group as kind of a woodsy background music.

Everyone was in a good mood until one guy mentioned a funeral. Things simmered down to somber for awhile. I had a huge double meat cheeseburger with chips and iced tea, followed by freshly made coconut pie for dessert. That was during the hunting season, so, in addition to the regular stories, hunting stories were exhumed about a hunter getting lost, becoming spooked, freezing solid or going home deerless. The owner of the café told the group he had shot a deer that past Saturday.

"Had nine points anda spread of eighteen and a half inches."

"What'd ya use?"

"Thirtyoughtsix–gonna mount the head–I was sittin' ina tent box for a coupahours. 'Round five this buck walked inda clearing and I popped 'im." The group applauded. Later, as I paid my check, I asked him about the deer.

"I took 'im home, skinned an' quartered 'im and put 'im on ice to bleed good, then took 'im to the processor. I'll get as many steaks as I can out of 'im anda rest I'll mix with fatty hamburger for patties." In answer to my question,

"No, ya can't sell it. Ya either eat it yerself or give it away." There were no women customers in the café.

## Warnings
### (Perimeter Tour 1994 and some of Fall Tour 1995)

**"Be careful,"** had a rather ominous sound when uttered in East Texas. Maybe it had something to do with the closed-in feeling caused by the forests–the inability to see farther than a few feet for great stretches–connoting mystery and, at worst, a shadowy evil. Common sense told me that life was not more dangerous in East Texas than anywhere else, but when anything did happen, it tended to be accompanied with a sense of gloom and foreboding.

One man in Groveton on the south boundary of the Davy Crockett National Forest, could not imagine my traveling without a gun.

"I've taken the training for carrying a concealed weapon and I can hardly wait to get my gun. Things can happen to you out there," motioning toward the forest up the highway, "and you gotta be ready. You better carry a gun. If the logging trucks don't get you–there's plenty of people who'll shoot you just for the hell of it."

On another day, at a small town on the north end of the forest, a grizzled guy with a huge gut held in place by a greasy T-shirt and suspenders, told me not to camp out at the roadside rest area north of Jacksonville, which was exactly what I had intended to do.

"A friend of mine was beat up there by a bunch of sonsabitchin' teenagers. They used a bat with nails in it–broke his arm and left him for dead. So, be careful in Jacksonville."

"When did that happen?"

"Two weeks ago." As he talked I couldn't help but notice most of his teeth except for the two upper canines were missing, which added something darker to the story. I decided not to camp at Jacksonville. It would be a motel for me that night.

Three years later, the little town of Jasper would be forever cloaked by the evil deed of three white men beating a black man, chaining him to a pickup and dragging him two miles to his death while parts of his body sheared off.

In 1995 just after I had biked through Silsbee near the Big Thicket, eleven youngsters were arrested after the brutal thrashing of a Quarter Horse. Run into barbed wire and hopelessly tangled, the 14-year-old horse, named Mr. Wilson, was beaten to death with sticks. One of the youngsters was a girl and some were younger than ten. When asked why they had killed the horse, they couldn't come up with a reason.

I stopped once at a café just west of the forests to have a cup of coffee. I struck up a conversation with a retired Houston area sheriff. When he found out what motel I had spent the night in, he laughed. "Boy, were you lucky. A highway dead-ends at that motel. Three trucks have already gone through it just this year." No wonder the room rate was low, I thought. My only concern at the time was the open space at the bottom of the door that might admit a snake or rat. The sheriff and the waitress took turns telling me how dangerous it was for me to be out on the road.

"Crazy people will run you right off the highway." The waitress refilled my cup. It was her turn.

"Ever camp at Granger Lake?" I had.

"You can't use the bathrooms because of the rattlesnakes. They have to use push brooms every morning to get them outta there." The retired sheriff added his comment.

"And the only way you can kill one is by accident, plus they got a big rat problem." To myself I thought rattlesnakes swallowed rats, perhaps Granger Lake needed more rattlers, not less.

Some of the nicest people I met on my tours lived in East Texas. I was never threatened or run into and any close shave I had could only be described as an accident. Yet, after listening to warning after warning it was hard to concentrate on a magnificent sixty-foot-tall magnolia tree without wondering what or who was standing behind it watching my every move.

## Some Dogs I Liked and Some I Didn't
(From all tours)

One day I encountered two dogs intent on a nibble. One was a big black chow and one was a pit bull–two dogs who don't understand friendly. I decided not to be friendly either so I commanded them to "STAY" and it worked. Usually, the dogs I encountered on my tours were farm dogs who, supposedly guardians of their homestead, were more interested in running along side barking away as if on a lark. To those dogs I issued friendly greetings and a good time was had by all.

I did have a dog grab my foot just east of El Paso while the lady of the house continued working in her lawn–ignoring the attack. I shook free and gave that dog a very picturesque lecture, intended for the lady more than the dog. I have a very loud deep voice and a good vocabulary. The dog went back in the yard and peed on her pants leg. Riding out of one of the national forests in East Texas, I pedaled up to a service station to buy some snacks and refill my water bottles. As I turned to leave, I saw a young, short-haired, brown and black hound at the door. I said something nice in dog language and he perked up immediately. I petted him a couple of times and scratched his ears. I couldn't help it. He was just too neat to ignore. However, I should have noticed no collar and no apparent owner standing around. When I boarded my bicycle, I had a new bike mate signed up.

A small but persistent incline kept my speed down so it was quite easy for him to trot behind me. A mile went by and I could not speed up sufficiently to lose him. I began thinking how nice it would be to have a dog with me on my trip.

I recalled the days of my youth when a stray appeared at our door and my brother and I begged and begged to keep him. We named him Dagwood, but never called him that–it was always "that's a good boy or here boy." My dad decided one day we didn't need Dagwood and we all piled into our 1928 Hudson and took a trip way out in the country. We let Dagwood out and sped off. My brother and I watched Dagwood trying to catch us but growing smaller and smaller in the distance. We cried. Mother cried. Dad didn't.

Several weeks went by and lo and behold, one day Dagwood showed up. He was thin and worn and had been in some fights. My brother and I rushed out to welcome him home, but he wouldn't look at us. It nearly broke our hearts. That time we got to keep him for good. Eventually, he returned our love.

Those memories flooded as I tried to pedal away from that young hound. I fantasized picking him up and letting him stand on his hind legs on my rolled up sleeping bag just behind the bicycle seat with his fore paws on my back. I didn't think he would do that. Even if I could have found a place for him to ride, would a motel allow him inside the room? The temperatures at night were below freezing. What about shots? Where could I get them? Was I stealing someone's pet? From time to time, I would lose sight of him only to see that he had taken up a position immediately behind the rear wheel–his earlier enthusiasm waned but doggedly he trotted on. I knew it was too far for him to follow me to my next stop. After four miles, I came to a UPS regional depot and turned in. I asked one of the men loading trucks if he would hold the hound until I was out of sight. He understood completely and because all East Texans love dogs, easily made friends, gave the dog something to eat from my snack container and took him around the building out of sight. I pedaled away.

I thought about that dog for days. I still do. I wonder whatever became of him. He would have been such good company. We would have had wonderful conversations. I hope he's alive and well and belongs to some boy who takes him hunting in the Piney Woods.

In two more days I encountered two mutts with no manners. They rushed at me with teeth flashing. One grabbed my foot. I kicked him away, barely averting a fall. Down the road I saw a short piece of rubber hose and figured that would be a good defense against any further attacks. Generally, I carried what I referred to as a dog minder. It was a three-foot piece of fiber-glass rod. It was light, but strong. I'd never had to strike a dog with it. Simply pulling it out and twirling it menacingly had worked every time. Some one told me that a dog can't concentrate on two things at the same time. So, if he or she were concentrating on the rod my foot escaped attention. I didn't think it would work on attack dogs–so, I stayed away from them.

Anyway, at that point in time and for some forgotten reason, I did not have the dog minder with me, so I picked up the hose. Making sure it was sturdy enough to do the job, I gave my leg a good whack. It was perfect. I noticed my leg stinging. Looking down, I saw my lower leg covered with fire ants. I had evicted them from their winter condominium and they were incensed.

Another time I rode at night and took the exit road into Columbus, near Houston. My head light batteries were running out of juice making me strain to see the highway. I slowed down so as not to hit something or run off the road. I heard a dog bark from a house set far back off the highway. The barking got louder so I reckoned he was coming after me. Trying to discourage a dog at night without being able to see too well, didn't seem to be a good idea. The bark indicated a rather large-sized animal. Fight or flight? I fled.

I put the shoe sole to the pedal, hoping I missed anything in my path. The sound of barking stopped but I could hear those toe nails behind me clicking on the hard pavement. I'm sure I could have been caught, but I did have a head start and perhaps interest waned after I passed the property's boundary. It was rather exciting for awhile–over taken on the moors by the Hound of the Baskerville's–my childhood terror story.

## The Cradles of Independence
### (Fall Tour 1995)

When I toured East Texas in 1995, I made sure I could include some of the great historic places prominent in the early days of this new land. J. Pinckney Henderson, Texas' first governor lived there. Of course Sam Houston and Davy Crockett were in evidence, too. Gonzales was known as the Lexington of Texas because of a battle over a cannon. Later, the men of Gonzales answered the call for help from the Alamo and were killed there. San Felipe (pronounced with typical Texas creativity as San Phillip) is known as the birthplace of Anglo-American Settlement in Texas.

San Felipe de Austin was named for Stephen F. Austin who located his first Texas settlers there in 1823. Washington-on-the-Brazos provided the site where the Declaration of Independence received the signatures of the early Texas leaders. Later the Constitution of the Republic got its start there. From 1842 to 1846 it served as the capital of the Texas Republic. There's a great museum there in the shape of the Texas Star. I thought all those places could aptly be called Cradles of Independence.

Just before I rode to the Stephen F. Austin State Park near San Felipe, I thought it would be fitting to have a Spanish omelet for breakfast–helped out with potatoes, biscuits and jam and my customary gulps of steaming black coffee. All for $4.75. It was spitting rain on October 29, 1995 and the wind gusts were in the neighborhood of 30 miles per hour. I wore a light riding jersey and my cycling shorts.

# Wandering Around Stephen F. Austin State Park
## (Fall Tour 1995)

My first night in the park it rained gently, but persistently, all evening. My tent leaked and that's why I carried a chamois cloth– soaked up water like a sponge. The park appeared empty–just the way I liked it. The bathrooms were all mine. In the morning a park employee went through two large trash bins collecting aluminum cans. Three hours later, he was still at it. There were lots of crows about. I listened as they exchanged information.

According to the folks at the San Felipe post office and information center, there would be a birthday celebration in a few days for Stephen F. Austin. He would have been 202 years old. They were hoping for a large turn out.

I took a great nature walk in the park. I tried to name the trees, like bois d'arc or Osage orange or horse apple or what I called them back in Indiana as a kid–a hedge apple tree. The wood was hard and orange-colored. The Indians used it for bows. We had a rope swing in ours. Other trees were ash, elm, oak, hackberry. One tree had a huge poison ivy vine crawling up. The vine was as big around as my thigh. As far as I was concerned that was carrying preservation too far. I looked inside Stephen F. Austin's log cabin. It was eighteen by forty-two feet with a nine by eighteen foot open dog trot dividing it in the middle. Inside, I noticed a nine by twelve foot loft.

Outside and behind it was a sixty-foot walnut tree with scads of walnuts on the ground. The marker read: "On this site stood a town hall built about 1830 in which were held the first and second conventions of Texas, 1832 and 1833 and the consultation of 1835. The provisional government functioned here until March 2, 1836 when the Republic was formed at Washington-on-the-Brazos. The building was burned with the town March 29, 1836, to prevent it from falling into the hands of the advancing Mexican Army."

I looked out on the park road and there came an orange maintenance truck. The crew got out and proceeded to eat lunch.

They were all speaking Spanish. I waved and checked to see if I had any matches.

Located next to a huge fifty-foot oak was the Stephen F. Austin Memorial statue. The pedestal was of pink granite and the statue of bronze had a green patina. On the back of the large pedestal were these words: "He planted the first Anglo American colony in Texas. 'The Old Three Hundred.' In his several colonies he settled more than a thousand families. He was, from 1823 to 1828, the actual ruler of Texas and thereafter, its most influential leader. His own words are a fitting epitaph. 'The prosperity of Texas has been the object of my labors, the idol of my existence–it has assumed the character of a religion–for the guidance of my thoughts and actions.' And he died in its service. No other state in the union owes its existence more completely to one man than Texas does to Austin."

On the back of an obelisk in front of Austin's statue: "Stephen F. Austin, Impresario.

If he who by conquest wins an empire and receives the world's applause, how much is due to him who by unceasing toil lays in the wilderness the foundation for an infant colony and builds thereon a vigorous state." -Henderson Yoakum.
I went by a small open bricked well dug by the original settlers. It was three feet wide and about seven feet deep and restored by the Sealy Chamber of Commerce in 1928–the year I was born. I dropped in a 1959 quarter.

### Lunch Without a Spoon
(Fall Tour 1995)

I took a long hot shower, washed out my clothes and had lunch. I had mislaid or forgotten my spoon. You would think with all my traveling, I would have made sure I had this essential utensil along. Why not get another? The nearest spoon place was three miles away and I just didn't want to make the effort–besides it was a challenge to see how I could fare without it. Things went well. I could spear the sardines and the chunks of tuna easily enough with my Swiss army knife. For the can of peas, I fashioned a scoop from the lid–being careful not to cut myself on the sharp edges. For the can of corn I decided to tip up the can and let the corn roll in. Corn being flat on the sides and kind of angular didn't roll. It occurred to me I should have done that with the peas–too late. So, lying down I tipped the can higher. Nothing. I opened my eyes and peered at this wall of immovable yellow nutrients. Just then, avalanche. Kernels cascaded around my mouth and up the sides of my face and onto my chest.

After dinner at night I always practiced my harmonica. "Silent Night" was my favorite. True, Christmas was two months off, but I would have it down by then. I still had trouble getting the scale right. There were practically no critters in the park–two mosquitoes, very few ants, a few gnats, a bee or two, one chigger–damn, and one or two flies. Not bad at all. Late fall is definitely the time to camp. Winter is even better–unless it's cold. I biked to Sealy on the day I left and stopped for a really good breakfast and picked up a few plastic spoons.

## A Pedal in the Cold
### (Fall Tour 1995)

After visiting statues I took off for Magnolia and had a late lunch in an IHOP where a bunch of high school kids also stopped for a snack, having been to a girls basketball scrimmage over in Waller– noted for its old-fashioned Christmas celebrations.

As I prepared to leave, a group of girls crowded around me outside and wanted to know what I was doing. They were shivering with cold and I was in my thin riding shirt and short pants.

"Where do you sleep?"

"By the side of the road," stretching it a bit. The girls were aghast.

"Do you have a home?" I hesitated and admitted I had one. Naturally, they wished me well and told me to be careful. I promised.

That night I heard a wildcat scream. Great sound.

Leaden skies sprinkled on me as I rode toward Montgomery the next day. It was now November and getting a bit chilly–great for riding. I talked with a fellow whose family still lived on one of the original Spanish land grants–we had pie and coffee together.

I wheeled right through the Sam Houston National Forest. Each place I stopped the men were talking about deer hunting–mostly how miserable they were sitting motionless for hours in the rain and cold with numb feet, even in insulated boots. Somehow my riding shirt and short pants were overlooked as being ridiculous in that weather. As I pedaled along I would hear shots ringing out in the woods. Usually a series of three, blam. . .blam. . .blam–then, silence for a while. I hadn't seen a deer since the Stephen F. Austin State Park. I heard a joke once about two hunters pulling a deer they had just shot by the hind legs. The buck had a huge rack which kept getting caught in the ground and the bushes. Another hunter happened by and said it would be easier if they pulled the deer by the head. They took his advice and after a while one said "That was good advice–this is a lot easier." "Yeah," responded his pal, "But we're gettin' farther and farther away from the pickup."

My hands got cold so I put on mittens and a bright orange hunting vest which acted as a wind buffer as well as a safety precaution against cold and desperate hunters. Tall pines lined the narrow highway. The hills were gentle. Wildflowers were still blooming–chiefly Indian blanket and Indian paintbrush. The smell of wood smoke permeated the forest as each little house stuck back in the woods sent a blue-gray plume circling lazily up to the tops of the trees.

I felt in great shape. My new hip gave me new life. The mittens were warm. My feet were wet and cool but several degrees this side of numb. It was cold enough that I kept the pedals turning–no coasting–changing gears to keep the pressure on and my blood circulating. I was in the "panting" mode for the entire trip through the forest.

In the afternoon, I arrived in Huntsville, noted for its prison and stopped at a fast food franchise just in time to join several buses of kids who had been in a band contest in Houston. The school had won a number two in the second division. I congratulated the young man who volunteered the information. They were very well-behaved and cheerful, just like the girls' basketball team in Magnolia. So much for the gloom and doom of East Texas.

## Old Fort Parker
(Fall Tour 1995)

The story of the abduction of Cynthia Ann Parker had interested me ever since my introduction to Texas history. Before arriving at the fort eighty miles west of the Davy Crockett national forest on a cold November day in 1995, I stocked up on five fried apple pies, four tins of sardines and two cans of refried beans. Do I not live well or what? On the fort grounds I found a place under a gigantic elm to pitch my tent and planned to stay a couple of days, reliving history. After getting settled, I toured the buildings. Although the original fort was long gone, the second restoration, completed in 1967, had an authentic look and feel.

I climbed into the block houses and peered out the small windows, wondering what it must have been like on that spring day in 1836, when a band of Indians appeared atop a rise in the east. One of the Indians waved a white flag, and foolishly, one of the men inside the stockade opened the gates and went out to meet him. The Indian wanted beef, a place to camp and directions to water.

The settler returned with the beef and was immediately surrounded and lanced to death. The Indians stormed through the gates of the fort before they could be closed. The men working the fields did not know of the attack until they returned in the evening. Some inside the fort escaped. Most were killed. Cynthia Ann Parker, only nine, watched as the intruders killed her parents. The Indians took her and a few others off to sell.

96

The early settlers of Texas counted the risks and decided having land and a new way of life overshadowed the probability of an early death.

The Parker fort, like some others in the early days, was private, built by several families who had come to Texas at the behest of their leader, Daniel Parker, a preacher in a Predestinarian Baptist Church in Illinois. Upon arriving in the new land, they spent some time erecting the stockade–constructed along the lines of the forts in the mid-west during colonial times. It consisted of cedar logs split and sunk into the ground side by side and three feet deep and soaring up for twelve feet. Inside were two rows of cabins and two block houses, the latter rising above the stockade walls. The rule was never to open the gate if Indians were present. One fellow apparently failed to grasp this rather simple dictum. On May 19, 1836, he got a refresher course.

They carried Cynthia Ann far away and eventually a Comanche adopted her. As a teenager she married a chief of the Pahuka band. She changed her name to Naduah and bore three children: two boys, Pecos and Quanah and a girl, Prairie Flower. Cynthia Ann and her daughter were recaptured in 1860. Prairie Flower was two years old. They returned to their relatives in East Texas, but could not adjust to the former way of life. Nadua (Cynthia Ann) knew little or no English and yearned to return to her husband. She never saw him again. Four years later, she starved herself to death. Six months before, Prairie Flower died at the age of six.

Quanah, devoted to his mother, never gave up his small-boy name she gave him which meant "sweet smelling." He also took her surname Parker. He became the last great chief of the Comanche. After being forced onto a reservation in 1874, he turned his attention to teaching his people how to adapt to the new culture around them and since he saw how his mother adapted to Indian ways Quanah decided his people could do the same–in reverse.

A great warrior, but even a greater leader in peace, Quanah Parker traveled across the United States and met with hundreds of people; married seven times and had numerous children before dying in1911, just seventeen years before my birth. He was buried beside his mother in Oklahoma.

In the middle of the night, the wind came up and great gusts shook my tent. The temperature dropped and by morning it was below freezing. The wind had shifted to the north and with such a great tailwind, I decided to leave the fort immediately. With numb fingers I packed up and pedaled out of the park, onto the highway and flew south toward Austin with good speed–pushed by the arctic blast. Indescribable.

### A Great Decision
(Perimeter Tour 1994)

Back now to the perimeter tour of the year before and the primary narrative. I left the forests of East Texas going north. It was late spring, 1994. I pedaled to a small lake named Murvaul nearly hidden off the road on a narrow black-topped state highway, I found it more or less by accident. Once there, I decided to stay a few days. The camping was free in a grove of towering trees. The lake had two bird colonies on an island. One colony consisted of thousands of white cattle egrets nesting in the trees. The second colony consisted of adult vultures which lined up on my shore along a fence railing each morning before flying to the island. There they fed on baby egrets which had fallen from the nests during the night. Sort of a win-win situation. The vultures were fat and the island didn't smell–too much.

Two stores supplied my needs. One emphasized bait and tackle–and later breakfast–for me. I noticed the wife fixing her fishing guide husband breakfast and asked if I might not be included. She said that would be fine and charged me a dollar for bacon and eggs, toast and coffee. I said that was not enough, but she wouldn't accept more than $2.00.

Idyllic. However, I was in a funk for several days. I knew I had extended my trip longer than planned. It was time to go back to Austin and get that new hip. Was it Wolfe who said a person couldn't go home again? Well, I didn't want to go home. What to do? I poured over maps. Counted my money. Looked at my bike's condition and made a decision.

I would do the whole perimeter of Texas! I estimated the total distance at 4,000 miles. That was farther than across the United States! Elation! Immediately the heavy carcass of depression lifted off my shoulders and lurched over the horizon to find some other unfortunate soul.

My plan: pedal to Texarkana, have my bike rebuilt and proceed west along the top of Texas. There would be two places to stop before Texarkana–Caddo Lake and Wright Patman Lake. The latter would mean a leisurely ride into Texarkana so that a whole day could be spent working on my bike if need be. In the phone book I located a bike shop in Texarkana and made a tentative appointment to be confirmed the day before I was slated to arrive.

TYLER.TX

I would pass close by Marshall and Longview, both cities boom towns in the 1930s with the discovery of oil. Now the area was host to hundreds of manufacturing firms. One of the most famous was R. G. LeTourneau. Years before I remembered listening to Mr. LeTourneau give a speech at my school.

On a later tour I passed through Tyler to the west which was notable for its roses. On 22 acres, the largest rose garden in the United States, there were 38,000 rose bushes representing some 500 varieties of roses.

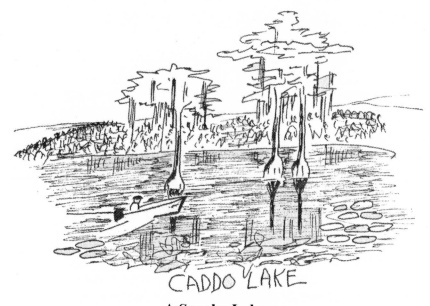

CADDO LAKE

**A Spooky Lake**
(Perimeter Tour 1994)

I packed up at Lake Murvaul, said goodbye to a bunch of newly-found friends and took off north to Caddo Lake and Uncertain–believe it or not, the name of the town at the southern edge of the lake. I was certain of that and also certain I would ride to Uncertain. I proclaimed that in no uncertain terms. I bet the people of Uncertain were certainly sick of humorous remarks about their town. I resolved with certainty not to mention it once I arrived.

Years ago, the town got its name when the paddle wheelers came up the river from Louisiana. The water level varied so much that it was never certain the boats could tie up–so what better name for such a landing than Uncertain. Anyway, I certainly wanted to go there. The village sits on the banks of a wonderfully mysterious lake called Caddo, after the Caddo Indians who used to live in the area. The lake looks primeval, but was probably formed by the New Madrid earthquake in 1811. In 1860 there was a river boat tragedy when the **Mittie Stevens** burned near Swanson's Landing with the loss of sixty lives. The water was only a few feet deep and everyone could have waded to shore, but no one on board knew that because the water was opaque.

Fresh water mussels caused a stir in the early 1900s because people found they contained pearls. Later, oil rigs were planted in the lake itself during the hey day of Texas' oil boom years.

Now thankfully, peace reigned on what was one of the most beautiful and haunting water ways in Texas.

It was May 31$^{st}$, 1994. I arrived after a 62 mile ride–some of it on a narrow two-lane highway. Trucks made me a bit nervous, but I survived without a scrape–not a bad ride. The temperature was in the 80s with a nice breeze. A small grocery store provided me with a quart of buttermilk, two bananas and a pint of ice cream. The lady owner called her friend who lived down the street and who had camping places by the lake's edge. I pedaled down the tree- shrouded street to the Shady Glade RV park and its defunct restaurant. Camping fee $5.00.

I put my tent right by the floating boat dock, five feet from the edge of the lake. The water looked like strong tea, which of course, it was–a tea made from all the leaves and moss and water plants constantly falling into the water and decaying. Rising out of the mirror-like surface of the lake were tall cypress trees with big knees at the bottom and wispy Spanish moss festooning their branches. A large white egret flew by, followed by a graceful blue heron.

The lady at the grocery store said not to worry about alligators– they were way back in the lake. I hoped they knew they were supposed to stay back there. I needed to watch for Cotton Mouths, though. Cotton mouths? Snakes? I remembered as a kid being scared to death about going into the attic where I knew something big lurked waiting to chomp on boys–and going in anyway. Fear can be delicious at times. I felt like that, camping by a lake I couldn't see into, full of water-loving ghostly trees draped in moss that looked like cobwebs and cotton mouth snakes looking like so many white blossoms–daring me to pick one. And there would be the alligator with no sense of direction that might show up at my tent door around midnight. Would anyone hear my feeble call for help as I was dragged into this giant pot of tea? It was the monster in my childhood attic all over again. Delicious.

Lily pads with yellow flowers floated on the lake surface. Looking at the lake from my camp site, it didn't seem all that large. Later I found out numerous channels wound throughout the lake and one could easily get lost. The park service did put up markers to minimize the danger. Over forty-two miles of waterways, flanked by majestic cypresses–watery Appian Ways–beckoned.

In the late afternoon, a young man steered his boat up to the ramp and made ready to haul it out. We visited and he asked if I had ever been out in the lake. When I said no, he invited me to take a ride. Danny Butler was a volunteer fireman in Marshall and had grown up in those parts. He knew Caddo lake so well, he didn't pay any attention to the markers. We roared off, up and down the spacious boulevards. Because of the mirror quality of the water in front of the boat, the trees were perfectly reflected, almost causing vertigo. Which was the sky–which the lake? Were we skimming the tops of trees–upside down?

Without the boat ride I would not have appreciated the lake nearly so much. I wondered what it would be like out there after dark–way back where the alligators lived–drifting–watching the trees move by–the waving moss–perhaps with a ghostly full moon.

That night brought a grand recital courtesy of thousands of frogs. I lay a long time listening, not wanting to drift into sleep. In the morning the unmistakable calls of ravens, sounding like crows suffering with congestion, awakened me.

### Day Off and Eating Meatloaf at Wright Patman Lake
(Perimeter Tour 1994)

At the barest showing of light, as the cypress trees dripped with dew and the last frog chorus died away, I got up. The clothes I had hung out the night before were still damp, so I decided to wait until nearly nine to leave. It's nice to have an excuse not to leave such a magical place. Maybe my clothes wouldn't dry until the following month. Finally, I left. Traffic seemed to be in a good mood with lots of waves and smiles–even the logging trucks were considerate. I arrived at the Rocky Point campground on Wright Patman Lake around five. Got a flat–fixed it. I noticed, however, that the rear tire was pretty chewed up because of my running over a broken bottle. It bulged and that didn't look good. Once settled in the park, I took it off and booted it hoping it would last until I got to Texarkana in the morning. When I checked my calendar I realized my money would not be in the bank until a day later–solution: two lazy days at Rocky Point instead of one. Bike touring is so cool.

My tent was on a bluff overlooking the lake. I hoped I wouldn't sleep walk. Several of the RVs around me had colored lanterns which blinked as the evening approached. In the half-light of dusk, I fixed a large pot of macaroni with mushroom gravy and ate it all. I wrote in my journal until it got too dark to see the page.

I finally relaxed and slowed down, listened to the soft lappings of the lake water–the subdued voices of my fellow campers–a wisp of music–soft chirps overhead as birds settled down for the evening. I drifted off to sleep at last.

The new day dawned and I just lay there for awhile waiting for the world to wake up around me. I had nothing to do and I thought I would just enjoy the day. In the trees, hundreds of birds tried to outdo each other with song as if they were happy to be alive in such a place. Before bicycling, I never noticed birds nor trees nor flowers; certainly not insects.

So, today I looked at and named a raven, a crow, a bluebird, blackbirds, an osprey, a Great White egret, bluejays, song sparrows, a Bewick wren, a chickadee, a redheaded woodpecker, a Great Blue heron. I watched two squirrels play tag. One outwitted the other. There were ants here, so I decided I would do some observing since the day had no pressures. I tried several of my favorite experiments in order to confirm further my biased opinion that some ants were smart, some were dumb, some were hard workers and some just fooled around. I concluded human beings and ants had some things in common after all.

That night folks from three RVs traveling together and camped next to me brought over dinner. The plate was stacked with meatloaf, fried green tomatoes, pinto beans, and hot-water cornbread. They were from Bloomberg and Bidien, Louisana and Smyrna, Texas. We had a great visit, telling stories and laughing into the evening hours. At the end they wished me well on the trip and to be careful. It was a very pleasant evening and I went to bed early. I looked up through the mesh at the top of my tent at the leaves of the tree I was under. All was still. I thought of tomorrow and the great ride ahead of me. I could hardly wait.

## Texarkana
### (Perimeter Tour 1994)

Up at the crack of dawn, I arrived in Texarkana by eight. I got my money, ate breakfast and arrived at the bicycle shop when it opened.

The Ozark Bicycle shop's owners greeted me–a brother and sister, both in their eighties. Most of the bikes they had for sale were mountain bikes, catering to the needs of their young customers. It amazed me to see and hear them in the shop. They knew the latest in bicycle technology. O. B. Baxter had an engineering background. He invited me to come into the back of the shop and watch him repack the front and rear wheels, adjust the derailleur, put on two new tubes and tires and just generally go over the whole bike. He handled my bike as though it were a fine violin. What a joy it was to watch him work. His sister stayed in the front of the shop working on the books. She taught a Sunday school class, wrote poetry and religious songs. She wrote *The Money Tree.*

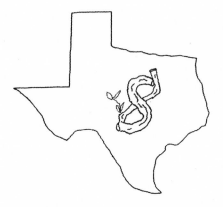

## *Following the Red River*
### (Perimeter Tour 1994)

Along about noon I left the bike shop with total confidence in my rebuilt two-wheeler, riding to the Tourist Bureau's office on Interstate 30 to complain about the Texas Department of Transportation's policy which barred me from erecting a tent at a highway rest stop. The offending signs did allow for exceptions, but required a permit. I found out later permits didn't exist. I had heard that the law, passed by our state legislature, took aim at prostitutes hanging out in tents at rest stops who hassled the drivers of trucks. "I couldn't say no, your Honor, please, we need a law."

Maybe hippies used to homestead at rest stops, or perhaps the homeless erected shanties. Whatever. The law entered the books. Now, aging hippies and the homeless were forced from public view– banned beneath bridges. The hassling of big trucks stopped. Truckers could sleep or toss and turn, safely. Big rigs pulled into rest stops with assurance that rest was imminent. Truckers needed their rest so they wouldn't smash into people. Prostitutes would not let them rest. I granted that. The truckers left their diesel engines running all night or for ever how long they wanted to stay at the rest stop, winter for the heater or summer for the A/C system. Trailers and mobile homes could do the same. I counted myself a traveler too, in need of rest. Who knew but that I, being sleep deprived, might run into a trucker on the highway, possibly denting something? With rest I would pose less of a safety hazard–also, since I had no engine to run while I rested, I didn't produce more pollution for the world. You would think there would have been a sign welcoming bicycle tourers to pitch a tent and slumber for a few hours. But no. Like a lot of legislation performed by overworked and underpaid legislators, bills do not pretend to look beyond the original band-aid solution. My being left out of the "rest your weary bones" provision was, what you would call, an oversight. I explained all of this to the attractive attendant at the Tourist Bureau and ended up with the phrase–"I am a *bona fide* traveler in the state of Texas and I am being discriminated against." Magic words. She called headquarters in Austin and I got an "unofficial" verbal permit to camp with a tent right along side trucks and motor homes.

*Actually, they really envy me.*

106

## Time to Eat
### (Perimeter Tour 1994)

Famished and riding out of Texarkana, I only lasted a few miles. My calorie tanks read empty as I pulled into a Love's Truck/Car/Travel Center off I-30 at the town of Hooks. I ate four tuna fish salad sandwiches (buy one get one free) which would tide me over until a more ample repast was available.

A big rainstorm developed while I ate, but I was dry and happy and listening to the 1950s music which brought back pleasant memories of my innocent years. It stopped raining. The sun came out and with the tuna salad sandwiches safely stashed inside, I jumped back on my bike and pedaled away ready for my next adventure. Getting back on my bike–especially after a food break–always caused me to have this sense of something new and exciting just waiting over the next hill. Sometimes this feeling evaporated almost immediately and sometimes it lasted for miles. Dekalb, twenty-three miles away would be far enough that day. Dekalb, pronounced, DEEcab had no place to camp and I rode on to Avery, the next town, not too far away, but I noticed my sense of new adventure was waning. I came upon my first road-side rest stop–which I now had permission to use, but it was much too shallow and appeared to be the favorite turnaround for the local teenagers. Even with permission, I didn't look forward to fending off curious and hormone-driven young folk from Avery–I passed it up.

I rode on. Getting worried. The sun sank. I rode on. The city limits sign announcing Annona appeared. It rained and wouldn't you know it, no motels, no RV parks, no place to rest my weary head were to be had.

## A Gracious Host
(Perimeter Tour 1994)

I told the clerk at the convenience store my dilemma and she
introduced me to a Mr. Brem who was, at that very moment, putting
gas in his car. He welcomed me to pitch my tent at his place. He lived
six miles out of town off Highway 44–a quiet and peaceful ride with
scenery that looked like a picture post card. My sense of adventure
returned and after a very pleasant pedal, I arrived at his home just as
darkness settled into the valley.

After I set up my tent in his driveway, we talked into the night.
As we visited, Mr. Brem fixed dinner consisting of zucchini, yellow
squash, boiled new potatoes, sweet onions–all raised in his garden
and just picked. Thick slices of ham accompanied the vegetables. We
discussed real estate and in the morning I helped load an antique
stove into his truck before we said goodbye. A very gracious host. I
left at six-thirty for Clarksville and breakfast fourteen miles away.
Late yesterday afternoon I had felt the beginnings of despair. Now,
the horizon beckoned with a smile and I felt great to be riding a
bicycle in such a friendly community.

When I arrived at Clarksville, I was still in a great mood and
eagerly anticipated a wonderful country breakfast. I was not
disappointed. At a small cafe, I ordered eggs, sausage, biscuits, cream
gravy, orange juice and coffee. There can never be anything so
satisfying as a country breakfast after an early morning ride.

## The Ku Klux Klan
(Perimeter Tour 1994)

Next stop–Paris! Yes, Paris was in Texas–and an Eiffel Tower
poked into the sky. Before reaching Paris I stopped in Detroit.
Pronounced DEEtroit. Most words in East Texas have the emphasis
on the first syllable. I loved it.

Some people told me that the Ku Klux Klan was meeting in

Clarksville and Paris and to be careful. I flew a confederate battle flag as part of my six flags over Texas. I rolled it up and stuck it in a bag. Later I got the regular Confederate flag to fly. The battle flag stirred up the fanatics. Show me any fanatic and I'll show you an eight cylinder engine with a few cylinders misfiring and a smoky, smelly exhaust.

In Paris I talked with two elderly gentlemen who asked a lot of questions about my trip. One blind and the other with an electronic voice box wanted to know if I ever talked to schools. I said I had not on this trip, but I would like to do that. A little over a year later I got that opportunity in Navasota about 200 miles or so south of Paris.

### A School Visit–A Year Later
(Fall Tour 1995)

A year later in the fall of 1995 I made a swing around the east central part of Texas. After leaving Washington-on-the-Brazos, and before going south to Hempstead to rid myself of fleas picked up at a miniature horse farm run by nuns, I biked into Navasota and like a magnet, the local Diary Queen drew me in. A class of 5th graders from the school next door paraded in right after I got all settled around my big hamburger and fries. Their teacher, Katie Webb, had promised a treat for successfully completing a project. I remembered my fifth grade teacher. She was young, attractive, had a great figure and took no guff from anyone. Ms. Webb took me back to long-ago feelings. There she was surrounded by happy students including dreaming boys. We visited for a few minutes and she invited me, if I had the time, to come over to the school and address some of the classes for the next hour. I accepted. The principal, Tom DeOlloz, thought it an excellent idea, too. So I brought my loaded bike into the library and in trooped the students. Some had been studying explorers–so now they faced a true real-life explorer of sorts–a celebrity–an explorer in the flesh. They gaped.

The hour went by too fast and after I left they made a special display area with a map of Texas showing where I had traveled. How invigorating to watch the kids–alert–eager to learn and boundlessly enthusiastic. As I write this they are Seniors. Seems like yesterday. I remembered the old gentlemen a year before putting the idea in my head. I have talked to several schools since.

## Lake Crook at Paris
### (Perimeter Tour 1994)

After I arrived in Paris I turned right on highway 271 and pedaled to Lake Crook–about 5 miles north of the city. No charge for camping–scenic, secluded and I had a lake to look at. However, there were no facilities–not even picnic tables. I had three small containers of water– no cooking and no washing–with water. It would be an alcohol bath that night–one of several I would take on my trips. I went for days once without a conventional bath or shower and stayed perfectly clean and refreshed. I would wash a set of clothes (shorts, socks, bandana, and shirt) in a service station's or a convenience store's restroom, dry them as I rode then "alcohol" myself at night. I used a half bottle of rubbing alcohol for each bath–which included "shampooing" my hair.

At dusk, on Lake Crook, I heard a woman singing. I couldn't see her, but her clear voice drifted across the park–melancholy songs– mournful at times. She made me feel happy and sad all at the same time.

## Too Much to Eat
### (Perimeter Tour 1994)

At a Wal-Mart I replenished my supplies including shirts, shorts and socks. Lake Bonham was 40 some miles west and that would be my next stop. The highway from Paris to Bonham had no towns, no stores, no service stations, no outdoor advertising. I rode without stopping, drinking water as I pedaled. By the time I got to the town of Bonham, hunger ruled the roost. At a super market I loaded up on

110

everything my famished eyes desired and went outside to eat it on a bench in front of the store. Customers came and went. A lady walked by, stopped for a moment to watch and announced, "I think I'm going to be sick." I rode very slowly on to Lake Bonham four miles north of the city and spent a very quiet evening inside my tent. I didn't need a late evening snack.

### A Visit with Sam Rayburn
(Perimeter Tour 1994)

I got up at five-thirty to the sound of rain on my tent. It quit by six-thirty and I was on the road by six-forty five. It rained again from seven-fifteen to seven-forty-five. I took a photo of Sam Rayburn's later home–he was the legendary Speaker of the House of Representatives for seventeen years, longer than anyone in the history of the House. He sponsored most of Franklin D. Roosevelt's New Deal legislation, the only president I knew growing up.

Twenty miles east of Gainesville, a tire developed a slow leak. I fixed it. I fixed it. I fixed it–three times I fixed it. Considering I unloaded the bike completely each time, it was remarkable I didn't kill something.

The next rest stop made up for my attack of flatireitis–shady trees, grass, quiet–deep enough that passing cars would not disturb and right across the street a Laundromat and store! I discovered a few snake holes, I thought, near my tent but I plugged them with dead limbs from the trees. No snakes showed up or whatever else lived down there. That day a handsome red-tailed hawk had soared right in front of my bicycle.

I got up at four-thirty and went across the street for coffee and visited with a young man who had just bought a bike, but because of back problems, couldn't ride it. He wore a brace and contemplated surgery. At daybreak I hit the road. My campsite target waited for me five miles east of Henrietta.

## The Cow Talker
(Perimeter Tour 1994)

I mooed at cows that morning. Some ran away tails held high. Others stopped and came toward me with an answering moo. My knowledge and appreciation of cows continued to increase.

I learned some key differences between East Texas and West Texas. The creeks and rivers in East Texas have water in them. At the rest stop I tried answering a bob white. He flew away. I guessed that meant I owned the territory–the dominant bob white. I met a lot of people that day as I wheeled in to rest and eat. They all appeared interested in what I was doing and wished me a safe and happy trip. I saw parts of the plains too. The trees thinned out. I went through the Cross Timbers–two parallel bands of woods running north and south. I don't know why they were called that unless people kept saying "There's a couple of bands of timber you gotta cross if you go thataway." Made sense to me.

## The Big Cities
(Perimeter Tour 1994)

As I did my tours in Texas, I gave a wide berth to the large cities. Consequently, I drifted throughout the land in another time. The hills, mountains, valleys, rivers and streams had not changed much in the last several hundred years and it was easy for me to imagine myself back in a simpler period, but without the hardships that went along with those days.

I thought about the great cities of Texas as I traveled and realized with the exception of Austin, and some other medium-sized cities, I had not ridden in any of them. What would it be like to ride down town in Dallas, Fort Worth, El Paso, Houston and San Antonio? I read about bicycle couriers in New York City and how fast they got through traffic. I guessed that most major cities had a select cadre of such dare devil riders–looking like modern day gladiators with their protective pads, straps and battered helmets. And I knew there were hike and bike trails and bicycle clubs, but I wondered more about bicycle commuters–that intrepid group who straddled their bikes each day and rode to work perhaps ten or twenty miles away into the heart of a large city. Also, I wondered if there were some people who regularly did their grocery shopping, or banking or any of those small errands on bicycles, as I did in Austin.

As I pedaled along the Red River with the Dallas/Fort Worth metroplex a mere fifty miles south of me, I tried to imagine taking a left and going down there for a few days–just biking around. Where would I stay? How would I stay off the huge spaghetti highways–or could I use them? Would the people welcome me and wish me well? I knew I could go anywhere in Texas outside those cities and be comfortable on my bike. Perhaps it was just a matter of getting used to the environment. I imagined a successful commuter, say, in San Antonio, or a young housewife in Houston doing bike errands there. What might seem old hat to them would be new and possibly threatening to me. I supposed the same would be true for them if I plopped them down in the middle of one of our National East Texas forests or on a desert highway with 50 miles of sage brush and mountains in front of them.

Perhaps I should visit those cities–spend a week or two in each one–searching out the byways, the trails, alleys and bike lanes; interviewing couriers, bicycling housewives and commuters. I could check out landmarks, parks, libraries, hostels, bed and breakfast places, bike shops and tall buildings–gather wild west city stories. That could make an interesting book. I just might do it. If you, the reader, want to do it ahead of me–be my guest.

## More Rest Stops
(Perimeter Tour 1994)

Majestic red oaks with lots of acorns shaded the Henrietta rest area. The next day I didn't go very far, just thirty-eight miles to the west side of Wichita Falls and another rest area.

Since I got my "unofficial" permit to use them, I did exactly that. Free camping meant more money available for food. I liked that.

**Bite Inventory**
(Perimeter Tour 1994)

I took inventory of my bites. I had bites from a fire ant, a regular ant, three chiggers, a black fly, probably a spider and a few mosquitoes. Before touring I absolutely hated mosquitoes, but they and black flies have one thing in common–the itch only lasts for ten minutes if you don't scratch. The fire ant and the chigger can last five to seven days. Comparable to those two and maybe worse was my experience with deer flies three years later on my trip through the sand hills of Nebraska. Utter agony. In all of my tours: no snake bites, no dog bites, no bear hugs, no leaping into the water by an alligator, no tarantula bites, and no car or truck bites. So, I guessed I needed to say thanks. Thanks.

While on the ride to Wichita Falls I practiced my Rottweiler bark and my wolf howl. My Rottweiler impersonation could make a Chihuahua faint. My voice is not high enough for an authentic sounding coyote, but I'm working on it along with some bird calls.

I needed more company. I was also very hungry for salads. Salads didn't seem to be available in convenience stores. When I arrived the next day a few miles on the other side of Vernon, I pulled up at one of those all-you-can-eat-pizza-buffet places. When asked, I opted for the salad bar and nearly demolished it. Four plate loads! I still needed more company.

## The Motor Home Menace
### (Perimeter Tour 1994)

The wind increased from 20 to 30 mph in my face which slowed me. That gave me time to think. I thought about motor homes. I concluded they ranked number one as a menace to cyclists. Often they tow a car behind which makes them as long or longer than an eighteen wheeler. The man or woman behind the wheel of a large truck had to pass rigorous tests of skill before he or she steered onto the highway. I thought the test for a motor home was more nearly like "Blow on this mirror and see if you can fog it. Good, you're ready to burn rubber."

One went around me towing a Cadillac. We were on a curve and the Cadillac drifted over onto the shoulder just missing me by inches. I'm sure the driver didn't realize the phenomenon of the rear part of a long load wanting to "cut corners." Another motor home on a narrow road stayed in the right lane even though no traffic faced him. He did not think it important to move into the passing lane to get around me. Hey, a bicycle won't even dent a fender. I believed no one wanted to do me harm. Some (not all) of these drivers were way over the hill when it came to driving skills, but most will continue getting their licenses renewed as long as they can locate the starter and the loo. They white-knuckle their way across the country behind the wheel of those behemoths, trying to sip some chicken soup prepared in the kitchenette. I didn't know the solution to that. I did know I had to stay alert. Most of the time I was. In fairness, there were a lot of motor home drivers who had excellent skills and were courteous and safety conscious. A friend and cyclist told me a motor home driver and crew will feed you at night at a rest stop and run over you the next day on the highway. Several fed me and not one ran over me–yet.

## A Wet Welcome
### (Perimeter Tour 1994)

The next day, Childress, tucked in at the bottom of the Texas Panhandle, would be my goal. As a welcoming gesture, a storm blew in. The western sky turned black and the wind howled. Rain came slanting. I put on a poncho. The trucks passing me caused it to rise up and cover my face. So, pedaling along a slick highway, in the face of a stinging storm, I had the added excitement of periodically fighting to get the poncho away from my face so I could see where the bicycle pointed. Twice, passing trucks blew the poncho completely off. I knew when to quit. I braked. Astraddle my bike with my feet spread wide on the shoulder of the highway, I hunkered down to wait it out. I was unaware that a motorist had stopped behind me until he was at my elbow. "Need some help?" I thought God had relented and was speaking at last. I nearly fell over.

The storm went by. The sun shone again. A Hostess Cup Cake delivery truck honked as it went by and a large carton of cupcakes landed just off the highway in front of me. Was it any wonder why I loved Texas and Texans? At another time close by, an attorney stopped and gave me a five pound sack of beef jerky.
"You can't enter the panhandle without some jerky." I ate it all in two days.

## Quanah
(Perimeter Tour 1994)

I made it to Quanah before the next downpour. On my Great Plains trip three years later I would go through Quanah. Also, on my second trip last winter I had pedaled through the town. I found that incredible to have ridden on a bike to a town three times which was 500 miles away from Austin. Even more incredible to me was the fact that my first tour lacked only 80 miles from making it four times to Quanah. I don't think anyone in Quanah knew that.

I sat there in the Quanah café and service station eating a couple of sandwiches, watching the rain come down and remembering some close-by events of those tours and the tour still to come.

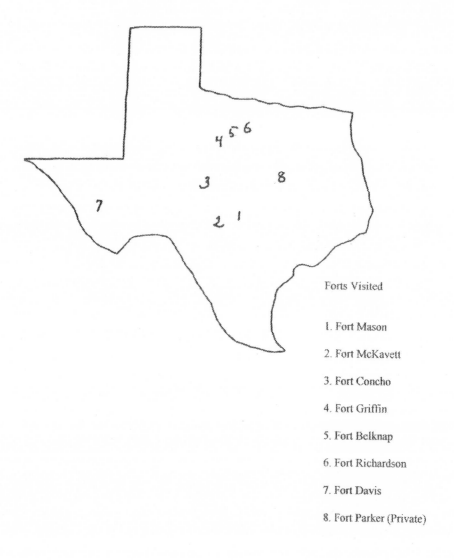

Forts Visited

1. Fort Mason

2. Fort McKavett

3. Fort Concho

4. Fort Griffin

5. Fort Belknap

6. Fort Richardson

7. Fort Davis

8. Fort Parker (Private)

*The author's tent at Seminole Canyon near Del Rio. On the right at the horizon, a train. To the left the headquarters building, one mile away.*

*The author in sub-freezing weather at Fort Parker in East Central Texas.*

*Windmills are being replaced by truck engines.*
*What a fully loaded bike looks like.*

*The Albany Courthouse in December 1993.*
*Most Texas courthouses are really handsome.*

*The author at the Navasota Public School.*
*To the left, a map showing the tours.*

*The author taking a breather. A compass hangs around his neck.*
*He didn't want to get lost in the Big Thicket of East Texas.*

*Taken near the town of Comanche.*
*The Comanche were excellent horsemen.*

*Rocky Point Camp site at Wright Patman Lake–*
*the day before the author's ride to rebuild his bike.*

*The author's apartment on December 30, 1993.*
*The end of a tour–unpacking–glad to be home.*

*The handsome author making a note for this book in East Texas.*
*A chigger on the visible knee itched like crazy.*

*A pump jack in West Texas.*
*Each pump jack has its own distinct sound while pumping.*

*The granite slab next to her mother's obelisk marks the site where Katherine Ann Porter's ashes are buried at the Indian Creek Cemetery south of Brownwood.*

*Daisy the dark Great Dane and Duffy the Red Heeler stand guard at Mayfield's Country Store, forty miles south of Ozona.*

## *More Indians*
(Summer Tour 1993)

On August 11, 1993, about 100 miles south of Quanah and 200 miles west of Dallas in a town named Roby, where about half the town won the state lottery a few years later, I finished my country breakfast at the Silver Star Cafe and Gift Shop. Outside, I aimed the bike at the rising sun toward Fort Griffin about 80 miles to the east and north. My first tour in Texas was three-fourths completed. I had three more military forts to visit before heading back into Austin. For all I knew that first tour could have been my last tour in Texas. I had no plans for another–I could not have imagined 7,000 more miles and four more tours. It's good sometimes not to see into the future. Too exciting. Too tiring.

At present, I had other things occupying my mind. The heat, as it always did, took its toll by late afternoon as I wheeled into Albany.

Fuzzy thinking usually afflicted me after several hours of pedaling, especially when the temperature was high. That afternoon it was 105 degrees. I still had 20 some miles to go.

I took the wrong highway out of town and struggled about 6 miles in the wrong direction before realizing my error. Twelve miles in an air-conditioned automobile are nothing. Twelve miles (about one hour) on a loaded bike on a hot afternoon were downright discouraging. The consequence of my misdirection: I pedaled 92 miles that day instead of 80.

TEXAS LONGHORN

## Fort Griffin
(Summer Tour 1993)

At last, Fort Griffin, now a state park, appeared, and not a minute too soon. I found a camping spot, showered, washed out my clothes, devoured the contents of several cans and was soon lulled to sleep by the soft lowing of the official herd of Texas Longhorn cattle, the slightly dissonant harmonies of a coyote family and the bass notes of bullfrogs squatting on the Clear Fork banks of the Brazos River.

Early next morning, I set off to explore the fort. Some buildings had been restored. I saw right away, however, that Fort Griffin had never been a very handsome place. In 1874, the army declared it unfit for human habitation, but it stayed open for seven more years. The "windjammer" mast on the parade ground resembled the one at Fort

McKavett, (see Chapter 14) only this one had more bracing. Fort Griffin was established July 31, 1867 with temporary buildings of wood. The immediate demands to serve the needs of the frontier were so great that only six of the more than 90 structures were of stone.

## Essential Black Troops–The Buffalo Soldiers
### (Summer Tour 1993)

Black troops distinguished themselves there, as they did at a number of frontier forts. As a matter of fact, black soldiers carried the load in every Texas military fort. The Indians called them buffalo soldiers because their curly hair resembled that of the buffalo. The Indians respected them as worthy adversaries of great fighting skill and stamina, again, analogous to the buffalo (actually bison). Life at the fort demanded much–young men soon looked old. The part played by black Americans on the frontier shocked later generations. History books for some time downplayed their significance or just plain ignored it. Suffice it to say that the west would have been much harder to settle if it had not been for these valiant soldiers. The officers–which we read about in the history books, were white.

The troops patrolled nearly all the time. They escorted government mail, protected surveying parties, watched over cattle drivers and chased Indians. Dust storms blotted out the horizon for several days at a time. Cold winters brought death to horses by freezing. Soldiers put up with cramped living spaces–up to six men per 100 square feet of space. That's 10 feet by 10 feet–smaller than most of our present-day mother-in-law rooms. Mealtimes barely met that definition–certainly not joyous occasions.

Breakfast consisted of beef, bread and coffee. When lunchtime rolled around (called dinner back then), the menu offered coffee bread and beef. For dinner (called supper), a trooper could look forward to bread and coffee–no beef.

Troops stationed in Texas had a rating for some of the forts. For pure luxury, in their eyes, Fort Sam Houston ranked number one. Fort

Davis in the mountains in the high plateaus of the west ranked high because of the climate. Fort Griffin fell off the page and into hell, undoubtedly the worst place to serve in Texas.

Near the fort, the town called Fort Griffin, but known better by such names as The Flats or The Flat and, sometimes, Hidetown got its nicknames honestly. Massive buffalo (bison) kills took place on the plains and Fort Griffin became the depot or shipping center for the uncured hides. In between shipments, the hides were stacked higher than a two-story building and numbered more than 200,000 at a time. Over the years, millions of hides called Hidetown home while awaiting shipment east. The buffalo hunters also collected the tongues as a delicacy, allowing thousands of carcasses at any one time to rot on the plains. The Western Cattle Trail went through the area and the town became a favorite stopping off place for a little fun. With the rotting hides and press of cattle, one could smell Fort Griffin for miles. Enormous clouds of flies enveloped man, beast and hide. The wise person kept his/her mouth shut. Western folk usually use words of one syllable and try to get by with only a couple of those words in a conversation. The "Flats" and other fly-infested hide depositories contributed to that verbal paucity, no doubt.

Buffalo hunters, prostitutes, gamblers, off-duty soldiers, desperados, and cattlemen called Fort Griffin home. Touring the saloons, one could bump into future movie stars like, Wyatt Earp, John H. "Doc" Holliday, "Bat" Masterson and "Big Nose" Kate Elder.

I visited the headquarters building and talked with vivacious Sonya Hargrove who knew the history of Fort Griffin well. She told me a story about a saloon named the Bee Hive. Over the front door hung a sign picturing a bee hive with bees flying around. Under the hive, a poem: "In this hive we are all alive/ Good whiskey makes us funny/ If you are dry step in and try/ The flower of our honey."

On January 17, 1877, Billy Bland, a ranch foreman and Charlie Reed, a cowboy, stepped inside the Bee Hive and tasted too much of the "flower." Out came the six-shooters and the two began yelling, cussing and shooting out the saloon lights. A young lawyer named Dan Barrow, just married, had stopped in to purchase some whiskey and decided to sit down and watch for a spell before going home. In the center of the room sat a dishonorably discharged Lieutenant of the 10th Cavalry. With the gunfire increasing, the deputy sheriff showed up accompanied by the county attorney to help make arrests. When the two got to the saloon, they saw that Charlie Reed stood near the front and Billy Bland lounged near the back door which led into the dance hall. He pointed his six-shooter at another light.

The sheriff walked toward Billy Bland and told him to throw down his gun. Naturally, this didn't sit too well with Billy so he decided to shoot at something else instead–namely, the sheriff. The bullet nicked the law officer. Immediately, everybody who had a gun began using it.

The young lawyer who had just stopped in to get some whiskey and had made the mistake of staying, had a bullet hole in his forehead and was deader than winter grass. The discharged soldier writhed on the floor shot through the back. In a couple of hours he died. Billy Bland rolled around in great pain. They carried him to a hotel where he begged someone to finish him off. He didn't die until the next morning. The county attorney suffered three bullet holes. One went through a lung near his heart. Everyone figured he would die and put him on a haystack out back. The next morning when a friend came by to bury him, he felt a lot better. Apparently the cold air stopped the bleeding. Charlie Reed who started the fracas with his pal–now dead– escaped with nary a bullet hole.

The folks at Hidetown acted as though nothing out of the ordinary had happened and ignored the dead and the dying. Cowboys still shot off their guns as they raced their ponies through the streets. In the saloons the music never missed a beat. Some Texans refer to those times as the "good ol' days."

# Fort Belknap
## (Summer Tour 1993)

On August 13, still on my first tour, I mounted my trusty two-wheeled pony and left Fort Griffin and Hidetown bound for Fort Belknap just 60 more miles to the northeast. Although there was no camping at Fort Belknap, an exception was made for me. I met Barbara Ledbetter, the archivist for the fort and county and had some productive sessions with her. I bought a couple of her research books and studied them.

A stone wall enclosed the fort. While there I walked the wall around the grounds. Only I and some children have done that. One of the more interesting highlights at the fort had nothing to do with its military history. On one part of the grounds grew the most gigantic grape arbor I had ever seen. It measured 120 feet by 130 feet. The ceiling, composed entirely of intertwining grape vines, spread across the entire arbor nine feet high. The sun shone through, striking the ground with thousands of silver dollar-sized circles of light, which danced on a thick brown carpet of dried grape leaves.

There were 15 massive vine trunks supporting the canopy, some measured 6 to 7 feet in circumference, rooted like columns in a spacious building throughout the arbor. The arbor stood open on all sides allowing the cooling breezes complete access. Large clusters of blue Mustang grapes hung down throughout. I ate a few of the tart grapes which caused my eyes to squint and my mouth to pucker.

The arbor began growing in the 1920s. Then, and for sometime before the restoration of the fort, a naturalist cared for the vines. He eschewed clothing and bathed in the Brazos River. If company called, he donned a potato sack. He got into a scrape with the law during the days of prohibition, because of the wine he made. In my mind's eye, I could see the peace officers sitting under the cool arbor, sipping the improved grape juice with the potato-sacked naturalist and negotiating some sort of an agreement, beneficial to all parties.

Fort Belknap, the largest military post in northern Texas until the

Civil War, served the community today as a grand place for civic functions like picnics and family reunions. One building housed a museum. Among the usual artifacts of frontier life, I saw a number of photos of people who lived during the settlement days of Young County, apparently plucked from old family albums. As I walked along, I noticed the facial expressions of these early pioneers. The portraits of the women shared a common look. Perhaps it was the fashion of the day to appear exceedingly serious, depressed, melancholy, sad, and opaque. If so, no one deviated from what was expected. I noted no joy, laughter, desire, or contentment on any pioneer woman's face. I hoped the sober images had more to do with having to stand "rock-solid" still in front of a primitive slow-exposure camera than with the hardships of frontier life. Riding around on smooth highways on a high-tech bicycle seemed extremely easy after imagining what those early settlers had to endure.

### Fort Richardson
(Summer Tour 1993)

Forty-one miles northeast of Fort Belknap another outpost, Fort Richardson, was next on the list. In less than five hours I arrived, set up my tent in a woodsy area south of the fort and had plenty of time to explore. The most impressive building turned out to be the hospital. An overhanging pitched roof supported by graceful pillars nearly all the way around the building set it off from the other buildings. This porch provided a restful and peaceful atmosphere and I took advantage of it to sit for a time in one of the wooden chairs. Recuperating soldiers, no doubt, sat there rocking in the cooling winds while watching the activities on the parade ground.

Other buildings I toured included the officers' quarters, the morgue, commissary, bakery, guardhouse, a reconstructed barracks and, a safe distance from all the buildings, the powder magazine building.

At Fort Richardson, General of the Army George Tecumseh Sherman, the same general who gave "Scarlett O'Hara" fits at Tara and burned Atlanta, decided that something needed to be done to quell Indian raiding parties which swarmed over the Red River from their reservations in Indian Territory (Oklahoma). The law forbade following the Indians across the River.

The defining moment came when the General, on a tour of the very same forts I visited, narrowly escaped being attacked by one of those raiding parties, saved only because a medicine man said bigger game approached. A wagon train of corn traveling from Jacksboro, near Fort Richardson, to Fort Griffin received the "big game" designation and the Indians attacked it the next day. The Salt Creek Massacre became bad news for the Indians–winning the battle lost them the war. Estimates of 25 to 100 Indians ambushed the 10 wagons and 12 men driving them. Seven drivers were killed. One was tied to a wagon wheel and his tongue cut out, then, burned alive. One had his head split open. All were mutilated. Of course, whites had been known to do the same sort of things to the reds, but this fight had dreaded repercussions for the Indians.

The raiders escaped into Oklahoma where the Kiowa chief, Satanta, bragged about it to the Indian agent. But this time retribution in the person of an angry general pursued the Indians to Fort Sill and the reservation, arrested the chiefs involved, and had Colonel Ranald Mackenzie escort them back to Jacksboro for trial. On the way, one of the chiefs, Stank, gnawed the flesh from his hand and slipped out of the cuffs. As he grabbed a knife, he was shot dead. The two remaining chiefs, Satanta and Big Tree, were tried and convicted in Jacksboro and sentenced to death, later commuted to life imprisonment. Two years later, both chiefs walked out, free. Big Tree became a Baptist Sunday School teacher. Satanta, the probable inspiration for Larry McMurtry's Blue Duck character in his book, *Lonesome Dove*, continued raiding until caught again. This time he leaped head-first to his death from a second story hospital window.

Colonel Mackenzie began a campaign to clean out the rest of the Indians in Texas. In conjunction with other commanders, he descended into Palo Duro Canyon, south of present-day Amarillo on September 28, 1874, where Comanche Chief Quanah Parker's Antelope band prepared to spend the winter. On my second tour in December, I camped at the bottom of the canyon for a few days imagining the scene. As the troops came into the canyon, the Indians rushed up the walls to gain a height advantage for the coming fight. Instead of engaging in battle, Mackenzie's troops seized nearly all the horses of the band, around 1,400 and shot them. He destroyed the Comanche's winter stores of food and burned the teepees (tipis). The troops climbed out of the canyon and rode back to their forts.

The Indians, facing winter without food or horses, had no choice but to give up and walk to Oklahoma. From that point on the Indian problems in Texas largely disappeared. The Indian's life of wild freedom had come to an end.

In preparation for my first tour, I read some Texas history. With each stop I experienced these historical events leaping off the pages of my books and right into my life. I found many interpretations and biases–a brutal period with all sides sharing in the brutality. Indians, settlers and soldiers shared equally in the atrocities. As I studied the old accounts, listened to old stories and walked along beside crumbling foundations and restored buildings, ghostly voices called out for revenge, forgiveness and justification. Musing over this turbulent period, I began to appreciate the complexity of the issues. I wondered what I would have done had I lived in Texas in the 1800s.

If I'd had a choice would I have been a Great Plains Indian, scornful of death, ready to do battle to preserve my free ranging style of life, or a settler, willing to undergo any hardship to stake out a piece of land to call my own?

For those who lived in those days on either side who were open to a peaceful and just solution, I would offer a memorial replete with ringing eulogies of admiration and amazement.

## The Mighty Wind at Memphis
(Winter Tour 1993)

I endured a lot of wind experiences on my tours in Texas. A couple from this part of the state will give you an idea of how exciting life on the plains in a tent or on a bicycle can be. There will be others as we continue around on our trip. One I want to share with you which I wouldn't know about until the following year–but since I'm writing this now and not then–I'll let you in on it ahead of time. If that ends up confusing you, just sit back and be amazed at the stories and sort the chronology out later or never.

If I had to pick one element in my cycling tours that demanded my attention daily it would be the wind–pushed and punched by it; blown away by it; even kissed lightly and passionately by it–my constant traveling companion.

I cursed it; praised it; sang to it; listened to its siren call early each morning and late each night. I feared it above everything else as it swept across the vast space of the Great Plains and forests.

Its constant presence became the defining memory of all my trips and in the end I felt I could accept it unconditionally–this seeming friend and enemy–in reality, neither for me nor against me. Soft or harsh in my face, it stirred me to life and scared me with death or injury. At times I couldn't handle it at all. One of those times occurred on my second tour–this time in the winter time and at the bottom southeast corner of the panhandle just a bit farther west from Quanah.

In December I arrived at a town called Memphis and I received permission to camp in the city park. The weather was breezy and crisp and it felt good. In the late afternoon, a huge cloud bank blossomed in the southwest. The sky turned yellow and orange and filled up with tumbling, fast-moving dark grey-blue clouds reaching almost to the ground. At first, the wind came through the tops of the trees in the park like a horde of lost souls. Next, it came in low. Dead leaves swirled. My tent buckled, collapsed and brushed against my head as I extinguished my stove and tried to balance a pan of boiling water. Bolts of lightning coursed across the sky and rocketed to the ground. Great tearing sounds ripping through the clouds ending in booms that shook the ground–pounded against my chest.

The clouds gave up their bulging load and a heavy downpour flooded against the trees. A solid waterfall of rain dashed hard against the tent. My bike, braced against a tree and I thought, tied securely, fell down flat. The lightning and thunder quit for a moment or two, then a tremendous brightness and a simultaneous monstrous crash startled me so, I spilled the boiling water on my ankle. The clouds turned orange as well as dark blue. The sheets of rain also appeared to be a dirty orange–probably the top soil from the bare fields after the cotton was picked. Water began to come into my tent corners. After several minutes the rain stopped. The lightning and thunder moved off, flickering, complaining and rumbling. The wind continued to blow.

### A Wondrous Sight
(Winter Tour 1993)

The sun, almost touching the horizon, suddenly reappeared, huge and red. Turning to the east I saw the sky filled with a perfect double rainbow. I had never in my life seen such a brilliant display of colors. At the bottom was violet followed in layers: indigo, blue, green, yellow, orange, and red. The second rainbow appeared on top and all the colors repeated again–all against a midnight blue sky–the retreating storm. I watched mesmerized until it faded from view. I bandaged my burned ankle. An hour later a flock of geese, in a serene V formation, flew over, honking.

The next morning, the wind had veered into the west still strong. The temperature moved into the flushed-cheek and red-nose region. I would be pedaling in a northwesterly direction that day–not good. As I left the park and entered downtown Memphis, I noticed people having a tough time opening and shutting their car doors. Thirty to forty miles per hour–strong but manageable, I thought. I ate breakfast at the local Shamrock service station and café. Outside I could see the flags on a building across the highway blowing straight out. I reasoned since I had only 27 miles to reach Claredon, my destination for the day, I could make it even if my pedaling speed were cut to six miles per hour. It would take five or six hours, counting rest stops, but what else had I planned to do? I got on my bike prepared to meet my non-enemy and non-friend.

As I expected, the gusting wind held me to about six miles per hour. By this time in my travels, my legs were strong and I knew I could pedal hard like that all day–with a break or two. I dropped to four miles per hour. I learned later that the wind had increased to 60 miles per hour, with gusts up to 70–right in my face. It got colder. The roof of the Pizza Hut blew off. The banners were in shreds. I had on ski goggles and a woolen face mask which permitted me to continue. At times, even though I used my lowest gear, the bicycle wanted to come to a complete stop. I had to fight to keep it on the highway. I don't remember any traffic.

## Good-bye Highway, Hello Ditch
### (Winter Tour 1993)

Just when I thought it couldn't get any worse–it got worse. I weighed 185 pounds. My bike, loaded with supplies, weighed nearly 160 pounds. Suddenly, the wind just picked the two of us up and deposited us in the weed-choked right of way. Amazingly, I was still aboard heading into the ditch at a right angle to the wind. I wrenched the handlebars hard to turn away from the deepening ditch and back toward town. Even with the rocky soil and the knee-high weeds and grass, the bike plowed through as if I were on the highway. I had to use the front and rear brakes to bring it to a halt.

Laboriously, I walked the bike back onto the highway and faced the wind. Riding was out of the question. There was a small service station seven miles out of Memphis and I thought I would just walk to it–another three miles–pushing my bike. This lasted about three steps. I couldn't even push it. By then I had been on the highway for two hours and had traveled a little over four miles. It's not too hard to make a decision when faced with those facts. Inclining the bike to a 45 degree angle toward me, I snailed across the median to the east-bound lane. Once across, on the graveled shoulder, and the bike pointed back toward Memphis, I attempted to get back on the saddle. With all the supplies on the bike, I could not throw my leg over the seat, but instead had to lift my leg across the frame, and in so doing had to take my hands off the handlebars where the brake levers were.

## Look Out Memphis–Here I Come
### (Winter Tour 1993)

The minute I released the brakes to lift my leg over the top tube, the bike would take off. I had to scramble to corral it before it ended up in town like a riderless horse. I tried this procedure again and gave up. I noticed a directional sign at the side of the road. It vibrated like crazy, but still held fast to its metal pole. An idea flashed. Inch by inch I positioned the bike next to the pole. I wrapped an arm around the pole and braced the bike against it. At last I could lift my leg over and squirm atop the saddle without the bike galloping off. I held to the pole with all my strength. When all was ready, I simply let go. The bike tore through the gravel. Rocks flew. The bike wriggled like an animal possessed. I held on and in one quick turn of the handlebars we leaped upon the highway. The bike quickly picked up speed until at times I saw 40 miles per hour register on my cyclometer. We zoomed up and down hills. I just sat there–never turning a pedal. Too bad it was such a short ride back to Memphis. I exceeded the speed limit as we entered town. What a ride. I was sorely tempted to keep on going to Dallas and maybe Florida.

### Sharing with a Mountain Lion
(Winter tour 1993)

The wind blew hard from the west all the rest of the day. I stayed in the café, where it was warm, eating sandwiches and drinking coffee, watching the ripped flags outside until time to bike back to the park and camping for the night.

The wind still strong, I chose a small canyon east of the park outside its boundaries. The wind roared overhead, but it didn't touch the tent. The next day, the wind moderated to a 15 miles per hour Texas breeze, but it definitely felt like December. I returned to the cafe for breakfast and to warm up. Asked where I'd spent the night, I described my snug canyon. "Good God man, we got a mountain lion that holes up there." True or not, I knew I would still have taken my chances on a shivering panther than stay another night clasped in the teeth of that panhandle wind.

East Texas
Mountain Lion

142

## Storms at Night
(Great Plains Tour 1997)

Before I began my bicycle trips in Texas and beyond, I didn't give storms much thought.

Safe behind masonry walls–sound and sight proofed from all but the most dramatic of jagged thrusts of blue white, white yellow and the bombardment of sound–coming from the tumbling storm clouds with their sheets of rain, sleet or hail–I, well insulated in my cocoon, continued to watch T.V., read a book, sip wine or soup, while just beyond my thick walls Mother Nature rearranged the atmosphere.

A different awareness of storms emerged when I exchanged the cement and brick walls for a thin piece of fabric stretched onto a support system of willowy fiberglass poles, staked flimsily to the ground by nothing more than a pitifully small number of 10 inch-long aluminum nails or cheap plastic spikes and thin cord, which, taken together, we all know as a tent. Most tents are for long peaceful evenings with wafting breezes, romantic candle light, some snacks, drinks and time for playing a harmonica or guitar. Of course, arctic expedition tents are indestructible and perhaps I shall get one the next time I venture out onto the plains. The drawback–they're small, causing calluses to form on my knuckles as I crawl about.

I learned that the usual touring tents and storms were incompatible. Yet storms came and bashed against the thin tent walls, or else threatened with percussive protestations, until fitful sleep finally tuned out the receding murmuring arguments.

Although I have been in storms during the daytime, while actually pedaling, most storms struck at night when I felt the most vulnerable and fragile. Luckily, my first storm in a tent was rather benign, though mighty exciting at the time. If one of those full-blown shriekers had hit me on those first days of touring, I am sure I would have shipped bicycle and equipment to Austin and caught the next bus home.

The nearest I came to being caught in a tornado happened on my

Great Plains trip of 1997. Again, I was about 100 miles south of Quanah and close to Abilene where I had just weathered a severe storm the night before. My new tent had ripped and one of the supporting poles had snapped. I pedaled about 30 miles north of the city, stopped, repaired my tent and set it up for the night. As on the previous night, a heavy bank of clouds approached. I turned on the radio and listened for weather reports. There were utility poles being blown down west of me. Tornados had been sighted and persons in my area were advised to seek shelter in a reinforced building. I got inside my tent.

The wind arrived. I stood in the center of the tent and braced my arms against the ceiling, clasping the supporting poles–hoping my strength would keep them from collapsing and breaking. We do crazy things, but for awhile it worked. Then, successive gusts like hammer blows smashed into me. I dived to the ground with the tent collapsing on top. Lying flat and the tent having a fit, I grabbed all my gear and piled it on the west side so the wind would have a harder time getting under the floor. The wind screamed. Everything held for a few moments and I thought I was going to make it without much damage, but another brute-force gust hit. The poles shattered, the tent tore open and torrents of rain came in.

After showing me who had the upper hand, the storm moved on. Water puddled on the floor, I stacked up luggage and crawled on top and spent the rest of the night with the top of the tent–actually, the side of the tent–six inches above me, funneling drips of rainwater onto my face. There were no mosquitoes.

## The Treasure Hunters
### (Summer Tour 1993)

While on my way toward Dallas to meet my son before pedaling back to Austin on my first tour in the summer of 1993, I stayed near Possum Kingdom Lake in a town the name of which I was sworn not to disclose. Possum Kingdom Lake was about 80 miles south and east of Quanah and about 50 miles due west of Dallas.

I stopped at a combination bar and café for a breakfast of biscuits, eggs, bacon, gravy and coffee. A young man, I guessed maybe in his thirties with a well-used small-brim Stetson pulled low, wearing clean but worn jeans, a blue denim shirt and scuffed hiking boots, seated himself two stools down from me at the bar and ordered his breakfast from the mother-earth waitress. They joked back and forth, but in a friendly caring sort of way that indicated a long relationship. He decided to have an omelet with hash browns rather than with biscuits and gravy. The waitress went back to the kitchen to deliver the order when he turned to me.

"That your bike out there?"

"Yep, I'm on a tour of Texas." We talked about how much it weighed, where I'd been, where I was going, the usual questions and comments I had grown used to.

"Well, I'm on my way too. Been here for six months taking care of my dad, but he just died–I'll be leaving in another day or two." I expressed my condolences.

"Oh, it was just a matter of time, he knew it wouldn't be long and he died peacefully in his sleep. Had a good and full life. We never were too close while I was growing up, so we had time to get to know each other and we both felt right when we knew it was getting close. No pain–just stopped breathing–and that was that–so now, I'm ready to take up where I left off."

"Are you from someplace in Texas, or will you be traveling out of the state?"

His breakfast arrived and he turned his plate around so the hash browns were on the left.

"Nope, I'll be staying in Texas. I'm a treasure hunter and I'll be trying my hand again at liberating some of that Spanish gold buried down by the Llano River." He introduced himself. I'll call him Jack–not his real name.

"Well, I'll have to say, Jack, you're the first treasure hunter, I've met. How do you know where to go and how to find it?" His manner

145

of speech and bearing marked him as an educated man–some college or maybe a degree. He had a good direct look. We talked until our plates were empty and we had started on our second coffee warm-up. He had read several books on Texas treasure, he especially liked the stories gathered by J. Frank Dobie. He had found maps in some libraries and in attics and at estate sales and from other treasure hunters who were too old to continue the quest.

"Some of them got close to a lot of gold, but time just ran out and they had to give up–I assured them if I found anything by using their directions, they'd certainly get a share–one old fellow provided several details which I think will help out a lot. There's been enough research done to convince me that there's gold out there–buried by the Spanish–stashed away by train robbers–hidden by confederates during the Civil War. Of course, If I find silver it won't be worth much–unless I find the two-thousand bars that weigh fifty pounds each–but, I'm not counting on that. But gold, that's a different story, and gold is what I'm after this time–prices are still good and you don't have to find much to make your troubles go away."

"So, is it a secret, Jack, where you're going to start? I mean, don't tell me if it's something you have to keep secret."

"Actually, I've two places where I've already done some work and a third place that looks kind of interesting–no, it doesn't have to be a secret as long as I don't go into detail. Ever hear of the San Saba Mine? It's supposed to be an old Spanish silver mine near the San Saba ruins outside of Menard. There's even reports of up to 14 silver mines out there." I told him I had ridden through there just a few weeks before. He kicked at the bar rail with his boot.

"The Indians knew where some of the mines were located because they had silver bullets at times and also silver jewelry. Sometimes it's called the lost Bowie Mine. Story goes how Jim Bowie learned where a mine was with a rich vein of silver that had a touch of gold in it. Nobody has ever found it. Bowie himself said he had been shown the mine by the Indians, it was full of millions of dollars worth of silver, but when he went to find it with an expedition, he couldn't locate it again. He died at the Alamo, before he could try again." The waitress filled our empty cups and walked back to the kitchen area. Jack sipped, shutting his eyes against the steam.

REAL PRESIDIO de SAN SABA

"What I'm working on is a stash of gold that was gathered by the missions in the southwest region and buried in a vault close to the old presidio. All the priests and Indian converts were killed in a Comanche uprising, so all records as to where that vault was located were lost, or so everyone thought. Actually, the directions were sent to mission headquarters in Mexico and were smuggled out years later–but doctored up–that's what I just found out. I'm certain I have the right key that has been hidden all those years. I've been working on it for the last six months I've been here with my dad and I've finally figured it out–so in a couple of days I'll be on my way and in a few weeks you'll be reading about what I've found." He smiled with anticipation and satisfaction.

"After that I'm going to Castle Gap and then there's a stash up by Palo Duro Canyon I want to get to before winter."

Jack held out his cup for one more warmup. I motioned to the returning waitress to fill mine, too.

"Well, good luck," I said. "Hope you find it–sounds like you know what you're doing. Maybe you ought to write a "how to" book on treasure hunting." He laughed, but behind that laugh and in those eyes I could see determination and an unwavering faith that he did know what he was doing, indeed, there was gold out there. I decided to read up on the still-hidden treasures in Texas once I got back to Austin.

A person would be hard put to find a more intriguing endeavor–especially if one had, somehow, got hold of a really good secret map. I could see how the hunters would give up everything for the sure and certain possibility of finding what no one else had been able to locate. It would be not only the money and the wealth such a discovery would bring, but also the notoriety, the fame, showered on that one individual, forever set apart from all the thousands who had dreamed, connived, struggled and who eventually gave up because the human body refused to climb that last hill, descend into that last pit, crawl into that last cave or shovel one more load of Texas rock.
In a few months I would be in the Palo Duro Canyon, camping in the wintertime in the great panhandle of Texas. I would wonder if the treasure hunter had already been there and if he had found that "stash."

"One thing," Jack said, standing up ready to leave. "I'd appreciate it if you don't mention this town or the restaurant–might make things tough on the folks around here if word got out." I promised and he left.

I drained my cup and left a tip. The waitress came over.

"His daddy died day before yesterday. He took it pretty hard. They got real close at the end. He's a good man."

Cowboy Biker

**The Cowboy Biker**
(Summer Tour 1993)

While I waited in Mineral Wells a few hours later for my son, I met a cowboy biker that put me to shame. I called this person a cowboy biker because he looked like a cowboy and he was riding a bicycle. Sweat-stained broad-brimmed western hat, blue jeans, faded tan shirt with a bandana tied around his throat, well-used boots and a ruck sack tied to his back from which protruded the barrel of a shortened .22 rifle, made me think of a western pioneer or perhaps of a drifter on his way to his next ranch job. He had no fancy color-coordinated panniers such as I had, but he did have a nice moustache. He rode a mountain bike with front wheel suspension. "I like it cause I can ride off the road if I need to." The "need to" meant getting his dinner: squirrels, rabbits or doves, which he would shoot with his .22 rifle. He would skin or pluck the animal, build a fire and roast it. He bathed in creeks and rivers, and when necessary used them for drinking water. He had been on the road for three years, having been discharged from the army after a long hitch. "I decided I wanted to travel and also I didn't want to be around too many people."

His rucksack was small, couldn't hold much–surely a poncho or coat for cold days. I noticed a bed roll strapped over his rear wheel.

149

All cowboys have a bed roll–and a slicker and some jerky. He said he had no stove, no tent, no change of clothes.

"Just wash'em out every few days–or ride in the rain–works just fine. Might have to sit in the bushes while they dry." I asked how he traveled in the winter time.

"Easy, I just head south and keep on agoin' till it warms up–it's a good life, mostly."

As we visited I was keenly aware of all my camping luxuries. I felt like a softie. A tenderfoot. A dude rancher. Could I skin and roast a squirrel–assuming I could aim straight enough to knock it out of a tree with a single shot .22? Could I plunge into an icy stream or bathe in a still pond with Cotton Mouth snakes slithering by? I wondered how many young men like the cowboy biker roamed the world and what they were seeking. I knew how much I enjoyed being out on the road–not like this cowboy biker, of course, but still out there. On that trip and on the others I took, I noticed that it took two or three weeks to get into the rhythm of the open road. Something I could not have imagined before the first trip. Perhaps people should take off two or three weeks before a vacation to give their systems a chance to slow down or speed up sufficiently. At the end of the vacation another week or two week period to become acclimated to the work place again would also be in order. Even so, to my way of thinking, it still wouldn't come close to the feeling I got on a long tour that lasted months–a way of life I hoped a lot of people would get to experience–even if it had to be in an RV. But , who can afford to stay on the road? Guess it depends on what one is willing to exchange for it.

Yes, I liked the company of friends and being at home in a warm bed and air-conditioning and all the rest that modern technology offers, but I also know the pull of the open road as it whispers its siren's song in every quiet moment. Small wonder why folks hit the road as a cowboy biker, a bicycle tourer such as myself, a motorcycle adventurer, or an RVer with all the comforts of home packed inside.

## Dinosaurs
(Summer Tour 1993)

After visiting a few days with my son, he took me to the Dallas city limits and I began my trek homeward to Austin. I stopped at Glen Rose to camp at the Dinosaur State Park. There were real prehistoric dinosaur tracks in the shallow river. I pulled off my shoes and socks and put my feet in one of the meat-eating dinosaur tracks–Acrocanthosaurus, a precursor of T. Rex. Wow. The track had three huge toe marks.

No theme park engineer developed those tracks for tourists to marvel at. Those magnificent brutes actually, really, walked there. If I could have been there–and I'm glad I wasn't–I could have put my feet in that track! Millions of years later, I could still do it. I did it. Talk about a spooky feeling. A sort of mystic feeling came over me as I pretended to touch something very much alive and roaring one hundred million years before.

I invited some Japanese tourists passing by to join me–to do what I had done explaining how it was a great life-experience to wiggle your toes in the toes of a killer. They just looked at me, kept their shoes and socks on and walked away. I wouldn't make a good missionary. Maybe they didn't know English. Maybe they thought I was stuck and went for help. No one came.

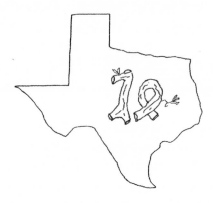

## *Up the Side of the Panhandle*
(Perimeter Tour 1994)

At Childress thirty miles west of Quanah, a new world opened up to me. A simple turn to the right and there stretching north and west lay the great panhandle of Texas. To so unpoetically name a region common to several states as a handle to some sort of pan though instantly conjuring up that utensil and recognizing the aptness of the name to describe a sliver of a state that juts away from the main body and often seen as superfluous to that body, let it be said that the so-called panhandle of Texas was anything but.

As Texas has been often described as "that whole other country" so the panhandle was a world unto its own. Back in the days when the leaders of the new Republic of Texas did their dreaming, Texas tried to expand into New Mexico–taking half of that state and then wanted to extend northward, wiping out the present day Oklahoma panhandle and taking over a huge swath of land right through the middle of

Colorado before coming to a stop in Wyoming west of Laramie. Now that would have been a real panhandle. Fortunately or unfortunately, debt ridden Texas had to pull in its horns and those grandiose plans for an empire didn't come to pass. One could say the handle got way too big for the pan.

As at Quanah, I rode three times through Childress, staying at the city park on two of the tours. In the last chapter I told how I had continued on 287 to Memphis, the second tour (1993), and had a bout with a super wind storm and eventually got to Amarillo in the middle of winter. The other two trips, the perimeter third tour (1994) we're dealing with chronologically, and the Great Plains tour (1997) where I was riding north to leave the state, completed the three visits. I don't think anyone in Childress was aware of my passing through anymore than they were in Quanah. As far I as I know–no historical marker has been requested.

## Park with a Lake
### (Winter and Perimeter Tours 1993, 1994)

I liked both times I stayed at the Childress City park. Ducks and geese paddled about on the lake, softly quacking and honking. A territorial goose chased anyone getting too close. I knew where to camp both times in order to escape its wrath. In the winter, the yellow-brown grass provided me a soft mattress beneath my tent and material for interesting Christmas cards sent to head-shaking friends. Hundreds of blackbirds wheeled through the air disappearing into the cat tails at the lake's edge for a while before darting off in huge undulating chattering black clouds to distant trees and back again.

During the perimeter tour, I received permission to camp in the covered pavilion since the storms had been rolling in each night. The park supervisor rescinded that not knowing my status as a Childress three-time visitor and therefore somewhat of a celebrity. The pavilion, my informant stated, could be used by groups only, and sure enough, I wasn't a group. No groups came either–so the pavilion sat pristinely empty all night–its mandate intact. I camped near another covered area which, although too small for my tent, did offer a place of escape if the weather turned foul. It didn't. Very peaceful evening. Did my laundry–hung it out to dry. The ducks watched from the still waters. We exchanged a few quacks, since I try to stay in touch with several different animal species as much as possible. Once inside my tent for the evening, I quacked softly and the whole flotilla came across the pond and spent the night close by.

While in Childress I availed myself of another salad bar and reduced the establishment's inventory of veggies significantly.

### The Magic of the Great Plains
#### (Perimeter Tour 1994)

Eager for an early start, I popped up at five-fifteen and attacked Highway 83 north by six-fifteen. A quick stop at a convenience store for a cup of coffee and a fried apple pie and I was ready to tackle the panhandle.

The sun jumped from the horizon as a gleaming dazzling white ball. Low hills to my left and right clothed themselves in soft blues and grays. Only the outlines of trees stood out–sort of floating–like in a Chinese landscape watercolor. Quail caught my attention with whistles and whirring wings. Cattle lowed in their pastures. Kildeer, a cactus wren–way up there–and warblers sang their hearts out. A soft haze appeared. The breeze shifted to the north–into my face–and increased from breeze to wind. I didn't care. I was in the Texas Panhandle. It was a beautiful morning.

### Clouds Were A-Comin'
#### (Perimeter Tour 1994)

Thick roiling gray clouds tumbled toward me from the north, moving rapidly. The once brilliant haze-filled sky turned dark and angry looking. I was in for it I thought. The clouds marched in double time and the wind gusted–and everything sped by without shedding a single drop of moisture. The sun reappeared as if nothing had happened. The birds sang. The watercolor trees took their places again. A new company of clouds appeared, bearing down on me from the north. The storm swept by on the left with much pomp and circumstance. The sun came out again.

In a few more minutes another battalion of clouds dark and menacing formed on the northern horizon. This time they went by on the right, bumping into each other and doing a lot of complaining. Where else could a person have a ride like that? The wind shifted to the northeast. I stopped and took a picture of a beautiful unnamed meandering creek twenty miles north of Childress. Some West Texas streams had water in them after all.

### Pioneer Park
(Perimeter Tour 1994)

I bought groceries in Wellington another ten miles up the panhandle. I planned to stop at Pioneer Park north of Wellington, but when I arrived it was closed for a family reunion. Could I have been a long-lost relative?–maybe, but instead of crashing the party, I chose to go on. By this time the wind had shifted to the east and in a few more minutes, to the southeast. A tailwind! Three years later I camped at the park. On both tours, I had breakfast at Shamrock.

### Speed Record
(Perimeter Tour 1994)

On the perimeter tour I decided to camp for the evening about 12 miles north of town. A good ride for the day 70 miles. The next day I would try for Follett in the extreme northeast corner of the panhandle–80 miles away. But first there was the descent into the town of Canadian on a beautiful sweeping section of the highway– like a boulevard. In my Great Plains tour three years later I

155

established my fastest speed ever on that decline–forty-six miles per hour! I thought about the combined weight of bike and rider approaching 350 pounds–those pounds riding on those two skinny tires and a small trailer tire.

I had another chance for the speed record in Montana, but my rear tire blew up half-way down the hill. Fortunately, I was able to coax the bicycle to a stop without losing control in about an eighth of a mile–seemed like forever at the time.

### A Really Big Dinosaur
### (Perimeter Tour 1994)

By the way, at the top of the descent into Canadian one can catch a glimpse of a huge sculpture of a plant-eating dinosaur on a mountain top. Quite striking and surprising if you weren't expecting it. And who would be?

### Higgins Bound
### (Great Plains Tour 1997)

After Canadian the tours that had shared that highway split. The one we are following for narrative purposes went on to Follett. The Great Plains tour of three years later veered off to the right and went out of the state into Oklahoma and north to Canada. What an adventure that was. I want to follow that one for just a few miles because it illustrated so well panhandle hospitality.

In 1997 I left the town of Canadian, planning on spending the night at a rest stop about six miles before reaching Higgins on Highway 60 and about the same distance from the Oklahoma border. Higgins is just about as close to Oklahoma as one can get without being a Sooner. I pedaled to the rest stop only to find it closed. I had no choice but to go on, even though the day light soon changed to dusk. Higgins had around 500 people, according to my map, so, probably not big enough for a park or a motel, I thought. Perhaps I might have to go on into Oklahoma at night and try to reach Arnett–another 12 or so miles away.

## How About a Hamburger
(Great Plains Tour 1997)

As the sun sank out of sight, I found myself within yelling distance of Higgins. But before I tried that out, a voice yelled at me. "How about a hamburger?" I turned into a small park on my left which had escaped my notice. Several people gathered about picnic tables. I had pedaled 95 miles that day and lots of things began to escape my notice. I was about pedaled out. The man who yelled was Vester Smith, Commander of the American Legion Post 509 of Higgins. I judged about 30 people gathered there–husbands and wives. They had just finished their picnic and had a lot of food left over. So, I had a hamburger with cheese and pickles, coffee, potato salad, baked beans and chocolate cake. I visited with Dee Phelps, chaplain, and Leroy Koch, historian, who took my picture. Most everyone just sat around watching me eat and plying me with more food–like a gigantic family that couldn't do enough for a prodigal son.

## The Sheriff
(Great Plains Tour 1997)

The first person I met, however, was James Robertson, Sheriff of Lipscomb County. Sheriff Robertson, surely a casting director's dream come true for a western Clint Eastwood-type lawman; except Sheriff Robertson was better looking. Quiet, friendly, reserved with eyes that didn't miss a trick–tall and slim with a western straw hat and a gun-filled holster on his hip, he welcomed me to the group.

## The Appreciative Teen-Aged Girls
(Great Plains Tour 1997)

Everyone was solicitous and invited me to put my tent up in the small park. The Sheriff promised to ride by and check on me. He said

157

teenagers used the park to smoke cigarettes and drink beer, but he'd keep an eye on things for me. I put up the tent. That night the moon was full. I left off the rain-fly so I could look up and out through the mesh top. At 3:30 the moon shone so brilliantly, I had to get out my binoculars again. I had used them earlier when it first rose and the folks were still there. I had passed the binoculars around and everyone enjoyed looking.

One car came by and honked. One drove by and called out "Hello." I answered with "Howdy." A pickup of teenagers drove in and girls got out and into another pickup that had been parked there for awhile. Apparently, boys from somewhere had met them and everyone had gotten into one pickup and had taken a drive. The girls called out to the boys before both pickups drove away, thanking the boys for coming over and for the "nice time."

There was a railroad about 100 yards away and a couple of freights rumbled by, but I didn't mind at all. I got up at 4:30, packed and slipped into Oklahoma at daybreak, refreshed with a good dose of Texas caring.

### On to Follett
(Perimeter Tour 1994)

Going back to the town of Canadian we'll pick up the trail of our main narrative–the perimeter tour of 1994. I saw on my Texas map a small blue dot that designated a rest stop about eight miles east of Follett–way up in the corner of Texas. After Follett and the rest stop there would be only the Oklahoma border and if I crossed over I would be on the inside corner of that state's panhandle.

### No Showers
(Perimeter Tour 1994)

I had pedaled every day since Wright Patman Lake south of Texarkana. No days off. No showers either–just alcohol baths at night

158

and in the morning and washing my clothes out wherever I could. I would not take a regular "water" shower or bath until I reached Dalhart on the west side of the panhandle. That would be sixteen days without a shower. Amazing for someone who had to shower everyday before these tours started.

## The Melting Highway
### (Perimeter Tour 1994)

The second week of June in the panhandle meant hot, or it could mean snow. That particular second week for me voted for hot. The highway melted. I had put fenders on my bike to ward off rain–little did I realize they would be effective against rocks in my face. The road tar stuck to my tires. My sticky tread picked up loose gravel which, without the fenders, would have been rifled at my face as centrifugal force sent them flying off the tire. With fenders, the rocks rode all the way around and were discharged like sub-machine gun bullets in a straight stream in front of me. What a weapon. Instead of running over armadillos I could shoot them with rocks–not that I would harm those gentle creatures.

Once that day the tire picked up a rock too big to "pass." I came to a sudden loud grinding halt. To dislodge it I had to back the bike up until it freed itself. Speaking of melting highways, I stopped once without realizing how soft the highway had become. I put the kickstand down and proceeded to open a can of ravioli. While checking on something, I placed the open can on the seat. I turned just in time to see the bike do a slow roll-over as the kickstand went right through the pavement. I grabbed for the can, and succeeded in spilling the ravioli sauce all over me. From that moment on, I carried a flat piece of wood to put under the kickstand. We learn as we go, but we never seem to learn enough to prevent the unexpected. Of course, if we did prevent the unexpected we wouldn't know it would we? In hot weather I always get weird thoughts.

## The Postmistress Did My Laundry
### (Perimeter Tour 1994)

I entered Follett and halted at the Post Office. The Postmistress offered to do my laundry on her lunch hour. No one at my neighborhood post office in Austin ever did that. I could take it with me to the rest area and dry it out there. I said sure and thank you. I toured the town and ate in the park. Follett was charming. Definitely not dry and dusty. Great trees, boutique shops. Friendly people. In an hour everyone knew I had invaded the town. They waved. They smiled. I smiled and waved back. It's a great ritual too often neglected. The young Baptist minister also acted as the town's reporter and did a story on me for the local newspaper. He, too, rode a bike. After my visit, I think his stock went up. I rode out to the rest stop eight miles east for my first night.

## The Corner of Texas
### (Perimeter Tour 1994)

Oklahoma waited four miles away. I thought about riding to the border, but not just the border, I wanted to stand on the exact corner of Texas. To do that meant I would have to hike across somebody's ranch about four miles north after I reached the border on state highway 15. I wondered if anyone had ever done it. I wondered if there was a marker or a statue out there in a pasture, maybe something looking like that black slab in the space odyssey movie. I could have held a ceremony—probably the only one held at that corner in recorded history. Maybe gold was buried there. I wondered, but I was also tired. I wondered too much at times.

## The Shelter East of Town
### (Perimeter Tour 1994)

It was windy at the rest stop. It contained a picnic table with a roof and a concrete floor and a barbeque pit. All around me it was kind of bleak. I liked bleak. If one looked closely, bleak was anything but bleak. I watched the swallows dive beneath a bridge at blinding speeds. Soon I had my laundry flapping in the freshening breeze. In thirty minutes I took it down–perfectly dry. It felt home-like, me sitting there, folding laundry at the picnic table in my house without walls. The two cars that went by that afternoon waved. I waved back.

## Snowstorm Tales
### (Perimeter Tour 1994)

I had a meal at the Panther Cove Café in town and met a rancher who told me a couple of snow stories. In the first one, he was coming from Shattuck, Oklahoma on February 17, 1978. When he reached the border, just four miles east of me on this very highway, the road was closed because of snow. He stayed there for three days. A helicopter finally rescued him. I thought about a helicopter descending on my tent in the middle of a blizzard out there–"you been here since summer? My God!–."

The second time took place in 1945. A train of twenty cars hauling cattle and pulled by two engines got caught in a terrible storm and derailed. He had to spend the night with the cattle, completely covered in snow. A person had to love cattle to do something like that. I rode back out to the rest stop. Almost there, I met a steer right in the middle of the road. I stopped and we looked at each other for a long while. I assured him that if he ever got stuck in a blizzard I would help out. He walked off and I went on.

I spent a restful, but windy night at the shelter and rode into town to the café early the next morning. The sun came up bright in a blue sky and promised a hot day for my ride west across the very top of

161

the panhandle. My destination, Perryton, only 47 miles away not counting the eight from the shelter into Follett.

## A Tale of Compassion
### (Perimeter Tour 1994)

At the café I talked with the owner, cook and waitress–Donna Cornett. She said there were nine racing motorcycles in her family. Years ago she fell off a motorcycle backwards, riding as a passenger at 100 miles per hour. Almost killed her. She doesn't ride anymore–unless she's the one driving.

As I ate breakfast, Donna told me about a homeless man who had come to Follett some years before. He was walking to Missouri and dying of cancer. The community of Follett took him in. He stayed with Donna's family for a month and at another family's home for a month. They got his social security checks coming and found him a house to rent. He began working at odd jobs in the community. He painted the inside of the Panther Cove Café. He worked almost to the day he died. They got him to a cancer clinic in Amarillo and he died there, but in a letter he had written while there was his request to be buried in Follett–so his ashes arrived in town. The local people donated money for a cemetery plot. A service was held and almost everyone attended. He had found a home in the great heart of Follett.

## Across the Top of the Panhandle
### (Perimeter Tour 1994)

As I left Follett, the wind came up and tried its best to blow me off the highway. My new tires were larger than the original ones and held the road well. When a truck passed me from behind, my riding shirt would come up to my helmet. I moved with the gusts instead of trying to hold a straight line. It saved my strength. I got the idea from watching how the swallows the day before at my shelter used the wind to help them navigate the bridge opening. They zigged and zagged to maintain position before making the dive. The wind howled and moaned through the utility wires as I zigged and zagged my way west. I stopped and picked up what I thought was a clump of lespedeza–a member of the legume family. I remembered it growing in Indiana for hay. Also I picked what looked like side oats. I picked some other plants and grasses and a yellow blooming plant on my way to Booker.

When I arrived I met Brad Schultz of the Bar S Ranch at the convenience store. He looked at my fistful of plants and went out to his truck for a book on plants given him by his dad. The side oats was also called cheat. The lespedeza was called Creeping Alfalfa. We named the other things I had picked up. Before riding I never paid any attention to wild flowers and plants growing by the side of the road. And who would have thought there would be someone driving around with a plant book on a pickup's front seat? He gave me a Bar S pen, which I still have.

## The Rest Stop from Hell and an Angel
### (Perimeter Tour 1994)

On my way to Perryton, I saw on my map a blue-dotted rest stop north of town. I thought at last I can ride with the wind at my back. At the time it was blowing good at about 40 miles per hour. The ride proved effortless. I found out though that flies also go with the wind and several landed on me and the bike as we zoomed north. Hitch-hiking flies dimmed the ride some.

When I arrived at the rest stop, it appeared more of a pull-over stop–just wide enough for a car to get off the highway–littered and dirty. A few hundred yards farther on, I could see a country beer joint. Being that close to bleary-eyed customers at closing time didn't appeal to me. I sat beside a noisy tree–the leaves slapping each other silly in the wind–and felt downright depressed. As I tried to figure out what to do, a pickup stopped and the driver offered a ride back into Perryton. I didn't hesitate a second.

I was worn out and knew I couldn't pedal against that wind. We stowed the bike and gear in the back. I climbed in the front and closed the door. Silence. Wonderful. The sound of silence. The wind had roared all day. When I closed the pickup's door–instant calm–instant peace. No wind. Back in Perryton, Robert Steele drove me to the city offices where I secured a camping spot in the park. There were four spaces available. I got the last one.

## Day Off to Snooze and Visit
### (Perimeter Tour 1994)

After sleeping through the night, I decided to stay in Perryton the following day and take naps in between chores. Two RV neighbors left early in the morning before I woke up. One couple remained. I could hear the husband yelling, cussing and groaning at his "pop up" camper which refused to "pop down." The wife's voice was supportive and very quiet. I could hardly hear her. After awhile he achieved success and my last two park neighbors left. During the day a small boy stopped by to chat about bikes. He had one he had built himself with special gears, he said.

"I got a slipping gear, so I can stop fast, a snow gear for winter and a water gear to get through high water." A girl came up and asked about my trips in Texas. As I mentioned the places I had traveled she kept saying, "O my gosh, I can't believe it" over and over. Was she not a good conversationalist or what? Reminded me of my dad's favorite conversationalist. The neighbor was our mailman in Bargersville, Indiana. When dad started talking, Mr. Brown would interject with, "Well, I'll be dogged" after every pause dad took for breath and with just about every inflection available to the human voice. Dad could talk all day to Mr. Brown. I could have talked all day to that young lady in the panhandle.

## Indiana: Dead Calm Most of the Time
(Perimeter Tour 1994)

The next morning I left. The wind had died down to 20 miles per hour. You can't get much lower than that on the plains. I went to college in Enid, Oklahoma after growing up in Indiana where the wind shows up occasionally, but generally there are long periods of dead calm. I would spend an inordinate amount of time each morning to get my straight hair "trained" to approximate a wave with the help of liberal doses of reddish hair oil that was a little like 3-in-1. I knew I had too much on if it began to seep onto my cheeks or run down my forehead. The trick was to get enough on to plaster the hair down, but not too much causing girls' faces to contort in disgust. With every hair in place, I would go to school and have no trouble maintaining my pompadour "do" for most of the day–much like the Fonz in the TV series, who, as he peered into the mirror, comb at the ready, realized his hair was still perfect.

When I graduated from high school I went out west to Oklahoma close to that state's panhandle where the wind roared daily. I thought the constant wind would drive me nuts. But I got used to it and after awhile, took it for granted. I did develop a new hairstyle called "wind-blown." After a few years I paid a visit to Indiana and thought I would suffocate. Where was the wind? I could hardly wait to get back to where it "comes sweeping " across the plains. But, sometimes it blew too long and too damned hard–even for me.

## Great Plains Towns
(Perimeter Tour 1994)

After my day off I biked to Spearman on Highway 15 . Some pesky flies went with me. Repellent helped. The countryside was gently rolling–mostly flat and I could see forever. I stayed at the spacious city park in Spearman and the next day rolled into the town of Gruver, at one time the richest town per capita in the United States back in the 50s and 60s because of oil and gas wells. Not that rich anymore, Gruver was still a prosperous and friendly community. In town I met Cindi Ferguson, the manager of Gopher's, a state-of-the-art convenience store (with deli). She called the local reporter and I gave another interview. Surely they will remember me in Gruver should I ever return.

On my way to Stratford I saw a ring-necked pheasant flying in the field next to the highway–graceful tail and iridescent colors. I heard what sounded like a truck doing about 50 miles per hour in a field–a truck motor all right, but stationary–used to pump water to irrigate the crops. Water was precious in the panhandle and I knew folks figured getting it was worth the noise. Traveling in a car, the sound of the engine wouldn't have been noticed. Someday the water will be gone, but the huge irrigated fields will remain, nourished by huge pipe lines bringing desalinated water from the Gulf. The resulting mounds of salt on the coast will be processed into something wonderful, car fuel maybe, or non-melting highways, who knows?

Out of hearing range of the engine, I heard the birds again. Red-winged blackbirds had a sustained note followed by chirps. Sometimes they sounded like an old-fashioned screen door spring being stretched–kind of a zinging sound. But those old screen doors were pretty rare so maybe I'd have to say it sounded more like the "zinging" my computer made as it tried to connect to the Internet–most computers have that turned off, however, so you just may have to listen to a blackbird yourself and figure out your own simile. A pheasant sounded like the back-in-the-throat laugh adolescent boys made when they wanted to be noticed by girls. The meadow lark had four up and down notes like the beginning of the Sound of Music song about do re me. After the fourth note there followed a kaleidoscope of notes usually in a descending scale. It sounded like an orchestra playing four notes on a single flute before cramming a thousand notes in a mad dash to the end. That furious dash lasted about one second. It was glorious. I met a fellow in the panhandle who said his dad could whistle an approximation of the meadow lark's call.

"When he gets to that part where all the notes come at once, his cheeks flutter and vibrate like crazy."

Measuring my water intake on a hot day, I figured I got around 39 miles to the gallon. I finally had my water problems behind me. I no longer worried about water nor did I get thirsty. I carried plenty. I got used to the extra weight on the bicycle. Believe me, it was well worth it to show up in a town still lumbering along with a gallon still untouched.

Along the way to Stratford in that wide-open land I noticed miles and miles of pastures on one side of the highway and miles and miles of milo and wheat on the other. For several miles now, I had crossed the Caprock Escarpment and I was in the high plains of Texas–the Llano Estacado or Staked Plains, so called because of the uplift that resembled a stockade. There was a time when people thought the early Spanish explorers had actually driven stakes in the plains so they wouldn't get lost.

At Stratford I put my tent up in a small field graciously offered by its owner. A couple of blocks away, I had met Nadine Bishard, manager of the Gopher's there. She had negotiated my being able to stay in the lot where I had a nice big tree to camp under. A local lawman in the store had refused my camping in the city's park. It was the only time in all my travels in Texas that city park camping was refused. I wondered if my not having had a shower for several days had anything to do with it. I decided not because after he left, a nice-looking customer turned to me and said he was like that all the time. "He's an asshole."

Leaving Stratford, I saw the remains of the big rain and hailstorm that came through on May 10, over a month before. Hail the size of tennis balls. Some as large as grapefruit. Hail drifts up to four feet high and ten inches of rain. I thought about being caught out in the open when such a storm came by. I stopped thinking about it. On my right the fields were still flooded to a depth of 5 to 6 feet–75 yards wide–from the railroad tracks to the highway and six miles long. At the six mile point a ditch had been cut six feet wide and eight feet deep to drain a lake which had formed a mile on down the road. The highway I was on had been impassable until a couple of days before. A truck loaded with hay passed. Smelled good. A truck loaded with cattle passed. Didn't smell good. The highway was hard and smooth– great to ride on. Pale lavender flowers bloomed in profusion at the roadside. Crickets and frogs near the water had a never-ending symphony playing.

### Small Place Big Café
(Perimeter Tour 1994)

I pulled into a café in Conlen–not on my map. There was a big statue of a cowboy outside. Vinyl cloths with a red and white checkered design covered the several small tables. There were ten counter stools, too. Enough room to seat at least thirty people–way out there where there was nothing. Two attractive women ran it. One explained. "The regulars come in around 7 to 9 each morning and the dinner crowd shows up around noon. They pack this place both times. They eat exactly the same thing every day–don't even order–we know what each wants and have it ready when they come through the door. They're mostly farmers and ranchers who live around here."

### Hey Texline
(Perimeter Tour 1994)

I got to Dalhart and angled northwest to the western corner of the Texas Panhandle–a town called Texline. The difference between Follett and Texline was striking. Follett–lush and green. Texline– brown and dry. It looked like what you might expect a high plains west Texas town to look like. Dust, sand, and windblown. What trees still existed appeared drab and beaten down, but tough and hanging on. Texline–a town straight out of western mythology where tumbleweeds blew along main street and the law faced the bad guys in a showdown.

## A Bruce Willis Look-Alike
### (Perimeter Tour 1994)

In the café, I had a good visit with the local sheriff who invited me to sit a spell at his table–facing the door. Also in the room was a hitch hiker who looked a little like Bruce Willis, down on his luck. The Bruce look-alike was blond and had a three-day growth of stubble. He had blue eyes which had a hard time looking directly at anyone. His pants and shirt were faded and dusty. His ruck sack collapsed on the seat beside him. Would there be a showdown? He was on his way to Houston where he had some business contacts. He hitchhiked but he didn't like to talk to the drivers who were always asking stupid questions. His favorite word was "man."

"...you know how it is, man, I mean, man, you gotta make conversation, man, if you ride up front, man, I'd rather ride in the back–no obligation that way, man, to talk."
He stopped "conversing" with me long enough to ask a guy looking out from the kitchen if he could wash the café's windows for a sandwich.

"You'll have to talk to her," motioning to a Miss Kitty-type woman, presumably the manager. Before he could repeat the question, a fat driver of a pickup sashayed in to buy some gas. Immediately, the would-be window washer saw an opportunity.

"Can I have a ride to Dalhart, man?" The fat pickup guy said sure and the drifter turned back to me.

"See you around, man, and good luck–hey man, we can put your bike in the back, man," suddenly, as if it were up to him to offer the pickup.

"No, that's fine. I don't have to be anywhere–it's the traveling that's important."

"O.K., see ya, man." He and the fat guy drove off–no showdown today.

I moseyed on down the road to a rest stop back toward Dalhart and spent a peaceful wild-west night beneath the stars.

The next morning I felt something moving in my helmet as I pedaled away. I stopped immediately, fearing a spider, a wasp, you know, man, the worst. It was just a moth, man, just a moth. Man, was I relieved.

## Russia and China in Five Years
### (Perimeter Tour 1994)

In Dalhart, again, I camped at the Elm Tree RV park. I got set up. Went to the bath house, took a long, long, long hot shower–my first in 16 days. Heaven! Heaven! At first I felt uncomfortable with all that water splashing on me. I shaved, brushed my teeth, did my laundry, (there were magazines in the laundry room and I read a lot of farm news–how much tractors cost and stuff), repaired tears in my tent and clothes, threw away a pair of socks so smeared with tar they were impossible to clean, and went over my bike. I felt at peace with the world.

I met a fellow camper from Nebraska who came through Dalhart a lot. This was the only part of Texas he had seen and thought it was like the panhandle everywhere in the state. Naturally, I had to enlighten him. He mentioned how important it was in Nebraska to have 100 degree weather to insure a good corn crop.

Later in the day another car moved in and I watched the man and woman set up a nice-sized tent. He had a bicycle. Over I went to introduce myself. I knew he would be friendly.

He told me how he wanted to tour Russia and China and backpack on the Appalachian Trail. He could hardly wait to retire–in about five years. He rode his bike to work in Plano, Texas, and had been on several of the long bike rides around the state like the "Chain Ring Challenge" and the "Hotter-n-Hell Century" out of Wichita Falls. If I do my big city tours, I will definitely look him up since Plano is part of the Dallas/Fort Worth metroplex.

## Dust Storms
### (Perimeter Tour 1994)

For dinner I went into town to a café buffet. As I was leaving, stuffed to the gills, I noticed in the vestibule at the front some pictures of the dreaded dust storms of the thirties. One photo grabbed my attention. The date beneath: April 14, 1935–the year I entered first grade in Indiana totally unaware of what had happened in Texas. "What's Texas?"

The photo showed a huge black ground-to-the-top-of-the-sky mass rolling across the plains and in the foreground the town of Dalhart, still shining in the sun, but soon to be engulfed. A woman behind me paused.

"Do you remember those? I do. I'll never forget how awful it was. We scooped up buckets and buckets of dirt in the house. It got into everything. Our faces were black and the grit between our teeth was terrible."

Back at the RV park I visited with my new friends some more; called it a night; got up at four-forty the next morning; packed and rode away to Dumas–the only close town that had an ATM. It was Monday June 20, 1994.

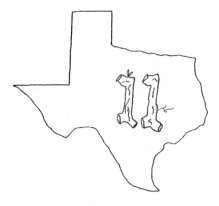

# Down the West Side of the Texas Panhandle
## (Perimeter Tour 1994)

### First an Itch

For some time on the perimeter tour I had trouble with the outside of my left forearm itching. It mystified me because there was no rash, no swelling. It looked perfectly normal, except it would redden from the scratching. The more I scratched and rubbed the more it itched accompanied by a terrible burning sensation. A bad combination. I didn't want to break the skin possibly causing an infection. My concern was scratching it too hard at night while asleep. About the only way I could get it calmed down was to soak a wash cloth with alcohol and lay it on the arm like a poultice, after which I could drift off.

I tried itch relievers from drugstores, but nothing worked until I applied the alcohol treatment. Maybe the sun caused it–sun poisoning–maybe I was nervous–maybe I would die of itching. I bought a white long-sleeved sweat shirt in Dalhart changing from my short-sleeved riding shirt. Presto, the itch stopped for good–what a solution. I'm so ingenious at times it hurts my head. A side benefit: the shirt held moisture which cooled me in the dry heat. I remembered talking to my mother shortly before she died and how her legs itched at times.

"I scratch them until they are raw and pour alcohol on them." At last I knew how she felt. She died years ago, bedfast and blind. I still have visions of her lying there in the night, her legs itching and unable to do anything.

*Dammit. Rain is good. Dammit*

**Shower as You Go**
(Perimeter Tour 1994)

Several miles north of Hartley on my way to Dumas and the ATM (and money!), the clouds opened up for a warm voluptuous summer rain. I yanked off my new sweatshirt and gloves and rode for a long time delighting in Mother Nature's impromptu shower. I pretended it was just for me. As I neared the city limits, the sun came out, I dried off and put my shirt back on. Could I have had this pleasure encased in a car? Only the windshield wipers would have had fun.

At Dumas I ransacked the ATM, bought groceries, ate lunch and went south toward Amarillo. I made a stop near the Tascosa trail. "The Tascosa-Dodge City Trail. Established in 1877 beginning at Tascosa just 25 miles southwest on the Canadian River. Stage coach, freighters, cattle herds, buffalo hunters, desperados, gamblers, lawmen, frontiersmen–all used this trail." Apparently, women couldn't use it or chose not to. Maybe I could write a story about the day a woman said, "By God, I'm going to use that Tascosa Trail." She was shot.

## Snake Talk
### (Perimeter Tour 1994)

At his store, near the marker, I met Terry Atkins and we got to talking snakes. I hadn't seen one on this trip, but I did on my Great Plains trip. He told me about running over one at night.

"I thought it was a stick, but just before I hit it I realized it was a huge rattlesnake. It bumped up against the underside of my Maverick. I had a hole in the floorboard and I was afraid it would somehow get inside the car, so I drove the rest of the way with my foot on that hole."

I told him if I used that in a fictional short story sometime, I'd have the snake come through that hole and while doing 50 miles per hour, I 'd have the driver reach down and grab that snake and wrestle it as it coiled about his neck, fangs dripping venom.

"What would happen?"

"Depends on whether I liked you in the story or not."
Terry fashioned "Wahoo" boards with inlays of various beautiful woods–a marble game–maybe like Chinese checkers.

"Used to play that game for hours with my grandmother. She was Cherokee," he said.

174

## For the Birds
(Perimeter Tour 1994)

I left and set up camp at a rest area about a mile farther on. Beautiful clouds, pleasant breeze. I happened to pitch my tent right beneath the nest of two western kingbirds. They did not approve of my location if I could tell anything about bird words. I hoped the top of my tent wouldn't resemble a snow-capped peak in the morning. I awoke to soft chirping. I had been made a part of the family. The top of the tent was spotless. Thank you kingbirds–may your children grow up to be as thoughtful as you.

My front tire was flat and fixing it set me back nearly an hour. I couldn't find the leak and finally gave up and put in a new tube. The culprit was a short thin wire used in truck tire casings which littered the road. As I gingerly felt inside my tire, my finger found it. Damn. So, in with a new tube and I would find the leak later when I could submerse the old tube in water.

Having the birds for company was nice. Having a flat tire was not. The good and the bad and eventually both accepted. Appreciation would not be possible without the presence of both, I supposed–still... Oh yes, I think the kingbirds were pleased to see me go.

## Amarillo
(Perimeter Tour 1994)

I biked up and down up and down into the northern edge of Amarillo. Upon reaching the city limits I called the neat parents of my true love and left a message on their answering machine. I had stayed with them on my winter trip to Amarillo the previous year. I also tried to call Jodi Thomas, a romance writer I had met when I camped at the Palo Duro Canyon the year before in the winter of 1993. What a difference in the weather. Now, I had to watch out for melting highways–puddles of tar that threatened to swallow me. Civilizations far in the future might unearth this strange creature with

175

wheels perfectly preserved in a tar pit–similar to the famous tar pits in Los Angeles that still yield prehistoric monsters. I would be put on display.

## First Time in Amarillo
(Winter Tour 1993)

The first time I entered Amarillo was from the south the previous year. I had bicycled west through the middle of the panhandle from Memphis–remember the wind–to Claredon then to Claude and to a most welcome sight–a café with two names–take your pick: Hitching Rail Café or Petras Mexican Café on Farm and Ranch Road 1151. I had a great and warming Mexican breakfast with lots of steaming black coffee after pedaling 29 miles across the startling golden wheat-stubbled winter fields and brilliantly clear blue skies from Claude. My temperature gauge read 18 degrees. I didn't freeze but I did stay numb at the extremities. It was a never-to-be-forgotten ride. Cold and perfect.

## Palo Duro Canyon
(Winter Tour 1993)

Leaving Amarillo on that first trip, I went to the Palo Duro Canyon to camp a few days. I wanted to be in the vicinity where years before Comanche Chief Quanah Parker and his band had wintered. The canyon site is deceptive. The canyon appears suddenly as if by magic from the flat plains. That feature kept it secret for many years. I descended, having to use my brakes to negotiate the hair-pin turns. At the bottom, I proceeded past five low-water crossings to my campsite–deep inside the park. I hoped there would be no winter flooding.

The climb out would be two miles up a ten percent grade. Complicating my departure would be a malfunctioning derailleur eliminating my lowest gear. It would take some muscle to climb that canyon wall.

The Prairie Dog Town Fork of the Red River gurgled peacefully nudging ice shards near my tent belying its great force in cutting that fantastic canyon. Maybe it could flood, even though at two feet deep and two feet across, the stream appeared quite harmless to me. Those low water crossings, however, said watch out. The temperature at night 20 degrees and 30 to 40 degrees during the day in the warm sun, with no breeze–it felt great. I repaired another flat and fixed my derailleur–restoring my low gear. I began to feel self-sufficient.

At dusk and early in the morning coyotes kept me company with their renditions of "Where have all the rabbits gone?" One night a male Great Horned owl called–a higher sounding garbled "who-who" requesting a date with a female acquaintance. They had talked earlier. She, being larger, had a lower voice. That night, she didn't answer. Too cold for sex, I surmised.

GREAT HORNED OWL

**A Word Photo**
(Winter Tour 1993)

In the morning as the sun peeked into the canyon I photographed in words what I saw through my tent door. Gray-brown leaves of the sycamore trees hanging on, falling; gold, tan and gray colored grasses crowding against the burbling stream and across the park road; juniper trees, always green, some twenty feet tall, spaced among the leafless trees whose bare branches reached for the sky; in the distance toward canyon walls, the small hills dark-blue with some green; the cliffs grayish-blue–hazy; the sky almost white touching the cliff tops;

slanting cirrus clouds tracing across the light blue sky just above; the sky turning a brighter blue toward the west; in the silence the sudden call of a woodpecker sounding like a small boy urgently squeaking his toy car to a stop–except repeated five to eight times– followed by a loud insistent knocking as a busy beak searched for insects in a tree trunk; close to the stream the land–sandy loam, damp, brown, mostly sand; a road-runner, neck and tail outstretched, dashing beside the road and into the brush after a brief stop to peer at my tent.

### Leaving the Canyon
(Winter Tour 1993)

After a couple of days I packed up and bade good-bye to that serene canyon which had been home to Indians and later a cattle ranch and now a park for all to appreciate. The climb out would be a matter of concentrating, conserving my strength and grinding out the two miles of the steady steep climb. I didn't make it. I lacked a mere 200 yards. Tourists did me in by coming up behind in a car and following me, following me, following me. I tried too hard. Discipline disappeared. Breathing came in gasps. My legs starting aching. Concentration no longer centered on the hill but on that car and its occupants and what they were saying and thinking. "How can he do that? That bike must weigh a ton! Why doesn't he have a car? Why doesn't he go faster? Why doesn't he get off and walk?" Lacking those 200 lousy yards, I did just that. I stopped. I got off. I walked. They passed me. Damned tourists.

### A Great Ride
(Winter Tour 1993)

I rode to Hereford and stayed at the spacious Veterans Park. Next day I rode through Friona and down the panhandle past the Muleshoe National Wildlife Refuge. In the clear cold air a strange chortling sounded, maybe ten feet to my side. What I heard were the calls of hundreds of sandhill cranes as they circled over head a thousand feet high–tiny white and gray dots in the sky's immensity. The ride down the west side of the Texas Panhandle on that crisp day was another unforgettable experience. A simple, beautiful 87-mile ride with the wind at my back. A biker's dream come true.

PUMP JACK

### The Lost Symphony
(Winter Tour 1993)

I set up in a roadside park at Denver City. Across from me, the largest carbon dioxide plant in the world blinked and steamed throughout the evening. Behind me an oil well pump jack with a distinctive and mesmerizing series of wails, squeaks and groans filled me with musical inspiration. During the night I became so fascinated with that repeated haunting musical motif I wanted to alert some symphonic composer to fly to West Texas and capture those dissonant notes and compose a whole symphony around them a la Schönberg. In my mind that night I knew it could become as well-known as the opening phrase of Beethoven's Fifth–only much more interesting. By now someone has oiled that pump jack, I bet. The world lost the greatest symphony because I didn't follow up. The cold eventually numbed me into unconsciousness. Ice had stuck to my rolled-up tent all day and that evening added another layer.

## Fickle Wind
### (Winter Tour 1993)

The next morning, stiff with cold and lacking a few vital synapses, I loosened and pulled out the stakes before lowering the tent. The wind which had blown moderately hard the day before toward the south, had changed directions in the night and now blew everything back north–including my tent. I ran, hobbling, yelling–my poor bones creaking–my hip complaining–as I chased that fool tumbling tent up the side of the highway. Luckily, no T.V. camera crews had stationed themselves nearby hoping for a "filler" feature. A hectic period passed and I corralled the tent. I was warmer, too. I rethought my options. Don't go south to Seminole–too windy. Go north–no, been there. Can't go west–this is a Texas trip and New Mexico's just an icicle throw away. Go east. Yes, the wind would be at my side and tolerable. Off I went. The tumble up the highway had knocked most of the ice from the tent. Good can come from bad.

## Christmas on the Plains
### (Winter Tour 1993)

The day before Christmas Eve I stopped and received permission to put up my tent beneath a blue spruce Christmas tree look-a-like on a church lawn in the town of Welch after a pedal of only 46 miles. I ate a Snickers bar for dinner and went to bed. That night it snowed. The name for those hard frozen granules was corn snow. (I almost said corn flakes, hah.) In the morning the temperature on my gauge inside the tent said 15 degrees. What was I doing out there? I got up and worked as fast as possible to keep from turning to ice. Periodically I had to stop and rub my gloved hands together vigorously while jumping up and down. I got things packed and was ready to roll up the stiffened tent when a pickup truck stopped and a man, who later introduced himself as Robert Ramirez, jumped out and said he had an extra burrito he would share, but first he wanted to take it a block away to Turner Supply and use their micro-wave to heat it up.

By the time I had the tent packed, he was back with hot coffee and the hot burrito–probably his breakfast. I was nearly overcome by this show of thoughtfulness. I still tear up a bit when I think about it. I cradled the hot burrito in my bare hands to warm them up before I ate it and drank the coffee. When I had pedaled into this wonderful little town the night before I had noticed the welcoming sign: "Welch– Home of Pride and Prosperity." It should have read: "Welch–Home of Caring People." Of course, you don't put words like those on signs. A great Christmas Eve gift, anyway, and I'll never forget it. Thanks, Robert Ramirez.

## The Girls of Gail
### (Winter Tour 1993)

After Christmas day, which I spent in a motel watching TV and thoroughly loving being inside out of the cold and slumbering in that wonderfully soft bed, I rode to Gail, a town pretty much run by women. A television station had done a story on it. The county highway superintendent was a woman; the postmaster was a woman; the service station was owned and operated by a woman; the café in which I was eating a golden brown one-inch-thick chicken-fried steak was owned and operated by a woman.

There were two token men on the city council. No doubt this condition of women taking over proved Darwin's natural evolution process and the fact cream does rise to the top. I wondered if I would become a slave of some sort if I moved to Gail. Bertie Copeland of the café looked friendly enough, but what guarantee would I have I wouldn't end up as a token? What was really behind that attractive face and those smiling eyes? Only two men showed up in the café while I was there and they quickly got their sandwiches and made for the door, mouthing lame excuses like needing to do the laundry or getting the shopping done. I went on to Austin, but I may go back someday.

## Enough of Winter
(Perimeter Tour 1994)

After passing through Amarillo for the second time–this time on the perimeter tour during the summer of 1994, I took a right as I had during the winter tour and pointed the bike toward Hereford, but in a roundabout way–first going west to Vega before turning south to Hereford. I was unable to make it all the way to Vega because of the horrendous hill I encountered trying to get around Amarillo on the west. It slowed me down considerably. Tired, hot and out of sorts, I approached Wildorado about 20 miles west. I checked with a motel since the rest areas were too shallow to camp in–not safe to my mind. In one of my economy moods, I asked the motel manager if I could put my tent up on the motel's property for free. He said no. That irritated me. I must have been suffering from heat stroke. If I had been in his place, I would have said the same thing. What was I becoming–a mooch? I had been free camping too long–a habit hard to break. I rationalized I still helped the economy because I spent the motel money on food. Made sense to me. He still said no. He had no restaurant. Maybe I was a cheapskate. I got to know one in Austin a few years later and let me say, it was not a pretty sight.

## Willie Nelson Visits with the Waitresses
(Perimeter Tour 1994)

A block away from the inhospitable motel, I stopped at a restaurant and asked if I could camp on the property, promising I would eat dinner and come in for breakfast. The manager said sure– so there I was, a persistent little devil–getting my free ride again but helping the economy.

I dawdled over dinner, eating, visiting and having a good time, in no hurry to be alone in my tent, besides, it was way too hot yet.
One of the waitresses at the restaurant, attractive, too thin, sick (she said), had just moved from Amarillo. She was a singer and a writer of

poetry. Her husband had left her and took their daughter with him. She wanted another baby. She wanted a singing career and would be ready to sign with a record company maybe next year. For the present, she wanted to calm down and smell the roses for awhile.

Another waitress, also attractive, with high cheekbones, large eyes and sharp features, perhaps some Indian ancestors. "Yes," she said, when I asked. "Dakota," came over to visit. She had a wolf dog at home.

"Sixty percent wolf and forty percent German Shepherd." She explained she liked wolves and had them off and on as pets.

"I like them because they are so wild. You can't take hold of their throats–they'll tear you to pieces." I resolved never to grab a wolf by the throat.

"You can't discipline them in the house either. They feel trapped and will attack. Outside it's Okay." I made a note to keep wolves outside.

She had children and read the Bible to them. If she read something like "slow to wrath" she would stop and explain what that meant. She liked to hear birds at night and early in the morning from her porch. She and her husband just bought their home in Wildorado. It reminded her of her own childhood home and she wanted her children to have a similar experience.

In the restaurant I had on my white sweat shirt with a red bandana around my forehead and another one tied around my neck. I hadn't shaved for a couple days or maybe three and my beard was coming in white. I had a pony tail, too–about a foot long. One of the waitresses said there was talk among the customers I was Willie Nelson. So, she asked if I were he.

If I had walked in there with a guitar and had sung a song, I might have gotten not only a free tent space but a free dinner as well. I didn't have a guitar and even if they took one off the wall–just hanging up there in case Willie Nelson might drop in some night looking for a free dinner and place to camp–but there wasn't any hanging up there–I couldn't have played it anyway.

One other problem, I didn't know the complete words to any Willie Nelson song and even I had, I couldn't sound like him. Besides, I was taller–I thought. After another cup of coffee I sauntered to my tent in the vacant lot next to the restaurant, humming. I practiced "Crazy" on my harmonica.

## Hereford Again
### (Perimeter Tour 1994)

This time in the summer, I went back to the Veterans Park. A few mosquitoes greeted me. Last time I camped there during the winter tour it was 22 degrees and my banana froze solid. I ate it anyway, although it was difficult to peel. Later, on that winter trip, I learned to put the fruit in my sleeping bag along with my water bottle and my shoes–at times it was quite snug in there with all those extras. I had to lie carefully so as not to mash the grapes between my toes. The cold of that trip changed places with the muggy hot of summer. The clouds gathered and along about 2 a.m. I awoke to a steady rain. My legs and face itched terribly. For a moment or two I thought the itching I experienced earlier on my arm had spread. I grabbed my flashlight and discovered mosquitoes on my legs. Slapping commenced. I found six more on the walls of the tent. I sent them to Valhalla as mosquito heros fallen in battle. Apparently, I had not closed the front flap sufficiently and the mosquitoes had raided. At daybreak the storm ended and the sun came up. The wind was from the north and since I was on my way south that was perfect.

## Some Neat Towns and a Wind Storm
### (Perimeter Tour 1994)

During the next several days I stopped at several free RV parks as I biked southward. Dimmit had the prettiest park, but that caused its undoing. The local teenagers loved it so much as a hangout the traveling public couldn't use it.

Littlefield had the best. An RV park right in town. Waylon Jennings' name graced the sign. I got to visit with a lot of fine folk coming and going. A traveler could stay free for four days. I stayed four days.

Levelland on down the road had a park, but not as convenient, being two miles outside of town. No place to shop or eat. I spent a very nervous evening there as the only camper. In the middle of the night a pickup came in and slowly circled the park coming within two feet of my tent–presumably the town's watchman.

About three quarters of the way down the western side of the panhandle I came to Brownfield. A large city park looked good and I got permission to camp. All during that period of biking from Hereford, the temperatures soared. Everyday broke a hundred degrees. By the time I got to Brownfield it was 114 degrees by noon. Much too hot to bicycle. I holed up at the library all afternoon, reading. The librarians were gracious and I found a great number of my favorite authors.

As I sat at a reading table a group of elementary students arrived as part of a summer's reading program. They passed my loaded bike outside and when they ascertained I rode it, they surrounded my table. The person in charge of this spirited group looked relieved the youngsters had found something of interest. The usual questions poured forth from those eager young minds. "What do you eat?" "How much money do you have?" "Why don't you get a pickup to carry all your stuff?" "Where do you sleep?"

In answering the last question, I mentioned I would be staying in the city park. Wide eyes greeted this announcement.

"I wouldn't stay there. It's too scary. A girl got raped there. And they murdered her, too. Yeah, and now the park is haunted." Everyone agreed with that. "Yeah, you can hear her screaming at night." I guessed the horrible event could act as an effective park curfew–a good way to keep youngsters out of the bushes.

Despite the warnings, I went off to the park and erected my tent. I tried to pound the tent stakes into the hard ground and finally gave up after getting a minimum number only two or three inches into the rock-like soil. Wouldn't rain anyway, too hot.

Because of the hot weather, I slept with no clothes on. At midnight my temperature gauge still red-lined at 90 degrees. Suddenly, it began to cool off fast. A rushing wind storm tore through the park, later judged at having gusts up to 70 mph. What a surprise, although one should never be surprised about anything that happens in the panhandle.

I awoke as the tent crashed down upon me in one instant and soared heavenward the next. The front door was facing the wind and was held not by a zipper, but by Velcro®, which immediately popped loose and in effect said to the wind: "come on in." In it came and blew the tent up like a hot-air balloon. I could see myself rolling out of control and into the creek that ran through the park. The stakes came out of the ground and everything suddenly ripped loose. I grabbed at the tent fabric and pulled it down upon me to keep the wind from blowing it into the next county. I snapped a pole, but no matter. Better a snapped pole than a cartwheeling tent. There I lay, clutching the tent, but unable to reach the rain fly which was flapping like some demented pterdactyl above.

At this point a patrol car with its blue and red blinking lights pulled up. A policeman with flashlight in hand approached. I was still naked and I didn't know for sure what could be seen through the thin tent fabric. He wanted to know if I were all right and if I needed any help. Lying there amidst the debris of my tent and supplies, I yelled, "I'm fine, but if you could hand me a corner of that rain fly, I can hold it until the wind stops." I had to repeat several versions of this because he couldn't hear over the roar of the wind. Finally, in a tiny lull, he heard and handed me some of the flapping material, and yelled at me there would be a big rain soon, got back in his cruiser and drove off. I held on for another thirty minutes until the wind began to moderate. Rather than risk the coming downpour drowning what was left of me and the tent, I released my hold. The wind still gusted at 40 miles per hour. Frantically, I searched and found my clothes, packed everything up on my bike and took off for an all night convenience store I had passed coming into town a few miles back, fully expecting to be thoroughly soaked any moment by a cloud burst.

## A Very Convenient Store
### (Perimeter Tour 1994)

Two young girl clerks, standing behind the counter, commiserated with me as I informed them of my misadventures and my desire, if they would allow it, to spend the rest of the night inside their store. They would allow it. At first I thought they were teenagers.

After getting acquainted, Susan and Carolyn (not their real names) began to share some of their adventures with me. I soon realized they were not quite as young as I had thought, or else they had started on life's rocky road at a very tender age.

Susan began by informing me about the state of her reproductive organs and how much they had been altered. She also had a lot of tumors and cysts, one of which had been taken out before she started work at the store three days ago. "They just cut me open and took it out and I went to work the next day." I agreed it was amazing as well as admirable. Despite her difficulties, Susan was very attractive. She was also divorced. "He punctured one of my lungs and broke a rib." Susan is seeking custody of a child, which the husband is fighting. They've had one hearing and going back for another, plus some mediation sessions. Her husband returned after she kicked him out and began threatening her some more, so she shot him, but not fatally. He didn't come back. Before getting pregnant she worked in a topless bar in Odessa. She's been held up twice at gun point and robbed–her van stolen. "Just left me there in the middle of the street." Susan said she had a scholarship to the Law School at the University of Texas. After graduation, she would do well, I thought.

The wind still blew outside and my bike got a good coating of orange panhandle. The other girl said her problem was too much

188

weight. Carolyn planned to start on a diet, tomorrow. "I don't produce enough progesterone, and I have too much estrogen. I get weird sometimes and really chew people out–don't know why–just happens." I said I hoped it wouldn't happen tonight. Carolyn laughed. She, in turn, gave me an itemized list of her reproductive problems. "The doctor has tried to heal them–even using a laser, but I'm still not cured–not contagious or anything like that–just precancerous. Haven't had them looked at again for over a year." Susan and I suggested strongly that she get an appointment immediately and get checked out. Carolyn said she was bored with life, but loved her husband and child. "I really got big when I was pregnant. I hurt if I didn't eat. I love candy too much."

The east began to lighten and the wind slowed some more. Early morning customers came by. I went outside and wiped most of the orange dust off, then came in to say goodbye. We all hugged and were glad the storm had brought us together. "The night went a lot faster, because you were here," said Carolyn. "Good luck. Be careful and come back," said Susan.

### Fly Attack
### (Perimeter Tour 1994)

The day would be hot–but not as hot as the day before. The strong wind had changed the weather. The heavy overcast had an orange tint. The wind died down to 5 mph with gusts to 10. The 38 miles to Seminole would be mostly uphill. About 12 miles out from town, I got very sleepy so I stopped and unrolled my air mattress for a brief nap. Apparently, the flies got a good rest last night while I battled the wind. I often wondered where those little creatures hid out during wind storms. Where did the birds go? I didn't consider this too long. I got out my fly swatter and began reducing the fly inventory. In a few minutes I had sent 87 flies into permanent naps. I got up, put the mattress back on the bike–unused–and, thoroughly refreshed, pedaled into Seminole. I spent the afternoon in the library again.

## Libraries, Cheap Novels, and Revisiting
### (Perimeter Tour 1994)

Paperback novels were for sale for a dime apiece. How could I resist a deal like that? I purchased three romance novels and read them all before I got back to Austin. Staying at libraries during the hot hours of the afternoon became a daily treat. What a great idea. Why hadn't I thought of it earlier? A perfect way to thwart the Texas sun. As the day cooled, I rode on to a rest area south of town and had a good evening, although I had to fix another flat caused by a goat head. I stopped often as I proceeded toward Pecos. It would be my second time in Pecos. Actually, my first trip would parallel the perimeter trip from Odessa to Pecos and my Great Plains tour three years away would intersect them both at Monahans halfway between Odessa and Pecos. Who could have predicted I would be crossing my own trails out in West Texas three times?

OUT WEST

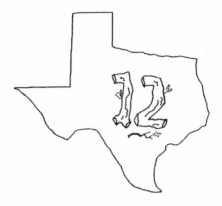

## *Southwest Texas*
(Summer Tour 1993)

On my first summer trip into southwest Texas in 1993, I had the distinct feeling of moving back in time the farther west I went. I think, subconsciously, I fully expected to run into old-time cowboys and Indians.

I say subconsciously because as I rode my bicycle; moving along about the speed of a trotting and sometimes walking horse; for long periods my only company being wild animals or stock and the vistas which in that brief time of 150 years had not changed one whit; enduring times of thirst, the beating-down merciless sun, the fury of wind, lightning, thunder and rain–the feeling of utter aloneness in a desert that was neither friend nor foe, but lay there waiting, waiting for me to make one mistake; all taken together–I was transported into that other time, perhaps mythological, but nevertheless real for the romantic that the tourist of today cannot appreciate nor appropriate at 70 miles per hour sipping a bottle of imported water cooled in an onboard ice chest while listening to music or an audio book being transmitted to his or her air conditioned metal cubicle from hundreds of miles away or from a spinning CD. Would anyone care to diagram that sentence? I wouldn't. I just wanted to see some old-time cowboys and Indians.

While camped once at Seminole Canyon way up high a mile from the gate and registration center, I spotted a luxurious motor home pull in. It stayed for a few minutes while a man went inside. Back to the motor home he came–tiny at that distance–and a swing up the hill and around my camping site then down again and out. The whole procedure taking twenty minutes. They saw Seminole Canyon. Maybe they took some snapshots through the windshield. He probably picked up a brochure or two.

They did not walk down into the canyon–too hot. They would not look at seven sunrises and seven sunsets. They didn't see the red racer wriggling across the path. They did not have time to contemplate the clouds, watch a gathering storm, feel the hot wind on their skins, smell the desert greasewood, mark the shadows as they crept up and down the canyon walls, squint into the sky at the circling vultures and hawks, nor time to listen to the cactus wren, nor did they awaken in the middle of the night enthralled as the glittering stars wheeled overhead. None of the ambiance trickled into their souls. They did not visit Seminole Canyon no matter what they wrote in their leather bound journal.

It takes effort and time to appreciate that "whole other country." Most of us hate the first and don't have the second. Clouds were forming again that afternoon. Maybe a storm would hit. A cactus wren and I looked at each other.

### Pecos From the South
(Summer Tour 1993)

I want to leave our narrative of the perimeter tour for a couple of days and invite you to join me as I pick up the adventures from the first tour in the summer of 1993–one year before the perimeter trip we are using as the backbone of this book. Wending my way past Langtry, through Sanderson and my awful bout with cramps, I had my sights set on Pecos as the quintessential spirit of the west.

After the horrible evening before and just a few hours of fitful sleep–ever watchful that the cramps might return, I awoke and strangely, felt good as new. I went back to the cafe for breakfast before sunrise and again, I felt the deceptive cooling breeze. Everyone but me spoke Spanish. I have to learn that language some day. My waitress was the same one I had the night before–obviously she worked long hours. I wolfed down scrambled eggs with salsa, fat bacon fried crisp, golden crunchy hash brown potatoes drowned in cream gravy, which I peppered heavily in case the morning flies were tempted , toast with butter and jam, topped off with several mugs of steaming black coffee. Exercising strenuously on a bicycle allowed me to eat just about anything in huge amounts. On a long trip, I would usually lose 20 pounds even though I ate everything in sight.

### Climbing Out of the Canyon
(Summer Tour 1993)

All packed up, I pedaled through the one long main street in Sanderson. Canyon walls reared fearfully high and jagged on both sides. A flash flood hit the canyon in 1954, killing 20.

I spotted my turn-off to highway 285, which would take me to Fort Stockton, 64 miles northwest through open range with no towns or houses. At the last service station, I stopped to buy some snacks and inquired about highway conditions. The non-smiling manager assured me the hills I grunted over yesterday didn't compare with what awaited me today.

"Worse?" I said.

"They're a lot worse. You're gonna have to walk up a few." He allowed this to sink in.

193

"First, you gotta climb out of this canyon–that'll be about a 12 mile climb. You got a straight downhill for maybe four miles with big cross winds that'll blow you right off the road into the canyons." I watched as his meaty and oil-stained hand moved forcefully from right to left and down toward the floor. He looked at the floor. I looked at the floor. More canyons–and I'm down there all crumpled up.

"So watch out." I nodded. He looked up. "You'll face a killer hill just before Fort Stockton–you'll walk that one, for sure." I guessed I didn't get blown into the canyons after all. Small comfort when I considered the killer hill which waited for me. I peered at the tacked-up map on the wall and found the notation close to Fort Stockton, "Five Mile Mountain."

I bought a can of beans, a can of corn and from a built-in cooler, two brown-spotted bananas, said thank you and pointed my bike toward my dubious future.

I ground my way up and out of the main canyon that holds Sanderson for 12 miles and sure enough there was the down hill hurtling straight as a Comanche arrow almost disappearing across the distant valley floor. I took a good grip on the handlebars, braced my knees against the top tube to add stability, steered into the middle of the highway–no traffic–and turned my *Randonnee* loose. At three miles I touched the brakes as I passed 40 miles per hour headed toward fifty with another mile to go. Forty was fast enough, besides, I had to watch out for those cross winds. At that speed, a bicycle tire appeared mighty fragile, too. An exhilarating ride.

As the highway leveled off, I relaxed and had a look around. A dead porcupine, first of three today, lay squashed, perhaps misjudged a speeding pickup last night.

I stopped at the side of the highway at noon and opened a can of refried beans. Good energy source–also ate some crackers and a Granola bar–all washed down with some great gulps of delicious warm water. Off to my right I heard the strident staccato song of a cactus wren. A mockingbird, the state bird of Texas–so terribly

194

misnamed–should be called something like "virtuoso extraordinaire," tuned up to explore a few intricate sonatas–music especially for me in my own private dining space 30 miles north of Sanderson and 30 miles south of Fort Stockton. All around, low hills, cacti, canyons, mesquite trees, rocks and sand, displayed in subtle shades of green, brown, yellow, red and orange close up, and purple, magenta, lavender and blue far off. Up above–a hot round brassy sun.

Being out there, with no other human being, just the sounds of the birds and the unfolding panorama of sky and land fading away beyond eyesight, had to be one of the most peaceful and life-affirming moments of my Texas tours.

I understood the peaceful part, but I knew the life-affirming part had a lot to do with the bleakness, the harshness, the unforgiving kill-you-in-a-minute terrain that dared me to stay alive. I realized that since I was still alive, though tenuously so, with only a bicycle to get me out of there in time, my awareness of life as awesomely fragile and precious reached heights and depths often impossible in my ordinary workaday world.

Pedaling on, keenly conscious now of my insignificance and vulnerability in this vastness, I noticed shadows sweeping across the highway. They belonged to circling vultures–those graceful and patient disposers of the dead. Their sailplane wings riding the desert thermals, their naked red heads and scrawny wrinkled necks swiveling about, the unseen but all-seeing eyes searching for a life that has called it quits, sent a slight shiver through my sun-baked bones.

The second shadow emanated from a magnificent blossoming cauliflower cumulus, sweeping northward at about my speed, so that by a small adjustment, I stayed beneath that cooling behemoth for several miles while the pavement cooked 50 yards in front and behind me. Occasionally, I slipped from beneath this canopy, because of my preoccupation with troubling thoughts that began to invade the journey. I kept seeing the words, Five Mile Mountain, on that wall map back in Sanderson.

## The Killer Mountain
### (Summer Tour 1993)

Troubling scenarios formed and played themselves out in my head. A five-mile high mountain? Quickly dismissed–no Mt. Everest in Texas. A five mile long mountain? That must be it. Five miles of up, up, up, during the hottest period of the day. If true, it would take me three hours to either ride it or walk it. I worried about my water supply. Two quarts had to be saved for the ascent. I stopped again and ate the two bananas I had bought in Sanderson–no cramps needed tonight. Can I walk five miles on my sore hip? Maybe I should hitch a ride. A truck will stop, load on my bike and equipment, then it'll take off without me! I could stash my equipment in the desert and ride an unloaded bike to the top. I could come back for my supplies the next day after resting. Or, I could hire a truck to come back. Maybe someone would do it for nothing. Either way, when we would get to the hiding place, some scoundrel would have already found my stuff and made off with it. I could just camp out in the desert tonight and tackle the mountain in the morning. What about rattlesnakes and scorpions and Mexican black ants? I don't have enough water to stay overnight. Each scenario ended in disaster.

In the meantime, an unnoticed ride took place. Because the highway flattened out and the breeze pushed me from the south, I glided along at 20 to 25 miles per hour. My fastest level ride yet, but I ignored it. I was interested only in the mountain. Once in awhile, I thought I saw it. A purplish haze on the horizon–yes, my dreaded mountain, but it slid by on the right. The second mountain near Six-Shooter Draw, melted away on my left. I strained to see the hated mound. I watched my cyclometer. It had to show up soon. Ten more miles to Fort Stockton. Seven more miles to Fort Stockton. Where in the hell was that mountain? I did climb a regular-sized hill for a couple of miles, but I'd hardly call that a killer mountain. The killer mountain, still beyond my vision, taunted me.

Unbelievably, the Fort Stockton city limits appeared. No

mountain. I wheeled up to a motel. The lady behind the desk squinted at me.

"How on earth did you climb up that mountain?"

"What mountain?" I answered. Whereupon she and a clerk walked around the desk to look at my legs.

"He didn't notice the mountain–can you believe that?" They stared at my legs. I stared at my legs.

BUS SERVICE

### Fort Stockton
### (Summer Tour 1993)

The folks at Fort Stockton endeavored to resurrect and maintain a western town of the early 1900s. Well, let's say half the town was in on it. The other half has been busy building super stores on I-10. Where Fort Stockton sits, a Comanche trail intersected the old San Antonio Road. The Butterfield Overland Mail Route thundered through there with weaving stagecoaches drawn by six fast horses. A military post established in 1859 tried to keep the peace between the ranchers and the Indians. The Indians liked the area because of Comanche Springs–once one of the largest in Texas. I pedaled around looking at the town and passed by a sculpture designed to awe tourists.

Paisano Pete, a Texas-sized statue of a roadrunner 20 feet long and 11 feet high towered at Main street, commemorating the bird that eluded the wily coyote, and struck fear in the hearts of western rattlesnakes, which it ate for breakfast, lunch and dinner.

When I questioned "Texas-sized," as perhaps stretching truth beyond acceptable boundaries, a leather-faced old man who sat on a bench with me in front of a service station, seemed a bit put out. "You don't understand," he drawled. "We gotta raise a bird to that size to kill the big rattlers out here." I rested my back up against the cool brick wall. "Well, how big are the rattlesnakes?" I said, taking the bait.

With half-lidded pale blue eyes, he gazed up into the sky where the sun would be around mid-morning and put on a serious look.

"I could tell you a rattler story, but that's all it'd be. And only a fool would believe it." He glanced in my direction. " I could tell you about a rattler so big as to swallow a sheepherder or a whole cow at one sittin'," he spat in the dust. "I reckon I could tell you one like that if you want, but it wouldn't be true. Anytime you hear tell a rattler longer than ten foot or bigger around than a goat's belly, you can bet somebody's pullin' your leg. Nosiree, they's big enough without being redic'lus about it." He scratched his leg and sat without a word for awhile.

"A few years back when I was aworkin' the range, me and the boys come up on a average-size rattler that was actual tryin' to swaller a sheepherder–and that's a fact. In them days we wasn't exactly friends with sheepmen, so we thought we'd just sit around and watch.

"Course, we knowed he couldn't do it–like I told you. But nobody had told that rattler. He kept at it til near dinner time afore he gave up. That herder gave us the what for cause we hadn't pried him loose. He died anyway, so wasn't no need to get riled. Back in them days we believed more in live and let live and didn't mix up in other folks' business more than a fella had to. Okay, it's not much of a story, but if you want a true one, there it is." He spat and leaned back, lost again in yesteryears. "Them was good days. Hard, but good." I straightened my back. "If you came up on a rattler today, trying to swallow a sheepherder, what would you do?" I asked. "I'd probly pry him loose sooner." I got up, stretched and went inside to get us a couple of beers.

*What's behind that tree? Why is that bird staring?*

### On to Pecos
(Summer Tour 1993)

Last night I slept well in a cheap but comfortable motel. Tonight I would camp outside in my tent in Pecos.

PECOS CANTALOUPE

Pecos, home of the world's first rodeo. Highway 285 stretched out before me spanning gentle rises and depressions. I foresaw a great and fast ride of 53 miles across the arid range–no towns–no people–again, just mile upon mile of uninterrupted serenity. I imagined sampling the world-famous Pecos cantaloupes, for Pecos is to cantaloupe as Swiss is to cheese. What luck. The harvest season began in late July and would run through September. I'd get to taste the first crop.

A few miles out of Fort Stockton, my speed increased to 25 miles per hour. I felt great. In peak condition–a fantastic sensation.

From time to time, I swerved to miss a millipede crossing the highway. Those worms had been with me off and on since Seminole Canyon. They have brown ridges interspersed with yellow fissures. Birds won't eat them because they taste so bad and if you run over one, you'll carry the smell for miles.

Hidden from my view, I heard a raven call–a guttural quack. A raven also sounds a little like a crow with a sore throat. A crow is one of my favorite birds and by association, so now is a raven. Growing up in Indiana, I heard the crows cawing to each other–always a long ways off–in some neighbor's corn field past a stand of blackened trees on cold misty days of late autumn. Like a distant train whistle in the middle of the night, their calls suggested mystery, adventure, freedom and travel to the ears of a small boy. Most people I know don't care for crows and I guess they don't hanker after ravens either, but I do. I wouldn't mind coming back as a crow in another life. I'd be smart, canny and just out of reach, filling young heads full of longing to know what lay beyond fog-shrouded and darkened woods. I stopped for lunch. I listened to the quiet. The temperature touched 100 degrees according to my thermometer. A pickup appeared on the horizon–just a speck–no sound. I waved at the driver as he sped by. He returned it–a slight lifting of the index finger from the steering wheel, but it was enough and all that's expected.

With all the heat, I thought it would be good to take a swim in Lake Toyah, which was on the way to Pecos. On the map it showed up huge. I pedaled right up to where it was supposed to be. No lake– just a big dry depression and a long bridge over it. I would need to return after a gully washer for that swim.

*Yeeeeeehah!*

## The Errant Steer
(Summer Tour 1993)

The range was fenced along this stretch. On both sides of the right-of-way as far as I could see grew thick gama grass with brilliant green stalks and bleached blonde seed heads. The stems bent before the south breeze which caused a ripple effect–a long narrow sea divided by the highway. I felt like Moses crossing the Red Sea–the grassy waters parting as I swept along.

Up ahead I saw a young steer. Somehow the blocky, white-faced yearling had sneaked through the fence and, totally oblivious to the roar of a passing eighteen wheeler, was voraciously gobbling up mouthful after mouthful of the sweet green grass. Across the fence a few envious steers with heads hanging, lolled about with not a single blade of grass to turn into cud–a big lesson in over grazing. This whole range could be undulating knee-deep in prairie grasses, just like the right-of-way. There must be a reason why the ranchers would rather have their land barren. Tax credit? Stupidity? Beats me.

In the meantime I was being a bit of a sneak myself. Stealthily, I was approaching the steer. Out of the corner of his eye, he caught sight of me. His head shot up, mouth half-filled with grass. I must have been the first bicycle he had ever seen. What is this quiet and strange thing rolling toward me on the highway? A belching truck had posed no threat, but my bike switched on the hard-wired genetics of ancestors. "Beware of anything sneaking up on you, especially if it's making no noise. Run like hell." Once this message got swallowed along with the grass, the steer raised tail, dug in all four chubby feet and sprang into gear. Down the road we went. As luck would have it, I was on a slight incline and doing only 18 miles per hour–the exact speed of the steer. Ten yards separated us–neither widening nor narrowing. I could not seem to gain an inch. It would do no good to stop. I had to pass the steer sometime, but how? This could go on forever. I saw myself chasing that steer all the way into Pecos, twenty miles away.

Only one thing needed doing–I had to pass that steer and the sooner the better. I strained on the pedals until my legs ached, but I didn't back off. Slowly, my loaded bike gained speed: 19 miles per hour–19.5 miles per hour–20 miles per hour. The gap narrowed. If I could just keep it up. I reached the tail, the flank, the shoulder. Finally, we were nearly eye to eye. Strings of froth were coming from his nose and mouth. Maybe mine too. I bent over the handlebars to decrease the wind pressure and gave it all I had. Leg muscles burned. Thank God I wasn't racing a Texas Longhorn. That long-legged lean animal with the six-foot horn span would have been good for half a state at least. Suddenly, the steer reached down deep into his panicked heart and came up with a supreme effort causing me to slip back to his rump. I gave my leg muscles a lecture and again we gained. No more spurt from him. As I reached the wild eye, showing white all around, it happened. His two front feet planted themselves– without informing the two in the rear. According to the laws of motion, inertia and gravity–not a smart thing to do. My steer added tumbling to his repertoire. I zoomed ahead. My first bicycle race and stampede.

For the next seven days I had a great time in Pecos telling any stranger who would listen all about it.

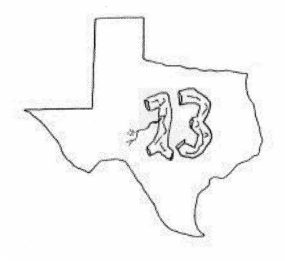

## *Pecos from the North*
### (Perimeter Tour 1994)

A year later on my way south from Seminole on the perimeter tour, I took the business route through Monahans. It was July 4, 1994 and I thought a pedal down main street with parades, cotton candy, horses prancing, high school bands tooting would be uplifting. I found three or four cars–without drivers–parked on the street. The town looked completely deserted. Bits of trash got caught in small dust devils and whirled about–but that was about it for a parade. I stopped at a convenience store–the only place of business open–and had a snack. The temperature baked the pavement outside at 110 degrees.

Coming from the opposite direction a year earlier, I had stopped at Monahans State Park and played for a time in the 70 foot-high sand dunes. That night, not wanting sand in everything, I had stretched out on a picnic table in my Texas flag shorts, rolled up in a sheet. The full moon beamed down so brightly I could actually read by it. There was a small breeze and only one or two mosquitoes. At four a.m. the desert had cooled a lot and I lay there shivering–too cold to get up and rummage for more blankets or clothes. I persevered until dawn. I found two quarters in the sand beneath my table.

JACK RABBIT

### Tra-Park
(Perimeter Tour 1994)

Pecos was an easy ride from Monahans and on the perimeter trip, I didn't stop to survey the sand dunes again. Once in Pecos I headed for the RV park I had stayed in the previous year and surprised Chuck and Linda Bratland, the managers. I'm sure they didn't expect to see me again out in the wilds of west Texas two years in a row.

Linda and I had several hours of conversation covering religion, philosophy, wild life, Texas history and anything else that popped into our minds. I went to the local museum and library, watched jack rabbits, ate my fill of those wonderfully sweet Pecos cantaloupes direct from the fields, learned about the sulfur mines and smelled French-fried onion rings being processed in a plant not far enough away. Pecos had a park, swimming pool, a small zoo, an airfield for local ranchers and no movie house. I understood that one might be reopened soon. According to Pecos history, the first rodeo in the nation debuted there on July 4, 1883–still a popular annual event. I stayed several days on my first trip but, only one night on the second. I thought the people of Pecos, special.

*Don't look back. . .Don't look back. . .*

### Newt Keen
(Perimeter Tour 1994)

After leaving Pecos I rode northwest paralleling the Pecos river to get close to the New Mexico border and continue west to El Paso. Apparently it was tarantula mating season because every few feet I met scampering male tarantulas crossing the highway in search of waiting females–which could, and probably would, eat them after copulation. I weaved to miss them, their future would be precarious enough.

At noon under a blazing sun I hitched my bike to the hitching post outside a weathered wood building in the dusty town of Orla. Orla could easily pass for a ghost town or western movie set. The word Café, in faded painted letters on the facade and a small bleached-out "open" sign stuck in a window said howdy to my empty stomach. If I hadn't detoured to Pecos I would have missed Orla and I would have never met Newt Keen–a for-real cowboy cook and rancher. Standing behind the counter, his denim pants and shirt protected by a liberally grease-splattered blue apron, Newt Keen barked another howdy and a come-on-in. He called to a young man to set a table and to take my order. His helper, fresh-faced and tanned, a young cowboy complete with black Stetson, work pants, worn shirt and working boots, moved quickly and politely. Was he in training to become a waiter? At a glance I could tell this was not some slick franchise attempt to create a western motif.

His were authentic ranch-hand clothes and after his stint at waiting tables, he would no doubt saddle up and ride off to round up some livestock on a nearby spread–maybe bring back a steer for Newt Keen's hamburgers.

"You won't get hamburgers like these in any big town. Picked out the beef myself. Best there is, and call me Newt." He waved a huge gnarled hand toward the kitchen or maybe, toward his ranch. I sidled up to the counter, instead of a table and immediately ordered two hamburgers with everything on them. I sipped hot coffee while Newt, a straight six feet tall and as rangy as a desert Longhorn, got busy at the stove down at the end. Our conversation continued.

"Used to ranch a lot and I still do a little. I got into cookin' for a dude ranch for a time, but quit. City guys wouldn't even help. Had a big tub of beans on the fire and was trying to fry meat and pan-bake biscuits," here Newt paused and sent a stream of brown snuff juice at something under the counter. Whatever it was–he hit it.

"Do you think they'd stir that tub of beans for me? Heck no–just sat there on their behinds doin' nothin'and grinnin' like fat jackasses."

We talked about the big blow I went through while camped at Brownfield.

"Yeah, boy. That was pretty good, but I've seen worse. One time it was so bad, I saw a hen lay the same egg three times cause she had her backside to the breeze."

The weather lines around his eyes got deeper and I could see the hint of a smile. I found out he used to have a café in Mentone, over in Loving County just across the Pecos River. Loving County contained 700 square miles and a 100 people to run around on them. Twenty of those lived in Mentone, the county's only town. Someday, I'm going out there and meet everyone in Loving County before they pass on. Orla was in Reeves County, one of the larger Texas' counties with 2,600 square miles and included the town of Pecos. The largest county in Texas was bigger than some states–Brewster–down in the Big Bend area with nearly 6,000 square miles to roam around in. I think I would like to stay awhile in either Orla or Mentone or wherever Newt Keen hung out.

My hamburgers arrived and I got some chips and more coffee. As advertised, the beef was first-rate. We talked about ranching and how it's changing.

"Now we got new-fangled things to work with–not like the old days," another arrow-straight spit at the hidden container.

"Used to break horses and castrate them with my pocket knife and I do yet." Newt pulled out a worn, but obviously well-honed folding knife.

"I can castrate faster and better with this than you can using one of those fancy nut-crackers." I didn't doubt him and took a decisive bite out of my hamburger. All too soon those hamburgers, chips and coffee disappeared and I had no reason to stay around any longer. Newt came to the front door with me and stuck out his big brown hand which nearly hid mine. His grasp was hard but not crushing.

"You be careful and stop by anytime." I assured Newt Keen that I would do that. I knew he had a lot more stories to tell about a way of life that keeps changing, maybe not always for the better.

## Wild and Uninhabited
(Perimeter Tour 1994)

I saddled up my bike and galloped northwest on a little-used highway that appeared as a thin line on the map. I had forty-one miles to ride that afternoon with no houses, service stations or sign of human activity. I listened to the cactus wrens, the harsh calls of ravens and watched a few vultures wheeling in the super-heated sky. I stopped 25 miles out just to listen to the silence–the birds were having their afternoon siesta–the wind had nearly stopped. It was a magic moment for me. The land stretched out mostly flat to rolling with brush, cactus, and mesquite. Brown, yellow, gray-green and various shades of orange dominated the landscape. I gained altitude with every mile. Off in the distance in a whitish-blue sky, I could make out the humping Guadalupe peaks–a soft light blue on the horizon to the west. I packed three gallons of water on my bike. Most of it would be gone by the time I reached the New Mexico border and the junction with the highway that would take me to the Guadalupe Mountains National Park. Periodically, I stopped for snacks, consuming two oranges, a can of spaghetti, two fried apple pies, wheat thins and a can of tuna.

CORNUDAS, TX.

## Border Café and the Mountains
(Perimeter Tour 1994)

The temperature that afternoon reached 108 degrees. By the time I got to the Border Café at the junction, I needed food. A few minutes rest and a substantial dinner prepared me for the final ten miles to the highway rest stop just a few miles short of the Guadalupe Mountains National Park. I felt a cooling breeze as I turned west toward the mountains–very much appreciated. I arrived at the rest stop at nine-fifteen that evening. I had been on the road since six-thirty that morning. I had biked 90 miles–a steady climb to the mountains. No support vehicle with lemonade had accompanied me. Tomorrow I would camp in the park at the foot of El Capitan, the highest peak, then zoom down and out of the park in a wild rushing ride the next day, stopping in Salt Flats for breakfast after which I would pedal on to an oasis in the arid ranch lands of west Texas for lunch where I would meet my next unforgettable person–a woman of prodigious energy, May Carson, mayor and owner of Cornudas.

## Western Ladies
### (Perimeter Tour 1994)

After my fast descent out of the park and before I reached the Salt Flats, I stopped near a road crew one of whom informed me he saw a motorcyclist swept into the canyon alongside the highway by the force of the cross winds. True, I had seen the wind socks standing straight out as I swooped down the mountain side, but the *Randonnee* had never wavered. Luckily for me, I hadn't encountered a really strong gust. Twenty miles down the road I came to a historical marker telling about the El Paso Salt Wars of 1877.

I stopped at another weathered café where Joyce Gilmore, a grandmother and a rancher, fixed me up with some eggs, bacon, hash browns, toast and coffee for five dollars. She told me she had lived no where else. Her son had his own ranch, but had just injured his hip, so she had been helping him while still maintaining her small store and her ranch. Her daughter-in-law watered the stock and built two miles of fence where the cattle had gotten out searching for water.

"Now they're trucking in water, but at least they have some grass left." Mrs. Gilmore's ranch had water but no grass.

"Too bad we can't get those two ranches together. Would kind of solve our problems." A small stoic laugh. Mrs. Gilmore had fallen a couple of days ago herself and had several scrapes and bruises to show for it. In the meantime life went on and no thought was given to quitting or complaining.

## Free Camping at Cornudas
### (Perimeter Tour 1994)

Down the highway another 20 miles or so, I could see some green trees and a small red water tower. It was almost four p.m., July 7, 1994–three days before my birthday. The barren land was over heating as it does every summer day, so I was quite relieved when only one more mile separated me from that oasis I had been watching for so long. I pulled up outside the café, went inside and met May Carson. A gruff but friendly blonde, full of energy and with a great figure poured into Levi's, threatening every seam, informed me I could camp out back in the desert under any tree I could find. When I asked the price she grinned. "It's free to all tenters who ride bikes, and we don't get many." She hurried back to the kitchen. I looked at the large menu and wondered what to order. Jerie Lewis, (I'm not kidding here) an attractive seventeen-year-old with dark eyes and straight black hair, came over to help me.

She recommended the famous Cornudas Chile Burger (note: not chili) and pointed to a write up carefully placed under plastic at the counter. It was by Sunny Conley of the Las Cruces Sun News.
"Thick green halved chiles peeked out from underneath the bun's toasted top and cheese dribbled down–the meat was juicy and hot off the grill–not greasy."

Actually, after the famous burger arrived, and before the first tasting, I could testify he did not do the sandwich justice. In addition to the sweet chile slices and cheese, there were onions, tomatoes and lettuce, all bunched atop a humongous hunk of grilled beef–almost too big to wrestle–and my hands weren't small. A large supply of fries looking more like a golden log-jam blocked the hamburger from falling off the plate. For dessert: home-made pecan pie and coffee. The chef, Rick Cornelius, nephew to May, came out to get acquainted. Naturally, I said he was a food magician. He had a big smile and a firm handshake. After dinner it was still too early to go out back and find a tree for my tent, so I wandered around the café. Up near the ceiling May had accumulated a collection of gimme caps–each one encased in plastic. Over 3,000 hung up there, she said, each proclaiming a special message about seed, feed, tractors, cattle, oil field equipment, assorted organizations and places. At the bar, glass cases stuffed with freshly baked chocolate chip cookies, hard candy, luscious looking muffins, sweet rolls and freshly baked pies tempted anyone walking by. I walked by and succumbed.

Red and white-checked gingham overlaid with clear plastic-covered the tables. Inserted beneath the plastic were testimonials–some printed–some hand written, extolling the virtues of May Carson, the café, and the town of Cornudas, named for the mountains out back. The café had been written up a lot by the press. The table legs were clothed in blue-jean pants legs and stuck into cowboy boots. Boots also held flowers on each table. Photos covered the walls. One showed 100 Harley Davidson bikers who had dropped in for lunch one day. John Wayne had a big signed photo. Along with the photos were testimonials:

"To Mayor May–A wonderful cook. Should've had you on the Great Wall," this written on a photo of Kevin Foster leaping along the Great Wall of China on his mountain bike. Another card: "Verona, Italy–Here I am, Hernando from Verona, Italy. Thanks again for your fantastic scrambled eggs and coffee. I'll never forget Cornudas, Tx."
There were several photos of participants in the annual Chili Cook-Off held out behind the café each year. A portion of a wall had shoulder patches of every description. In an adjoining room hung western paintings and a good selection of western greeting cards and gift items. Outside next to the small rustic service station and the restrooms, May had made a small motel into a series of cozy gift

shops–each with its own theme. There was a board walk and a rail fence fronting each shop. A sampling of the signs nailed, screwed and roped to the "authentic faux fronts" above the gift shop doors: Grandma Keeney's Kandy Kitchen, R. B. Longs Livery Stables, Campbell Brothers Feed, Qing Qings Chinese Laundry, Fosters Bank and Trust, Assay Office - Gold and Silver, Miss Jo's Bath House, Dry Gulch Saloon and Hotel, Jay Williams M.D. and Undertaker. The names of the proprietors were May's friends who lived on ranches close by.

Some of the shops had gravel floors, some had Indian rugs. Each inhabited a space no more than ten feet square–intimate and beckoning. Antique bureaus held glass ware, dolls and trinkets. There were stuffed toys, jams and jellies, western clothing, western sculptures, paintings and furniture. Surrounding the gift shops, service station and café several tall trees waved in the desert breeze– Russian olive, cottonwood, arborvitae, mesquite, ponderosa pine, and salt cedar (tamarack) which blooms a bright pink in the spring. I would like to see it.

Later, I put my tent under one of those. The landscaping included desert plants and a variety of cacti. May even had an irrigated patch of lawn, lovingly tended next to her trailer home just behind the café. Her nephew had his own trailer and so did Jerie–the three of them made up the entire population of Cornudas. To the north were the blue-clad Cornudas Mountains. May had painted several signs expressing her western philosophy: "Keep your dog on dog walk and out of picnic area or we will add shotgun dog souffle to the menu at the Road Kill Café. Kids–please teach the adults to stay out of the cactus garden and off of fences. May's Law." "This is not Burger King–you don't get it your way–you take it my way or you don't get it!"

"If you came here to bitch, you have already used up 98% of your time. I would like to suggest you use the remaining 2% to find the door." "I'm somewhat of a bullshitter myself, but occasionally I enjoy listening to an expert." "Cover your hide or stay outside."

"Notice to all parents–unattended children will be sold into slavery."
"Keys to restrooms free to customers. All others $1.00. Please
conserve the water. Thank you." This last sign introduced a story I
liked.

## The Famous Toilet Tale
(Perimeter Tour 1994)

In either direction forty miles separate desperate travelers from
restrooms. A lot of cars and trucks stop and the occupants have only
one or two things on their minds. Worried and preoccupied faces
open the café's doors and gape at the $1.00 sign. May has to truck in
all the water, hence the sign about restroom protocol. The last thing
on the minds of these stoppers is a soda before taking care of
business–that's all they need, another can of fizzing pop. One day a
woman in distress promised to buy something afterwards. Instead,
she threw the keys in the front door and went to her car. A waitress
and a firm believer in May's Law, dashed out and confronted the
reneging woman and got an earful of verbal abuse from the now
relieved non-customer. The waitress ran back into the café, picked up
a shotgun and tore out again to shoot a load into that gal's behind.
She probably would have, too, but she couldn't get the safety off.
Meanwhile one very scared woman paid the dollar and roared off
toward El Paso.

The next day the sheriff came by. He empathized but cautioned
the waitress that even with a valid hunting license, she shouldn't
shoot a tourist. "Now, if you'd just smacked her a good one, that'd
been all right."

Rick and I went out to meet four guys from El Paso at a ranch
landing strip. The red bi-plane was a beautiful civilian version of a
Beech UC-43 Traveler with a top speed of nearly 200 miles per hour.
They had flown in just for lunch. Good thing they hadn't come for
breakfast. Rick had tried to gather eggs that morning and every one
had a small hole. The resident bull snake, five feet long and thick of

waist, had found them first and sucked them dry. May liked to keep the snake around to control the rattlesnake population.

One morning before I walked in from my campsite for breakfast, a foursome from the United Kingdom sat down for their morning meal in this strange land called Texas. May looked out from the kitchen and noticed all four were standing with their backs against the wall staring at something beneath the table. May hurried over to see what was the matter. One of the women pointed and in a shaky voice said, "There seems to be a rather large spider down there."

May saw the tarantula and scooped it up with her hand and deposited it outside. The front door to the café had about an inch clearance at the bottom and it was a common occurrence for tarantulas to slip in at night. The woman was asked why she hadn't screamed when she looked down and saw this slow-moving black beastie crawling across her foot. "I wanted to, but nothing would come out." What a story to be repeated at numerous dinner parties in merry old England for years to come.

## The Soon-to-be-Famous Recital
### (Perimeter Tour 1994)

The café boasted a Yamaha electronic keyboard. It had 99 rhythms and 128 voices. We played around on it after closing hours. While Rick played, May and I danced rumbas. Jeri joined me in some country swing dances. The Yamaha had a large selection of pre-recorded music and I had a good time pretending to play those pieces. I got pretty good at it. So good, that one evening during the dinner hour, I gave a "concert," which included my magnificent theatrical gesticulations, for the diners. The customers were convinced I played all those tunes in all those styles. One customer told his date he knew I was performing that night which was why he drove her out there from El Paso as a special treat. I played through the entire menu of pre-recorded music which took about an hour and included everything from classical to Latin, pop, blues and country.

214

When the music started to repeat I decided to quit, but forgot where the power switch was, so I just got up and left. The music continued. The customers appeared stunned then burst out laughing. The fellow who had bragged on me to his girl friend told me I was lucky he hadn't brought his gun.

I stayed at Cornudas for seven fun-filled days. I helped in the café. I painted more signs. May and a neighbor took me with them to the city market in Juarez to shop for more collectibles to put in the gift shops. As recompense for helping out I received all my meals free. I celebrated my birthday there and after hours on that evening a banquet was prepared in my honor. On the menu: grilled steaks with purple onions, grilled chicken strips, huge baked potatoes, cauliflower, broccoli, carrots–all steamed to perfection, lettuce and tomato salad and plenty of beer. I ate four chicken strips and two large rib-eye steaks.

Rick came all dressed up looking like a movie cowboy. Also present were May and Jerie (all of Cornudas) and two long-time friends of May's. We were on a spacious patio ringed with decorative white crushed rock pathways next to black volcanic rock. Indirect lighting highlighted the shrubs and trees around us. Four flags waved from their 30 foot standards: United States, Texas, Cornudas and the Chili Cook-Off flag, the latter a jalapeno pepper on a red field. As we sat there, a large tarantula ambled beneath May's chair and between her feet proceeding with its measured slow-motion gait to the center of the patio. Jerie headed for safe ground. Eventually, Rick gently directed him toward the bushes. The sun was just setting and doing so with such an array of color we grew silent and watched. Rose, lavender, burnt orange, purple, mother of pearl clouds, yellow, light pink and up in the sky turning from teal blue to cobalt, there hung one of the planets almost as large-looking as if we were using binoculars. The wind came up slightly and we brought down the flags. What a marvel, new friends who gathered like old friends and Mother Nature in all her splendor with one of her hairy critters helping me begin a new birth year. I was 66, going on 40.

The day of departure finally arrived and off I pedaled early one morning. Two miles up the highway on my way to El Paso, I stopped and looked back at that tiny green spot beside the road. The rising sun already made it shimmer in the air. Yep. An oasis.

Newt Keen, Joyce Gilmore and May Carson, probably unknown to each other, but one with the land. Independent, no pretense, tell it like it is, always ready to help, but taking guff from nobody. These are Great Plains people, blessed with stubborn, abrasive ways and big hearts, resourceful, solid as the rock mountains around them, with a never failing courage to face freezing winters and hot, dry summers with a steady look. They have grit.

## *Far West Texas*
### (Perimeter Tour 1994)

The wind gently pushed me to El Paso. Rolling to flat roads. Temperature at 100 degrees, but it felt comfortable. El Paso along with its border sister city Juarez was home to more than two million persons, most of whom resided across the Rio Grande in Mexico. The size intimidated me as I pedaled, so I chose not to enter it. I reached similar decisions for all of Texas' large cities. The only city I felt comfortable biking in was Austin–and that was a gradual love affair stretched over a ten year period. Nevertheless, El Paso/Juarez was possibly one of the most interesting places to visit in Texas. Truly, it was a "whole other country," a marvelous country, and with the free trade now with Mexico the area was sure to mushroom to a gigantic center of trade and culture. I took Loop 375 south to the border and hooked up with I-10, my highway back to San Antonio about 600 miles away.

The rest stop on I-10, going east and a few miles from El Paso, was nice–small sand dunes, large mulberry trees, green grass. In the distance, looking south across the Rio Grande into Mexico, I could see a string of small villages and a patch-work of irrigated fields. I delayed setting up my tent until nightfall. During the late afternoon hours, the wind increased so much I couldn't put it up at all. I moved my loaded bike inside the entryway to the men's restroom and read some from one of my ten-cent novels. The restroom light gleamed brightly. I said howdy to anyone coming in to use the facilities–sort of a bookish doorkeeper.

## The Ferrets Arrived
(Perimeter Tour 1994)

One man told me he was driving straight through from San Diego to a town in Ohio for a reunion–hadn't been back since 1958. He was a bit anxious about what his old friends would look like.

A couple with three thin frenetic children and a passel of ferrets stopped. I think they had six or eight or twelve ferrets–they moved around so rapidly I couldn't keep track. The children turned the ferrets loose on the restroom floor for exercise. The room, usually with its definitive essence, now smelled quite wild as the musk of the ferrets permeated it. The children acted as wild as the ferrets and the family members had "Ferret Musk No. 5" liberally applied, which gave them sort of a prehistoric cave-family smell. During the screaming, chasing, and tossing of ferrets by the children, the young woman and I visited. She was taken with the idea of camping with me, but her traveling companion (who was fixing a tire or something) wanted to move on and thus a very interesting chapter in this book will never be written.

The woman told how the police arrested her the day before because she drove topless. A truck driver (the prude) had reported her. Tonight she wore a tube top on her slim but well-formed tanned body.

"It was too hot to wear anything." She tugged at the tube top. "I didn't see anything wrong with it. They look just fine." For a moment I thought she was going to slip her top off just to prove that it was perfectly natural and not in bad taste at all. The moment went by. I think I was disappointed. How could I pass judgment without objective evidence?

After collecting every ferret, counting and recounting, the wild carful sped off into the night. The scent of our encounter hung around. I put my tent on the outside of the restroom up against the wall out of the wind. Someone had dumped motor oil close to where I placed my tent, but it smelled better than ferret.

### A Biker in Need and a Fantastic Store
(Perimeter Tour 1994)

The next day I rode to Fort Hancock. Before entering town, off I-10, I stopped at a service station where I found another cyclist. He had been in every state except Alaska and Hawaii. His back prevented him from driving so bicycling served as his transportation. His back provided Social Security disability payments–his only source of income. He had already spent all his money for the month and he sat there with two flat tires.

"So, what are you going to do?"

"I don't know."

I gave him ten dollars since he hadn't asked for a handout. Who knew? He might make a hundred dollars a day, sitting there with his two flat tires and telling his story over and over. Sometimes, I could be a cynic. Maybe the ten dollars would prevent me from having a bad feeling down the road. It was good to give back. Lord knows, people helped me.

At three p.m. on July 15, 1994, I sat in the shade at the Fort Hancock Mercantile Store in downtown Fort Hancock–one of the more eclectic stores in all of Texas.

Established in 1883 and after the second purchase in 1916, the store became the property of a woman and passed down through the years from daughter to daughter. Any guy marrying one of those daughters automatically had a career. The present owner–just got it last year–was Tootsie Farris. Her husband Kevin hired on as shopkeeper. Their daughter, Emma, would be the next owner. Accidentally, the store contained a bountiful supply of antiques–the unsold merchandise down through the years still remained on the shelves and in nooks and crannies. Kevin told me going into the attic storage space was like going back to the early days of Texas.

"There's a trunk up there filled with clothes and stuff that belongs to a school teacher. She left it in 1920–said she'd be back. We're still holding it for her." He told me how for a time the store was the only one in town.

"We had the only telephone–it's still there." He pointed to a shelf behind him.

"People could get a casket here by coming in and telephoning El Paso. It would be on the train the next day."

*I just know this will turn out well*

### Night Ride
(Perimeter Tour 1994)

I left to pitch my tent just outside of town, but I got a funny feeling. I had funny feelings about places before and I always sided with them when it came to choosing a camping site–not that I caved in to superstitions–I just knew I would toss and turn all night–

220

wondering. Anyway, I decided to go on. Although already late in the afternoon, I thought I would have enough daylight to reach another spot–twenty miles–or even Sierra Blanca, another ten miles after that. The trip would be mostly up hill. The setting sun behind me bathed the mountains in front with shimmering shades of gold and lavender. Ten miles out into the nothingness, I got a flat. It took forty minutes to repair. I had to unpack the bike completely to take off the rear wheel and put on a new tube. The Sierra Blanca and Quitman Mountains kept me company as dusk approached too quickly. Soon, a mellow half-moon appeared over the mountains as I cycled into the night. I gained altitude which made my ride slow. I did not arrive at my rest area until eleven-thirty. A wondrous ride, illuminated by the soft light of the moon–out in the middle of the desert–the mountains, hours before painted in gorgeous colors, now loomed about me in deep shadow and shining ivory. No wind. No sounds.

### Whistling at Badgers
(Perimeter Tour 1994)

Just three miles before the rest stop I pedaled into an all-night convenience store and had a few hot dogs. The manager warned me to stay out of the grassy areas at the rest stop because of badgers. "Just whistle–it scares them off." Yeah, right.

I raised my tent. I flashlighted the perimeter of my camping area, but saw no green or yellow eyes looking back. I whistled a tune for insurance. Heck, maybe whistling worked. Stars brightened as the moon began setting. A great day. A great night. Glad I listened to my feelings.

AUSTIN, TX

## Perimeter Completed
### (Perimeter Tour 1994)

I worked my way along I-10 through Fort Stockton–my second visit. At this point I had completed the perimeter ride around Texas. Big Bend National park where I had started last March lay south of me about 100 miles away. The rest of my trip into Austin of some 400 miles (not direct) would be icing on the cake.

I must have been looking worn, since more people wanted to give me food and offered rides. Perhaps travelers on the Interstate were not used to seeing bicycles. The traffic became lighter as I traveled east, particularly when I-20 branched off for the Fort Worth/Dallas area. At times the shoulder consisted of loose gravel and I rode up on the highway itself. Trucks and cars, although few, pulled into the passing lane giving me plenty of room. I watched my rear view mirror carefully, just in case.

## The Land of Opportunity
(Perimeter Tour 1994)

At a large supermart/service station about 20 miles past Sheffield, I met a young man, over six feet, blond, blue eyed, friendly, from Czeckoslovakia–now from California–and his big rig. He had arrived in the United States as a tourist three years before and toured the country on a motorcycle. An accident depleted his visa time and his funds. He couldn't get a work visa, so he took a chance on the immigration lottery which awards 40,000 visas per year and won.

He went to truck-driving school, the $3,000 tuition paid for by a government on-the-job training program. He had been driving coast to coast for the past six months. He took produce east and whatever back west. He drove 20 hours at a stretch, more than allowed, I thought. When I left him at Sheffield he had to be in California by 6 a.m. the next day–about 1,000 miles away. A few months ago, his parents came over to visit and rode in his truck. He received his first American credit card a week ago. He thought the United States was the best place in the whole world. He had a degree in civil engineering, but loved his job as a truck driver.

He gave me a tour of his rig–a huge Freightliner–luxurious with deep red leather upholstery, television, stereo, two bunks, VCR, refrigerator, storage and a closet for clothes. He planned to return to Czechoslovakia for a visit–maybe next year.

Well maintained rest stops along I-10 made them a joy to use. I rode all day and relaxed in the evenings, usually visiting with others who pulled in for the night or for a few hours of rest.

On my first trip I entered the city of Ozona on I-10 from the east. This time I pedaled in from the west. That first tour seemed a long time ago. I visited three nearby Indian Forts on that first tour: Fort Mason and Fort McKavett some miles east and 75 miles or so north, Fort Concho in San Angelo. Labor Day weekend at Lake Brownwood State Park and my visit to the grave site of Katherine Ann Porter also

223

took place on that first tour in 1993 and not all that far from where I stopped now in Ozona on the final leg of the 1994 perimeter tour.

The next chapter will pick up the narrative again as I examine the "coming home" days of each tour. For now, let's go back and visit those forts, laze around on Labor Day weekend at Lake Brownwood and cycle down to visit Ms. Porter.

FORT McKAVETT

### Fort Mason and Fort McKavett
(Summer Tour 1993)

On my "trial run" tour in the summer of 1993, I finished looking at my very first Indian fort to the west, Fort Mason, and was suitably impressed. I touched Texas history at last. Sitting on the veranda of the restored officers' building, I imagined Colonel Robert E. Lee (Fort Mason being his last command before joining the Confederate forces) sitting where I sat, looking out over the hazy blue hills for any sign of marauding Indians. I looked and listened, but only a brilliant dragonfly, flitting about, and the call of a mockingbird tested my powers of observation and less-than-perfect hearing.

My next fort on the list that summer, a year earlier, was south and west of Menard. I would always remember Menard as a sensuous experience since I had to ride by on the north side of extensive sheep pens across which the richly flavored southern breeze blew. One cannot hold one's breath and pedal for two miles, but one tries.

I arrived at Fort McKavett 60 some miles west of Mason on the one day of the week it was closed to the public. I heard this from Steve Crothers at the Fort McKavett Trading Post. On vacation from his job in Dallas as a computer analyst, he filled in for his brother, Pete, who normally ran the place. Their great grandfather served at Fort McKavett before the Civil War.

He told me this while he ladled out a bowl of beans from a big pot. "Been simmerin' since I opened up–should be ready–help yourself to an onion and some bread. Eat all you want. Here's some coffee, too." He wore his black hair in a ponytail under a well-used Stetson. He looked at me through designer black-wire-rimmed glasses.

A raw-boned rancher, sprawled at a wooden table worn smooth by countless elbows, told Steve he'd about decided to buy the old TV set that was for sale over at a Brady antique shop. "They tol' me it was the first kerosene-powered TV in the county. I tol' them that I'd take it if they could find some new wicks for it." After the laughter subsided, I was cautioned by the narrator to be on the lookout for rattlesnakes. "They're going to be your greatest danger." I heeded the warning as real. In all my Texas tours, I never saw a live rattlesnake. Steve invited me to pitch my tent in the front yard of his house about a quarter of a mile down the highway and directly across from the fort. "We'll have quail for dinner tonight," he added.

I rode down to his house, which he planned to fix up. The previous owner decided to homestead in the cemetery. Only a few houses grouped themselves near the fort ruins. Availability depended on someone dying. For temporary curtains, Steve hung large flags: Great Britain, United States, Mexico, and others I didn't recognize. True to his word, he prepared quail for dinner, also green beans with mushrooms and almonds, corn, whole wheat bread–already buttered, Coors Lite and brownies for dessert. I rigged up my five-gallon portable shower in a small stand of trees and stretched a clothesline. I went to bed clean and with clean riding clothes drying outside my tent door.

The next morning, Steve hollered from the porch that breakfast was ready. We had deer sausage, potatoes, eggs with onions, buttered toast and plenty of hot black coffee. Well fed, I walked across the highway to the extensive grounds of Fort McKavett.

FORT MASON, TX.

At its peak in the 1880s, the fort consisted of 40 buildings and hundreds of soldiers. Today, 12 buildings have been handsomely restored and 18 others have been stabilized as ruins. A thick tree-trunk flag pole that looked like a mast from a windjammer, soared over the parade grounds. The flat grass-covered expanse that reached to distant rows of buildings on all sides, resounded in my mind to the beat of drums, the call of bugles and the pawing of horses impatient for patrol.

In the headquarters building, the attendant, whom I believed at first to be a young teenager, but was an adult single mother with a two-year-old, looked up from a substantial book and related the history of Fort McKavett as if she had lived it first hand. Sarah was a history buff and wanted to go back to college. "I love to read and usually have three or four books going all the time." She commuted to work in a Chevy pickup. I thought she also rode horses and hunted, but I might have imagined that. To me she looked like a Texas pioneer, strong-willed, clear-eyed, not easily turned aside by circumstance.

Later that day, while I loitered inside the Trading Post, a young man, appearing to be down on his luck, came in. He had walked from Menard, 23 miles away, after the sheriff had invited him to leave town. Steve gave him some money, a big hamburger, cigarettes and a 25-mile lift over to Interstate 10 where he'd have a better chance to catch a ride. In the stories of the old West, when a stranger showed up at your campfire, you gave him some grub and a little extra to take with him. At Fort McKavett, 19th century hospitality was alive and well.

### Fort Concho
(Summer Tour 1993)

August 4, 1993, found me in the city of Sterling about 50 miles northwest of San Angelo where Fort Concho awaited. I received permission to camp in the city park from the teenaged manager of the local Diary Queen. At the park I set up my tent beneath a pecan tree near the community baseball field. A father and son were playing catch. The restrooms contained no showers, but there was a sprinkler system in the grassy park with powerful jets of water spewing in great circles. Changing into my Texas flag shorts, I hopped into the middle of the ice-cold spurts, following them around and around while soaping and rinsing. I washed my riding clothes the same way– invigorating. Later, I wondered if the water was the kind used on some golf courses–partially treated. Surely not in Sterling.

That night, across a fence, not more than 20 yards away, a small herd of cows choired me to sleep. At daybreak, I repacked my panniers, rolled up my tent and bedroll, pumped up my tires, checked and tightened bolts and nuts, oiled the chain, powdered my behind with baby powder and dabbed on sun block–things I did every morning, but who wants to hear it every day?

I arrived in San Angelo during rush hour and inadvertently did my part to hold up traffic by having to go through road construction on Knickerbocker Road on my way to Lake Nasworthy and my campsite for a few days. To visit Fort Concho, located in the heart of the city, I traversed this same stretch of street a couple of times, but not at rush hour.

The fort has been almost completely restored. I looked at the barracks filled with rows of narrow, wood-slatted beds covered with four-inch thick mattresses stuffed with hay. There was a small chest at the foot of each bed that held most of the frontier soldier's worldly goods. At the head of each bed were pegs from which swords and gun belts dangled. Each year there were reenactments of military life at the fort. Horses, drums and bugles created quite a show. At night the "soldiers" returned to their air-conditioned homes and TVs in town.

Fort Concho now comprises 23 original and restored structures—some were used by community organizations. Established in 1867, the fort was abandoned in 1889 with the band playing, "The Girl I Left Behind Me."

In the museum, the period-dressed attendant with beard, moustache and ponytail, upon learning of my trek by bike, confided that he and his wife would like to get on horses and ride across the United States. "Just like back in the good old days." He gestured at the memorabilia around him. "It's the only way to appreciate nature and the country." He thought the government should make it possible to retire at 40 when a person was still young enough to travel. I let that pass, but I thought I was traveling and also past forty. We both decried the discovery that unknown persons had painted graffiti recently on some of the fort's buildings. "Don't know what the world's comin' to when even a place like this gets splattered by those morons." He pulled at his beard. "Oughta hang 'em."

After seeing the six forts on that first tour and spending some time with my son in Dallas, I had a leisurely ride back into the hill country of Texas instead of going directly south to Austin. I don't remember my rationale for doing that, but it did set me up for the most enlightening week-end of any of my tours. I had arranged several months in advance for a camping spot at Lake Brownwood State Park just north of the city of Brownwood.

## Labor Day Weekend at Lake Brownwood State Park
### (Summer Tour 1993)

I set up my tent beneath an oak, a mesquite and an elm in such a way I would be guaranteed shade for at least 60 percent of the day. The lake, light-dappled, shimmered 100 feet away, while the sun, tempered by the continuing north wind maintained a welcome warmth.

I showered and washed my clothes, hung them up next to my tent, sat down and waited for all the campers to show up. I was used to camping in nearly empty parks. I learned to guard my solitude. What would this experience be like? I looked at the mass of picnic tables and the grills spreading out in the distance and tried to imagine a family hunched around each table and barbeque pit–a mass of humanity. Why would that be fun? Two and one half days and three nights for them–three days and four nights for me. Most of my last day and all of my last night would be without the vast horde. That thought would see me through the coming onslaught.

That first evening, my new neighbors turned on their radio full-blast, listening to a local football game. I asked them to turn it down. They did–and even apologized–so maybe the weekend would be manageable after all. Three or four kids raced around the park roads on their bicycles. Not bad, except one had training wheels with no tires–just metal against road–which sounded as if he were plowing it up. The ensuing racket excited a small dog to rapid-fire barking. It would be a long week-end.

The sun, meanwhile, without uttering a sound, painted the sky with reckless abandon as it set. I heard no comment from anyone, I would have thought someone would have said Oh or Ah, but no, nothing. Of course, I didn't comment. I saw so many sunsets on that trip my silence could be justified, I sniffed. Tonight was prelude. The next two and one half days would be hectic big time, what with water skiing, motor boat riding, swimming, eating, drinking, horsing around and the rubbing on of lots of sun tan lotion.

Pickups continued to roll in pulling sleek-looking motor boats, pontoon boats, even a canoe. Coolers, baskets, tents, bed rolls, women and children deposited themselves at the reserved picnic tables. Pickup and boat would trundle toward the lake where fellow campers watched the launchings, obviously judging the skill of each truck driver backing into the lake just far enough and with just the right amount of braking, to send the beautiful boat softly sliding off the trailer and into the waiting water with hardly a ripple.

Meanwhile back at the camping spot, picnic tables groaned under stacks of food and drink. Tents billowed into being–one for the super-excited children. Maybe it would rain all week-end and they would all leave. "Hear my prayer, O Lord." Just call me an old grouch.

More pickups. More trailers with huge boats. More children. Greetings as campers recognized each other. Most everyone called Brownwood home. My bicycle looked out of place next to the multi-engined ski boats and the powerful pickups with larger than normal tires. At my spot–no pickup, no trailer, and no boat.

I noticed a neighboring camper south of me trying to figure out how to park three pickups on his slab. I went over and invited him to put one on my slab. He did and thanked me. I thanked him for making my camping spot look somewhat normal. Now, if I could only get a boat trailer and some kids, I'd look just like everyone else. Some people arrived in air-conditioned RVs with satellite dishes so as not to miss their favorite TV shows. Some strung up colored lights, just like Christmas. It looked festive–noisy, but festive.

I got out my copy of *Zen and Motorcycle Maintenance,* switched on the battery-operated reading lamp and tried to read. Impossible. After awhile, I switched it off and just lay there listening to folks getting settled. The next thing I knew, morning arrived with a vengeance. Up and at 'em–the morning bugle call, telling us all to hurry because the week-end would soon be gone–and not to lose a single moment. Motors started in the boats to make sure they would start. The training wheel kid was plowing up the road in front of my tent.

I sat up, fully awake, heeding the summons–to do what? I unzipped my tent door and looked out. Not a cloud in the sky–no rain today. I got dressed–it was the least I could do to join in.

A dead oak tree would provide my only shade until noon, in the afternoon an elm with lots of leaves would take over–just as I planned. The sun bounced off the dead branches of the oak just enough to provide the morning warmth I liked. In the afternoon, the elm would block the sun completely and a cool breeze would waft around me. What an expert camper.

On the agenda: visit the swimming beach just around the point and bike over to the park store to get food. I think I picked up a chigger last night or at Proctor Lake the day before. I watched a pickup driver backing a boat-ladened trailer between two stumps. Good job.

A multi-colored hot-air balloon crossed the lake barely above the water, its gas jets firing great blasts. As it neared the edge of the lake a sustained blast raised it lazily and safely above the sharp-pointed trees. To my left a fishing dock sticking ten feet up from the water held two early-bird fishermen concentrating on the bobbing corks below.

An ample man walked by from the bath house, freshly showered, clad in a red swim suit, a large fluffy towel draped around his bare shoulders. He smelled of after shave and talcum powder. He sported a two-inch damp ponytail. His great white body jelloed its way along the park road. Tonight that body would be red and proud of it. All around me, the laughter and squeals of children and the happy yapping of dogs filled the air. The lake seethed with boats and skiers. I put on my swim shorts, packed up my ruck sack with sandals, water, a can of tomatoes, a can of refried beans and some crackers. I added my writing materials and a book–hoisted the bag onto my naked back and headed for the swimming beach where I found a vacant and shaded picnic table. Soon, a boy and a girl who rode the bicycles around my tent, approached. After all, I rode a bike too, so in their eyes, I was one of them. The eight year-old blonde wanted to know if I had a wife. I said no and that I was free to do whatever I liked.

"And what God tells you to do," she responded. She recounted the story of a surfer who had been lost on the east coast during Hurricane Emily.

"He didn't do what God told him to do," she said soberly. The boy, also eight, but smaller than the girl, and quite eager to have her as his girlfriend, shook his head affirmatively. They had met yesterday.

"Is she your girlfriend?" I asked him. Too quick for him, she answered.

"No. I'm a girl and he's a friend," and laughed. I thought of the many years that poor boy would have to go through trying to out talk and out think women. Not giving up, however, the boy straightened narrow shoulders and came forth with a tale of his own.

"There was a boy last year who drownded right here in this lake. He went under and drownded. Out there where it's really deep. He drownded all the way to the bottom." For a moment he had her attention.

"When they found him all that was left was bones." The girl wanted to know if I were an Indian.

Back at my campsite, I settled down to spy on my neighbors some more. Across the road pickups had been coming and going with regularity. New people showed up and left. Others took their place. Some returned. The original campers included a young gregarious husband with a generous waist, his red-headed wife and two or three children. Loud rough talking meant to be funny, I supposed, ricocheted off my dead oak tree. One of the newcomers addressed one of the children:

"Listen, punk, don't mess with me, I'll tear your head off, get it kid?" Raucous laughter met this show of macho brain power. Two of the women, both platinum blondes, blared away with their cigarette voices at one another, at the men, at the kids.

On my side of the road and one space away a couple in their 40s paid them no mind. They had a boy about four, one about six and two girls aged eight and ten. In the afternoon the husband left on an errand. The mother put the boys in a small tent unprotected from the sun while the girls got a larger one in the shade. The mother sat under a tarp stretched between two trees which shaded her and sipped on a soda. It was nap time. The girls giggled and practiced head stands. The boys scuffled, whined and announced they wanted out.

"We don't want to take a nap—it's too hot in here."

"If you don't go to sleep right now, you know what I'm gonna do? I'm gonna kill you." A few minutes later, again to the whimpering boys:

"Oh you have broken the zipper on the tent—when your father comes back he will kill you for sure. You will go home dead boys. I'm gonna get my belt and you'll be sorry. Go to sleep or no hot dogs or marshmallows or swimming later. You hear?"

When the father came back to the camp, nothing happened. Immediately, the boys and the girls left their tents. The dreaded consequences of the returning father melted away. The younger boy wanted a soda.

"You've already had one—this one's mine," said the mother.
Night came on. Across the way, angry voices pierced the air with many references to and about body apertures and what you could do to them. Some strident voices called upon the Deity to damn this one and that one. Curses swirled around our end of the park like so much backed up sewage. This was the second night—one to go and Monday night wouldn't come soon enough for me.

Recriminations, threats and accusations continued unabated in the darkness. Finally, truck doors opened and slammed shut, engines started, roaring the disapproval of the offended. Two, maybe three, pickups took off. Over the rumble of engines I heard:

"You drunk 12 bottles of my f—— Coors Lite." Answered by:

"I don't drink f—— Coors Lite." As the truck sounds receded, things quieted down until 2 a.m. when a load of visitors arrived to join the couple and their children behind me. A new language awakened me.

"Glory be to God, God Bless and Thank the Lord, Praise Jesus' name." followed by murmured "Amens." Finally, we all went to sleep.

In the morning the women behind me had put on dresses and one of the new visitors stood in front of the small group, preaching away. After a few minutes of exhortations, two hymns ascended to the leafy canopy, shakily at first, but soon grew in volume and confidence. A thoroughly humbled young husband from across the way came over to my tent and said how sorry he was for all the commotion last night–especially he felt bad because of the religious folk having to listen to it. I told him not to worry. Life was life. We talked for awhile and he said he hoped he could go back to school some day and get a real education–maybe be a pilot. We went back together to his picnic table and sampled left overs. Turned out, his wife had invited a bunch of her relatives to come by and he hadn't appreciated it.

"I should never have invited them to come see us–you treated them like sh–." I took a sip of coffee. The wife walked around the picnic table and confronted her husband at close range as he spread some butter on a piece of biscuit.

"You made fun of my family. My sister knew what she did was wrong–you didn't have to rub her nose in it like a dog's face in sh–." I had been eyeing a dark brown sausage patty and decided to pass. In the silence that followed, I offered advice.

"Try not to make up with your in-laws until after Christmas–you'll save a bundle on Christmas cards and gifts."
They both laughed and the tension eased. I left while I was ahead.

The two kids I talked to yesterday rode up on their bikes. We talked bike stuff for awhile–number of gears, how to climb hills, how far I had ridden. Bob, the boy, said he would like to ride across the country some day. Brandi, the girl, gave me the impression she had a greater interest in Bob today. This latest bit of news about his possible future inspired her.

"Me too. That would be really fun–if our parents would let us." We continued our visit, one of many that day. Two eight-years-old and a guy of sixty-five talking as equals and all because we rode bikes.

Later, I pedaled to the park store for a couple of hot dogs and got in a conversation with a woman who had two girls. Slim and with a combed out perm, she informed me of her divorce–that someone killed her father when she was two and that her mother had taken all four children to Mexico where they were marooned on an island for a week existing on snails and scrambled birds' eggs. Other problems plagued her to be passed from generation to generation.

"I keep a journal–it helps."

Back at my tent, two couples, surprisingly, not from Brownwood, invited me over for a cold one. They said they had been discussing me all day.

"We have decided you are either an artist or a writer." Apparently, others, besides me, spied on neighboring campers too.

I received an invitation to dinner from the young fighting couple. "We've got a ton of food since all the relatives left–you might as well help us eat it." We had a good time visiting. The sun went down again spewing colors all over the sky–the last night of condensed bodies had arrived.

In the morning I made the rounds saying my goodbyes. I met Brandi's folks and Bob's grandparents at the other end of the campgrounds.

"So you're the bike rider we been hearin' about." I wondered if Bob was able to turn Brandi from a friend into a girlfriend.
The young couple from across the way said they hoped to see me again and to stop and visit them anytime I came through Brownwood. We exchanged addresses. The husband of the religious family came over and presented me with a diet drink and three cookies.

"My girl Janey made these two and this one's from my wife." I took a picture of the girls and some of their newly made friends. The husband said he would include me in his prayers when he got back home. I thanked him.

Everyone hurried–packing up. One by one, the pickups hauling dripping ski boats bumped out of the park to the highway–to home and to work the next day. Sundown witnessed a nearly empty park. The trash barrels overflowed with napkins, empty beer cans and soda cans, punctured inner tubes, boxes and paper plates and a worn-out swim suit or two. Silence spread across the lake. I could hear the waves breaking on the shore again. At last I would have my solitude at Lake Brownwood–what I had been waiting for–yearning for. I took a sip of my diet drink and nibbled a cookie, the wife's, I thought. Actually, the weekend hadn't been half-bad. Not half-bad at all. To tell the truth I was a little lonesome.

## On to the Cemetery
(Summer Tour 1993)

A few miles south of Brownwood I came across a marker which pointed down a side road as the place where Katherine Anne Porter was buried. So, I hung a left and entered one of the most quiet rides I have ever had. Absolutely no traffic. I pedaled up to a couple of men working on a fence and we talked and laughed for some distance after I went by. They wanted me to stop and help. I called out that I'd be glad to except my brakes didn't work.

Several miles went by and no cemetery. Also, no more signs. Down the road I saw a man standing by his mailbox. Since it was so quiet, I called out while still several hundred feet away, so as not to startle him. I startled him. I asked about the cemetery and he gave me directions. He said he and his wife used to live in Colorado, but wanted something secluded, so had bought this place.

"And it's really quiet–except in the fall–then it's hunting season in the fields over there," pointing across the road.

236

"Blam. Blam. All day. Real estate agent forgot to mention hunting season, but we still like it."

At last I saw the cemetery as I topped a small hill. Situated on a rise with a commanding view, fenced and gated, the well-kept Indian Creek cemetery appeared as the epitome of peace and quiet. Entering, I judged about two hundred grave markers and monuments dotted the golden grass cover. How would I find Katherine Anne Porter's? I walked down toward the center, turned right for fifty feet and picked out an obelisk. It belonged to her mother. A simple upright granite slab rested next to it with Katherine Anne Porter carved on it along with the dates: May 15, 1890 - Sept. 18, 1980. Below the dates: "In my end is my beginning." A slight breeze rustled through the dry prairie grass. In the distance the hills, layered in ever lighter shades of blue, provided a frame for this country painting. The few trees wore the mottled brown and yellow dress of a Texas autumn. The seeds of wild flowers waited patiently in the ground for next spring and the renewal of life. I felt certain Katherine Anne Porter renewed her life by planting a memory in me and in others who have visited her in this prairie cemetery. I promised Ms. Porter I would read her stories and her novel, *The Ship of Fools*, again when I got back to Austin. And I did.

# *Coming Home*
## (The Five Texas Tours 1993 (2), 1994, 1995, 1996)

All my tours ended in Austin. I rode up to the front door of my apartment at the conclusion of each one. This chapter will attempt to capture my experiences of each of those final days of "coming home" again.

An exception will be the coming home from the Great Plains tour. I want to hold that back until I visit those plains again. The final days contained a mix of emotions simplistically stated as "glad this tour is over and sad this tour is over."

While on the road I missed my close friends terribly–I could hardly wait to see them again. I missed my bed–normal food–movies, concerts, plays, discussion groups–even dressing up. While at home I missed the challenge of facing Mother Nature–the excitement of every new day–the sense of freedom and discovery inherent in the open road.

238

Powerful emotions drew me homeward. Powerful emotions voted to stay gone forever. All my tours ended with an uneven ambivalence weighted sometimes in favor of home and sometimes in favor of the road, but both were always present.

## Returning from the First Tour
(July 6- Sep 15, 1993- 72 days- 1,816 miles)

*September 15, 1993*

The wine tasted great at the Fall Creek Vineyards, owned by Ed and Susan Auler, friends who lived in Austin and commuted to their state-of-the-art vineyard and winery. At a later date I helped "stomp" the grapes at one of their open house wine celebrations. Children especially had a good time watching their legs turn purple. Down the road in Tow, I camped on the north edge of Lake Buchanan–the largest of the Colorado River lakes that stretch northwest of Austin. The first night a giant wind and rain storm came across the lake and slammed into my tent. It was a wild night and since, by that time, I had been in a few storms, I relaxed and read while my tent had conniptions. The mercury retreated the next day to 55 degrees.

I walked around meditating, soaking up my surroundings, knowing that the next day would be my next to last day on this tour. My plan: to ride into Austin in two days, staying overnight at Marble Falls. In the late afternoon I just watched and listened. The leaves danced in the trees. The wind whistled through the branches–I heard the lapping of the lake onto the beach–dogs barking–birds calling. I had nothing to do. No pressure. I walked out on the shore looking for a piece of driftwood I could take back to Austin. The sunlight turned golden. I could feel a sense of melancholy invading my heart.

The town of Tow catered to fisherfolk and others who enjoyed being near a good-sized lake. At seven on September 15th I packed my tent for the last time and boarded my faithful companion. My bike carried me all the way to Austin, arriving at my apartment by four–

almost 85 miles and a day early. The temperature at Tow in the early morning–50 degrees. When I left Austin on July 6, it had been hot, hot, hot. I stopped in Burnet for breakfast: biscuits, gravy, omelet with everything they could stuff in it, hash browns and coffee. I waited until I arrived in Austin to eat again.

Arriving in Marble Falls too early to stay at the motel–I decided to go on. My friends planned to meet me the next day on the bridge I had crossed on July 6 pedaling for the first time out of town. I looked for another motel on my way in to Austin. None. So, I continued pedaling. In the cool weather, the miles sped by. My legs didn't get tired at all as I raced south.

A cyclist joined me on Bee Cave Road about eight miles before the Austin city limits and we rode together almost to my apartment. He asked a thousand questions about the trip. Inside my apartment that had been silent for 72 days, I sat down, looked around and began calling all my friends. "Guess what! Yeah, I'm a day early. Had a great time–glad to be home."

I went out to my driveway and began unloading the bike. I fixed my own dinner of rice and soup and ate alone. I felt a lot of different emotions that evening. The trip was over and I had actually ridden my bike all the way to Pecos and back. I couldn't get over it. I felt ecstatic one moment and depressed the next. What would I do next? I had no idea. At first, there had been the desire to cross the country. Maybe I would do that. The trial ride had been a success. Almost 2,000 miles! Wow. I touched my sun-bleached panniers, my equipment.

My bike looked as if it were ready to go again, it had borne me up and down hills without complaint. After unloading everything, I brought the bike inside where it took up its place near my bed. Tomorrow it would get a bath, a polish and a good oiling and then we would go together to breakfast. My car. Sold. Would I buy another? I didn't know. Too many questions to answer. I stayed awake a long time that night–wondering, remembering, realizing things were different now. Tomorrow I would see my friends again.

## Returning from the Second Tour
(Nov 19- Dec 30, 1993- 42 days- 1,290 miles)

*December 30, 1993*

While still away from Austin, I made a list of recommendations to myself. My first note indicated how I felt toward the end of that winter tour.

"I am really glad I don't have to camp anymore on this trip."

In the summer I faced the heat, ants, and other insects. In the winter I faced the cold and too many hours in the tent. On the plus side–no ants or other insects. I decided I needed a larger tent so my bicycle could be brought inside. I wanted a better light and if I toured in the winter again I had to have some sort of heat lantern I could use to warm my hands as I put the tent up and took it down. I shivered when I thought of that tent ice-encrusted. I wanted a better bed too, especially in winter when the nights were longer. Next time I must have a chair–with a back. Apparently as the list grew I realized I would be taking more tours. I just didn't know where or when. The traveling bug had bit.

On December 30, I got up at six-thirty. Ate the same kind of country breakfast I had at the end of the first tour. It was colder than I expected so I donned a ski mask and goggles as well as thermal underwear beneath my riding clothes. I had spent the night in a motel in Goldthwaite northwest of Austin. The hills seemed unusually numerous and steep and I had a hard time with them. They slowed me down so much I became concerned about reaching home. My funds were low and I didn't think there would be an ATM handy. Small towns were just beginning to put them in. I made another note not to enter Austin that way again. At a stop for a snack, a clerk told me about a cutoff I could take over to Georgetown. There, I could use the access road beside I-35 into Austin.

Six miles out of Georgetown, darkness descended. The nights came quickly on short winter days. I rode into town with my lights on

241

and tried to keep out of the way of rush hour traffic–a hectic experience. Riding in heavy traffic in the dark, not knowing how well I showed up in the headlights of overtaking cars and trucks–feeling the cold coming again–not pleasant, not pleasant at all. I pedaled and stayed as close to the edge on the automobile-filled four-lane city street as I could. No shoulders, no bike lanes. Wide storm drain gratings? I hoped not. I gritted my teeth more than once as the cars moved around me, too close, I thought, although I felt they did the best they could. Not a bicycle street. I held up traffic, but no one honked. Perhaps inside those warm cars, they pitied that cold cyclist. I thought about staying at a motel, but the prices this close to Austin were for more than I had with me. I had to ride on home. First, I had to face the bridge across the river. The access road ended at the water. I had to pedal up on I-35, perhaps one of the most traffic-choked interstate highways in the country. Trash, including bricks, rocks and bottles littered the narrow area I had to ride in. Cars and trucks only four or five feet away roared past me at highway speeds. My bike hit a brick, but never wavered. What a bike. It had never faltered in over 3,000 miles at that point and I knew it wouldn't let me down now. Mercifully, the bridge ended and I found the access road again.

At times the access road dipped below I-35 to such an extent that my pavement pitched into total darkness. My headlight dimmed. The batteries gave up. Even with fresh batteries, my bike light could not match the oncoming blinding headlights and tall floodlights that made the interstate bright as day–and all else as black as midnight at the bottom of an ocean. It seemed as though I were in that cold black ocean. I heard the crunch of gravel and knew I had lost my pavement. I stopped and got off, walking ahead with my small camping flash light and shielding my eyes against the glare of the interstate. Not more that five yards directly in front of me there yawned a giant open storm drain several feet across and several feet deep. If I had not stopped, I bet I would have hurt my helmet. I continued to walk in places where the glare of the highway plunged the access road into a black void. As I got closer to Austin, I was able to see better. No longer did I have to stop and feel my way through a black pocket. My spirits lightened and I began humming and thinking about stopping for a hamburger. I rode south on Lamar boulevard and I did stop and I did have that hamburger. I wasn't even cold although the temperature had fallen below freezing. I knew that without looking at my gauge because I had some ice cream in my back pack and it stayed frozen.

I got home to my apartment by ten-thirty. Tomorrow would be New Year's Eve. I had ridden 110 miles that day, actually pedaling eleven hours of the over 15 hours on the road. Forty of those miles had been on busy city streets and highways after dark. Beginning to relax in my now warming apartment, I picked up the phone and dialed a few friends. It was wonderful being home and hearing their welcoming voices. Settling down on my bed I read my mail, which included a nice stack of Christmas cards. Into my back pack I rummaged for the ice cream. It tasted really good.

### Returning from the Third Tour
(Mar 29- Aug 3, 1994- 128 days- 3,937 miles)

*August 3, 1994*

The perimeter tour which formed the main narrative of this book, neared its end. I had camped at Ozona and readied myself for the ride into Austin. One small and pleasant detour remained.

I rode to Kerrville from Ozona on I-10 then turned south instead of north to Austin and home. Obviously, I didn't want to go home yet, although I had been gone four months. The ride to Medina was through gentle valleys and tree-covered hills–surely one of the most scenic areas of Texas. Tom and Barbara Fuller arranged a festive party with friends from surrounding ranches and San Antonio.

We watched the stars from their extensive deck with its swimming pool that stretched out over the crystal-clear Medina River forty feet below. Later, after my tours, I returned to house-sit their dramatic home and to feed the wild mustangs Barbara kept across the road. In the back of this book in the poetry section I tried to put into words how I felt about that experience.

Also after the tours I rode back to that area, near Utopia, for one of my several visits with Donna Edgeman at her Pennyloafer Farm. She and Larry Edgeman are two of my closest friends. On a bright and sunny winter's morning bundled on the porch drinking that first cup of hot coffee or at night, grouped about a glowing pot-bellied stove sipping wine and telling stories or taking a quick dip on a dare in the ice-cold Sabinal River, these and other wonderful moments made my visits into wonderful memories. One Christmas was especially meaningful.

I left Medina and camped five miles east of Bandera. The oak trees formed a solid canopy of leaves over me where I set up the tent. One more night after that and I would be back in Austin. I could see the surrounding hills between the trunks of the trees. In effect I had a beautiful natural house in which to dwell that night.

In the morning, the clouds appeared smoky. The sun blazed burnt orange and the sky turned lavender, purple, pink and orange. I left my campground at 7:30. At Pipe Creek I saw a small cafe with dozens of hanging plants arranged across a veranda. I couldn't pass by. So, breakfast was ordered and soon the bacon and pancakes arrived with plenty of coffee. A couple more stops and I arrived at the rest area south of New Braunfels on I-35. The restroom facilities were closed for construction and a line of Porta-Potties took their place. I pitched my tent on the grass next to one of the covered picnic tables.

I had drifted off to sleep when a voice awakened me.

"You can't camp here." Groggy with sleep, I looked out the back mesh window of my tent and saw a man squatting right next to it.

"What?" The statement was repeated as my brain began to click on a few switches.

"You can't camp here."

I said that I usually did not camp on the grass, but on the concrete apron of the covered picnic area when I realized I was

244

coming face to face with the no camping–no erecting of any structure–unless you have a permit–ordinance.

"Oh yes," I said, "I know what you mean. I can't erect a tent unless I have a permit. Well, I have a permit." A moment of silence. "I never heard of anyone getting a permit." I explained how I had received permission from the Department of Transportation's Tourist Office to camp in any rest area in the state at my discretion. I named the official who had given me permission (unofficially). I asked the security guard's name and complimented him on being the only one in the state of Texas who had questioned me. I told him about writing a book about my travels and that I would put him in it. We became friends. I forgot to write down his name.

Early next morning I headed north to Austin. I rode the access road beside I-35 to the Austin city limits and eventually got on the Hike and Bike Trail which came very close to my apartment. I entered the front door at one-thirty that afternoon. I couldn't call anyone. My phone had been disconnected. I sat down, turned on the TV and had a snack. I could have stayed on the road a lot longer I thought. I had fourteen flats on that trip.

## Returning from the Fourth Tour
(Oct 28- Nov 12, 1995- 16 days- 697 miles)

*November 12, 1995*

On this tour I had my new hip and it felt fantastic. On the next to last day I stayed in a motel with quite reasonable rates only to learn later that trucks had a habit of crashing into it since it sat at a highway dead-end. No trucks got me that night. I was more concerned with the wide space at the bottom of the door. Surely it was too cold for varmints to be out.

On the last day I would have only 65 or 70 miles to reach home. The temperature sank into the 20s at night and up to the 40s during the day. Good riding weather. I used my regular bicycle shorts, short-sleeved riding shirt with a thermal undershirt and fingerless gloves. It was chilly, but invigorating. Everyone I met bundled up with only their eyes showing.

At the motel I scarfed down my last two tins of sardines. I also had two oranges, two fried apple pies, a can of refried beans and a quart of buttermilk with crackers. I wondered if I would miss my eclectic menu once I got home. Nope.

When I left the next morning the temperature hovered at 35 degrees. I put on more clothes for awhile, but the constant pedaling warmed me up after about 8 miles. My spirits were high and I sort of ate my way into Austin that day.

One little cafe typified the laid back acceptance of strangers and locals into one family gathering. In one booth two guys were conversing in Spanish at times, laughing and talking in English, too, with the other customers. Behind me a grizzled white man was playing a video game with a middle-aged black woman. They teased each other about the other's ineptness. There was the typical good 'ol boy joshing a heavy-set black man about a boat.

"You'll never buy that boat. You're too heavy. Three hundred pounds at least."

"I don't weigh a pound over two fifty." A cowboy type with a large western straw hat, jeans, black boots and red satin wind-breaker jacket joined in the fun. Another man piped up at the black woman playing the arcade game.

"You're not the gambler your brother is." Laugh.

"I just play for fun." They asked me about my trip and to be really careful on the highway. We sat around drinking the weak coffee. It was only twenty cents a cup. I went on down the street and had another breakfast.

At lunch time I rolled into Taylor and decided on Mekeska's Barbeque restaurant. In the room next to the dining room I could hear a keyboard playing "San Antonio Rose" and "Have I Told You Lately That I Love You?" Those were followed by others all in the same key and rhythmic beat. I stopped listening and ate my great chopped beef sandwiches. On down the road I stopped in at Rice's Crossing and bought some cheese. The store would soon be gone. Moved to another location if funds could be raised because of its historical value.

I finally made it to Highway 290 east of Austin. The wind was now at my side and no problem. Traffic was. At one narrow bridge I had to wait for a lull in the line of cars and trucks before I dared cross it. Absolutely no extra room—not even to walk. Traffic whizzed by at 70 miles per hour. I waited thirty minutes. I raced the sun to my apartment and just made it. I thought it was darker, but I had forgotten to remove my sunglasses. I was glad to be home. My apartment looked and felt terrific.

### Returning from the Fifth Trip
(Jan 28- Feb 10, 1996- 14 days- 706 miles)

February 10, 1996

I had stopped at a Food Mart on the beltway around San Antonio for a snack before proceeding up I-35 to Austin. As I got up to pay, an attractive young woman insisted on paying for me and wanted to talk. We sat in a booth while I told of some of my experiences. It was her birthday and she had just left a party held in her honor by some of her women friends. She lived in New Braunfels and when she found out I planned to camp there as I had before, she insisted I stay the night with her and her husband. When I arrived in New Braunfels and called, she gave me directions to her home. She had just called her husband who worked in Austin and told him she had met this nice biker and had invited him/me to spend the night.

Just as I reached the driveway, the husband pulled in and jumped out of his car.

"You're not a serial killer are you?" When he had received the telephone call from his wife, he had raced home breaking the speed limit, his imagination working overtime. When everyone settled down and I had assured the husband that I was "safe," they took me to dinner, invited friends to come over, and we had a really good time. I got to play my harmonica. What a neat way to end a trip. But, I had one more warming experience awaiting me.

As I pedaled into Austin and stopped at a busy intersection, a new SUV filled with a family pulled up beside me. In a melodious Spanish accent, I heard, "Welcome to Texas."

Once I began my tours in Texas, I found the history of the state riveting. I am sure that growing up in Indiana, I learned something about the history of my birth state, but all I seemed to remember was the nick-name "hoosier" and that Johnny Appleseed had passed through near the dawn of history scattering seeds–which was why we had an apple tree on our front lawn.

Texas was different. Texans fought a foreign power and became a nation in its own right–the only state to do so. The struggle for Texas independence has been a highlight in the history lessons at all Texas schools. I still collect the facts, the maybe facts, the stories and legends that make up the proud heritage of my adopted land. Texas means family. Now, I have friends not only at home, but all over the state. I'm also glad Mother Nature ain't my mom.

I biked every day while living in Austin. In the fall of 2002 I biked to Wimberley south of Austin–an all day ride to talk with a publisher at a book fair about this story. If you're reading it, I was successful. For Thanksgiving, I rode to Oklahoma to visit part of my family. A round trip of only a 1,000 miles–but a tour! I had a few sore muscles and lots of turkey.

I liked being with some of my grandchildren, my former wife, my daughter and son-in-law so much I decided to move to Oklahoma–a few days before Christmas, 2002, to finish up my present writing projects. I plan to do some touring in Oklahoma while I'm there. In a year or so, I'll be back exploring the Great Plains again! Come with me!

## The Bawdy and Romantic Scenes
## from a Stalled Texas Novel

On one of my trips, I camped out in the Palo Duro Canyon alongside the famed Prairie Dog Town Fork of the Red River–the same fork that Chief Quanah Parker and his Antelope band of Comanches camped near before being surprised by Colonel Ranald Mackenzie and his troops in 1874. Leaving the canyon, I chanced to meet a romance writer in Canyon City. I got one of her highly rated novels and I thought it was pretty neat. Later, I read a novel by a great western writer, and I thought that was pretty neat too. Could I write like those guys? Don't I wish. That's why my novel is stalled. Nevertheless, I continued reading, ingesting and digesting Texas history. Maybe some day I'll get after that novel in earnest. I did do a couple of scenes and I do have the entire book blocked out. It covers three generations of Texans and includes the Revolution, the Indians, the Civil War, interracial marriage, bigotry and acceptance–even a ravenous Mexican ant hill. I mean, we're talking big novel here–a giant. Maybe I should take to my bed in a cork-lined room as did

Marcel Proust and scribble my own search for time lost.

Under the influence of the western writer's strong and gritty style, I wrote a camp scene where the hero, seventeen-year-old, Robert Bullaque, was part of a volunteer army under Stephen F. Austin in the late fall of 1835. The volunteers were camped outside

ALIBATES FLINT

San Antonio de Bexar for seven weeks with a dwindling force that had begun with over 800 eager adventurers and believers while the officers decided when, or if, to attack the Mexican army holed up within the city's fortified walls. The volunteer Texans were strong-willed, rowdy and often entertained the idea of leaving since no fighting seemed imminent. Gathering around the fires at night in groups, they whiled away their time listening to ribald stories which would lighten the prevailing gloom enough for them to stay another day. November became December and some of those days and nights were getting cold–so, story, fire, coffee and perhaps something from a hidden keg bound them together, but not for much longer. Indeed, in a few days, following this scene, our hero mounted his horse and headed back toward his plantation home in Louisiana, just two days before the fight for San Antonio finally took place ending with victory for the Texans and setting the stage for the battle of the Alamo when Santa Anna arrived in the early spring of 1836 to take San Antonio back.

The scene: the volunteer army camp outside the walls of San Antonio de Bexar–tents pitched far enough away so the balls from the Mexican muskets can't reach. It is the very end of November and there's a rumor that the army will attack soon, but that's been heard before.

To pretend that what I have written comes anywhere near the superb prose of the western writer I had read is ludicrous. But amateurs have to begin somewhere. The same is true about the "true" romance style of an award winning romance writer. To think that I could write a romantic scene as powerful as the ones she turned out is the height of presumption. I ask all romance writers to forgive and, if possible, forget. But, hey, Rome wasn't written in a day.

ଓଃ         ଓଃ         ଓଃ

Over the small yellow fire, a blackened pot swayed, held by two pair of sticks tied together to form two Xs. Each X was planted firmly in the ground on either side of the fire and cradled between them a defective ramrod spanned the flames. From the middle of the ramrod hung the pot filled with bubbling water turning brown from the crushed coffee beans dancing on the bottom.

Five volunteers, four young and one in his late 30s huddle in close, the light from the fire flickering across their wind burned cheeks and noses. One has on greasy-black buckskin, another, trousers made of sail cloth, stiff from the cold. One wraps a shawl blanket about him, a jorongo, he took that morning from the local tejanos–as well as two chicken eggs and a plump chicken. Each one an individual in mind as well as in clothing, thought Robert Bullaque, sitting apart and thinking about heading home.

"Back to home by Christmas," he whispers to himself and picks up his long rifle. It seems to him he cleaned it at least a hundred times in the last few days. His sun-browned hand slips easily along the striped maple stock with the intricate silver inlays. The gun was his father's going away gift when he said he was leaving for Texas to fight in the war of independence. His father tried to talk him out of it, but Robert was adamant.

"Wonder what he'll say when I come riding home?" He didn't care. He was sick of camping out here in the wind and the rain and now the cold–looking at those damn walls.

The people's army. It sounded so grand at the time. A chance for adventure, maybe even for some cash. A few days ago most everyone left camp to intercept a Mexican column with pack animals–silver they thought–headed for San Antonio to pay the army inside. The packs were captured and opened. Just grass inside. Grass. To feed the horses in the city. What a joke.

This whole thing was turning into a big joke. He turns sideways to see the moon rising, quietly, indifferently. Robert rubs the barrel of the long rifle, which already glistens.

The laughter from the fire signals the yarns are beginning. Usually old Tom held the younger men in rapt attention detailing another of his supposed exploits with women. Tonight would be no exception. Robert listens, too.

"I slipped in. It was might near midnight. Just like we agreed. There she was on the bed with nary a stitch on. Like a creamy white plucked chicken–just layin' there waitin'."

"How'd you know she's naked with nothin' on if it was dark and midnight?"

"There was a moon, sap head, just like tonight," and Tom waves his arm toward the east.

Then after a moment's hesitation, "purtiest moon you ever did see." The others around the fire stare hard at the questioner who dared interrupt.

"Get on with it, Tom, what happened," they plead, eager as kids watching a juicy watermelon divided up.

"Well, there she was. Kind of spare, but invitin' none the less. I took off my trousers and she commenced to dodgin' this way and that and all the time gigglin', I swear, I couldn't get home. Ever time I tried, she'd squirm away. After about three or four minutes that seemed like an hour to me, I was really gettin' het up. I thought I'd pop for sure. Then she stopped all of a sudden to listen to a fool mockin' bird outside the winder, and when she did that I jumped in with both feet, you might say. Like ramming home a double charge in ol' Betsy." Lots of sighing can be heard from the listeners.

"Well, her head kind of jerked back and her eyes rolled up into her head and her eyeballs looked all white, and there was kind of a low cryin' goin' on way back in her throat. I'm tellin' you boys, it was really somethin'." Choking and clearing of throats circle the fire. Nobody says anything.

"But that's not the dangdest thing about it." Here Tom pauses to take a good gulp of coffee from his tin cup. Four bodies sit like marble statues, hardly daring to breathe, lest they upset Tom and he won't go on. He did it once before and they learned to keep quiet, which is what they would do tonight, no matter how long he swallowed on that coffee.

"Well, I no sooner got in there, right up to the hilt, you might say, when she grabbed me with them skinny legs–I'd call 'em spider legs. She grabbed me with them spider legs and wrapped 'em around me and hog tied me so I couldn't get loose even if I'd wanted to–and I didn't want to." Legs around the fire fidget and sounds of great approval fall out of every mouth.

"Well, she commenced to rockin' and rockin' till you'd think I'd got sea sick. But instead, I was buildin' up like a volcano and finally I couldn't hold it any longer and I exploded like an 18 pounder loaded with too much powder. I swear I bet they coulda heard me all the way to the church house."

The boys pound each other on the back and slap their legs, spilling their coffee, but they don't seem to mind. After things settle down again–they can't resist.

"Then what?" they yell.

Another sip of coffee and a clearing of the throat.

"Well, I tried to collect myself a little. Got untangled and I was just layin' there gettin' my breath back when I heard a noise on the porch. It was her big bug husband comin' back afore sunup from huntin'. I come to life purty quick believe you me. I followed my pants out that winder and cut dirt outa there faster than a jackass rabbit."

"Did you get away?"

"I shore did–I'm here ain't I?"

More slapping and laughing and back pounding. Then a hidden jug appears and some welcome corn juice makes the rounds.

Shaking his head, Robert smiles in spite of himself. The weariness and discontent of the day was lifted for awhile with this ridiculous tale. "He did tell it good, he did tell it good," he repeats to himself, outside the warming circle of light. By the time he rolled up in his heavy blanket for the few fitful hours before dawn, he knew the smile disappeared. His lips clamp hard again. One more day. One more night. For several moments he stares upward where the top of his tent flaps, hidden in the darkness.

&#x2683;  &#x2683;  &#x2683;

## Some Notes I Made in my Journal Earlier

The overcast sky promised another clammy day, as I crawled out of my tent in east Texas. Today, I would pedal to Goliad. Along the way I would relive the fall of the Alamo, then Colonel James Fannin's defeat near Goliad and the subsequent massacre after surrendering to the advancing Mexican army. I camped on the banks of the San Antonio River–the same river some of Fannin's men had leaped into to escape the firing squad that killed 400. Fannin had requested his watch be sent back to his family, that he be shot in the breast and given a Christian burial. The officer commanding the firing squad pocketed the watch. Fannin was shot through the face and his body burned on a pyre along with the rest of his men. Tonight the frogs sang me to sleep. The next day I visited the site of Fannin's grave. A man standing beside me said, "We're standing on holy ground."

Much later I rode into Nacogdoches just north of the national forests in east Texas. And that is where we pick up our story of Robert Bullaque again–the hero of my novel–although he hasn't acted like a hero yet.

Robert had saddled up and ridden away from San Antonio on December 3, convinced that the city would never be taken. Of course two days later, it was and the Texans prevailed. Too bad for Robert. To make matters worse–on his way to the east Texas border, his black gelding stumbled and threw him. He hit his head on a rock, knocking him out cold. His large unsheathed Bowie knife cut quite a gash in his upper leg and he lost a lot of blood and could have died had it not been so cold. Luckily he was found and brought to Nacogdoches to the home of physician, Dr. William Baille, a transplanted New Yorker. Living with the good doctor was his very attractive niece, 16-year-old Kaye Baille LeCage.

She nursed Robert tenderly, expertly changing the bandage on his leg, using a tent of lint to keep the wound open and draining. Robert got better, but when told of the news of San Antonio he went into a funk. Christmas came and went. Then he reinjured his leg trying to get back on his feet–very stubborn young man. Spring came and he heard of the Alamo's defeat and later the slaughter of Fannin's men at Goliad. He also heard that Sam Houston was getting his army together either to lay over in Louisiana or to attack Santa Anna. Robert made up his mind to join as a permanent volunteer and stay in Texas to fight. It was the least he could do. So by the time Houston broke camp at Groce's farm, Robert was once again fit for battle and ready to ride out on the morrow to join him. This, of course, was upsetting to the niece, who by that time, had come under the spell of the strong-willed and handsome fighter for independence. Robert, too, had been affected in the heart region and although loathe to leave was, nevertheless, determined to reclaim his good name on the field of honor.

I thought I would write the scene where the two lovers were saying goodbye the night before Robert galloped off at break of day. I always like the early dawn hours best to begin my bicycle journeys. Robert was a lot like I am.

In addition, I decided to use the romance novel style. I'll have to make up my mind before I start writing seriously on the novel whether to use more blood and guts passion or highly emotional sexual tension descriptions, guaranteed to cause squirming.

Kaye could not help noticing the top of her bodice tightening. She could feel her nipples crowding against the lacing. She was excited. She was scared. She wanted Robert, tall, handsome, but painfully shy, Robert, to touch her breasts on this last night. She needed to have them fondled, lovingly and lustfully. And she wanted Robert to do it. To do it now. But she knew he wouldn't.

Now that his leg had healed, he would ride south in the morning to join up with Sam Houston's army as a permanent volunteer. Everyone in Nacogdoches knew Houston had spent weeks at Groce's Crossing getting his army in shape and now he was ready to fight at last, despite rumors to the contrary.

Kaye dreaded for Robert to be a part of that. He had been fed up first with Austin and then Burleson at San Antonio for not taking the city. It had been one delay after another. Finally, when Burleson did decide to attack, his officers had said no. Robert wasn't the only one disgusted. Around 200 had ridden or walked away on December 3rd last year. Robert included.

Now it was time to redeem himself–to ease the guilt he felt for turning his back on San Antonio. If General Houston would have him, he would march south to settle things with Santa Anna. "Where has the time gone?" thought Kaye. "I know I've fallen in love with this man–his mind–his spirit." But tonight, she realized there was another demanding force at work in her body. She wanted to be one with him. Kaye could hardly contain herself, but she could not do anything overtly. It would not be lady-like to say simply and honestly, "Please, dear Robert, put your hands on me–on my body. I want you so much. Please, hold me. Please, undo my dress. Take me. Let me feel your strong sun-burned fingers. Please. Please."

No, no matter how much the fever raged inside her, she could never say a word or do anything. No matter how much her heaving breasts, near to exploding, teased her to mouth the words, surely to drown her in the flood waters of love–would send her spiraling out of control in a dizzying dance of desire. "Why is this feeling so insistent–so overpowering? Why can't I think–why can I only feel–and I want to–must–feel more?"

Was it the thought he might be killed and she would never know his love–the feel of his body next to hers? Her brain whirled as in a storm. Kaye bent close to Robert and for just an instant, her bosom, tight as a drum head, brushed against him. A small, helpless sounding cry escaped her lips. She closed her eyes to hide her longing.

Apparently, thinking Kaye was about to faint, Robert reached out awkwardly to steady her. Kaye turned slightly to one side. His hand–his large, gentle, brown-fingered hand–instead of grasping her shoulder, completely surrounded her right breast. It was all Kaye needed. Her hand of its own volition and before she could stop it, came up to cover his and to hold it there just as he was trying to pull free. Kaye's face felt on fire. She knew she must be crimson. She looked Robert straight in the eye and with fierce determination kept his hand where it was. Slowly, ever so slowly, she moved his wonderfully strong fingers around her swelling little hill, while humming in ecstasy.

Robert needed no further urging or instruction. He cupped his hand securely over her virgin, yielding form. Hungrily, Kaye leaned against him, panting as if each breath might be her last. Down deep in her throat, a moan, wild and dark, a sound a million years old, began singing its powerful, unrelenting melody no man could resist. She jerked with a delicious spasm–jerked again–and yet again. Then, to her surprise and shock, she felt her free hand tear at her bodice, pulling away the fragile blue ribbons until her two milky-white and pulsating breasts, quivering with hard pink buds of desire, burst forth, overflowing, into Robert Bullaque's shaking but welcoming hands. He leaned down to kiss those fully erect buds, which waited and yearned for his lips.

୬     ୬     ୬

I don't believe I'll let nature run its course in this scene. Maybe a little more heaving and sighing, fondling and kissing. Kaye has made her point. Surely, Robert is convinced that this fulsome girl with the red ringlets is more than a nurse to him. So, having a monstrous integrity and being aware of the vicissitudes of warfare, I'll have him quote something–maybe in Latin or French–about waiting and that their next meeting will be all the sweeter for it. How about *la patience est a mere, mais son fruit est doux.* Patience is bitter, but its reward is sweet. Perfect. Certainly, he would rather blurt out *Carpe diem!* In the end he will let Kaye make the final decision and, she too, will opt for the wiser course, although she is, by this time, feeling more akin to Mount St. Helens a moment before KABOOM.

Just so you know, Robert made it through the battle at San Jacinto where Santa Anna was defeated and captured. He went back to Kaye as a hero, got the 640 acres the army promised him and they married. That time nature was allowed free reign resulting in three children. I wish I could say that everybody lived happily ever after– but that wouldn't be much of novel would it? I'm not quite certain how it would turn out. Guess I'll just have to write it some day–soon as I figure out the right genre.

## *Moments on the Road*

The following few pages offer a compilation of some of my thoughts as I caught a glimpse of my surroundings while riding or camping. We see, hear, touch, smell and taste so many fleeting experiences in life, but we usually are so preoccupied or pressed for time that the moment comes and goes and is soon forgotten. I tried to keep a notebook handy and would jot down just a word or two to remind me, then when I sat down at the end of the day to work on my journal, those few words would bring those experiences back to me. Sometimes I would put them in some simple poetic form. I especially liked Haiku, even though I did not always follow the rules, for the form allowed an instant photo in words that would be, to me, as indelible and thought provoking as a photo using film. I have used other forms as well. These lines conjure up places, happenings, aspects of nature which may be lost to the readers, for they were not there. Nevertheless, I would like to share some of them. If, for no other reason, but to tempt folks to write down their own. I was fortunate to have Billie Clark, an Austin friend, and Lauren Ide, now living in New Jersey, sharing their poem thoughts with me which kept my muse refreshed and active. We have, when you think about it, only a few moments of what we call life. They should be treasured.

ଔ

When born I had some
Thirty thousand sunrises
And sunsets to see.
Twenty-three thousand have slipped
Away. I search for lost time.
Memories, asleep
Hovering comatosely
Wake up! Talk to me!
Seven thousand sunsets left
Seven thousand sunrises
Each day a treasure
To spend and save completely
A paradox I suppose.

ଔ

I pause to reflect
Life is made of small moments
Accumulated
Shelved for a time
Polished before tucked away.

ଔ

Open up my tent
Startle a squirrel up a tree
But first, nip a flea
Life is filled with great dangers
But an itch must be heeded
A Mayfly bouncing
Against my tent searching for
A mate–bounce! Bouncing!
Legs askew, wings aflutter
Driven by minute passion.
At dusk I heard him
Saw his small mockingbird shape
In a tree with her.
A mockingbird lass–a foot
Away–listening! Waiting!

ભ

Thrice cawing, the crow
A shadow shrouded echo
Seductive rebel
I ache to join its wildness
Some hear only a scoundrel
In the road cold, still
Mouth agape, sprinkled with blood
A 'possum lay dead
Inexperienced youngster?
Or tired-of-dodging oldster?
Indolent orange sun
Overweight, slouching, setting
Behind icy hills
The night comes soon and with it
My beating heart burns the frost.

ભ

ॐ

A dampness today
Heavy, magnifying sounds
An expectancy
The haunting call of a dove
A shriek behind those bushes
Must life be fitful–
A fever–a constant strife
A bubble bursting?
Should there not be times of peace
Cow-like in a green pasture?

ॐ

A common housefly
Sits sprucing, wiping, cleaning
I swat this marvel.
With some guilt I rid the world
Of tiny complexities.

ॐ

Black on black
Perching grackle
Above my
Tent door
In a dead
Tree
Looks this way
And that
Cleans a beak
Ruffles feathers
Waits.

‰

I breathe in and out
Deeper, yet deeper, as I
Ride my wet bike west.
A simple fortunate life
Hemingway's Old Man am I?
The wet wind blusters
Rain drops smack against my face
I like being old.

‰

Eight doves on a wire
Silent gathering watch me
Beneath their cold feet.
A string of gray pearls
Oblong irregular pearls
Fresh water dove pearls
High on a wire they huddle
Wait for the warm neck of spring
Like statues they sit
Gray upon gray against gray
Eight doves on a wire.
A time of waiting, waiting
No nest-building in their minds.

‰

Cold and bright morning
A red-bird sings out of sight
An icicle tune.
He sings for joy, I think.
It's too early for a mate.

On a tip top branch
Leafed in green–a small red flash
Sings: Come mate with me!

ꙮ

Like quicksilver
Rushing here and there
My life appears disappears
In nooks and crannies
Concerned not with destinies
Whether poor or rich
It doesn't matter
I wane I wax
Like the moon now
Slim crescent now
Full and bright
Comes yet the clouds
Some nights.

ꙮ

Cicada buzzing
Deafening its own small ears
Seventeen black years.
Thrust in sunlight and color
Carpe Diem, little bug

ꙮ

Coyotes off-key
In the half-light of the dawn
Welcome a weak sun
Out of sight beyond a hill
A furry choir rehearses
Coyote music
Discordant notes to my ears
Nature's harmony
Listen to the melodies
No major chords just magic.

అ

Only God can make
Trees–broken in winter storms
Who made all that ice?
Sometimes God has a tough time
Fulfilling expectations.

అ

Impudent flower
Squeezing through the concrete road
Budding bravado!
Braggart blossom–how dare you
Show me the impossible?

అ

In my heart there hums this siren song
My bonds are loosed–I'm free to go
The steam train whistle sounds soft and long
In my heart there hums this siren song
The cry of the loon from a secluded pond

A narrow country road snaking to and fro
In my heart there hums this siren song
My bonds are loosed–I'm free to go

ം

The moon is too bright
Hanging in the sky like that
And I am too cold
Staring at the stars
I blow my breath in the air
My private night cloud
I hold in my breath
No sound comes from moon or stars
Now no sound from me.

ം

Mud cakes my tires and
I steer my bike into a
Big puddle–so neat.
Then, I notice a
Man getting out of his truck
Swinging a ghost bat.
I didn't get wet and he
Just imagined a baseball
Were we kids again
And for a moment finding
Distant memories?
He was fifty or sixty
And I was seventy-three.

ം

Heavy headed fields
Green sturdy stalks turned to straw
Brassy seas breaking
Sun-burned wheat ripe and bursting
Brightly packaged soon as loaves
Bowing heads sun-baked
Whispering supplications
Golden field of wheat
A fragile congregation
Hear their prayers, O God of Bread

଼ଓ

A chorus of leaves
Whispering their canticles
Dispossessed spirits
Worshipers of summer
Squeezed free to roam the autumn
Sycamore brown leaves
Tick tock on brittle edges
In front of my bike.

଼ଓ

Single silken thread
The night spider leaves behind
It shines in the sun
I watch it float out of reach
Then out of sight. Wait for me!

଼ଓ

It is midnight dark
I hear a wild bird calling
Such a small lost sound
I lie awake listening
We are both alone tonight.

ೞ

My face is aching
I am smiling at the cold
Winter is no womb
To breathe the fierce wind is good
In this moment I am strong.

ೞ

Against the storm clouds
Ink-like and filled with thunder
Birds soar unafraid
Small and white in that tempest
Wild and free I see them yet.
Aflame with red rust
They stand rooted to the banks
Autumn cypresses
Whispering to each other
In a language I don't know.

ೞ

Ticks and flies
Ants and fleas
Gnats and chiggers
Poison Ivy also
And don't forget
That damn mosquito
Poems I make are kind of rough
But only God makes that other stuff.

ℭℨ

Raindrops. Pop! Pop! On
My rain hood. Raindrops stinging my
Chilled face to numbness
Rain drops hanging from
Darkened branches like gem eyes
Blink and wink at me.
Watching each other, they wait
For gravity's selection.

ℭℨ

On the brown sand beach
Wetted with soapy brown seas
Dried by mustard skies
Home to brown pelicans' cries
Here, I walk with my brown dreams.
The brown sand stretches
Along and into brown seas
Under brass brown skies
Galveston Island, Texas
Where only sea gulls are white.

ℭℨ

∝

Purring vibrato
Hidden in autumn's dusk
An owl calls.      Listen!

∝

Softly the dusk puts the valley to bed
Covers the hills–enfolds the flowers
Night eyes stare! Night ears listen!
Food for some–no dawn for others
Covers the hills–enfolds the flowers
Shadows and rustlings and gossiping voices
Food for some–no dawn for others
Soon a moon shining and silent
Shadows and rustlings and gossiping voices
A rabbit screams–a coyote howls
Soon a moon shining and silent
Off in the distance someone is singing.
Softly the dusk puts the valley to bed
A rabbit screams–a coyote howls
Off in the distance someone is singing.
Night eyes stare! Night ears listen!

∝

1. I am like the independently wealthy.
2. Nothing will take away my income–Social Security.
3. I live within my means and save money.
4. Should I need more–I have but to take any entry-level job.
5. I have no bills–no financial worries.
6. I have 3 months worth of income laid by for emergencies.
7. I can move with one month's notice.
8. I have a lovely room in a lovely home with no responsibilities. All house privileges. The rent covers everything.
9. My bicycle represents one month's income only.
10. I'm on Medicare so I pay only 20 percent of a reduced bill.
11. I eat what I want.
12. I can afford to buy books, give gifts, remember birthdays and take a bottle of wine to parties.
13. I read a lot of books. Listen to NPR and watch PBS.
14. I am comfortably clothed–albeit not in $1500.00 suits.
15. I can take a nap anytime I want to, do absolutely nothing day after day if I want to, stay up all night and sleep all day, compose mediocre poetry, attempt sexy books, and poke fun at the mirror.
16. I have several wonderful friends, a former wife who is one of my best friends, five grown children making their way without alcohol or drugs and nine grandchildren.

ଓଃ

&#x2123;

A red breast flashed by
 Caught it barely with my eye
Am I seeing spring?
Gloved and hooded, nipped by cold
I am eager to believe.
Another robin
I saw briefly–a surprise
It is not spring yet.
A harbinger in feathers?
Surely a bird mistaken
Yet, one more robin
I spied today on the ground
Skipping and stopping.
So, I am nearly convinced
Spring is here despite the cold

&#x2123;

Reading with open
Tent flap by my side, I feel
        And hear a cool wind.
Winter ghost dancing unleashed
Suddenly! Then a quiet.
Now, dry leaves partner
Dark brown, curled by swirling flings
They wind-waltz again.
The sounds and sights bewitch me
I'm in the leprechauns' glen.

&#x2123;

Four, maybe seven
Grackles seize left-over eggs
At the next table.
They fill up and fly away
I fork sausage and biscuits.
They come and they go
Come again, spearing the yellow
Mostly female birds.
Taking bits of egg to nests?
What a way to raise the kids!
I eat all my stuff
No left overs on my plate
Not even gravy.
I know sausage and biscuits
Can't be good for young grackles.

Waiting on traffic
I watch a mockingbird die
Struck by a windshield
It struggles for awhile as
Drivers' black tires mash the street.
Broken neck or stunned?
Hard to know as wings quiver
Desperate flutters.
Loosened feathers flee away
In Saturday's morning rush.
Again, it is hit.
Stilled–near a dime-sized red spot.
More feathers set free.
Now, across the wide hard street

*(continued)*
Another mockingbird sings.
Dark clouds bump and slide
The warming sun shines and hides
I stare and listen
Wondrous song–quiet dying
Life and death–singing, sighing.

ೞ

I'm remembering
In August, the cold winter.
My way of coping.
There are days when it's too hot.
Perhaps days when it's too cold.
But now–in August
Winter is in–hot is not.
Start the memories.
Off to the white-covered hills
The ski slopes, tingling fingers.
I feel cool although
Scorched August turns me to toast.
I wipe my brow–now.
So it's illusion–well, well.
How else to get through this hell?
My mind slides on ice
Cicadas wail around me
The August furnace!
I gather these fiery days
I shall need them next winter.

ೞ

Looking at the sun
Deceptively, it warms me
Fiercely exploding
The churning ball which gives life
Will kill us without blinking
The globe boils hot
Giant bubbles erupting
Unpredictable
Worry not about the sun
It will last longer than hair.

ᆭ

I hear dry voices
There off the curb–autumn leaves
Gossiping in gold

ᆭ

Cool early morning
Late afternoon now warming
The fog–sun-swallowed

ᆭ

Memory–the gift
Above all I have or had
Or shall have–the best.

ᆭ

They come, they go–birds
They stay for a little while
Flight is more than food.
Bright dots in their heads
Black-eyed sparrows blink at me
Puffed against the cold.

ഐ

Southwest of Austin, three hours away
Down in the hill country, I fed wild horses
Mustangs they were–four in number
Fed the horses oats and hay
High above the Medina River
In an open house with lots of glass
I swam in the pool and fed the cats
Two they were–one was feral
Fed the cats pellets and tuna
High above the Medina River
Where I could see the deer at dusk
Splashing and leaping lithe and clever.
Down in the hill country, I fed the dog
Cricket, her name, a golden retriever
Fed her and trained her to do as she dared
High above the Medina River
Where I walked, listened and checked the stars
And laughed at the deer who never cared.
I counted the cows–goats and the sheep
Out in the fields belonging to neighbors
And I fed nary a one–in the valleys so deep.
The days, they came, the days, they went
Down in the hill country, three hours away

Southwest of Austin. I wish I could stay.
Days of magic, eleven in number
Days of sunshine, clouds and mist
Flowers and trees and sounds in the night
Too much to remember too much to list
High above the Medina River
Where deer at dusk are a certain sight.

ɞ

My breath makes more noise
Than my bicycle.
Sometimes to far off places
Maybe just around the block
Or for groceries
Down a path or
Up a highway.
Dogs suspicious
Red lights, left turn lanes
Cars and trucks on busy streets
Make me cautious.
I swim with whales.
Then the sky
Open above me
Open everywhere I look
The rush of wind
In my ears and on my face
On my legs
Against my chest
Garbage cologne–deep-fried onion rings
Passing dumpster and café
In the country
Skunks, manure, fresh plowed earth
Stretching grass in May

*(continued)*
Wet with rain
Fields of flowers
Smell just to smell.
Sweat drips
Down my arms
Glistens on my knees
Taste it–warm and salty
Slippery all over my body
Skin shines in the sun
In the winter
Cold air like iced tea
Bathes my throat
Filling every tiny lung cup
Overflowing with the gift
I gulp with ferocious thirst
Touch my leg muscles
My arm muscles
Feel my belly lean and hard
I can't believe I'm in
My seventies.
My bicycle pure and simple
The wheels go around
A silent friend
The best kind
Never any advice
Childhood remembered on every ride
A time bending into yesteryear
Cradled in the arms of gnarled oaks
Sinewy streams
And secret places
A coveted life and excuses
To take yet another ride
Across boundaries

To hear mockingbirds and coyotes
See the deer leap. Eat
A country breakfast without guilt
Watch the sun set
And come up
It's time to start once more
Morning holds its breath
Unfolded ribbon road waiting
My heart is like a lover's.
Gliding through mysteries
Leaning into adventures
Over the hill
A cool and swift descent
Effortless
Renewed to climb again
Again, until I die.

☙

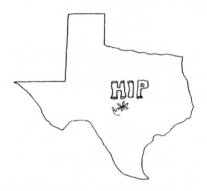

# *A New Lease on Life*

My journal for October 5, 1994 reads that I entered the Seton hospital in Austin, Texas at eight in the morning. My son, Rob, came down from Dallas, drove me to the hospital and stayed with me for my hip replacement operation. I went back to my room by three p.m. after what has been described as one of the noisier operations done today with a lot of sawing and hammering going on. Happily, the successful procedure took place while I slept. I had complete trust and confidence in my surgeon, Dr. Joseph Abell, Jr., now retired, and one of the highest rated hip replacement orthopedists in the country.

He had operated on my broken leg twenty some years earlier after my first and final parachute jump. His honeymoon began that night. I can't imagine how his wife took the news. "I'll be back in a little while–gotta go fix a leg." An indication of her future as a wife to medicine. I'd like to meet her someday and ask her about that night.

I felt a pain in my hip on April 4, 1993. At that time, I thought I had sprained something lifting weights or had over-exercised on my bike–getting ready for my first Texas tour. The pain persisted, but I ignored it. After my second tour in Texas to the panhandle, I thought I broke my wrist falling off a curb in Austin. After a confirming X-ray, I decided to get my hip X-rayed, too. The X-ray showed I had an advanced state of degeneration. The doctor prescribed powerful pain pills. He told me to give up thinking about any further bicycle tours. He said to take it easy. "For how long?" "From now on." I went home. I thought about it, read up on the side effects of powerful anti-inflammatory drugs and switched to Tylenol. I began keeping a detailed journal of my hip pain. Rereading the journal for this book, my poor condition amazed me. Some days, I had to lift my left leg with my hands. The pain prevented the leg from moving on its own. Nevertheless, I embarked on a gradual exercise program for the hip. Leg lifts. Knee bends. Bicycle riding. Walking. The pain persisted. I went camping for several days in the Big Bend area with a good friend. I loaded in the Tylenol, but I could only hobble about. I made two decisions. The first: to take a long bicycle trip from Big Bend south and east along the border and back into Austin–later I amended that trip to include the rest of the border of Texas. My second decision: to leave the doctor I had been consulting and to call Dr. Abell requesting a hip replacement as soon as possible after I returned from the tour. I told him I would be in good muscular condition and that I thought this would be a plus for the operation. After examining my hip, he agreed.

I returned to Austin four months later on August 3, 1994. I set an appointment with Dr. Abell for August 15. On August 29, my friend Dr. Clift Price had his hip replaced. I went to see him in the hospital and he said there was nothing to it. That made me feel good, even though I knew different. I inspected the facilities at the rehabilitation hospital on August 31. We decided on October 5 for the operation. I could hardly wait. On September 13, Clift got his crutches.

On September 26, I began my last series of tests with my primary doctor, Dr. Paul Harvill. I was ready for the operation. On October 3,

I had a pre-admissions meeting at the hospital and one with Dr. Abell. I purchased my one lottery ticket ahead because I knew the nurses wouldn't let me out of the hospital on the day of the operation to buy one. Thursday morning, after the operation had been completed the day before, I looked at the winning numbers in the paper. I got one number right. Usually nothing matched. I took that as a good sign. I had one chance in several million of winning, which meant I had a much better chance of being struck by lightning. But, if I didn't play I would have no chance at all. So, since I'm permanently enrolled in the lightning game, I thought why not have a chance on something less shocking–although winning the lottery would be quite a shock, too.

Before the operation, the anesthesiologist explained I would be given epidural anesthesia. This would numb my legs through the use of a small catheter inserted in my back and left in after the operation so I could administer my own pain reliever by pushing a button– much better than waiting for an over-worked nurse to arrive with a shot or pill. The sedative relaxed me so much I went off to dream land and didn't awaken until after surgery–just like waking up from a nap. No nausea.

The operation itself involved slicing open my upper thigh with a ten-inch cut, getting the muscles out of the way and cutting or sawing off the upper part of the thigh bone which has a knob on the end. To the rollicking tune of "John Henry, The Steel Drivin' Man," the surgeon drove a good-sized spike into the hollow of my thigh bone until it stuck tight, ground the socket on my pelvis; put in a nice plastic liner and bolted it on as you would a flange. The ball end of my titanium spike could be metal or plastic, mine was ceramic. Definitely, I got first-class components throughout. After securing everything and all spare parts removed, the muscles got reattached and the cut sewn up. A new life free from pain, free from hobbling about–after a few months of therapy, naturally.

While in the hospital I ran a fever for a couple of nights. I soon got bored with the bed. I received a wheel chair to run around in, but

I scared the nurses with my speeding and "graduated" to crutches and took daily walks. Every day, I felt better–the best part–no pain in the hip.

On October 10, I transferred to the rehabilitation facility where I received physical therapy which included swimming and occupational therapy, the latter taught me how to do for myself when I went home to my apartment. I made friends in the group of fellow replacement folks. We ate our meals in a common dining room. I sat by a pleasant woman who had a poor appetite. I ate my food and hers. It still didn't seem to be enough. I lost weight and my cholesterol went down. The doctor in charge also had received a replacement–more than one replacement–for the same hip. Energetic, reaching, twisting without thought and, consequently, his hip continued to dislocate. Good doctor, bad patient. I decided not to follow his example.

On October 18, 1994, the rehab staff discharged me and I became an out-patient, which meant I could come back to exercise and swim, which I did until October 31. A special city bus came by and picked me up and brought me home. In the meantime, I had started riding my bike, beginning the 21st day after surgery. The first time I pedaled around the block–like when I bought my first bike in 1992. In a couple of days, I increased my distance to four blocks.

On October 30th, I rode to the super market, a mile away, with my crutches strapped to my back. I couldn't walk yet, unaided, but I could ride. I bought wine, milk, cheese, meat, oranges, bananas, bread and kale. Free again! On November 17, I rode to the doctor's office for a check up–four miles away. He shook his head in disbelief. I could walk a little without a cane by that time. On November 21, I rode three miles to a local park and watched the installation of a group sculpture of Roy Bedichek, a naturalist, J. Frank Dobie, humorist and folklorist, and Walter Prescott Webb, historian–all three men were highly valued Texans. When alive, the three would gather on a boulder, dubbed the Philosopher's Rock, and hold forth in earnest discourse interspersed with a swim or two in the famous cold and clear Barton Springs pool–the precious gem of Austin. Because of the tours already taken, Texas history tugged at me. On November 30, I danced one rhumba at a Rotarian party. Thanks to my partner, I didn't fall over. Wonder of wonders–no pain. I reclaimed my life. I heartily recommended the operation to anyone I saw limping. "Don't wait until your muscles atrophy," I would warn.

Around 120,000 people have a hip replaced each year. In nearly all cases mobility is markedly improved and pain becomes but a memory. Persons as old as 80 and as young as Bo Jackson, who received a replacement when only 29, have had successful operations. Elizabeth Taylor and Liza Minelli have undergone the operation. After a few years some parts might need replacing. Each year I have an X-ray to make sure the hip is secure. "There's no warning–one minute everything's fine and the next you're yelling for an ambulance." The "new parts" replacement thing had me worried, but at my last X-ray–eight years after the operation, the doctor said there was no sign of weakening and it would last longer than I would." I knew if it gave out the following year and complained, he would only say, "I didn't expect you to last another year." If I do need a replacement part, it will be the flange and won't involve the titanium spike driven into my thigh bone. Apparently, minute particles of the plastic wear off and settle around the flange area, eventually loosening the screws to the point of failure. My particles haven't found out where the screws hang out–yet. Of course, if my hip gives way while I'm careening down a hill with dangerously deep chasms on either side–it could help sell more books–what a chapter.

By the way, surgeons encourage healthy activities following replacement. Among them: bicycling, swimming, scuba diving, golfing, bowling, sailing and also, for some, speed walking, tennis, volleyball, ice skating, hiking, backpacking, cross-country skiing, and ballet. A lot depends upon a person's general fitness level before the operation and how religiously he or she sticks with the physical therapies after the operation. Most surgeons would advise not to indulge in running, football, baseball, basketball, hockey, soccer, handball, racquetball, water skiing, and karate. Darn.

If you do none of the above and are content to walk about slowly, you will still smile broadly, because the pain will be no more. Now, my right hip appears to be in bad shape as seen in X-rays. As soon as I start limping I'll get another one of those new ceramic models with a titanium spike. That way my bicycle legs will match.

# *Bicycle Nuggets*

## *Just in Case You're Considering Hopping on a Bike*

I sold my Mercury in June 1993 in preparation for my first tour in Texas. The extra money helped purchase more equipment, besides, I could always buy another car when I got back.

The years slipped by and I haven't purchased that car. Somehow a new lifestyle sneaked up on me. Could that lifestyle sneak up on the nation–an alternative transportation mode as disturbing to mainstream America as drugs and nose rings? Don't count on it. Personally, I don't want too many bicyclists out there–but I would like to make room for you.

If someone had predicted my continuing carless state ten years ago, I would have shaken my head in disbelief. In most major cities, public transportation has made it possible for the average citizen to get about without an automobile, but out west, being without a car is like being a cowboy without a pickup, which most would say is incomprehensible. How else can one haul barbed wire, hay bales and tools to the high range?

Most of the spotless pickups I see in Austin, Texas, appear empty–their open beds shining without a dent or scratch, but again, I'm sure the occasional load certainly justifies the over all cost it takes to keep one stabled. I wouldn't mind having one myself. Do I not depend upon friends with automobiles to come pick me up in the heat of summer, or inclement weather, or freezing cold to take me to parties, dinners or the movies? Have I not gratefully accepted the offers to help me move–using my friend's spotless pickup? So, who am I to talk? And yet, most of my daily transportation needs can be met quite nicely by my bicycle. Even a horse could not have been more faithful than my touring bicycle–taking me all over Texas and beyond. If not in the mood to pedal I can always catch the bus and put my bike on the front. Being old means I ride busses free, too.

As a matter of fact quite a few students and workers in Austin commute to and from the workplace using a dependable bicycle and the Capital Metro bus system. Some do it out of economic considerations, although there must be members of a hard core group who leave car and pickup in the garage–steadfastly pedaling daily for a cleaner environment and a healthier lifestyle. If I had a pickup I hope I would be of that persuasion.

I derive much pleasure running errands and commuting, but have been known to invent reasons to ride–just for the sheer mind-clearing joy that comes from the wind blowing in my face. Riding can be a rejuvenating early morning or weekend sport–an opportunity to get back into the open, enabling one to call out hellos to neighbors working in their flower beds. Cycling just makes me feel better.

In upscale retirement communities, the preferred mode of transportation seems to be golf carts–some plain, some fancy. Liberated from the golf course, these open-to-nature silent machines provide similar benefits inherent in bicycling, except exercise. But for those who cannot exercise, golf carts can be a welcome alternative. After a lifetime of sedentary living it may be all a person can do. But even here we find retirees coming back to the bicycle and in some cases to state-of-the-art tricycles. So, maybe something is happening out there after all.

Perhaps the demand for ever increasing slabs of pavement could be mitigated by providing safe bicycle lanes to all parts of a city and beefing up public transportation for longer distances with bicycle carrying capacity.

Top-notch in-town cyclists can beat most motorized traffic today–especially during rush hour, but may need a shower and a change of clothes upon arrival at the office, which takes time–but maybe not anymore than trying to find a parking place for a car. The cost of parking a car for six months would go a long way toward purchasing a bicycle.

## My First Bicycle

My first bicycle, red and trimmed in cream, highlighted my twelfth year. Chromed streamlined headlights, a tail light, mud flaps with red jeweled reflectors that looked like a sultan's rubies and white-walled fat tires drew envious stares from my peers. The batteries in the lights lasted a long time because of prohibited after dark cycling. I switched them off and on in broad daylight to impress my friends. They, in turn, impressed me with flowing fox tails at the ends of their sweeping handlebars.

I had saved up my money by helping plant tomatoes in the fields around my hometown of Bargersville, Indiana.

Earlier, my younger brother and I rented bicycles from two neighbor boys for ten cents per hour per bicycle. Through diligent budgeting we saved this amount each week enabling us to escape the bonds of walking and running. Needless to say, we rode like bats out of hell for that full hour and when we returned the bikes we dripped with sweat and promised to be back the following week. It was great but not enough. We yearned for more–bikes of own. Only then, could we be truly free.

At the end of one summer, I had saved $12.00. Wonder of wonders, a boy across town had a bike to sell for $12.00. Mother said to offer $10.00 and go to $12.00 only if he refused to sell. I walked across town to the boy's home and there, leaning against the side of his house, was this great bike–at that time sans lights, and mud flaps–yet still the handsomest thing I had ever seen. With unsteady knees I climbed the steps and knocked at the door. When he peered through the screen, I asked if the bicycle were for sale–yet–and held my breath. He said yes and I said, "Well, I'll give you $10.00 for it, but if you won't take that I'll give you $12.00." He took the $12.00 and I could hardly contain myself riding my very own bike home. Everyone I passed commented on the bike and how expertly I rode it. Saving up more money allowed me to outfit it with the lights and the mud flaps.

Not a speck of dust marred its beauty if I could help it. That bicycle and I had a marvelous time. The boys in town who had bicycles would get together to play a game similar to hide and seek except we used the entire town as our playground–all the streets and alleys–remember those shaded alleys? When we spotted our target, maybe three or four streets away, the race began. We had to get close enough to nudge the other biker with our front wheel. Naturally, my bike proved to be the fastest. For a year or more, my bicycle and I stayed glued to each other. Surely, my younger brother also obtained a bike–but the experience of owning one completely wiped my memory banks clean as far as my knowledge of his owning a bike.

One summer day, I showed off in front of the local tomato canning factory by making U turns in an area where trucks came and went with their loads of tomatoes. First, the drivers weighed the load of tomatoes, then, they drove back on the scales to weigh the empty truck to see the difference before heading out to the fields again. They drove fast in order to get as many loads from the fields as possible each day. As I made one of my daring U turns, I heard a horn and a screech of brakes. One of the empty trucks, racing back to the scales, came within a foot of hitting me. I went home shaken and scared. I got mad. I didn't deserve having a bike if I couldn't ride it responsibly. I sold it the next day.

I did not own another bike until I entered college. I rode it for a couple of years. I sold it to help pay for my first car. As a ministerial student in Enid, Oklahoma, I landed my first church, a small congregation some 50 miles away, where I would be the student preacher on Sundays for $18.50. Goodbye bicycle. Hello Ford.

Forty-two years passed before I walked into that bicycle shop in Austin, Texas.

H. G. Wells said, "Every time I see an adult on a bicycle, I no longer despair for the future of the human race." Being an adult and not wishing to be despaired upon, I bought a bike.

"I am riding a bike and it is great fun. Everyone in America is riding bikes. It makes the grease come out of a fellow and is the greatest thing to produce a thirst for beer." Frederick Remington. It took awhile to get around to the beer. They do go together quite well—though not at the same time.

"But you'll look sweet upon the seat of a bicycle..." Daisy Bell. Someday, I may own a tandem and go find a Daisy.

## Some History

The high-wheeled bicycle claimed the speed record for over-the-road traveling in 1876. With the invention of the so-called safety bicycle, where both wheels were the same size, bicycle riding turned society upside down. Bicycle clubs mushroomed. Fashionable and important ladies and important and fashionable men belonged. Some of the clubs had indoor arenas which permitted riding on Sunday afternoons during inclement weather. The advent of daring bicycle bloomers worn beneath short provocative skirts instead of huge restrictive dresses freed women and stopped traffic. Susan B. Anthony said the bicycle did more to emancipate women than anything else. In 1895 the nation boasted 300 bicycle manufacturers. Americans, during the years 1890-96, spent more than $100 million on bicycles.

In 1896, the national bicycle organization known as the League of American Wheelmen held a convention in Louisville, Kentucky. Thirty thousand cyclists from out of town arrived. Louisville contributed another 10,000 riders. Other thousands stood alongside the parade route, waving and cheering. The papers reported on the convention for days. As part of the women's riding costume, corsets still pinched tiny waists while the well-dressed male cyclists wore flowing capes. Each club represented had its own costume and colors. On a regular day in Louisville, nearly 3,000 bicycle riders passed through one intersection between the hours of 5:30 a.m. and 8:30 a.m. on their way to work. A reporter said they acted as though acquainted, sending and receiving greetings and joking, since they could easily hear and see each other.

Even so, a lot of people did not believe bicycles belonged on the road. The League of American Wheelmen, today renamed The League of American Bicyclists, won over the populace by becoming a strong lobby for improved highways, reasoning that with good roads, farmers and truckers could get their produce and livestock to market faster and cheaper. Of course, better roads meant better bicycling too.

## The State of the Bicycle Today

The problem of moving people around from place to place remains, yet today. Perhaps bicyclists should once again become a strong lobby for better ways to use those highways and streets through public transportation and bicycle friendly thoroughfares. I have often heard people say they would ride if it were safe. Most people who do not ride have convinced themselves that riding even a few yards on a city's streets is tantamount to a death wish. They may be right. Those who ride anyway, apparently choose to ignore that dire consequence or else relish the thrill of escaping being smashed by a two-ton SUV on the way to work. "I made it," has a special meaning for those folks as they exchange high fives with their fellow daredevils before grabbing the morning cup of caffeine.

Although my current interest centers on day by day commuting and long distance touring, several other bicycle pursuits need mentioning. Racing, for example, has gained a strong pedal hold in the U.S. in recent years, thanks to the amazing efforts of Lance Armstrong, who, after surviving advanced testicular cancer, won the Tour de France, the most venerable and demanding bicycle race in the world today. Although one race, it commands the attention of the world. Mr. Armstrong may become the best rider in the history of bicycling. As of this writing five straight Tour de France victories attest to his awesome abilities.

In addition, each year thousands of cyclists race all over the world, increasingly in the United States. Specialized clothing, high-tech bikes, national magazines devoted to racing techniques, a club in practically every medium sized city, testify to the vigorous growth of the sport.

Among the younger set, BMX style racing counts millions of adherents. The elementary and middle school bike racks packed with these highly maneuverable low-slung bicycles serve as a witness to their popularity.

Almost over night, the phenomenon of the mountain bike changed the cycling world. A generation ago unheard of, today a monster contributing mightily to our culture in a furious attempt to mold the rugged, toned-up, slimmed-down, blood and mud body of the 21$^{st}$ century.

Mountain bike sales exhibit a cycling resurgence in the United States or maybe a renewed interest in inventing a new and more efficient method of body flogging, formerly the province of medieval monks. In 1983, 500,000 mountain bikes hit the trails. In 1993, 7,000,000 joined them. After the millennium dawned, sales reached 24,000.000.

Every weekend in foul weather or fair, hardy souls attach their mountain bikes to the top or back of the family vehicle and roar off to join other enthusiasts–hard muscled women and men–at some remote ranch, wildlife area, or park where single tracks abound–read paths–

and go racing away over stumps, rocks, through creeks, off steep embankments and across meadows filled with wild flowers, dead grass, or snow drifts. Hours later they return to their vehicles, compare bruises, blood splotches and caked-on mud and roar home, overflowing with virility and keen of eye.

Some older people indulge in this sport, but the more rigorous expressions of it strongly suggest an age when things heal faster. I saw a mountain biker once who could leap his bike into the bed of a pickup. Yes, the tailgate was down, but still.... Approaching the rear of a pickup with the intention of leaping into it should be attempted at speeds of less than five miles per hour–in case the rider misjudges the leap.

The name, Slickrock, near Moab, Utah, evokes heaven for the mountain biker because it seems like hell. Mountain climbers talk of 8,000 meter mountains with respect and yearning. So, mountain bikers speak of the Slickrock Trail in tones of quiet wonder, dread and fascination.

There nestled amongst dramatically sculpted boulders, where the summer heat melts tires, where some bikers disappear without a trace and turn up dead before being found, where canyons yawn to engulf the unwary, lay the king of all mountain bike trails. The dreaded, spectacularly awesome, Slickrock Trail weaves in and out and over the harsh landscape for twelve and six tenths miles. A trail that the most hardy can complete in less than three hours and the week-end warriors from back home struggle through in five hours or more, looking as if aliens had performed devilish experiments on them.

The first-time rider can expect to part company with the bicycle forty or fifty times on one circuit, hoping of course , one of those falls does not include a canyon. Oh yes, while the trail exhausts all but the most hardy with its sudden ascents that threaten to tear out one's lungs, or heart-hammering with its nearly vertical descents which ages one several months, it comforts a rider to know Slickrock Trail is not slick. The rock is hard–more like solidified and unyielding sand dunes. Small comfort. Mountain bikers have not lived–and died–until they trek to this mecca.

Another popular and growing segment of bicycle riding centers on fully supported tours. Some of these can be expensive, but no more so than any middle-tier luxury vacation. Tours of a week-end, a week, two weeks, a month or longer and offered by professional bicycle trip companies provide plenty of open road enjoyment. One could spend years going on these tours which take place in practically every country in the world. I keep looking for one that circles Greenland or pedals straight across Antarctica during the winter season. Not that I would go.

If I should become financially able I just might go on some of those tours where you stay at a bed and breakfast or some old castle and have gourmet treats supplied at regular intervals. I would only have to pedal 30 miles or so each day, and carry nothing on my bike while savoring the company of almost fit enthusiasts. Of course, if riding the entire 30 miles were too tiring, the support vehicle would pick me up whenever I wished and whisk me off to a masseuse to work on those sore muscles, followed by a nice steam, and a quick change into fresh casuals just in time to join the group for a seven course dinner served with appropriate wines. The cost of these jaunts includes renting the bike and equipment, too. Definitely, when I get the money and am old enough, I shall do that.

Tours come in gradations. The rustic tour means sleeping out in tents and eating wholesome but simple food. You bring your own tent and bike and equipment. On the high end, you drift through the countryside in the lap of luxury, pedaling but a few miles daily and stay in great hotels with gourmet feasting at the drop of a helmet. Probably no mosquitoes. Tours provide a wonderful way to meet interesting people and experience the great-out-of-doors. Bragging rights belong to you when you return home where friends gather around to hear of your rugged exploits. You will appear ruggedly healthy, too.

Still another kind of riding is joining a group of people on short or long rides perhaps to benefit a charity. Texas hosts one called the

Hotter'N Hell Century done in the middle of the summer. The ride is at Wichita Falls in north Texas and covers 100 miles in one day. A rider named Jasper Hubbert, 84 years old, completed the run in 1995. To train he pedaled 180 miles each week before the race.

RAGBRAI gets national attention each year. The initials stand for Register's Annual Great Bicycle Ride Across Iowa. Register's is the Des Moines Register newspaper. The ride began in 1973 when two columnists for the paper decided to ride across Iowa and persuaded a few hundred readers to join them. Slated originally as a one time journey, it caught on and continues, year after year. Today the riders number more than10,000 and come from all over the country. The small towns along the way look forward to the excitement of this annual invasion of their peaceful communities. It lasts seven days and covers about 600 miles.

Although fun, some spills are inevitable. At one railroad crossing 67 cyclists went down, those in the lead did not navigate the slippery railroad crossing and those that followed ran into them.

Fanciful and humorous costumes abound. The riders pedal all day and camp in football stadiums, parks, vacant fields–any large open space at night. Everyone eats constantly. Pancakes, muffins, Gatorade, fruit, bagels, ice cream, grilled turkey sandwiches, espresso, pies, cake, barbequed pork chops, corn on the cob–the menu goes on–which certainly entices me to join the group.

One town resident who watched the thousands wheel by said, "Up to now, about the only time we had excitement in this town was when one of those big semis rolled through with hogs in it."

At the end of the journey, one participant had a vision: "I want to do this for the rest of my life. Just ride and eat and meet people."

Since his bout with cancer, Lance Armstrong has joined others in "The Ride for the Roses" to benefit cancer research and cancer programs. He was diagnosed in 1996 and given a fifty percent chance for survival. In 2002 the event numbered 10,000 riders and volunteers taking part. Two million seven hundred thousand dollars provided a good start for the cancer programs. The ride takes place each year in Austin, Texas.

# Some Records

As in every field we find some who push the envelope, and bicycling enthusiasts have done what, for most of us, would be not only unreachable, but unthinkable.

In 1973, Allan Abbot, using a race car as a wind buffer, achieved a speed over a measured mile of 138.674 miles per hour.

With a streamlined body fitted to a recumbent bicycle, without being paced, a speed record was set in 1992 for two hundred meters at 68.72 miles per hour.

Around 1900, a super woman named Margaret Gast pedaled 500 miles in 44 hours and 45 minutes. (That's 268 miles per day).

Her other records include: 1,000 miles in 99 hours 55 minutes and 2,000 miles in 222 hours 51 1/2 minutes, the latter being 216 miles pedaled each day over a 12 hour period. What could she have done with a modern bicycle?

Thomas Godwin of the U.K. rode 75,065 miles in 1939. He averaged almost 206 miles per day for 365 days straight.

In 1884, Thomas Stevens on a high-wheeled "ordinary" rode around the world beginning on the west coast. At times he rode through Indian (Native American) villages. Usually, he rode on railroad tracks since there were few roads. Kind of bumpy, I would imagine. Another, named Lenz, tried to do a world tour shortly thereafter, but disappeared in Turkey.

# My Type of Riding

Local transportation and self-contained touring are the two forms of bicycle riding I do and about which I feel I can offer advice. I do my shopping, banking, errand running and visiting on a bicycle. Occasionally, I call up some biker friends and we do a morning ride together. My trips pedaling about town hardly exceed 20 miles per day. I do not race and I do not need to train anymore for long tours, with 15,000 miles of tours behind me. I use the first two or three weeks of a long tour as my training period– riding a small number of miles each day–at a slow speed–checking everything out–knowing I can fix whatever goes wrong. As my strength increases, so do my miles as well as my speed, so that, by the end of the tour I am in peak condition, ready to sink my iron-hard muscles once again into my soft bed at home.

If you have never done a long self-contained tour it would be wise to pack up your bike, pretending to leave home, but instead, pedaling about 15 miles out and 15 miles back for a few times, just to make sure everything is working okay. Before my first tour I practiced with a loaded bike for a couple of months and still experienced extreme exhaustion on the first day of the actual tour. Stress contributed–the fear of the unknown.

By the time I had reached my third, fourth and fifth tours in Texas, the stress and anxiety which usually preceded a journey had dissipated. I knew what I needed to take. I knew how to prepare my bike and I knew how to allow my body to settle in without injury. I have ridden nearly every day since October 1992. I have been slightly touched once by a car, and that may have been my imagination. Never hit. No serious accidents. I did have a hairline break in my wrist from toppling over once. Most of my falls have been exactly that–toppling over at a very low speed or when stopped completely. By far, the reason for my toppling centered on my inability to extricate my feet from the pedal clips in time. Once diagnosed as the culprits, I took those clips off. In eight years I have toppled maybe 10 times. A mountain biker expects that many falls in a single afternoon. If you're young, go for it. For me, I would rather minimize my contact with pavement or gravel.

At my best, I am a cautious, defensive rider. When not paying attention or taking some unwise risk, I put my life in the hands of others. I have been lucky to have escaped harm. I thank those drivers who spared me and I thank my bike which never failed me. Tomorrow, given the right circumstances, I could be flattened. I plan to be as careful as possible and hope the terminal accident never happens until I reach 100.

Allow me to bundle my advice into the three areas of getting started, on the road and riding friendly. I will use the long-distance tour as the illustration, although most of what I say will also apply to using the bike as a source of errand running close to home. The skills needed for racing and for extreme mountain biking call for special hands-on training because the margin for error diminishes to skinned-knee thin. If you contemplate excelling in either of these sports, my advice–get a professional trainer. Of course, if you just want to ride fast on club rides and spin through the green belt in your city park, fear not. If, however, you plan on blitzing the Slickrock Trail in Moab or joining a local racing team, get trained right.

## Getting Started

Now a look at getting started. When I bought my first bike at the beginning of my second childhood, I had been out of the bike riding business for over 40 years. I didn't bother to read anything or ask anything of anybody except the salesperson. I thought I knew enough. Wrong. If I had asked around–tried out a few bikes–picked up a national bike magazine off the rack–I would have saved several hundred dollars. I wouldn't have bought that bike. In two months I shopped for another one. So, spend the time instead of the dollars to do the research.

When you make your decision and that fantastic bike belongs to you, make sure it fits, the tires are properly inflated, nothing rubs, the seat fits your sit bones, you know how to use the quick release on seat and wheels. Practice taking the rear wheel off and putting it back on. Take it home, have a little get-acquainted ride for a few blocks, read the owner's manual from front to back. Practice fixing a flat. Take out and put in a chain link. Take a deep breath and try replacing a spoke–you'll need to have your wheel trued at the shop after this experiment, but it beats learning how when you're alone out there where the coyotes serenade in E flat minor.

Now the fun part begins as you start adding equipment, stylish pullovers of the latest wicking material, Lycra® riding shorts with chamois inserts, rain gear, booties, gloves, helmet, special shoes, eye glasses, lock, mirrors, lights, cyclometer, water bottles, cages, bell or horn, etc.. Suddenly, frighteningly, you discover you have spent the cost of your bicycle on the extras.

If you are going to do a long distance tour, you'll probably spend more than that same amount again by adding reading lights, fan, trailer, tent, sleeping bag, mattress pad, chair, pillow, stove, first aid kit, extra tubes and tires, tire patches, tools to fix whatever happens out on the road, harmonica, camera, binoculars, duct tape, wire, rope, more water bottles, panniers, racks, flashlight, Swiss army knife, toiletries, calculator, pens, notebooks, maps, address book, plastic bags, cell phone, radio, ax, dog minder, toilet paper, baby powder, pump, utensils, pots and pans, matches, fuel, snacks, insect repellent, fly swatter, towel and wash cloth and anything else you feel you can't live without–like a modem equipped laptop.

It's amazing what you can load onto a bike. My motto: take everything you can to make yourself comfortable. Once you get rolling the bike almost goes by itself–until you come to a hill. You will average 10 to 12 miles per hour. Count on 50 miles a day minimum–some days you might do a century. Allow yourself plenty of rest time and days off.

## On the Road at Last

Now to hit the road. As you gain experience you will add to this list. Some people I have known have never pedaled a loaded bike until the day of departure. Big mistake. An unloaded bare bike acts like a sports car–load it up and you have a tank. The unloaded bike whisks you about town like an autumn leaf in the breeze. The loaded bike on tour shudders and groans like a semi-trailer truck until it gets rolling.

When you approach a hill and your bike weighs 100 to 160

pounds, not counting your weight, you will discover how fast that bike wants to slow down. By not paying attention, the gear propelling you on a flat surface, gives up and says no to a hill. You will grind to a stop. Don't put more pressure on the pedals. Your knees don't like that kind of exercise and if you persist, they may decide to go home by bus. Learn to spin. That means higher revolutions in a lower gear. Learn to anticipate the hill–just look up ahead. Begin while on the flat to select a gear low enough to get you to the top. This takes practice. At first, just go to your lowest gear and spin your way to the top at around 3.5 to 4 miles per hour. Slower than 3.5 and you'll have trouble maintaining balance. Don't look at the top of the hill if you can help it, unless you like being depressed.

At a time like this I play games. I try to figure out in my head how many seconds make up a year. Believe me, no hill lasts longer than that problem. I almost got it once but got distracted and had to start all over. Inevitably, when you top a hill another awaits you in the distance. You don't appreciate hills in a car. Try to guess the distance to the top of the next hill. If you guess correctly, and who will be checking, you can reward yourself with ice cream in the next town. If you lose, ice cream makes a good consolation prize as well.

You can also try yelling with delight that you have received a special revelation that unequivocally announced the absence of all hills for the remainder of the day's journey. Repeat this assertion as each new hill appears. Yell louder. It tests your faith as you continue to groan from ridge to ridge. When you have had enough you can stop, eat a fried apple pie, a can of beans, or a box of donuts–anything that appeals to you at the moment and which you have thoughtfully stashed away in your panniers. Follow the snack with great gulps of water. On a trip where you have 20 or 30 miles between towns, carry at least three gallons at all times–you never, never want to run out of water. Remember, water weighs about 8 pounds per gallon.

Ride on the shoulder of the highway, however, if loose or nonexistent, ride up on the highway proper about a third of the way into your lane and watch your rear view mirror. As traffic comes up you want them to use the passing lane. If you try to stay close to the edge they may not move over.

I had a fellow do that in west Texas as I tried to ride as close to the edge as possible. He gave me no room as he whizzed past. A few hundred yards farther on he swerved into the passing lane to miss some mud dropped by a tractor. The mud would have soiled his car. Apparently, I wouldn't have.

Now, in the case of no shoulder and the traffic coming up behind you can't pass because of on-coming traffic, wait until the traffic from behind slows a little then go to the edge or off the pavement–your choice. If two trucks are meeting, don't wait for one to slow–go immediately off the road, stop and wait for them to go by. Be particularly careful to watch for traffic from behind pulling a mobile home, wide enough to take up one lane of traffic plus some or all of the shoulder. You may hear a horn. Get way off the highway and let the home pass. Other times it could be a truck hauling some kind of equipment that extends onto the shoulder. Not all truck drivers remember this, so you may not be signaled, which means it's up to you to watch your mirror. You can generally hear the truck, but not always.

*He sees me... He sees me not... He...*

I consider myself a good mirror watcher, but one time, in a day dreaming mode, a truck came up behind me which I neither saw nor heard. He had a block of machinery that extended far onto the shoulder. For some reason, I rode on the extreme edge of the shoulder, next to the grass, and that saved me from being decapitated. Not more than a foot or so separated us as he swooshed past. Maybe he thought he would miss me. Maybe he forgot about his load. It did shake me up and I gave myself a good talking to about watching that mirror.

If you want to attempt powering up a small incline by standing up to pump, remember to keep the bike completely vertical. Don't jerk the bike back and forth as they do in races–you will snap or bend your frame. Only on a bare bike can the rider stay vertical and jerk the bike back and forth. On a loaded bike, the steadier the bike the better.

Check your brakes. Realize that you can't stop on a dime. Realize, too, if you wish to check your speed on a descent, to alternate the front and rear brakes. This keeps your rims from getting too hot. Too hot and your tire melts. Clamp your knees against your top tube on descents to keep the bike stable for cross winds or rough pavement. Going too fast? Want to slow without putting all the pressure on your brakes? Sit up. Your speed will decrease by 10 miles per hour.

Fenders protect you from a wheel shower during a rain. How about when the road tar melts and your front tire picks up rocks and hurls them in your face? Nice to have fenders for that too.

I spent a couple of hours once digging tar from my tire treads. By running through gravel with my tar ladened tires, the rocks did it for me–kind of like washing pots and pans with sand. Mother nature helps out if you'll let her.

How to drink. Racers learn to drink and ride at the same time. And you can too. It's one of the first things a rider learns to do–slip that bottle from its cage, and pour a stream into your waiting mouth– all the while pedaling furiously. Forget it. A tourer is not in a hurry.

Stop and drink. The rest as well as the water will do you good. Also, if something threatens the bike's balance, it may be difficult to correct it with one hand when that front end has thirty or forty pounds of panniers on it. While stopped you can jot down that great thought you just had a mile back, but which will flit from you memory if you wait until you zip yourself in the tent tonight, you can also look at a flower–up close–or call out to a cow. Cows lead boring lives and welcome a little conversation. Making milk day after day after day becomes tedious. Moo.

Take good care of your bike and your bike will take care of you. Lubricating the chain ranks high on the must-do list. If your day involved grit and/or rain–lubricate. Examine your tires each time you stop for bits of glass or thorns that can be brushed off before they penetrate the casing. Test the air pressure in your tires several times a day. You won't need to use a pressure gauge. Just squeeze the tire. With practice you can judge the pressure quite well. A low tire on a loaded bike not only makes the bike harder to pedal, but can cause damage to the tire's side wall.

The headset (where the handlebar post rotates in the frame) needs to be checked often, since you have a lot of weight on the bike–tighten or loosen as needed. There should be no play when you try to move the bike forward and backward with the brakes on. Go over the whole bike checking for loose bolts and nuts every three or four days. Make sure the wheels rotate without rubbing. A brake pad can be askew.

If you repair a tube with a patch kit, follow the directions religiously. Use the enclosed file to roughen the surface of the tube at the hole. Give the smeared-on glue time to rest for five minutes–not two, not three, not four, but five–then put the patch on where you have spread the glue. Otherwise, it won't hold and you'll get to unpack everything from your bike and repair the tube again. As you ride stay in constant movement. Keep changing your hand positions and don't grip the handle bars tightly–pretend you're playing the piano. Move your head up and down and side to side, slide forward and backward on your saddle. Stand up and stretch with your pedals at three and nine for a few seconds.

Every two hours, powder your behind until you have a little cloud of white following you around–of course do not wear underwear–the seams will do you in. Eat something each hour. You can chew and drink five thousand calories or more a day and still lose weight. Riding at 12 to 15 miles per hour burns 12 to 15 calories per minute.

Before you put your supplies in your panniers, put them in sealable plastic bags. Remember to unseal at night to air out. Never ride with ear phones or a radio blaring. You need to be listening for traffic. Besides, the sounds of the country, especially bird calls sound better.

Wear gloves–helps you hang on and protects you if you should fall. Wear eyeglasses–the best you can afford with interchangeable lenses from clear to dark. Wrap arounds help with the wind and lessen distortion. Investigate some type of ear flaps to reduce wind roar–ear plugs won't work.

Wear an approved helmet. Buy the best you can afford. An accident will destroy it, but a hundred dollars will replace it. Doctors will charge you more to work on your brains.

## Riding Friendly

And now a few words on riding friendly. This could save your life, so pay attention.

When you find yourself on a busy highway for the first time, the noise of the cars and trucks can be almost overwhelming. Especially nerve racking, the vehicle which, as it passes, lets loose with a million decibels of horse power. You get irritated. You get mad. You feel like a second-class citizen. A car darts around you and makes a right turn immediately in front of you. You squeeze your brakes. You feel threatened and taken advantage of. The next car or truck that roars by like that or turns in front of you deserves a waving fist–or worse. Don't yield to this temptation.

Exceptions? Of course, but only if you wish to die. Generally speaking, those drivers meant you no harm. They may not have noticed you at all. The noise that you hear, the screech of brakes, the gunning of the engines, the horns, are just normal everyday noises on the highway. The difference? Your protective car shell. Inside that shell, luxuriating in the air-conditioning and listening to your favorite CD, you don't hear any of that stuff. Recognize that practically nobody out there wants to make your life miserable.

Never insist on the right-of-way. Always give in, not reluctantly, but graciously with a wave and a smile. If you grit your teeth as you smile, you need to go back to behavior school, but at least you made a start. This posture does not mean you are subservient, hesitant and afraid. It means you're smart. Ride with assurance and confidence. Be assertive, but ready to give way instantly–ready to apply brakes, ready to jump the curb, ready to bail out into a bush if need be, all without rancor, recrimination or vengeance burning in your brain like blinking neon signs. It takes practice. It takes rehearsing who you are and who you are not. You are not a car. You are not that two-ton SUV controlled by someone's big toe. You can not afford to indulge in the puerile antics of some drivers. Your life is at stake. Print this on your forehead before someone prints a bumper on your behind. Remain calm and friendly. Repeat that sentence as you ride. If a driver swishes by close enough to make you cringe, stay calm, stay friendly–no fist waving. If you arouse road rage in a driver, you cannot win. If a gray-haired grandmother needs to be taught a lesson in sharing the road, even if she visits you in the hospital with an apology or scatters a few flower seeds on your cemetery plot, her defense will always be, "I didn't see that bicycle, your Honor." She may be telling the truth. No matter. She will be forgiven. The record seems to show that most drivers will be forgiven no matter how visible you are and no matter how drunk, drug-addicted, cell-phone distracted or sleepy they may be.

A few years ago, a driver who tried to run down Lance

Armstrong and one of his riding buddies, was convicted and sent to prison. Unless you have won the Tour de France, I wouldn't count on that kind of justice. Besides, how would you like being out there, pedaling happily on your two-wheeler, when this guy gets out and back into the driver's seat?

See yourself as a quick-thinking, quick-acting songbird watching for the neighborhood cat. Pretend you are swimming in the ocean with whales–they don't mean to hurt you, but if you get too close, you are history. Assume that a driver suffers a heart attack, has just belched up the remains of a six-pack, can't see, hear, or count to ten, hates his mother-in-law or her son-in-law, has just received a pink slip and would like to kick something, applying make-up in the rearview mirror or talking to an inept employee on the cell phone, numb with drugs, has been over charged at the grocery store, has just held up the corner bank, or suffering totally unexpected labor pains. The purpose of this unending list? To ingrain on your brain the good sense to be an alert, friendly and defensive cyclist.

Once I had a driver cut in front of me as I approached a stop light. I continued to pedal, passing between the lanes of traffic and cutting in between him and the car in front which was stopped at the light–keeping him from turning right–*touche*. I didn't stop there. I passed the stopped car on the right and turned onto the street and into my bike lane. Once the light changed, the offending, and now offended, driver tore around the corner and passed me as close as possible swerving into the bike lane for a hundred yards, showing me in no uncertain terms who was boss of the highway. I waved my fist at him vigorously sending a message that I would beat him to a pulp if I could catch him.

At the next light, I caught up with him. He had turned his car into the curb so I couldn't possibly go around him. He was angry with me and I with him. The difference–he weighed two tons. I sat there, seething. He sat there. Neither of us made a sign. I cooled off some. Apparently, so did he. How stupid I had been. Road rage never helps the cyclist. If I had not tried to "even the score," none of that would have happened. I'm sure he felt he had enough room to get by that slow-poke on the bike. It was close. I could have applied the brakes. I could have smiled and waved even. I could have been friendly and meant it. I had not given myself a talking to before that ride. I could have ended up in the hospital. He would have said, "I didn't even see that bike, your Honor." It takes two to tango.

Check on your attitude. Don't ride with one. "Have a great day." makes for a great mantra. Say it. Say it. Say it. If you can't, stay off your bike and buy an SUV.

Hope you hop on a bike.

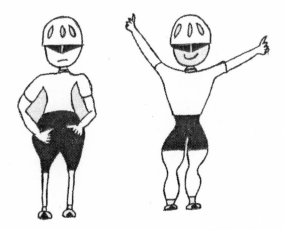

*Before and after biking.*

*The author's self-portrait*

# *About the Author*

Lloyd Mardis grew up in Indiana, spent thirty years in Oklahoma, and another thirty years in Texas. Now, he's back in Enid, Oklahoma, counting the days until he can travel for the second time on the Great Plains by bicycle.

His careers and vocations have included the ministry, advertising, marketing, public speaking, seminars, Real Estate, bicycle touring and finally writing.

This is his second book. He is the author of *The Burro and The Basket*, a children's book. He is now working on a series of novels to be completed by 2004, then it'll be pedal time again, and another book.

## Index of Places

Abilene, 144

Acuna, 52

Alamo, 64, 91

Albany, 129

Alpine, 15, 16, 18-22, 28, 36, 54

Amarillo, xii, 137, 162, 174-176, 183

Angelina National Forest, 84

Annona, 107

Apple Springs, 84

Amistad Reservoir, 40, 48, 53

Arnett,OK, 156

Austin, Too many references

Avery, 107

Bandera, 244

Bargersville, IN, 164

Beaumont, 83

Bentson Rio Grande State Park, 69, 70

Bidien, LA, 104

Big Bend Museum, 22

Big Ben National Park, 11, 12, 41, 76

Big Thicket, 84, 87

Black Gap Wildlife Management Area, 10, 11

Bloomberg, LA, 104

Boca Chica, 57, 73

Bonham, 110

Booker, 163

Bowie Mine, 146

Brewster County, 207

Brownfield, 186-189, 206

Brownsville, 52, 54, 57, 64, 72-74

Brownwood, 229, 230, 235, 236

Burnet, 240

Caddo Lake, 99-102

Cajun Triangle, 83

Canadian, 155, 156, 158

Canyon Lake, vi, vii, 2

Caprock Escarpment, 167

Carrizo Springs, 54

Casa Blanca Park, 57, 59

Castle Gap, 147

Catarina, 55-56

Childress, 116, 152-155

Chinati Foundation, 25

Claredon, 176, 140

Clarksville, 108, 109

Claude, 176

Columbus, 90

Comanche Springs, 197

Comanche War Trail, 29ff

Conlen, 168

Cornudas, 209-216

Corpus Christi, 76

Crooked Tree RV Park, 73

Dalhart, 159, 168-171, 173

Dallas, 21, 112, 113, 129, 142, 151, 225, 228

Davy Crockett National Forest, 84, 96

Dekalb, 107

Del Rio, xii, 28, 36, 39, 52-53, 64

Denver City, 179, 180

Detroit, 108

Devil's River, 39-40, 48

Dimmit, 185

Dinosaur State Park, 151

Douglass, 85

Dumas, 171, 173, 174

Dryden, 36

Eagle Pass, 54

Edinburg, 74

Edna, 78

El Capitan, 209

El Paso, 31, 52, 88, 112, 216, 217

El Paso Salt Wars, 209

Elm Tree RV Park, 170

Enid, OK, xii, 165

Falcon Lake State Park, 65-57

Fall Creek Vineyards, 239

Five Mile Mountain, 194, 196

Flat(s), The  (Fort Griffin),132

Follet's Island, 80

Follett, 155, 156, 158, 160-162, 168

Fort Belknap, 134, 135

Fort D.A. Russell, 26

Fort Davis, 21-23, 28, 132

Fort Chadbourne, 30

Fort Concho, 223, 227, 228

Fort Griffin, 129-134

Fort Hancock, 219

Fort Houston, 131

Fort McKavett, 131, 223-227

Fort Mason, 223, 224

Fort Richardson, 135, 136

Fort Stockton, 193, 195-200, 222

Fort Worth, xii, 21, 112, 113, 222

Freer, 59, 63

Friona, 178

Gage Hotel, 29

Gail, 182

Gainesville, 111

Galveston Island, 80-83

Galveston State Park, 80-83

Georgetown, 241

Giant (movie location), 25, 26

Gladys Porter Zoo, 72

Glen Rose, 151

Golden Triangle, 83

Goldthwaite, 241

Goliad, 77

Goliad State Historical Park, 77

Gonzales, 91

Granger Lake, 87

Groveton, 86

Gruver, 165

Guadalupe Mountains National Park, 208, 209

Hallie Stillwell Ranch, 12

Harlingen, 60, 74

Hartley, 173

Hebronville, 59, 63

Hempstead, 109

Henrietta, 111, 113

Hereford, 178, 183-186

Hidetown (Fort Griffin),    132, 134

Higgins, 156, 157

Hitching Rail Café/Petras Mexican Café, 176

Hooks, 107

Houston, 64, 90, 96, 112, 113, 169

Huntsville, 96

Jacksboro, 136

Jacksonville, 87

Jasper, 87

Juarez, 20, 215, 217

Katharine Ann Porter Gravesite, 223, 236, 237

Kerrville, 243

King Ranch, 73, 74, 75

Kingsville, 75

Lake Bonham, 110, 111

Lake Brownwood State Park, 223, 224, 229-236

Lake Buchanan, 239

Lake Crook, 110

Lake Murvaul, 98, 100

Lake Nasworthy, 228

Lake Toyah, 201

Langtry, 34, 36-37, 193

Laredo, 52, 55, 57, 59, 63

Last Frontier Store, 19

Levelland, 186

Limpia Hotel, 22

Lipscomb County, 157

Littlefield, 186

Llano Estacado, 167

Llano, 32

Llano River, 145

Longhorn Ranch Motel, 17

Longview,99

Los Angeles, 176

Loving County, 207

Luling, 59

Magnolia, 94, 96

Marble Falls, 239, 240

Marathon, 28, 29, 36

Marfa Lights, 26

Marfa, 21-28

Marshall, 99, 102

Mason, 225

Matamoros, 72, 74

Mayfield's Country Store, 40

McAllen, 69, 74

McDonald Observatory, 22, 23

Memphis, 138-142, 153, 176

Medina, 243

Menard, 146, 224, 227

Mentone, 207

Midland, 21

Mineral Wells, 149

Mission, 69, 71, 74

Monahans, 190, 203, 204

Monahans State Park, 203

Montgomery, 95

Muleshoe National Wildlife Refuge, 178

Nacogdoches, 85

Navasota, 109

New Braunfels, 244, 247

New York City, 112

Nuevo Laredo, 57

Odessa, 21, 190

Old Fort Parker, 96

Orange, 83

Orla, 205-207

Ozona, 39, 40, 223, 243

Paisano Pete, 197

Palo Duro Canyon, 137, 148, 175-178

Panther Junction, 12

Paris, 108, 109, 110

Pecan Grove RV Park, 22

Pecos, ii, vii, xii, 10, 80, 110, 193, 199, 201-203, 205-207, 240

Pennyloafer Farm, 244

Perryton, 162-164

Pharr, 74

Pipe Creek, 244

Plano, 170

Pioneer Park, Wellington, 155

Port Arthur, 83

Possum Kingdom Lake, 144

Proctor Lake, 231

Presidio la Bahia (mission), Goliad, 77

Quanah, 117, 129, 139, 144, 152, 153

Raymondville, 74

Reeves County, 207

Riata Restaurant, 22

Rice's Crossing, 247

Robstown, 76

Roby, 129

Rocky Point Campground, 103, 104

Roma, 65

Sabine National Forest, 84

Salt Flats, 209

Sam Houston National Forest, 84, 95

San Angelo, 30, 223, 227, 228

San Antonio, 41, 64, 112, 113, 217, 243, 247-248

San Felipe, 91

San Felipe Springs, Del Rio, 52

San Jacinto, 64

San Saba Mine, 146

Sanderson, vii, 34-36, 193-196

Sarita, 74,75

Satler, vi

Sealy, 93, 94

Seminole, 180, 189, 192, 203

Seminole Canyon, vii, 39-51, 192

Shady Glade RV Park, 100-102

Shamrock, 155

Shattuck, OK, 161

Sheffield, 223

Sierra Blanca, 221

Six Shooter Draw, 196

Silsbee, 87

Sinton, 76

Smyrna, 104

Spearman, 165

Staked Plains, 167

Stillwell Ranch, 12

Stephen F. Austin State Park, 92-95

Sterling, 227

Stratford, 166, 167

Study Butte, 13, 15, 36

Sul Ross State University, 22, 27

Sulphur Springs, viii

Surfside, 79, 80

Swanson's Landing, 100

Tascosa, 174

Tascosa-Dodge City Trail,174

Taylor, 247

Terlingua, 36

Texana State Park, 78

Texarkana, 99, 104, 107

Texas Hill Country, vi

Texas Panhandle, 10, 116

Texas Southmost College, 72

Texline, 168

Tow, 239

Town Lake (Austin), viii

Tyler, 99

Uncertain, 100

UT Campus at Brownsville,72

Utopia, 244

Val Verde Winery, 53

Vega, 183

Vernon, 115

Veterans Park, 178, 185

Vinegaroon, 38

Victoria, 78

Waller, 94

Washington-on-the-Brazos, 91, 92, 109

Welch, 181

Wellington, 155

Wichita Falls, 114, 170

Wild Horse Station, 16

Wildorado, 183, 184

Will's Point, viii

Wimberly, 249

Winnie, 83

Wright Patman Lake, 99, 102, 103, 158

Young County, 135

Zapata, 65-68

To order additional copies of
*Mother Nature Ain't Nobody's Mom*

Name _____

Address _____

_____

$21.95 x _____ copies =          _____

Sales Tax          _____
(Texas residents add 8.25% sales tax)

Please add $3.50 postage and handling          ____ _____

Total amount due:_____

Please send check or money order for books to:

**WordWright.biz, Inc.
P.O. Box 1785
Georgetown, TX 78627**

**For a complete catalog of books,
visit our site at
http://www.WordWright.biz**

Printed in the United States
1463500004B/103-126